Édition de Luxe

THE

VICOMTE DE BRAGELONNE

OR

TEN YEARS LATER

IN FIVE VOLUMES
VOL. III

BY ALEXANDRE DUMAS

WITH ILLUSTRATIONS

BOSTON
ESTES AND LAURIAT
1893

THE VICOMTE DE BRAGELONNE.

VOL. III.

CONTENTS.

VOL. III.

LIST OF ILLUSTRATIONS.

VOL. III.

THE VICOMTE DE BRAGELONNE.

CHAPTER I.

THE BATH.

At Valvins, beneath the impenetrable shade of flowering osiers and willows, which, as they bent down their green heads, dipped the extremities of their branches in the blue waters, a long and flat-bottomed boat, with ladders covered with long blue curtains, served as a refuge for the bathing Dianas, who, as they left the water, were watched by twenty plumed Acteons, who, eagerly, and full of admiration, galloped up and down the flowery banks of the river. But Diana herself, even the chaste Diana, clothed in her long chlamys, was less beautiful—less impenetrable, than Madame, as young and beautiful as that goddess herself. For, notwithstanding the fine tunic of the huntress, her round and delicate knee can be seen; and notwithstanding the sonorous quiver, her brown shoulders can be detected; whereas, in Madame's case, a long white veil enveloped her, wrapping her round and round a hundred times, as she resigned herself into the hands of her female attendants, and thus was rendered inaccessible to the most indiscreet, as well as to the most penetrating gaze. When she ascended the ladder, the poets who were present—and all were poets when Madame was the subject of discussion—the twenty poets who were galloping about, stopped, and with one voice exclaimed, that pearls, and not drops of water, were falling from her person, to be lost again in the happy river. The king, the center of these effusions, and of this respectful homage, imposed silence upon those expatiators, for whom it seemed impossible to exhaust their raptures, and he rode away, for fear of offending, even through the silken curtains, the modesty of the woman and the dignity of the princess. A great blank thereupon ensued in the scene, and perfect silence in the boat. From the movements on board—from the flutterings and agitations of the curtains—the goings to and fro of the female attendants engaged in their duties, could be guessed.

The king smilingly listened to the conversation of the courtiers around him, but it could easily be perceived that he gave but little, if any, attention to their remarks. In fact, hardly had the sound of the rings drawn along the curtain-rods announced that Madame was dressed, and that the goddess was about to make her reappearance, than the king, returning to his former post immediately, and running quite close to the river-bank, gave the signal for all those to approach whose duty or pleasure summoned them to Madame's side. The pages hurried forward, conducting the led horses ; the carriages, which had remained sheltered under the trees, advanced towards the tent, followed by a crowd of servants, bearers, and female attendants, who, while their masters had been bathing, had mutually exchanged their own observations, critical remarks, and the discussion of matters personal—the fugitive journal of that period, of which no one now remembers anything, not even by the waves, the witnesses of what went on that day—themselves now sublimed into immensity, as the actors have vanished into eternity.

A crowd of people swarming upon the banks of the river, without reckoning the groups of peasants drawn together by their anxiety to see the king and the princess, was, for many minutes, the most disorderly, but the most agreeable, mob imaginable. The king dismounted from his horse, a movement which was imitated by all the courtiers, and offered his hand to Madame, whose rich riding-habit displayed her fine figure, which was set off to great advantage by that garment, made of fine woolen cloth embroidered with silver. Her hair, still damp and blacker than jet, hung in heavy masses upon her white and delicate neck. Joy and health sparkled in her beautiful eyes; composed, yet full of energy, she inhaled the air in deep draughts, under a lace parasol, which was borne by one of her pages. Nothing could be more charming, more graceful, more poetical, than these two figures buried under the rose-colored shade of the parasol, the king, whose white teeth were displayed in continual smiles, and Madame, whose black eyes sparkled like carbuncles in the glittering reflection of the changing hues of the silk. When Madame approached her horse, a magnificent animal of Andalusian breed, of spotless white, somewhat heavy, perhaps, but with a spirited and splendid head, in which the mixture, happily combined, of Arabian and Spanish blood could be readily traced, and whose long tail swept the ground; and as the princess affected difficulty in mounting, the king took her in his arms in such a manner that Madame's arm was clasped like a circlet of alabaster around the king's neck. Louis, as he withdrew, involuntarily touched with his lips the arm, which was not withheld, and the princess, having thanked her royal equerry, every one sprang to his saddle at the same moment. The king and Madame drew aside to allow the carriages, the outriders, and runners, to pass by. A fair proportion of the cavaliers, released from the restraint etiquette had imposed upon them, gave the rein to their horses, and darted after the carriages which bore

the maids of honor, as blooming as so many virgin hunt-
resses around Diana, and the human whirlwind, laughing, chattering, and noisy, passed onward.

The king and Madame, however, kept their horses in
hand at a foot-pace. Behind his majesty and his sister-
in-law, certain of the courtiers—those, at least, who were
seriously disposed or were anxious to be within reach, or
under the eyes, of the king—followed at a respectful distance, restraining their impatient horses, regulating their
pace by that of the king and Madame, and abandoned
themselves to all the delight and gratification which is to
be found in the conversation of clever people, who can,
with perfect courtesy, make a thousand atrocious, but
laughable remarks about their neighbors. In their stifled
laughter, and in the little reticences of their sardonic
humor, Monsieur, the poor absentee, was not spared.
But they pitied, and bewailed greatly, the fate of De
Guiche, and it must be confessed that their compassion,
as far as he was concerned, was not misplaced. The king
and Madame having breathed the horses, and repeated a
hundred times over such remarks as the courtiers, who
supplied them with talk, suggested to them, set off at a
hand gallop, and the leafy coverts of the forest resounded
to the footfalls of the mounted party. To the conversations beneath the shade of trees,—to remarks made in the
shape of confidential communications, and observations,
mysteriously exchanged, succeeded the noisiest bursts of
laughter;—from the very outriders to royalty itself, merriment seemed to spread. Every one began to laugh and
to cry out. The magpies and the jays fluttered away uttering their guttural cries, beneath the waving avenues of oaks;
the cuckoo staid his monotonous cry in the recesses of the
forest; the chaffinch and tomtit flew; while the terrified
deer bounded riverwards from the midst of the thickets.
This crowd, spreading joy, confusion, and light wherever

it passed, was heralded, it may be said, to the château by
its own clamor. As the king and Madame entered the
village, they were received by the acclamations of the
crowd. Madame hastened to look for Monsieur, for she .
instinctively understood that he had been far too long
kept from sharing in this joy. The king went to rejoin
the queens; he knew he owed them—one especially—a
compensation for his long absence. But Madame was
not admitted to Monsieur's apartments, and she was informed that Monsieur was asleep. The king, instead of
being met by Maria Theresa smiling, as was usual with
her, found Anne of Austria in the gallery watching for
his return, who advanced to meet him, and taking him
by the hand, led him to her own apartment. No one
ever knew what was the nature of the conversation which
took place between them, or rather what it was that the
queen-mother said to Louis XIV.; but the general tenor
of the interview might certainly be guessed from the
annoyed expression of the king's face as he left her.

But we, whose mission it is to interpret all things, as
it is also to communicate our interpretations to our readers,—we should fail in our duty, if we were to leave them
in ignorance of the result of this interview. It will be
found sufficiently detailed, at least we hope so, in the
following chapter.

CHAPTER II.

THE BUTTERFLY-CHASE.

The king, on retiring to his apartments to give some
directions and to arrange his ideas, found on his toilette-
glass a small note, the handwriting of which seemed dis-
guised. He opened it and read—" Come quickly, I have

a thousand things to say to you." The king and Madame had not been separated a sufficiently long time for these thousand things to be the result of the three thousand which they had been saying to each other during the route which separated Valvins from Fontainebleau. The confused and hurried character of the note gave the king a great deal to reflect upon. He occupied himself but slightly with his toilette, and set off to pay his visit to Madame. The princess, who did not wish to have the appearance of expecting him, had gone into the gardens with the ladies of her suite. When the king was informed that Madame had left her apartments and had gone for a walk in the gardens, he collected all the gentlemen he could find, and invited them to follow him. He found Madame engaged in chasing butterflies, on a large lawn bordered with heliotrope and flowering broom. She was looking on as the most adventurous and youngest of her ladies ran to and fro, and with her back turned to a high hedge, very impatiently awaited the arrival of the king, with whom she had appointed the rendezvous. The sound of many feet upon the gravel-walk made her turn round. Louis XIV. was hatless: he had struck down with his cane a peacock butterfly, which Monsieur de Saint-Aignan had picked up from the ground quite stunned.

"You see, Madame," said the king, as he approached her, "that I, too, am hunting on your behalf!" and then, turning towards those who had accompanied him, said, "Gentlemen, see if each of you cannot obtain as much for these ladies," a remark which was a signal for all to retire. And thereupon a curious spectacle might have been observed; old and corpulent courtiers were seen running after butterflies, losing their hats as they ran, and with their raised canes cutting down the myrtles and the furze, as they would have done the Spaniards.

The king offered Madame his arm, and they both

selected, as the center of observation, a bench with a roof of boards and moss, a kind of hut roughly designed by the modest genius of one of the gardeners who had inaugurated the picturesque and fanciful amid the formal style of gardening of that period. This sheltered retreat, covered with nasturtiums and climbing roses, screened the bench, so that the spectators, insulated in the middle of the lawn, saw and were seen on every side, but could not be heard, without perceiving those who might approach for the purpose of listening. Seated thus, the king made a sign of encouragement to those who were running about; and then, as if he were engaged with Madame in a dissertation upon the butterfly, which he had thrust through with a gold pin and fastened on his hat, said to her, "How admirably we are placed here for conversation."

"Yes, sire, for I wished to be heard by you alone, and yet to be seen by every one."

"And I also," said Louis.

"My note surprised you?"

"Terrified me rather. But what I have to tell you is more important."

"It cannot be, sire. Do you know that Monsieur refuses to see me?"

"Why so?"

"Can you not guess why?"

"Ah, Madame! in that case we have both the same thing to say to each other."

"What has happened to you, then?"

"You wish me to begin?"

"Yes, for I have told you all."

"Well, then, as soon as I returned, I found my mother waiting for me, and she led me away to her own apartments."

"The queen-mother?" said Madame, with some anxiety, "the matter is serious, then."

"Indeed it is, for she told me . . . but, in the first place, allow me to preface what I have to say with one remark. Has Monsieur ever spoken to you about me?"

"Often."

"Has he ever spoken to you about his jealousy?"

"More frequently still."

"Of his jealousy of me?"

"No, but of the Duke of Buckingham and De Guiche."

"Well, Madame, Monsieur's present idea is a jealousy of myself."

"Really," replied the princess, smiling archly.

"And it really seems to me," continued the king, "that we have never given any ground——"

"Never! at least *I* have not. But who told you that Monsieur was jealous?"

"My mother represented to me that Monsieur entered her apartments like a madman, that he uttered a thousand complaints against you, and—forgive me for saying it—against your coquetry. It appears that Monsieur indulges in injustice, too."

"You are very kind, sire."

"My mother reassured him; but he pretended that people reassure him too often, and that he had had quite enough of it."

"Would it not be better for him not to make himself uneasy in any way?"

"The very thing I said."

"Confess, sire, that the world is very wicked. Is it possible that a brother and sister cannot converse together, or take pleasure in each other's company, without giving rise to remarks and suspicions? For indeed, sire, we are doing no harm, and have no intention of doing any." And she looked at the king with that proud yet provoking glance that kindles desire in the coldest and wisest of men.

"No!" sighed the king, "that is true."

"You know very well, sire, that if it were to continue, I should be obliged to make a disturbance. Do you decide upon our conduct, and say whether it has, or has not, been perfectly correct."

" Oh, certainly—perfectly correct."

"Often alone together,—for we delight in the same things, we might possibly be led away into error, but *have* we been? I regard you as a brother, and nothing more."

The king frowned. She continued :—

" Your hand, which often meets my own, does not excite in me that agitation and emotion which is the case with those who love each other, for instance——"

" Enough," said the king, "enough, I entreat you. You have no pity—you are killing me."

" What is the matter ?"

" In fact, then, you distinctly say you experience nothing when near me."

" Oh, sire! I don't say that—my affection——"

" Enough, Henrietta, I again entreat you. If you believe me to be marble, as you are, undeceive yourself."

" I do not understand you, sire."

"Very well," sighed the king, casting down his eyes. " And so our meetings, the pressure of each other's hand, the looks we have exchanged—Yes, yes; you are right, and I understand your meaning," and he buried his face in his hands.

" Take care, sire," said Madame, hurriedly, "Monsieur de Saint-Aignan is looking at you."

" Of course," said Louis, angrily; "never even the shadow of liberty! never any sincerity in my intercourse with any one! I imagine I have found a friend, who is nothing but a spy; a dearer friend, who is only a—sister ! "

Madame was silent, and cast down her eyes.

" My husband is jealous," she murmured, in a tone of which nothing could equal its sweetness and its charm.

"You are right," exclaimed the king, suddenly.

"You see," she said, looking at him in a manner that set his heart on fire, "you are free, you are not suspected, the peace of your house is not disturbed."

"Alas," said the king, "as yet you know nothing, for the queen is jealous."

"Maria Theresa!"

"Stark mad with jealousy! Monsieur's jealousy arises from hers; she was weeping and complaining to my mother, and was reproaching us for those bathing parties, which have made me so happy."

"And me too," answered Madame, by a look.

"When, suddenly," continued the king, "Monsieur, who was listening, heard the word 'banos,' which the queen pronounced with some degree of bitterness, that awakened his attention; he entered the room, looking quite wild, broke into the conversation, and began to quarrel with my mother so bitterly that she was obliged to leave him; so that, while you have a jealous husband to deal with, I shall have perpetually present before me a specter of jealousy with swollen eyes, a cadaverous face, and sinister looks."

"Poor king," murmured Madame, as she lightly touched the king's hand. He retained her hand in his, and, in order to press it without exciting suspicion in the spectators, who were not so much taken up with the butterflies that they could not occupy themselves about other matters, and who perceived clearly enough that there was some mystery in the king's and Madame's conversation.

Louis placed the dying butterfly before his sister-in-law, and both bent over it as if to count the thousand eyes of its wings, or the particles of golden dust which covered it. Neither of them spoke; however, their hair mingled, their breath united, and their hands feverishly throbbed in each other's grasp. Five minutes passed in this manner.

CHAPTER III.

WHAT WAS CAUGHT AFTER THE BUTTERFLIES.

THE two young people remained for a moment with their heads bent down, bowed, as it were, beneath the double thought of the love which was springing up in their hearts, and which gives birth to so many happy fancies in the imaginations of twenty years of age. Henrietta gave a side glance, from time to time, at the king. Hers was one of those finely-organized natures capable of looking inwardly at itself, as well as at others at the same moment. She perceived Love lying at the bottom of Louis's heart, as a skillful diver sees a pearl at the bottom of the sea. She knew Louis was hesitating, if not in doubt, and that his indolent or timid heart required aid and encouragement. "And so?" she said, interrogatively, breaking the silence.

"What do you mean?" inquired Louis, after a moment's pause.

"I mean, that I shall be obliged to return to the resolution I had formed."

"To what resolution?"

"To that which I have already submitted to your majesty."

"When?"

"On the very day we had a certain explanation about Monsieur's jealousies."

"What did you say to me then?" inquired Louis, with some anxiety.

"Do you not remember, sire?"

"Alas! if it be another cause of unhappiness, I shall recollect it soon enough."

"A cause of unhappiness for myself alone, sire," replied Madame Henrietta; "but as it is necessary, I must submit to it."

"At least, tell me what it is," said the king.

"Absence."

"Still that unkind resolve?"

"Believe me, sire, I have not formed it without a violent struggle with myself; it is absolutely necessary I should return to England."

"Never, never will I permit you to leave France," exclaimed the king.

"And yet, sire," said Madame, affecting a gentle yet sorrowful determination, "nothing is more urgently necessary; nay, more than that, I am persuaded it is your mother's desire I should do so."

"Desire!" exclaimed the king: "that is a very strange expression to use to me."

"Still," replied Madame Henrietta, smilingly, "are you not happy in submitting to the wishes of so good a mother?"

"Enough, I implore you; you rend my very soul."

"I?"

"Yes; for you speak of your departure with tranquillity."

"I was not born for happiness, sire," replied the princess, dejectedly; "and I acquired, in very early life, the habit of seeing my dearest wishes disappointed."

"Do you speak truly?" said the king. "Would your departure gainsay any one of your cherished thoughts?"

"If I were to say 'yes,' would you begin to take your misfortune patiently?"

"How cruel you are!"

" Take care, sire ; some one is coming."

The king looked all round him, and said, " No, there is no one," and then continued : " Come, Henrietta, instead of trying to contend against Monsieur's jealousy by a departure which would kill me——" Henrietta slightly shrugged her shoulders like a woman unconvinced. " Yes," repeated Louis, " which would kill me, I say. Instead of fixing your mind on this departure, does not your imagination—or rather does not your heart—suggest some expedient ? "

" What is it you wish my heart to suggest ? "

" Tell me, how can · one prove to another that it is wrong to be jealous ? "

" In the first place, sire, by giving no motive for jealousy ; in other words, in loving no one but the person in question."

" Oh ! I expected more than that."

" What did you expect ? "

" That you would simply tell me that jealous people are pacified by concealing the affection which is entertained for the object of jealousy."

" Dissimulation is difficult, sire."

" Yet it is only by means of conquering difficulties that any happiness is attained. As far as I am concerned, I swear I will give the lie to those who are jealous of me by pretending to treat you like any other woman."

" A bad, as well as an unsafe, means," said the young princess, shaking her pretty head.

" You seem to think everything bad, dear Henrietta," said Louis, discontentedly. " You negative everything I propose. Suggest, at least, something else in its stead. Come, try and think. I trust implicitly to a woman's invention. Do you invent in your turn."

" Well, sire, I have hit upon something. Will you listen to it ? "

"Can you ask me? You speak of a matter of life or death to me, and then ask if I will listen."

"Well, I judge of it by my own case. If my husband intended to put me on the wrong scent with regard to another woman, one thing would reassure me more than anything else."

"What would that be?"

"In the first place to see that he never took any notice of the woman in question."

"Exactly. That is precisely what I said just now."

"Very well; but in order to be perfectly reassured on the subject, I should like to see him occupy himself with some one else."

"Ah! I understand you," replied Louis, smiling. "But confess, dear Henrietta, if the means is at least ingenious, it is hardly charitable."

"Why so?"

"In curing the dread of a wound in a jealous person's mind, you inflict one upon the heart. His fear ceases, it is true; but the evil still exists; and that seems to me to be far worse."

"Agreed; but he does not detect, he does not suspect the real enemy; he does no prejudice to love itself; he concentrates all his strength on the side where his strength will do no injury to anything or any one. In a word, sire, my plan, which I confess I am surprised to find you dispute, is mischievous to jealous people, it is true; but to lovers it is full of advantage. Besides, let me ask, sire, who, except yourself, has ever thought of pitying jealous people? Are they not a melancholy crew of grumblers always equally unhappy, whether with or without a cause? You may remove that cause, but you never can remove their sufferings. It is a disease which lies in the imagination, and, like all imaginary disorders, it is incurable. By the by, I remember an aphorism upon this subject, of poor Dr. Dawley, a clever and amusing man, who, had it not been for my brother, who could not do without him, I should have with me now. He used to say, 'Whenever you are likely to suffer from two affections, choose that which will give you the least trouble, and I will allow you to retain it; for it is positive,' he said, 'that that very ailment is of the greatest service to me, in order to enable me to get rid of the other.' "

"Well and judiciously remarked, Henrietta," replied the king, smiling.

" Oh! we have some clever people in London, sire."

"And those clever people produce adorable pupils. I will grant this Daley, Darley, Dawley, or whatever you call him, a pension for his aphorism; but I entreat you, Henrietta, to begin by choosing the least of your evils. You do not answer—you smile. I guess that the least of your bugbears is your stay in France. I will allow you to retain this misfortune; and, in order to begin with the cure of the other, I will this very day begin to look out for a subject which shall divert the attention of the jealous members of either sex who persecute us both."

"Hush! this time some one is really coming," said Madame; and she stooped to gather a flower from the thick grass at her feet. Some one, in fact, was approaching; for, suddenly, a bevy of young girls ran down from the top of the hillock, following the cavaliers—the cause of this irruption being a magnificent hawk-moth, with wings like rose-leaves. The prey in question had fallen into the net of Mademoiselle de Tonnay-Charente, who displayed it with some pride to her less successful rivals. The queen of the chase had seated herself some twenty paces from the bank on which Louis and Madame Henrietta were reclining; and leaned her back against a magnificent oak tree entwined with ivy, and stuck the butterfly on the long cane she carried in her hand.

Mademoiselle de Tonnay-Charente was very beautiful, and the gentlemen, accordingly, deserted her companions, and under the pretext of complimenting her upon her success, pressed in a circle around her. The king and the princess looked gloomily at this scene, as spectators of maturer age look on at the games of little children. "They seem to be amusing themselves there," said the king.

"Greatly, sire; I have always found that people are amused wherever youth and beauty are to be found."

"What do you think of Mademoiselle de Tonnay-Charente, Henrietta?" inquired the king.

"I think she has rather too much flax-yellow and lily-whiteness in her complexion," replied Madame, fixing in a moment upon the only fault it was possible to find in the almost perfect beauty of the future Madame de Montespan.

"Rather too fair, yes; but beautiful, I think, in spite of that."

"Is that your opinion, sire?"

"Yes, really."

"Very well; and it is mine, too."

"And she seems to be much sought after."

"Oh, that is a matter of course. Lovers flutter from one to another. If we had hunted for lovers instead of butterflies, you can see, from those who surround her, what successful sport we should have had."

"Tell me, Henrietta, what would be said if the king were to make himself one of those lovers, and let his glance fall in that direction? Would some one else be jealous, in such a case?"

"Oh! sire, Mademoiselle de Tonnay-Charente is a very efficacious remedy," said Madame, with a sigh. "She would cure a jealous man, certainly; but she might possibly make a woman jealous, too."

"Henrietta," exclaimed Louis, "you fill my heart with joy. Yes, yes; Mademoiselle de Tonnay-Charente is far too beautiful to serve as a cloak."

"A king's cloak," said Madame Henrietta, smiling, "ought to be beautiful."

"Do you advise me to do it, then?" inquired Louis.

"I! what should I say, sire, except that to give such an advice would be to supply arms against myself. It would be folly or pride to advise you to take, for the heroine of an assumed affection, a woman more beautiful than the one for whom you pretend to feel real regard."

The king tried to take Madame's hand in his own; his eyes sought hers; and then he murmured a few words so full of tenderness, but pronounced in so low a tone, that the historian, who ought to hear everything, could not hear them. Then, speaking aloud, he said, "Do you yourself choose for me the one who is to cure our jealous friend. To her, then, all my devotion, all my attention, all the time that I can spare from my occupations, shall be devoted. For her shall be the flower that I may pluck for you, the fond thoughts with which you have inspired me. Towards her, I will direct the glance I dare not bestow upon you, and which ought to be able to rouse you from your indifference. But, be careful in your selection, lest, in offering her the rose which I may have plucked, I find myself conquered by you; and my looks, my hand, my lips, turn immediately towards you, even were the whole world to guess my secret."

While these words escaped from the king's lips, in a stream of wild affection, Madame blushed, breathless, happy, proud, almost intoxicated with delight. She could find nothing to say in reply; her pride and her thirst for homage were satisfied. "I shall fail," she said, raising her beautiful black eyes, "but not as you beg me, for all this incense which you wish to burn on the altar of another divinity, ah! sire, I too shall be jealous of, and want restored to me; and would not that a particle of it should be lost in the way. Therefore, sire, with your royal permission, I will choose one who shall appear to me the least likely to distract your attention, and who will leave my image intact and unshadowed in your heart."

"Happily for me," said the king, "your heart is not hard and unfeeling. If it were so, I should be alarmed at the threat you hold out. Precautions were taken on this point, and around you, as around myself, it would be difficult to meet with a disagreeable looking face."

Whilst the king was speaking, Madame had risen from her seat, looked around the greensward, and after a careful and silent examination, she called the king to her side, and said, "See yonder, sire, upon the declivity of that little hill, near that group of Guelder roses, that beautiful girl walking alone, her head down, her arms hanging by her side, with her eyes fixed upon the flowers, which she crushes beneath her feet, like one who is lost in thought."

"Mademoiselle de Vallière, do you mean?" remarked the king.

"Yes."

"Oh!"

"Will she not suit you, sire?"

"Why, look how thin the poor child is. She has hardly any flesh upon her bones."

"Nay: am I stout then?"

"She is so melancholy."

"The greater contrast to myself, who am accused of being too lively."

"She is lame."

"Do you really think so?"

"No doubt of it. Look; she has allowed every one to pass by her, through fear of her defect being remarked."

"Well, she will not run so fast as Daphné, and will not be as able to escape Apollo."

"Henrietta," said the king, out of temper; "of all your maids of honor, you have really selected for me the one most full of defects."

"Still she is one of my maids of honor."

"Of course; but what do you mean?"

"I mean that, in order to visit this new divinity, you will not be able to do so without paying a visit to my apartments, and that, as propriety will forbid your conversing with her in private, you will be compelled to see her in my circle, to speak as it were, at me, while speaking to her. I mean, in fact, that those who may be jealous, will be wrong if they suppose you come to my apartments for my sake, since you will go there for Mademoiselle de la Vallière."

"Who happens to be lame."

"Hardly that."

"Who never opens her lips."

"But who, when she does open them, displays a beautiful set of teeth."

"Who may serve as a model for an osteologist."

"Your favor will change her appearance."

"Henrietta!"

"At all events you allowed me to choose."

"Alas! yes."

"Well, my choice is made: I impose her upon you, and you must submit."

"Oh! I would accept one of the furies, if you were to insist upon it."

"La Vallière is as gentle as a lamb: do not fear she will ever contradict you when you tell her you love her," said Madame, laughing.

"You are not afraid, are you, that I shall say too much to her?"

"It would be for my sake."

"The treaty is agreed to, then?"

"Not only so, but signed."

"You will continue to show me the friendship of a brother, the attention of a brother, the gallantry of a monarch, will you not?"

"I will preserve for you intact, a heart that has already become accustomed to beat only at your command."

"Very well, do you not see that we have guaranteed the future by this means?"

"I hope so."

"Will your mother cease to regard me as an enemy?"

"Yes."

"Will Maria Theresa leave off speaking in Spanish before Monsieur, who has a horror of conversation held in foreign languages, because he always thinks he is being ill spoken of? and lastly," continued the princess, "will people persist in attributing a wrongful affection to the king when the truth is, we can offer nothing to each other, except absolute sympathy, free from mental reservation?"

"Yes, yes," said the king, hesitatingly. "But other things may still be said of us."

"What can be said, sire? shall we never be left in tranquillity?"

"People will say I am deficient in taste; but what is my self-respect in comparison with your tranquillity?"

"In comparison with my honor, sire, and that of our family, you mean. Besides, I beg you to attend, do not be so hastily prejudiced against La Vallière. She is slightly lame, it is true, but she is not deficient in good sense. Moreover, all that the king touches is converted into gold."

"Well, Madame, rest assured of one thing, namely, that I am still grateful to you: you might even yet make me pay dearer for your stay in France."

"Sire, some one approaches."

"Well!"

"One last word."

"Say it."

"You are prudent and judicious, sire; but in the present instance you will be obliged to summon to your aid all your prudence, and all your judgment."

"Oh!" exclaimed Louis, laughing, "from this very day I shall begin to act my part, and you shall see whether I am not quite fit to represent the character of a tender swain.   After luncheon, there will be a promenade in the forest, and then there is supper and the ballet at ten o'clock."

"I know it."

"The ardor of my passion shall blaze more brilliantly than the fireworks, shall shine more steadily than our friend Colbert's lamps; it shall shine so dazzlingly that the queens and Monsieur will be almost blinded by it."

"Take care, sire, take care."

"In heaven's name what have I done, then?"

"I shall begin to recall the compliments I paid you just now.   You prudent! you wise! did I say? why you begin by the most reckless inconsistencies?   Can a passion be kindled in this manner, like a torch, in a moment? Can a monarch, such as you are, without any preparation, fall at the feet of a girl like La Vallière?"

"Ah! Henrietta, now I understand you.   We have not yet begun the campaign, and you are plundering me already."

"No, I am only recalling you to common-sense ideas. Let your passion be kindled gradually, instead of allowing it to burst forth so suddenly.   Jove's thunders and lightnings are heard and seen before the palace is set on fire.   Everything has its commencements.   If you are so easily excited, no one will believe you are really captivated, and every one will think you out of your senses—if even, indeed, the truth itself be not guessed. The public is not so fatuous as they seem."

The king was obliged to admit that Madame was an angel for sense, and the very reverse for cleverness. He bowed, and said : "Agreed, madame, I will think over my plan of attack: great military men—my cousin De Condé, for instance—grow pale in meditation upon their strategical plans, before they move one of the pawns, which people call armies ; I therefore wish to draw up a complete plan of campaign ; for, you know, that the tender passion is subdivided in a variety of ways. Well, then, I shall stop at the village of Little Attentions, at the ham- let of Love-Letters, before I follow the road of Visible Affection ; the way is clear enough, you know, and poor Madame de Scudéry would never forgive me for passing through a halting-place without stopping."

"Oh ! now we have returned to our proper senses, shall we say adieu, sire ? "

"Alas ! it must be so, for, see we are interrupted."

"Yes, indeed," said Henrietta, "they are bringing Mademoiselle de Tonnay-Charente and her sphinx butter- fly in grand procession this way."

"It is perfectly well understood, then, that this evening, during the promenade, I am to make my escape into the forest, and find La Vallière without you."

"I will take care to send her away."

"Very well ! I will speak to her when she is with her companions, and I will then discharge my first arrow at her."

"Be skillful," said Madame, laughing, "and do not miss the heart."

Then the princess took leave of the king, and went for- ward to meet the merry troop, which was advancing with much ceremony, and a great many pretended flourishes of trumpets, imitated with their mouths.

CHAPTER IV.

THE BALLET OF THE SEASONS.

At the conclusion of the banquet, which was served at five o'clock, the king entered his cabinet, where his tailors were awaiting him for the purpose of trying on the celebrated costume representing Spring, which was the result of so much imagination, and had cost so many efforts of thought to the designers and ornament-workers of the court. As for the ballet itself, every person knew the part he had to take in it, and how to perform it. The king had resolved to make it a surprise. Hardly, therefore, had he finished his conference, and entered his own apartment, than he desired his two masters of the ceremonies, Villeroy and Saint-Aignan to be sent for. Both replied that they only awaited his orders, and that everything was ready to begin, but that it was necessary to be sure of fine weather and a favorable night before these orders could be carried out. The king opened his window; the pale-gold hues of evening were visible on the horizon through the vistas of the wood, and the moon, white as snow, was already mounting the heavens. Not a ripple on the surface of the green waters; the swans themselves, even, reposing with folded wings like ships at anchor, seemed inspirations of the warmth of the air, the freshness of the water, and the silence of the beautiful evening. The king, having observed all these things, and contemplated the magnificent picture before him, gave the order which De Villeroy and De Saint-Aignan awaited; but with a view of insuring the execution of this order in a royal manner, one last question was necessary, and Louis XIV. put it to the two gentlemen in the following manner:—"Have you any money?"

" Sire," replied Saint-Aignan, " we have arranged everything with M. Colbert."

" Ah! very well!"

" Yes, sire, and M. Colbert said he would wait upon your majesty, as soon as your majesty should manifest an intention of carrying out the *fêtes*, of which he has furnished the programme.

" Let him come in, then," said the king; and as if Colbert had been listening at the door for the purpose of keeping himself *au courant* with the conversation, he entered as soon as the king had pronounced his name to the two courtiers.

" Ah! M. Colbert," said the king. "Gentlemen, to your posts," whereupon Saint-Aignan and Villeroy took their leave. The king seated himself in an easy-chair near the window, saying: " The ballet will take place this evening, M. Colbert."

" In that case, sire, I will pay all accounts to-morrow."

" Why so?"

" I promised the tradespeople to pay their bills the day following that on which the ballet should take place."

" Very well, M. Colbert, pay them, since you have promised to do so."

" Certainly, sire; but I must have money to do that."

" What! have not the four millions, which M. Fouquet promised been sent? I forgot to ask you about it."

" Sire, they were sent at the hour promised."

" Well?"

" Well, sire, the colored lamps, the fireworks, the musicians, and the cooks, have swallowed up four millions in eight days."

" Entirely?"

" To the last penny. Every time your majesty directed the banks of the grand canal to be illuminated, as much oil was consumed as there was water in the basins."

" Well, well, M. Colbert; the fact is, then, you have no more money?"

" I have no more, sire, but M. Fouquet has," Colbert replied, his face darkening with a sinister expression of pleasure.

" What do you mean?" inquired Louis.

" We have already made M. Fouquet advance six millions. He has given them with too much grace not to have others still to give, if they are required, which is the case at the present moment. It is necessary, therefore, that he should comply."

The king frowned. " M. Colbert," said he, accentuating the financier's name, " that is not the way I understood the matter; I do not wish to make use, against any of my servants, of a means of pressure which may oppress him and fetter his services. In eight days, M. Fouquet has furnished six millions; that is a good round sum."

Colbert turned pale. "And yet," he said, " your majesty did not use this language some time ago, when the news about Belle-Isle arrived, for instance."

" You are right, M. Colbert."

" Nothing, however, has changed since then; on the contrary, indeed."

" In my thoughts, monsieur, everything is changed."

" Does your majesty then no longer believe the disloyal attempt?"

" My affairs concern myself alone, monsieur; and I have already told you I transact them without interference."

" Then, I perceive," said Colbert, trembling with anger and fear, " that I have had the misfortune to fall into disgrace with your majesty."

" Not at all; you are, on the contrary, most agreeable to me."

" Yet, sire," said the minister, with a certain affected bluntness, so successful when it was a question of flattering Louis's self-esteem, " what use is there in being agreeable to your majesty, if one can no longer be of any use? "

" I reserve your services for a better occasion; and believe me, they will only be the better appreciated."

" Your majesty's plan, then, in this affair, is——"

" You want money, M. Colbert? "

" Seven hundred thousand francs, sire."

" You will take them from my private treasure." Colbert bowed. " And," added Louis, " as it seems a difficult matter for you, notwithstanding your economy, to defray, with so limited a sum, the expenses which I intend to incur, I will at once sign an order for three millions."

The king took a pen and signed an order immediately, then handed it to Colbert. " Be satisfied, M. Colbert, the plan I have adopted is one worthy of a king," said Louis XIV., who pronounced these words with all the majesty he knew how to assume in such circumstances; and dismissed Colbert for the purpose of giving an audience to his tailors.

The order issued by the king was known throughout the whole of Fontainebleau; it was already known, too, that the king was trying on his costume, and that the ballet would be danced in the evening. The news circulated with the rapidity of lightning; during its progress it kindled every variety of coquetry, desire and wild ambition. At the same moment, as if by enchantment, every one who knew how to hold a needle, every one who could distinguish a coat from a pair of trousers, was summoned to the assistance of those who had received invitations. The king had completed his toilette by nine o'clock; he appeared in an open carriage decorated with

branches of trees and flowers. The queens had taken
their seats upon a magnificent daîs or platform, erected
upon the borders of the lake, in a theater of wonderful
elegance of construction. In the space of five hours the
carpenters had put together all the different parts con-
nected with the building; the upholsterers had laid down
the carpets, erected the seats; and, as if at the wave of
an enchanter's wand, a thousand arms, aiding, instead of
interfering with each other, had constructed the building,
amidst the sound of music; whilst, at the same time,
other workmen illuminated the theater and the shores of
the lake with an incalculable number of lamps. As the
heavens, set with stars, were perfectly unclouded, as not
even a breath of air could be heard in the woods, and as
if Nature itself had yielded complacently to the king's
fancies, the back of the theater had been left open; so
that, behind the foreground of the scenes, could be seen
as a background the beautiful sky, glittering with stars;
the sheet of water, illumined by the lights which were reflected in it; and the bluish outline of the grand masses
of woods, with their rounded tops. When the king made
his appearance, the theater was full, and presented to
the view one vast group, dazzling with gold and precious
stones; in which, however, at the first glance, no single
face could be distinguished. By degrees, as the sight became accustomed to so much brilliancy, the rarest beauties appeared to the view, as in the evening sky the stars
appear one by one to him who closes his eyes and then
opens them again.

The theatre represented a grove of trees; a few fauns
lifting up their cloven feet were jumping about; a dryad
made her appearance on the scene, and was immediately
pursued by them; others gathered round her for her
defense, and they quarreled as they danced. Suddenly,
for the purpose of restoring peace and order, Spring,

accompanied by his whole court, made his appearance. The Elements, subaltern powers of mythology, together with their attributes, hastened to follow their gracious sovereign. The Seasons, allies of Spring, followed him closely, to form a quadrille, which, after many words of more or less flattering import, was the commencement of the dance. The music, hautboys, flutes, and viols, was delightfully descriptive of rural delights. The king had already made his appearance, amid thunders of applause. He was dressed in a tunic of flowers, which set off his graceful and well-formed figure to advantage. His legs, the best-shaped at court, were displayed to great advantage in flesh-colored silken hose, of silk so fine and so transparent that it seemed almost like flesh itself. The most beautiful pale-lilac satin shoes, with bows of flowers and leaves, imprisoned his small feet. The bust of the figure was in harmonious keeping with the base; Louis' waving hair floated on his shoulders, the freshness of his complexion was enhanced by the brilliancy of his beautiful blue eyes, which softly kindled all hearts; a mouth with tempting lips, which deigned to open in smiles. Such was the prince of that period: justly that evening styled "The King of all the Loves." There was something in his carriage which resembled the buoyant movements of an immortal, and he did not dance so much as seem to soar along. His entrance produced, therefore, the most brilliant effect. Suddenly the Comte de Saint-Aignan was observed endeavoring to approach either the king or Madame.

The princess—who was robed in a long dress, diaphanous and light as the finest network tissue from the hands of skillful Mechlin workers, one knee occasionally revealed beneath the folds of the tunic, and her little feet encased in silken slippers decked with pearls—advanced radiant with beauty, accompanied by her *cortège* of Bacchantes, and had already reached the spot assigned to her in the dance. The applause continued so long that the comte had ample leisure to join the king.

"What is the matter, Saint-Aignan?" said Spring.

"Nothing whatever," replied the courtier, as pale as death; but your majesty has not thought of Fruits."

"Yes; it is suppressed."

"Far from it, sire; your majesty having given no directions about it, the musicians have retained it."

"How excessively annoying," said the king. "This figure cannot be performed, since M. de Guiche is absent. It must be suppressed."

"Ah, sire, a quarter of an hour's music without any dancing will produce an effect so chilling as to ruin the success of the ballet."

"But, come, since——"

"Oh, sire, that is not the greatest misfortune; for, after all, the orchestra could still just as well cut it out, if it were necessary; but——"

"But what?"

"Why, M. de Guiche is here."

"Here?" replied the king, frowning, "here? Are you sure?"

"Yes, sire; and ready-dressed for the ballet."

The king felt himself color deeply, and said, "You are probably mistaken."

"So little is that the case, sire, that if your majesty will look to the right, you will see that the comte is in waiting."

Louis turned hastily towards the side, and in fact, on his right, brilliant in his character of Autumn, De Guiche awaited until the king should look at him, in order that he might address him. To give an idea of the stupefaction of the king, and that of Monsieur, who was moving about restlessly in his box,—to describe also the agitated move-

ment of the heads in the theater, and the strange emotion
of Madame, at the sight of her partner,—is a task we must
leave to abler hands.   The king stood almost gaping with
astonishment as he looked at the comte, who, bowing lowly,
approached Louis with the profoundest respect.

"Sire," he said, "your majesty's most devoted servant
approaches to perform a service on this occasion with
similar zeal to that he has already shown on the field of
battle.   Your majesty, in omitting the dance of the Fruits,
would be losing the most beautiful scene in the ballet.   I
did not wish to be the substance of so dark a shadow to
your majesty's elegance, skill, and graceful invention;
and I have left my tenants in order to place my services
at your majesty's commands."

Every word fell distinctly, in perfect harmony and
eloquence, upon Louis XIV.'s ears.   Their flattery pleased,
as much as De Guiche's courage had astonished him, and he
simply replied: "I did not tell you to return, comte."

"Certainly not, sire; but your majesty did not tell me
to remain."

The king perceived that time was passing away, that
if this strange scene were prolonged it would complicate
everything, and that a single cloud upon the picture
would effectually spoil the whole.   Besides, the king's
heart was filled with two or three new ideas; he had
just derived fresh inspiration from the eloquent glances of
Madame.   Her look had said to him.   "Since they are
jealous of you, divide their suspicions, for the man who
distrusts two rivals does not object to either in particular."
So that Madame, by this clever diversion, decided him.
The king smiled upon De Guiche, who did not comprehend
a word of Madame's dumb language, but he remarked
that she pretended not to look at him, and he attributed
the pardon which had been conferred upon him to the
princess's kindness of heart.   The king seemed pleased

with every one present. Monsieur was the only one who
did not understand anything about the matter. The
ballet began ; the effect was more than beautiful. When
the music, by its bursts of melody, carried away these
illustrious dancers, when the simple, untutored pantomime
of that period, only the more natural on account of the
very indifferent acting of the august actors, had reached
its culminating point of triumph, the theater shook with
tumultuous applause.

De Guiche shone like a sun, but like a courtly sun, that
is resigned to fill a subordinate part. Disdainful of a
success of which Madame showed no acknowledgment,
he thought of nothing but boldly regaining the marked
preference of the princess. She, however, did not bestow a single glance upon him. By degrees all his happiness, all his brilliancy, subsided into regret and uneasiness ; so that his limbs lost their power, his arms
hung heavily by his sides, and his head drooped as though
he was stupefied. The king, who had from this moment
become in reality the principal dancer in the quadrille,
cast a look upon his vanquished rival. De Guiche soon
ceased to sustain even the character of the courtier : without applause, he danced indifferently, and very soon
could not dance at all, by which accident the triumph of
the king and of Madame was assured.

CHAPTER V.

THE NYMPHS OF THE PARK OF FONTAINEBLEAU.

THE king remained for a moment to enjoy a triumph
as complete as it could possibly be. He then turned
towards Madame, for the purpose of admiring her also a
little in her turn. Young persons love with more vivacity, .

perhaps with greater ardor and deeper passion, than others more advanced in years; but all the other feelings are at the same time developed in proportion to their youth and vigor: so that vanity being with them almost always the equivalent of love, the latter feeling, according to the laws of equipoise, never attains that degree of perfection which it acquires in men and women from thirty to five-and-thirty years of age. Louis thought of Madame, but only after he had studiously thought of himself : and Madame carefully thought of herself, without bestowing a single thought upon the king. The victim, however, of all these royal affections and affectations, was poor De Guiche. Every one could observe his agitation and prostration —a prostration which was, indeed, the more remarkable since people were not accustomed to see him with his arms hanging listlessly by his side, his head bewildered, and eyes with all their bright intelligence bedimmed. It rarely happened that any uneasiness was excited on his account, whenever a question of elegance or taste was under discussion ; and De Guiche's defeat was accordingly attributed by the greater number present to his courtier-like tact and ability. But there were others —keen-sighted observers are always to be met with at court —who remarked his paleness and his altered looks ; which he could neither feign nor conceal, and their conclusion was that De Guiche was not acting the part of a flatterer. All these sufferings, successes, and remarks, were blended, confounded, and lost in the uproar of applause. When, however, the queens had expressed their satisfaction and the spectators their enthusiasm, when the king had retired to his dressing-room to change his costume, and whilst Monsieur, dressed as a woman, as he delighted to be, was in his turn, dancing about, De Guiche, who had now re-covered himself, approached Madame, who, seated at the back of the theater, was waiting for the second part, and

had quitted the others for the purpose of creating a sort
of solitude for herself in the midst of the crowd, to meditate, as it were, beforehand, upon chorographic effects:
and it will be perfectly understood that, absorbed in deep
meditation, she did not see, or rather pretended not to
notice, anything that was passing around her.   De Guiche,
observing that she was alone, near a thicket constructed
of painted cloth, approached her.   Two of her maids of
honor, dressed as hamadryads, seeing De Guiche advance,
drew back out of respect, whereupon De Guiche proceeded
towards the middle of the circle and saluted her royal
highness; but, whether she did or did not observe his salutations, the princess did not even turn her head.   A cold
shiver passed through poor De Guiche; he was unpre-
pared for such utter indifference, for he had neither seen
nor been told of anything that had taken place, and consequently could guess nothing.   Remarking, therefore,
that his obeisance obtained him no acknowledgment, he
advanced one step further, and in a voice which he tried,
though vainly, to render calm, said: "I have the honor
to present my most humble respects to your royal highness."

Upon this Madame deigned to turn her eyes languish-
ingly towards the comte, observing. "Ah! M. de Guiche,
is that you? good-day!"

The comte's patience almost forsook him, as he continued,—"Your royal highness danced just now most
charmingly."

"Do you think so?" she replied with indifference.

"Yes; the character which your royal highness
assumed is in perfect harmony with your own."

Madame again turned round, and, looking De Guiche
full in the face with a bright and steady gaze, said,—
"Why so?"

"Oh! there can be no doubt of it."

"Explain yourself?"

"You represented a divinity, beautiful, disdainful, inconstant."

"You mean Pomona, comte?"

"I allude to the goddess."

Madame remained silent for a moment, with her lips compressed, and then observed,—"But comte, you, too, are an excellent dancer."

"Nay, madame, I am only one of those who are never noticed, or who are soon forgotten if they ever happen to be noticed."

With this remark, accompanied by one of those deep sighs which affect the remotest fibers of one's being, his heart burdened with sorrow and throbbing fast, his head on fire, and his gaze wandering, he bowed breathlessly, and withdrew behind the thicket. The only reply Madame condescended to make was by slightly raising her shoulders, and, as her ladies of honor had discreetly retired while the conversation lasted, she recalled them by a look. The ladies were Mademoiselle de Tonnay-Charente and Mademoiselle de Montalais.

"Did you hear what the Comte de Guiche said?" the princess inquired.

"No."

"It really is very singular," she continued, in a compassionate tone, "how exile has affected poor M. de Guiche's wit." And then, in a louder voice, fearful lest her unhappy victim might lose a syllable, she said,—"In the first place he danced badly, and afterwards his remarks were very silly."

She then rose, humming the air to which she was presently going to dance. De Guiche had overheard everything. The arrow pierced his heart and wounded him mortally. Then, at the risk of interrupting the progress of the *fête* by his annoyance, he fled from the scene, tearing his beautiful costume of Autumn in pieces, and scattering, as he went along, the branches of vines, mulberry and almond trees, with all the other artificial attributes of his assumed divinity. A quarter of an hour afterwards he returned to the theater; but it will be readily believed that it was only a powerful effort of reason over his great excitement that enabled him to go back; or perhaps, for love is thus strangely constituted, he found it impossible even to remain much longer separated from the presence of one who had broken his heart. Madame was finishing her figure. She saw, but did not look at De Guiche, who, irritated and revengeful, turned his back upon her as she passed him, escorted by her nymphs, and followed by a hundred flatterers. During this time, at the other end of the theater, near the lake, a young woman was seated, with her eyes fixed upon one of the windows of the theater, from which were issuing streams of light— the window in question being that of the royal box. As De Guiche quitted the theater for the purpose of getting into the fresh air he so much needed, he passed close to this figure and saluted her. When she perceived the young man, she rose, like a woman surprised in the midst of ideas she was desirous of concealing from herself. De Guiche stopped as he recognized her, and said hurriedly, —"Good-evening, Mademoiselle de la Vallière; I am indeed fortunate in meeting you."

"I, also, M. de Guiche, am glad of this accidental meeting," said the young girl, as she was about to withdraw.

"Pray do not leave me," said De Guiche, stretching out his hand towards her, "for you would be contradicting the kind words you have just pronounced. Remain, I implore you: the evening is most lovely. You wish to escape from the merry tumult, and prefer your own society. Well, I can understand it; all women who are possessed of any feeling do, and one never finds them dull or lonely when removed from the giddy vortex of these exciting amusements. Oh! Heaven!" he exclaimed, suddenly.

"What is the matter, monsieur le comte?" inquired La Vallière, with some anxiety. "You seem agitated."

"I! oh, no!"

"Will you allow me, M. de Guiche, to return you the thanks I had proposed to offer you on the very first opportunity. It is to your recommendation, I am aware, that I owe my admission among the number of Madame's maids of honor."

"Indeed! Ah! I remember now, and I congratulate myself. Do you love any one?"

"I!" exclaimed La Vallière.

"Forgive me, I hardly know what I am saying; a thousand times forgive me; Madame was right, quite right, this brutal exile has completely turned my brain."

"And yet it seemed to me that the king received you with kindness."

"Do you think so? Received me with kindness—perhaps so—yes——"

"There cannot be a doubt he received you kindly, for, in fact you returned without his permission."

"Quite true, and I believe you are right. But have you not seen M. de Bragelonne here?"

La Vallière started at the name. "Why do you ask?" she inquired.

"Have I offended you again?" said De Guiche. "In that case I am indeed unhappy, and greatly to be pitied."

"Yes, very unhappy, and very much to be pitied, Monsieur de Guiche, for you seem to be suffering terribly."

"Oh! mademoiselle, why have I not a devoted sister, or a true friend, such as yourself?"

"You have friends, Monsieur de Guiche, and the Vicomte de Bragelonne, of whom you spoke just now, is, I believe, one of the most devoted.".

"Yes, yes, you are right, he is one of my best friends. Farewell, Mademoiselle de la Vallière, farewell." And he fled, like one possessed, along the banks of the lake. His dark shadow glided, lengthening as it disappeared, among the illumined yews and glittering undulations of the water. La Vallière looked after him, saying,—"Yes, yes, he, too, is suffering, and I begin to understand why."

She had hardly finished when her companions, Mademoiselle de Montalais and Mademoiselle de Tonnay-Charente, ran forward. They were released from their attendance, and had changed their costumes of nymphs; delighted with the beautiful night, and the success of the evening, they returned to look after their companion.

"What, already here!" they said to her. "We thought we should be first at the rendezvous."

"I have been here this quarter of an hour," replied La Vallière.

"Did not the dancing amuse you?"

"No."

"But surely the enchanting spectacle?"

"No more than the dancing. As far as beauty is concerned, I much prefer that which these dark woods present, in whose depths can be seen now in one direction and again in another, a light passing by, as though it were an eye, in color like a midnight rainbow, sometimes open, at others closed."

"La Vallière is quite a poetess," said Tonnay-Charente.

"In other words," said Montalais, "she is insupportable. Whenever there is a question of laughing a little, or of amusing ourselves, La Vallière begins to cry; whenever we girls have reason to cry, because, perhaps, we have

mislaid our dresses, or because our vanity has been wounded, or our costume fails to produce an effect, La Vallière
laughs."

" As far as I am concerned, that is not my character,"
said Mademoiselle de Tonnay-Charente. " I am a woman;
and there are few like me ; whoever loves me, flatters me ;
whoever flatters me, pleases me : and whoever pleases-—"

" Well ! " said Montalais, " you do not finish."

" It is too difficult," replied Mademoiselle de Tonnay-
Charente, laughing loudly. " Do you, who are so clever,
finish for me."

" And you, Louise ? " said Montalais, " does any one
please you ? "

" That is a matter which concerns no one but myself,"
replied the young girl, rising from the mossy bank on
which she had been reclining during the whole time the
ballet lasted. " Now, mesdemoiselles, we have agreed to
amuse ourselves to-night without any one to overlook us,
and without any escort. We are three in number, we like
one another, and the night is lovely. Look yonder, do you not
see the moon slowly rising, silvering the topmost branches
of the chestnuts and the oaks. Oh ! beautiful walk ! sweet
liberty ! exquisite soft turf of the woods, the happiness
which your friendship confers upon me ! let us walk arm-
in-arm towards those large trees. Out yonder all are at
this moment seated at table and fully occupied, or preparing to adorn themselves for a set and formal promenade ;
horses are being saddled, or harnessed to the carriages—
the queen's mules or Madame's four white ponies. As
for ourselves, we shall soon reach some retired spot where
no eye can see us and no step follow ours. Do you not
remember, Montalais, the woods of Chaverney and of
Chambord, the innumerable rustling poplars of Blois,
where we exchanged our mutual hopes ? "

" And confidences too ? "

" Yes."

" Well," said Mademoiselle de Tonnay-Charente.   " I
also think a good deal; but I take care——"

" To say nothing," said Montalais, " so that when
Mademoiselle de Tonnay-Charente thinks, Athenaïs is
the only one who knows it."

" Hush!" said Mademoiselle de Tonnay-Charente, " I
hear steps approaching from this side."

" Quick, quick, then, among the high reed-grass," said
Montalais ; " stoop, Athenaïs, you are so tall."

Mademoiselle de Tonnay-Charente stooped as she was
told, and, almost at the same moment, they saw two gentlemen approaching, their heads bent down, walking arm-
in-arm, on the fine gravel-walk running parallel with the
bank.   The young girls had, indeed, made themselves
small—indeed invisible.

" It is Monsieur de Guiche," whispered Montalais in
Mademoiselle de Tonnay-Charente's ear.

" It is Monsieur de Bragelonne," whispered the latter
to La Vallière.

The two young men approached still closer, conversing
in animated tones. " She was here just now," said the
count. " If I had only seen her, I should have declared it
to be a vision, but I spoke to her."

" You are positive, then?"

" Yes ; but perhaps I frightened her."

" In what way?"

" Oh! I was still half crazy at you know what; so that
she could hardly have understood what I was saying, and
must have grown alarmed."

" Oh !" said Bragelonne, " do not make yourself uneasy : she is all kindness, and will excuse you; she is
clear-sighted, and will understand."

" Yes, but if she should have understood, and understood too well, she may talk."

"You do not know Louise, count," said Raoul. "Louise possesses every virtue, and has not a single fault." And the two young men passed on, and, as they proceeded, their voices were soon lost in the distance.

"How is it, La Vallière," said Mademoiselle de Tonnay-Charente, "that the Vicomte de Bragelonne spoke of you as Louise?"

"We were brought up together," replied Louise, blushing; "M. de Bragelonne has honored me by asking my hand in marriage, but——"

"Well?"

"It seems the king will not consent to it."

"Eh! Why the king? and what has the king to do with it?" exclaimed Aure sharply. "Good gracious! has the king any right to interfere in matters of that kind? Politics are politics, as M. de Mazarin used to say; but love is love. If, therefore, you love M. de Bragelonne, marry him: *I* give *my* consent."

Athenaïs began to laugh.

"Oh! I am speaking seriously," replied Montalais, "and my opinion in this case is quite as good as the king's, I suppose; is it not, Louise?"

"Come," said La Vallière, "these gentlemen have passed; let us take advantage of our being alone to cross the open ground and so take refuge in the woods."

"So much the better," said Athenaïs, "because I see the torches setting out from the château and the theater, and they seem as if they were preceding some person of distinction."

"Let us run, then," said all three. And, gracefully lifting up the long skirts of their silk dresses, they lightly ran across the open space between the lake and the thickest covert of the park. Montalais agile as a deer, Athenaïs eager as a young wolf, bounded through the dry grass, and, now and then, some bold Acteon might, by the aid of the faint light, have perceived their straight and well-formed limbs somewhat displayed beneath the heavy folds of their satin petticoats. La Vallière, more refined and more bashful, allowed her dress to flow around her ; retarded also by the lameness of her foot, it was not long before she called out to her companions to halt, and, left behind, she obliged them both to wait for her. At this moment, a man, concealed in a dry ditch planted with young willow saplings, scrambled quickly up its shelving side, and ran off in the direction of the château. The three young girls, on their side, reached the outskirts of the park, every path of which they well knew. The ditches were bordered by high hedges full of flowers, which on that side protected the foot passengers from being intruded upon by the horses and carriages. In fact, the sound of Madame's and the queen's carriages could be heard in the distance upon the hard dry ground of the roads, followed by the mounted cavaliers. Distant music reached them in response, and when the soft notes died away, the nightingale, with throat of pride, poured forth his melodious chants, and his most complicated, learned, and sweetest compositions, to those who had met beneath the thick covert of the woods. Near the songster, in the dark background of the large trees, could be seen the glistening eyes of an owl, attracted by the harmony. In this way the *fête* of the whole court was a *fête* also for the mysterious inhabitants of the forest ; for certainly the deer in the brake, the pheasant on the branch, the fox in its hole, were all listening. One could realize the life led by this nocturnal and invisible population from the restless movements that suddenly took place among the leaves. Our sylvan nymphs uttered a slight cry, but, reassured immediately afterwards, they laughed, and resumed their walk. In this manner they reached the royal oak, the venerable relic of a tree which in its prime had listened to the sighs of Henry the Second for the beautiful Diana of Poictiers, and later still to those of Henry the Fourth for the lovely Gabrielle D'Estrées. Beneath this oak the gardeners had piled up the moss and turf in such a manner that never had seat more luxuriously rested the wearied limbs of man or monarch. The trunk, somewhat rough to recline against, was sufficiently large to accommodate the three young girls, whose voices were lost among the branches, which stretched upwards to the sky.

CHAPTER VI.

WHAT WAS SAID UNDER THE ROYAL OAK.

THE softness of the air, the stillness of the foliage, tacitly imposed upon these young girls an engagement to change immediately their giddy conversation for one of a more serious character. She, indeed, whose disposition was the most lively,—Montalais, for instance,—was the first to yield to the influence; and she began by heaving a deep sigh, and saying:—"What happiness to be here alone, and at liberty, with every right to be frank, especially towards one another."

"Yes," said Mademoiselle de Tonnay-Charente; "for the court, however brilliant it may be, has always some falsehood concealed beneath the folds of its velvet robes, or the glitter of its diamonds."

"I," replied La Vallière, "I never tell a falsehood; when I cannot speak the truth, I remain silent."

"You will not remain long in favor," said Montalais; "it is not here, as it was at Blois, where we told the dowager Madame all our little annoyances, and all our longings. There were certain days when Madame remembered that she herself had been young, and, on those days, whoever talked with her found in her a sincere friend. She related to us her flirtations with Monsieur, and we told her of the flirtations she had had with others, or, at least, the rumors of them that had spread abroad. Poor woman, so simple-minded! she laughed at them, as we did. Where is she now?"

"Ah, Montalais,—laughter-loving Montalais!" cried La Vallière; "you see you are sighing again; the woods inspire you, and you are almost reasonable this evening."

"You ought not, either of you," said Athenaïs, "to regret the court at Blois so much, unless you do not feel happy with us. A court is a place where men and women resort to talk of matters which mothers, guardians, and especially confessors, severely denounce."

"Oh, Athenaïs!" said Louise, blushing.

"Athenaïs is frank to-night," said Montalais; "let us avail ourselves of it."

"Yes, let us take advantage of it, for this evening I could divulge the softest secrets of my heart."

"Ah, if M. Montespan were here!" said Montalais.

"Do you think that I care for M. de Montespan?" murmured the beautiful young girl.

"He is handsome, I believe?"

"Yes. And that is no small advantage in my eyes."

"There now, you see——"

"I will go further, and say, that of all the men whom one sees here, he is the handsomest, and the most——"

"What was that?" said La Vallière, starting suddenly from the mossy bank.

"A deer hurrying by, perhaps."

"I am only afraid of men," said Athenaïs.

"When they do not resemble M. de Montespan."

"A truce to raillery. M. de Montespan is attentive to

me, but that does not commit me in any way. Is not
M. de Guiche here, he who is so devoted to Madame ? "

" Poor fellow ! " said La Vallière.

" Why to be pitied ? "   Madame is sufficiently beautiful,
and of high enough rank, I suppose."

La Vallière shook her head sorrowfully, saying, " when
one loves, it is neither beauty nor rank ;—when one loves
it should be the heart, or the eyes only, of him, or of her
whom one loves."

Montalais began to laugh loudly. " Heart, eyes," she
said; " oh, sugar-plums ! "

" I speak for myself," replied La Vallière.

"Noble sentiments," said Athenaïs, with an air of protection, but with indifference.

" Are they not your own ? " asked Louise.

" Perfectly so ; but to continue : how can one pity a
man who bestows his attentions upon such a woman as
Madame ?   If any disproportion exists, it is on the count's
side."

" Oh ! no, no," returned La Vallière ; " it is on Madame's
side."

" Explain yourself."

" I will.   Madame has not even a wish to know what
love is.   She diverts herself with the feeling, as children
do with fireworks, from which a spark might set a palace
on fire.   It makes a display, and that is all she cares
about.   Besides, pleasure forms the tissue of which she
wishes her life to be woven.   M. de Guiche loves this illustrious personage, but she will never love him."

Athenaïs laughed disdainfully. " Do people really ever
love ? " she said.   " Where are the noble sentiments you
just now uttered ?   Does not a woman's virtues consist
in the uncompromising refusal of every intrigue that might
compromise her?   A properly-regulated woman, endowed
with a natural heart, ought to look at men, make herself

loved—adored, even, by them, and say at the very utmost
but once in her life, 'I begin to think that I ought not to
have been what I am,—I should have detested this one
less than others."

" Therefore," exclaimed La Vallière, " that is what M.
de Montespan has to expect."

" Certainly ; he, as well as every one else.   What ! have
I not said that I admit he possesses a certain superiority,
and would not that be enough ?   My dear child, a woman
is a queen during the entire period nature permits her to
enjoy sovereign power—from fifteen to thirty-five years
of age.   After that, we are free to have a heart, when we
only have that left——"

" Oh, oh ! " murmured La Vallière.

" Excellent," cried Montalais ; " a very masterly woman ;
Athenaïs, you will make your way in the world."

" Do you not approve of what I say ? "

" Completely," replied her laughing companion.

" You are not serious, Montalais ? " said Louise.

" Yes, yes ; I approve everything Athenaïs has just
said ; only——"

" Only *what ?* "

" Well, I cannot carry it out.   I have the firmest prin-
ciples ; I form resolutions beside which the laws of the
Stadtholder and of the King of Spain are child's play ; but,
when the moment arrives to put them into execution,
nothing comes of them."

" Your courage fails ? " said Athenaïs, scornfully.

" Miserably so."

" Great weakness of nature," returned Athenaïs.   " But
at least you make a choice."

" Why, no.   It pleases fate to disappoint me in everything ; I dream of emperors, and I find only——"

" Aure, Aure ! " exclaimed La Vallière, " for pity's sake,
do not, for the pleasure of saying something witty,

sacrifice those who love you with such devoted affection."

" Oh, I do not trouble myself much about that ; those who love me are sufficiently happy that I do not dismiss them altogether.   So much the worse for myself if I have a weakness for any one, but so much the worse for others if I revenge myself upon them for it."

" You are right," said Athenaïs, " and, perhaps, you too will reach the goal.   In other words, young ladies, that is termed being a coquette.   Men, who are very silly in most things, are particularly so in confounding, under the term of coquetry, a woman's pride, and love of changing her sentiments as she does her dress.   I, for instance, am proud ; that is to say, impregnable.   I treat my admirers harshly, but without any pretension to retain them.   Men call me a coquette, because they are vain enough to think I care for them.   Other women—Montalais, for instance— have allowed themselves to be influenced by flattery ; they would be lost were it not for that most fortunate prin- ciple of instinct which urges them to change suddenly, and punish the man whose devotion they so recently accepted."

" A very learned dissertation," said Montalais, in the tone of thorough enjoyment.

" It is odious ! " murmured Louise.

" Thanks to that sort of coquetry, for, indeed, that is genuine coquetry," continued Mademoiselle Tonnay- Charente ; " the lover who, a little while since, was puffed up with pride, in a minute afterwards is suffering at every pore of his vanity and self-esteem.   He was, perhaps, al- ready beginning to assume the airs of a conqueror, but now he retreats defeated ; he was about to assume an air of protection towards us, but he is obliged to prostrate himself once more.   The result of all this is, that, instead of having a husband who is jealous and troublesome, free from restraint in his conduct toward us, we have a lover always

trembling in our presence, always fascinated by our attractions, always submissive ; and for this simple reason, that he finds the same woman never twice of the same mind. Be convinced, therefore, of the advantages of coquetry. Possessing that, one reigns a queen among women in cases where Providence has withheld that precious faculty of holding one's heart and mind in check."

" How clever you are," said Montalais, " and how well you understand the duty women owe themselves ! "

" I am only settling a case of individual happiness," said Athenaïs modestly ; " and defending myself, like all weak, loving dispositions, against the oppressions of the stronger."

" La Vallière does not say a word."

" Does she not approve of what we are saying ? "

" Nay ; only I do not understand it," said Louise. " You talk like people not called upon to live in this world of ours."

" And very pretty your world is," said Montalais.

" A world," returned Athenaïs, " in which men worship a woman until she has fallen,—and insult her when she has fallen."

" Who spoke to you of falling ? " said Louise.

" Yours is a new theory, then ; will you tell us how you intend to resist yielding to temptation, if you allow yourself to be hurried away by feelings of affection ? "

" Oh ! " exclaimed the young girl, raising towards the dark heavens her beautiful large eyes filled with tears, " if you did but know what a heart is, I would explain, and convince you ; a loving heart is stronger than all your coquetry, more powerful than all your pride. A woman is never truly loved, I believe ; a man never loves with idolatry, unless he feels sure he is loved in return. Let old men, whom we read of in comedies, fancy themselves adored by coquettes. A young man is conscious

of, and knows them ; if he has a fancy, or a strong desire,
or an absorbing passion, for a coquette, he cannot mistake
her ; a coquette may drive him out of his senses, but will
never make him fall in love.   Love, such as I conceive it
to be, is an incessant, complete, and perfect sacrifice ; but
it is not the sacrifice of one only of the two persons thus
united.   It is the perfect abnegation of two who are
desirous of blending their beings into one.   If I ever love,
I shall implore my lover to leave me free and pure ; I will
tell him, and he will understand, that my heart was torn
by my refusal, and he, in his love for me, aware of the
magnitude of my sacrifice,—he, in his turn, I say, will
store his devotion for me,—will respect me, and will not
seek my ruin, to insult me when I shall have fallen, as
you said just now, whilst uttering your blasphemies
against love, such as I understand it.   That is *my* idea of
love.   And now you will tell me, perhaps, that my lover
will despise me ; I defy him to do so, unless he be the
vilest of men, and my heart assures me that it is not such
a man I would choose.   A look from me will repay him
for the sacrifices he makes, or will inspire him with virtues
which he would never think he possessed."

" But, Louise," exclaimed Montalais, " you tell us this,
and do not carry it into practice."

" What do you mean ? "

" You are adored by Raoul de Bragelonne, who worships
you on both knees.   The poor fellow is made the victim
of your virtue, just as he would be—nay, more than he
would be, even—of my coquetry, or of Athenaïs's pride."

" All this is simply a different shade of coquetry,
said Athenaïs ; " and Louise, I perceive, is a coquette
without knowing it."

" Oh ! " said La Vallière.

" Yes, you may call it instinct, if you please, keenest
sensibility, exquisite refinement of feeling, perpetual dis-

play of restrained outbreaks of affection, which end in smoke. It is very artful too, and very effective. I should even, now that I reflect on it, have preferred this system of tactics to my own pride, for waging war on members of the other sex, because it offers the advantage sometimes of thoroughly convincing them; but, at the present moment, without utterly condemning myself, I declare it to be superior to the non-complex coquetry of Montalais." And the two young girls began to laugh.

La Vallière alone preserved silence, and quietly shook her head. Then, a moment after, she added, "If you were to tell me, in the presence of a man, but a fourth part of what you have just said, or even if I were assured that you think it, I should die of shame and grief where I am now."

"Very well; die, poor tender little darling," replied Mademoiselle de Tonnay-Charente; "for, if there are no men here, there are at least two women, your own friends, who declare you to be attainted and convicted of being a coquette from instinct; in other words, the most danger- ous kind of coquette the world possesses."

"Oh! mesdemoiselles," replied La Vallière, blushing, and almost ready to weep. Her two companions again burst out laughing.

"Very well! I will ask Bragelonne to tell me."

"Bragelonne?" said Athenaïs.

"Yes! Bragelonne, who is as courageous as Cæsar, and as clever and witty as M. Fouquet. Poor fellow! for twelve years he has known you, loved you, and yet—one can hardly believe it—he has never even kissed the tips of your fingers."

"Tell us the reason of this cruelty, you who are all heart," said Athenaïs to La Vallière.

"Let me explain it by a single word—virtue. You will perhaps deny the existence of virtue?"

"Come, Louise, tell us the truth," said Aure, taking her by the hand.

"What do you wish me to tell you?" cried Vallière.

"Whatever you like; but it will be useless for you to say anything, for I persist in my opinion of you. A coquette from instinct; in other words, as I have already said, and I say it again, the most dangerous of all coquettes."

"Oh! no, no; for pity's sake do not believe that!"

"What! twelve years of extreme severity."

"How can that be, since twelve years ago I was only five years old. The frivolity of the child cannot surely be placed to the young girl's account."

"Well! you are now seventeen; three years instead of twelve. During those three years you have remained constantly and unchangeably cruel. Against you are arrayed the silent shades of Blois, the meetings when you diligently conned the stars together, the evening wanderings beneath the plantain trees, his impassioned twenty years speaking to your fourteen summers, the fire of his glances addressed to yourself."

"Yes, yes; but so it is!"

"Impossible!"

"But why impossible?"

"Tell us something credible and we will believe you."

"Yet, if you were to suppose one thing."

"What is that?"

"Suppose that I thought I was in love, and that I am not."

"What! not in love!"

"Well, then! if I have acted in a different manner to what others do when they are in love, it is because I do not love; and because my hour has not yet come."

"Louise, Louise," said Montalais, "take care, or I will remind you of the remark you made just now. Raoul is not here ; do not overwhelm him while he is absent ; be charitable, and if, on closer inspection, you think you do not love him, tell him so, poor fellow ! " and she began to laugh.

" Louise pitied M. de Guiche just now," said Athenaïs ; " would it be possible to detect an explanation of her indifference for the one in this compassion for the other."

" Say what you please," said La Vallière, sadly ; " upbraid me as you like, since you do not understand me."

" Oh ! oh ! " replied Montalais, " temper, sorrow, tears ; we are jesting, Louise, and are not, I assure you, quite the monsters you suppose. Look at the proud Athenaïs, as she is called ; she does not love M. de Montespan, it is true, but she would be in despair if M. de Montespan did not continue to love her. Look at me ; I laugh at M. Malicorne, but the poor fellow whom I laugh at knows precisely when he will be permitted to press his lips upon my hand. And yet the eldest of us is not twenty yet. What a future before us ! "

" Silly, silly girls ! " murmured Louise.

" You are quite right," said Montalais ; " and you alone have spoken words of wisdom."

" Certainly."

" I do not dispute it," replied Athenaïs. " And so it is clear you do not love poor M. de Bragelonne ? "

" Perhaps she does," said Montalais ; " she is not yet quite sure of it. But, in any case, listen, Athenaïs ; if M. de Bragelonne is ever free, I will give you a little friendly advice."

" What is that ? "

" To look at him well before you decide in favor of M. de Montespan."

" Oh ! in that way of considering the subject, M. de Bragelonne is not the only one whom one could look at with pleasure ; M. de Guiche, for instance, has his value also."

" He did not distinguish himself this evening," said Montalais ; "and I know from very good authority that Madame thought him insupportable."

" M. de Saint-Aignan produced a most brilliant effect, and I am sure that more than one person who saw him dance this evening, will not soon forget him. Do you not think so, La Vallière ? "

" Why do you ask me? I did not see him, nor do I know him."

" What ! you did not see M. de Saint-Aignan ? Don't you know him ? "

" No."

" Come, come, do not affect a virtue more extravagantly excessive than our vanity !—you have eyes, I suppose ? "

" Excellent."

" Then you must have seen all those who danced this evening."

" Yes, nearly all."

" That is a very impertinent ' nearly all ' for somebody."

" You must take it for what it is worth."

" Very well; now, among all those gentlemen whom you saw, which do you prefer ? "

" Yes," said Montalais, "is it M. de Saint-Aignan, or M. de Guiche, or M.——"

" I prefer no one ; I thought them all about the same."

" Do you mean, then, that among that brilliant assembly, the first court in the world, no one pleased you."

" I do not say that."

" Tell us, then, who your ideal is ? "

" It is not an ideal being."

" He exists, then ? "

" In very truth," exclaimed La Vallière, aroused and excited ; " I cannot understand you at all. What ! you who have a heart as I have, eyes as I have, and yet you speak of M. de Guiche, of M. de Saint-Aignan, when the king

was there." These words, uttered in a precipitate manner, and in an agitated, fervid tone of voice, made her two
companions, between whom she was seated, exclaim in a
manner that terrified her, " *The king !*"

La Vallière buried her face in her hands. " Yes," she
murmured ; "the king! the king! Have you ever seen
any one to be compared to the king ? "

" You were right just now in saying you had excellent
eyes, Louise, for you see a great distance ; too far, indeed.
Alas! the king is not one upon whom our poor eyes have
a right to hinge themselves."

" That is too true," cried La Vallière ; " it is not the
privilege of all eyes to gaze upon the sun ; but I will look
upon him, even were I to be blinded in doing so." At
this moment, and as though caused by the words which
had just escaped La Vallière's lips, a rustling of leaves,
and of what sounded like some silken material, was
heard behind the adjoining bushes. The young girls
hastily rose, almost terrified out of their senses. They
distinctly saw the leaves move, without being able to see
what it was that stirred them.

" It is a wolf or a wild boar," cried Montalais ; "fly!
fly ! " The three girls, in the extremity of terror, fled by
the first path that presented itself, and did not stop until
they had reached the verge of the wood. There, breathless, leaning against each other, feeling their hearts throb
wildly, they endeavored to collect their senses, but could
only succeed in doing so after the lapse of some minutes.
Perceiving at last the lights from the windows of the
château, they decided to walk towards them. La Vallière
was exhausted with fatigue, and Aure and Athenaïs were
obliged to support her.

" We have escaped well," said Montalais.

" I am greatly afraid," said La Vallière, "that it was
something worse than a wolf. For my part, and I speak

as I think, I should have preferred to have run the risk of
being devoured alive by some wild animal than to have
been listened to and overheard. Fool, fool, that I am!
How could I have thought, how could I have said what I
did." And saying this her head bowed like the water-
tossed plume of a bulrush; she felt her limbs fail, and her
strength abandoning her, and, gliding almost inanimate
from the arms of her companions, sank down upon the
turf.

CHAPTER VII.

THE KING'S UNEASINESS.

LET us leave poor La Vallière, who had fainted in the
arms of her two companions, and return to the precincts
of the royal oak. The young girls had hardly run twenty
paces, when the sound which had so much alarmed them
was renewed among the branches. A man's figure might
indistinctly be perceived, and putting the branches of the
bushes aside, he appeared upon the verge of the wood, and
perceiving that the place was empty, burst out into a peal
of laughter. It is almost superfluous to add that the form
in question was that of a young and handsome cavalier,
who immediately made a sign to another, who thereupon
made his appearance.

" What, sire," said the second figure, advancing timidly,
"has your majesty put our young sentimentalists to flight."

" It seems so," said the king, "and you can show yourself without fear."

" Take care, sire, you will be recognized."

" But I tell you they are flown."

" This is a most fortunate meeting, sire; and, if I dared
offer an opinion to your majesty, we ought to follow them."

" They are far enough away by this time."

" They would quickly allow themselves to be overtaken, especially if they knew who were following them."

" What do you mean by that, coxcomb that you are ? "

" Why one of them seems to have taken a fancy to me, and another compared you to the sun."

" The greater reason why we should not show ourselves, Saint-Aignan. The sun never shows himself in the night-time."

" Upon my word, sire, your majesty seems to have very little curiosity. In your place, I should like to know who are the two nymphs, the two dryads, the two hama-dryads, who have so good an opinion of us."

" I shall know them again very well, I assure you, without running after them."

" By what means ? "

" By their voices, of course. They belong to the court, and the one who spoke of me had a remarkably sweet voice."

" Ah ! your majesty permits yourself to be influenced by flattery."

" No one will ever say it is a means *you* make use of."

" Forgive my stupidity, sire."

" Come ; let us go and look where I told you. .

" Is the passion, then, which your majesty confided to me, already forgotten ? "

" Oh ! no, indeed. How is it possible to forget such beautiful eyes as Mademoiselle de la Vallière has ? "

" Yet the other had as beautiful a voice."

" Which one ? "

" The lady who has fallen in love with the sun."

" M. de Saint-Aignan ! "

" Forgive me, sire."

" Well, I am not sorry you should believe me to be an admirer of sweet voices as well as of beautiful eyes. I know you to be a terrible talker, and to-morrow I shall have to pay for the confidence I have shown you ? "

" What do you mean, sire ? "

" That to-morrow every one will know that I have designs upon this little La Vallière; but be careful, Saint-Aignan, I have confided my secret to no one but you, and if any one should speak to me about it, I shall know who has betrayed my secret."

" You are angry, sire."

" No; but you understand I do not wish to compromise the poor girl."

" Do not be afraid, sire."

" You promise me, then ? "

" I give you my word of honor."

" Excellent," thought the king, laughing to himself; " now every one will know to-morrow that I have been running about after La Vallière to-night."

Then, endeavoring to see where he was, he said, " Why, we have lost ourselves."

" Not quite so bad as that, sire."

" Where does that gate lead to ? "

" To Rond-Point, sire."

" Where we were going when we heard the sound of women's voices ? "

" Yes, sire, and the termination of a conversation in which I had the honor of hearing my own name pronounced by the side of your majesty's."

" You return to that subject too frequently, Saint-Aignan."

" Your majesty will forgive me, but I am delighted to know that a woman exists whose thoughts are occupied about me, without my knowledge, and without my having done any thing to deserve it. Your majesty cannot comprehend this satisfaction, for your rank and merit attract attention, and compel regard."

"No, no, Saint-Aignan, believe me or not, as you like," said the king, leaning familiarly upon Saint Aignan's arm and taking the path he thought would lead them to the château; but this candid confession, this perfectly disinterested preference of one who will, perhaps, never attract my attention—in one word, the mystery of this adventure excites me, and the truth is, that if I were not so taken with La Vallière——"

"Do not let that interfere with your majesty's intentions : you have time enough before you."

"What do you mean ?"

"La Vallière is said to be very strict in her ideas."

"You excite my curiosity and I am anxious to see her again. Come let us walk on."

The king spoke untruly, for nothing, on the contrary, could make him less anxious, but he had a part to play, and so he walked on hurriedly. Saint-Aignan followed him at a short distance. Suddenly the king stopped, the courtier followed his example.

"Saint-Aignan," he said, "do you not hear some one moaning ?"

"Yes, sire, and weeping, too, it seems."

"It is in this direction," said the king. "It sounds like the tears and sobs of a woman."

"Run," said the king; and, following a by-path, they ran across the grass. As they approached, the cries were more distinctly heard.

"Help, help," exclaimed two voices. The king and his companion redoubled their speed, and, as they approached nearer, the sighs they had heard were changed into loud sobs. The cry of "Help! help!" was again repeated ; at the sound of which, the king and Saint-Aignan increased the rapidity of their pace. Suddenly, at the other side of a ditch, under the branches of a willow, they perceived a woman on her knees, holding another in her arms who seemed to have fainted. A few paces from them, a third, standing in the middle of the path, was calling for assistance. Perceiving two gentlemen, whose rank she could not tell, her cries for assistance were redoubled. The king, who was in advance of his companion, leaped across the ditch, and reached the group at the very moment when, from the end of the path which led to the château, a dozen persons were approaching, who had been drawn to the spot by the same cries that had attracted the attention of the king and M. de Saint-Aignan.

"What is the matter, young ladies?" said Louis.

"The king!" exclaimed Mademoiselle de Montalais, in her astonishment, letting La Vallière's head fall upon the ground.

"Yes, it is the king; but that is no reason why you should abandon your companion. Who is she?"

"It is Mademoiselle de la Vallière, sire."

"Mademoiselle de la Vallière!"

"Yes, sire, she has just fainted."

"Poor child!" said the king. "Quick, quick, fetch a surgeon." But however great the anxiety with which the king had pronounced these words may have seemed to others, he had not so carefully schooled himself, but that they appeared, as well as the gesture which accompanied them, somewhat cold to Saint-Aignan, to whom the king had confided the sudden love with which she had inspired him.

"Saint-Aignan," continued the king, "watch over Mademoiselle de Vallière, I beg. Send for a surgeon. I will hasten forward and inform Madame of the accident which has befallen one of her maids of honor." And, in fact, while M. de Saint-Aignan was busily engaged in making preparations for carrying Mademoiselle de la Vallière to the château, the king hurried forward, happy to have an opportunity of approaching Madame, and of speaking to her under a colorable pretext. Fortunately, a carriage was passing; the coachman was told to stop, and the persons who were inside, having been informed of the accident, eagerly gave up their seats to Mademoiselle de la Vallière. The current of fresh air produced by the rapid motion of the carriage soon recalled her to her senses. Having reached the château, she was able, though very weak, to alight from the carriage, and, with the assistance of Athenaïs and of Montalais, to reach the inner apartments. They made her sit down in one of the rooms of the ground-floor. After awhile, as the accident had not produced much effect upon those who had been walking, the promenade was resumed. During this time, the king had found Madame beneath a tree with overhanging branches, and had seated himself by her side.

"Take care, sire," said Henrietta to him, in a low tone, "you do not show yourself as indifferent as you ought to be."

"Alas!" replied the king, in the same tone, "I much fear we have entered into an agreement above our strength to keep." He then added aloud, "You have heard of the accident, I suppose?

"What accident?"

"Oh! in seeing you I forgot I hurried here expressly to tell you of it. I am, however, painfully affected by it; one of your maids of honor, Mademoiselle de la Vallière, has just fainted."

"Indeed! poor girl," said the princess, quietly, "what was the cause of it?"

She then added, in an undertone, "You forget, sire, that you wish others to believe in your passion for this girl, and yet you remain here while she is almost dying, perhaps, elsewhere."

"Ah! madame," said the king, sighing, "how much

more perfect you are in your part than I am, and how actively you think of everything."

He then rose, saying loud enough for every one to hear him, "Permit me to leave you, madame; my uneasiness is very great, and I wish to be quite certain, myself, that proper attention has been given to Mademoiselle de la Vallière." And the king left again to return to La Vallière, while those who had been present commented upon the king's remark:—"My uneasiness is very great."

CHAPTER VIII.

THE KING'S SECRET.

On his way Louis met the Comte de Saint-Aignan. "Well, Saint-Aignan," he inquired, with affected interest, "how is the invalid?"

"Really, sire," stammered Saint-Aignan, "to my shame, I confess I do not know."

"What! you do not know?" said the king, pretending to take in a serious manner this want of attention for the object of his predilection.

"Will your majesty pardon me; but I have just met one of our three loquacious wood-nymphs, and I confess that my attention has been taken away from other matters."

"Ah!" said the king, eagerly, "you have found, then——"

"The one who deigned to speak of me in such advantageous terms; and, having found mine, I was searching for yours, sire, when I had the happiness to meet your majesty."

"Very well; but Mademoiselle de la Vallière before

everything else," said the king, faithful to the character he had assumed.

"Oh! our charming invalid!" said Saint-Aignan; "how fortunately her fainting-fit came on, since your majesty had already occupied yourself about her."

"What is the name of your fair lady, Saint-Aignan? Is it a secret?"

"It ought to be a secret, and a very great one, even; but your majesty is well aware that no secret can possibly exist for you."

"Well, what is her name?"

"Mademoiselle de Tonnay-Charente."

"Is she pretty?"

"Exceedingly, sire; and I recognized the voice which pronounced my name in such tender accents. I accosted her, questioned her as well as I was able to do, in the midst of the crowd; and she told me, without suspecting anything, that a little while ago she was under the great oak, with her two friends, when the sound of a wolf or a robber had terrified them, and made them run away."

"But," inquired the king, anxiously, "what are the names of these two friends?"

"Sire," said Saint-Aignan, "will your majesty send me forthwith to the Bastile?"

"What for?"

"Because I am an egotist and a fool. My surprise was so great at such a conquest, and at so fortunate a discovery, that I went no further in my inquiries. Besides, I did not think that your majesty would attach any very great importance to what you heard, knowing how much your attention was taken up by Mademoiselle de la Vallière; and then, Mademoiselle de Tonnay-Charente left me precipitately, to return to Mademoiselle de la Vallière."

"Let us hope, then, that I shall be as fortunate as yourself. Come, Saint-Aignan."

"Your Majesty is ambitious, I perceive, and does not wish to allow any conquest to escape you. Well, I assure you that I will conscientiously set about my inquiries; and, moreover, from one or other of those Three Graces we shall learn the names of the rest, and by the names their secrets."

"I, too," said the king, " only require to hear her voice to know it again. Come, let us say no more about it, but show me where poor La Vallière is."

" Well," thought Saint-Aignan, " the king's regard is beginning to display itself, and for that girl too. It is extraordinary; I should never have believed it." And with this thought passing through his mind, he showed the king the room to which La Vallière had been carried; the king entered, followed by Saint-Aignan. In a low chamber, near a large window looking out upon the gardens, La Vallière, reclining in a large arm-chair, was inhaling deep draughts of the perfumed evening breeze. From the loosened body of her dress, the lace fell in tumbled folds, mingling with the tresses of her beautiful fair hair, which lay scattered upon her shoulders. Her languishing eyes were filled with tears; she seemed as lifeless as those beautiful visions of our dreams, that pass before the mental eyes of the sleeper, half-opening their wings without moving them, unclosing their lips without a sound escaping them. The pearl-like pallor of La Vallière possessed a charm it would be impossible to describe. Mental and bodily suffering had produced upon her features a soft and noble expression of grief; from the perfect passiveness of her arms and bust, she more resembled one whose soul had passed away, than a living being; she seemed not to hear either the whisperings of her companions, or the distant murmurs which arose from the court. She seemed to be communing within herself; and her beautiful, delicate hands trembled from time to time, as though at the contact of some invisible touch. She was so completely absorbed in her reverie, that the king entered without her perceiving him. At a distance he gazed upon her lovely face, upon which the moon shed its pure silvery light.

"Good Heavens!" he exclaimed, with a terror he could not control, " she is dead."

"No, sire," said Montalais, in a low voice; "on the contrary, she is better. Are you not better, Louise?"

But Louise did not answer. "Louise," continued Montalais, "the king has deigned to express his uneasiness on your account."

"The king!" exclaimed Louise, starting up abruptly, as if a stream of fire had darted through her frame to her heart; "the king uneasy about me?"

"Yes," said Montalais.

"The king is here, then?" said La Vallière, not venturing to look round her.

"That voice! that voice!" whispered Louis, eagerly, to Saint-Aignan.

"Yes, it is so," replied Saint-Aignan; "Your majesty is right; it is she who declared her love for the sun."

"Hush!" said the king. And then approaching La Vallière, he said, "You are not well, Mademoiselle de la Vallière? Just now, indeed, in the park, I saw that you had fainted. How were you attacked?"

"Sire," stammered out the poor child, pale and trembling, "I really do not know."

"You have been walking too far," said the king; "and fatigue, perhaps——"

"No, sire," said Montalais, eagerly, answering for her friend, "it could not be from fatigue, for we passed most of the evening seated beneath the royal oak."

"Under the royal oak?" returned the king, starting.

"I was not deceived; it is as I thought." And he directed a look of intelligence at the comte.

"Yes," said Saint-Aignan, "under the royal oak, with Mademoiselle de Tonnay-Charente."

"How do you know that?" inquired Montalais.

"In a very simple way. Mademoiselle de Tonnay-Charente told me so."

"In that case, she probably told you the cause of Mademoiselle de la Vallière's fainting?"

"Why, yes; she told me something about a wolf or a robber. I forget precisely which." La Vallière listened, her eyes fixed, her bosom heaving, as if, gifted with an acuteness of perception, she foresaw a portion of the truth. Louis imagined this attitude and agitation to be the consequence of a terror only partially reassured. "Nay, fear nothing," he said, with a rising emotion which he could not conceal; "the wolf which terrified you so much was simply a wolf with two legs."

"It was a man, then!" said Louise; "it was a man who was listening?"

"Suppose it was so, mademoiselle, what great harm was there in his having listened? Is it likely that, even in your own opinion, you would have said anything which could not have been listened to?"

La Vallière wrung her hands, and hid her face in them, as if to hide her blushes. In Heaven's name," she said, "who was concealed there? who was listening?"

The king advanced towards her, to take hold of one of her hands. "It was I," he said, bowing with marked respect. "Is it likely I could have frightened you?" La Vallière uttered a loud cry; for the second time her strength forsook her; and moaning in utter despair, she again fell lifeless in her chair. The king had just time to hold out his arm; so that she was partially supported by him. Mademoiselle de Tonnay-Charente and Montalais, who stood a few paces from the king and La Vallière, motionless and almost petrified at the recollection of their conversation with La Vallière, did not even think of offering their assistance, feeling restrained by the presence of the king, who, with one knee on the ground held La Vallière round the waist with his arm.

"You heard, sire!" murmured Athenaïs. But the king did not reply; he remained with his eyes fixed upon La Vallière's half-closed eyes, and held her quiescent hand in his own.

"Of course," replied Saint-Aignan, who, on his side, hoping that Mademoiselle de Tonnay-Charente, too, would faint, advanced towards her, holding his arms extended,—"of course; we did not even lose a single word." But the haughty Athenaïs was not a woman to faint easily; she darted a terrible look at Saint-Aignan, and fled. Montalais, with more courage, advanced hurriedly towards Louise, and received her from the king's hands, who was already fast losing his presence of mind, as he felt his face covered by the perfumed tresses of the seemingly dying girl. "Excellent," whispered Saint-Aignan. "This is indeed an adventure; and it will be my own fault if I am not the first to relate it."

The king approached him, and, with a trembling voice and a passionate gesture, said, "Not a syllable, comte."

The poor king forgot that, only an hour before, he had given him a similar recommendation, but with the very opposite intention; namely, that the comte should be indiscreet. It followed as a matter of course, that the latter recommendation was quite as unnecessary as the former. Half an hour afterwards, everybody in Fontainebleau knew that Mademoiselle de la Vallière had had a conversation under the royal oak with Montalais and Tonnay-Charente, and that in this conversation she had confessed her affection for the king. It was known, also, that the king, after having manifested the uneasiness with which Mademoiselle de la Vallière's health had inspired him, had turned pale, and trembled very much as he received the beautiful girl fainting in his arms; so that it was quite agreed among the courtiers, that the greatest event of the period had just been revealed; that his majesty loved Mademoiselle de la Vallière, and that, consequently, Monsieur could now sleep in perfect tranquillity. It was this, even, that the queen-mother, as surprised as the others by this sudden change, hastened to tell the young queen and Philippe d'Orleans. Only she set to work in a different manner, by attacking them in the following way: —To her daughter-in-law she said, " See, now, Thérèse, how very wrong you were to accuse the king; now it is said he is devoted to some other person; why should there be any greater truth in the report of to-day than in that of yesterday, or in that of yesterday than in that of to-day?" To Monsieur, in relating to him the adventure of the royal oak, she said, " Are you not very absurd in your jealousies, my dear Philip? It is asserted that the king is madly in love with that little La Vallière. Say nothing of it to your wife; for the queen will know all about it very soon." This latter confidential communication had an immediate result. Monsieur, who had regained his composure, went triumphantly to look after his wife, and as it was not yet midnight and the *fête* was to continue until two in the morning, he offered her his hand for a promenade. At the end of a few paces, however, the first thing he did was to disobey his mother's injunctions.

" Do not tell any one, the queen least of all," he said mysteriously, "what people say about the king."

" What do they say about him ?" inquired Madame.

" That my brother has suddenly fallen in love."

" With whom ?"

" With Mademoiselle de la Vallière."

As it was dark, Madame could smile at her ease.

" Ah! " she said, " and how long is it since this has been the case ? "

" For some days, it seems. But that was nothing but nonsense ; it is only this evening that he has revealed his passion."

" The king shows his good taste," said Madame ; " in my opinion she is a very charming girl."

" I verily believe you are jesting."

" I ! in what way ? "

" In any case this passion will make some one very happy, even if it be only La Vallière herself."

" Really," continued the princess, " you speak as if you had read into the inmost recesses of La Vallière's heart. Who has told you that she agrees to return the king's affection ? "

" And who has told you that she will not return it ? "

" She loves the Vicomte de Bragelonne."

" You think so ? "

" She is even affianced to him."

" She was so."

" What do you mean ? "

" When they went to ask the king's permission to arrange the marriage, he refused his permission."

" Refused ? "

" Yes, although the request was preferred by the Comte de la Fère himself, for whom the king has the greatest regard, on account of the part he took in your royal brother's restoration, and in other events, also, which happened a long time ago."

" Well ! the poor lovers must wait until the king is pleased to change his opinion ; they are young, and there is time enough."

"But, dear me," said Philip, laughing, "I perceive you do not know the best part of the affair."

"No!"

"That by which the king was most deeply touched."

"The king, do you say, has been deeply touched?"

"To the very quick of his heart."

"But how?—in what manner?—tell me directly."

"By an adventure, the romance of which cannot be equaled."

"You know how I love to hear of such adventures, and yet you keep me waiting," said the princess, impatiently.

"Well, then——" and Monsieur paused.

"I am listening."

"Under the royal oak—you know where the royal oak is?"

"What can that matter? Under the royal oak, you were saying."

"Well! Mademoiselle de la Vallière, fancying herself alone with her two friends, revealed to them her affection for the king."

"Ah!" said Madame, beginning to be uneasy, "her affection for the king?"

"Yes."

"When was this?"

"About an hour ago."

Madame started, and then said, "And no one knew of this affection?"

"No one."

"Not even his majesty?"

"Not even his majesty. The artful little puss kept her secret strictly to herself, when suddenly it proved stronger than herself, and so escaped her."

"And from whom did you get this absurd tale?"

"Why, as everybody else did, from La Vallière, herself,

who confessed her love to Montalais and Tonnay-Charente, who were her companions."

Madame stopped suddenly, and by a hasty movement let go her husband's hand.

" Did you say it was an hour ago she made this confession ? " Madame inquired.

" About that time."

" Is the king aware of it ? "

" Why, that is the very thing which constitutes the perfect romance of the affair, for the king was behind the royal oak with Saint-Aignan, and heard the whole of the interesting conversation without losing a single word of it."

Madame felt struck to the heart, saying incautiously, " But I have seen the king since, and he never told me a word about it."

" Of course," said Monsieur ; " he took care not to speak of it to you himself, since he recommended every one not to say a word about it to you."

" What do you mean ? " said Madame, growing angry.

" I mean that they wished to keep you in ignorance of the affair altogether."

" But why should they wish to conceal it from me ? "

" From the fear that your friendship for the young queen might induce you to say something about it to her, nothing more."

Madame hung down her head : her feelings were grievously wounded. She could not enjoy a moment's repose until she had met the king. As a king is, most naturally, the very last person in his kingdom who knows what is said about him, in the same way that a lover is the only one who is kept in ignorance of what is said about his mistress, therefore, when the king perceived Madame, who was looking for him, he approached her in some perturbation, but still gracious and attentive in his manner.

Madame waited for him to speak about La Vallière first; but as he did not speak of her, she said, "And the poor girl?"

"What poor girl?" said the king.

"La Vallière. Did you not tell me, sire, that she had fainted?"

"She is still very ill," said the king, affecting the greatest indifference.

"But surely that will prejudicially affect the rumor you were going to spread, sire?"

"What rumor?"

"That your attention was taken up by her."

"Oh!" said the king, carelessly, "I trust it will be reported all the same.

Madame still waited; she wished to know if the king would speak to her of the adventure of the royal oak. But the king did not say a word about it. Madame, on her side, did not open her lips about it; so that the king took leave of her without having reposed the slightest confidence in her. Hardly had she watched the king move away, than she set out in search of Saint-Aignan. Saint-Aignan was never very difficult to find; he was like the smaller vessels that always follow in the wake of, and as tenders to the larger ships. Saint-Aignan was the very man whom Madame needed in her then state of mind. And as for him, he only looked for worthier ears than others he had found, to have an opportunity of recounting the event in all its details. And so he did not spare Madame a single word of the whole affair. When he had finished, Madame said to him, "Confess, now, that this is all a charming invention."

"Invention, no; a true story, yes."

"Confess, whether invention or true story, that it was told to you as you have told it to me, but that you were not there."

"Upon my honor, Madame, I was there."

"And you think that these confessions may have made an impression upon the king?"

"Certainly, as those of Mademoiselle Tonnay-Charente did upon me," replied Saint-Aignan; "do not forget, Madame, that Mademoiselle de la Vallière compared the king to the sun; that was flattering enough."

"The king does not permit himself to be influenced by such flatteries."

"Madame, the king is just as much Adonis as Apollo; and I saw that plain enough just now when La Vallière fell into his arms."

"La Vallière fell into the king's arms!"

"Oh! it was the most graceful picture possible; just imagine, La Vallière had fallen back fainting, and——"

"Well! what did you see?—tell me—speak!"

"I saw, what ten other people saw at the same time as myself; I saw that when La Vallière fell into his arms, the king almost fainted himself."

Madame uttered a subdued cry, the only indication of her smothered anger.

"Thank you," she said, laughing in a convulsive manner, "you relate stories delightfully, M. de Saint-Aignan." And she hurried away, alone, and almost suffocated by painful emotion, toward the château.

CHAPTER IX.

COURSES DE NUIT.

MONSIEUR quitted the princess in the best possible humor, and feeling greatly fatigued, retired to his apartments, leaving every one to finish the night as he chose.

When in his room, Monsieur began to dress for the night with careful attention, which displayed itself from time to time in paroxysms of satisfaction. While his attendants were engaged curling his hair, he sang the principal airs of the ballet which the violins had played and to which the king had danced. He then summoned his tailors, inspected his costumes for the next day, and, in token of his extreme satisfaction, distributed various presents among them. As, however, the Chevalier de Lorraine, who had seen the prince return to the château entered the room, Monsieur overwhelmed him with kindness. The former, after having saluted the prince, remained silent for a moment, like a sharp-shooter who deliberates before deciding in what direction he will renew his fire; then, seeming to make up his mind he said, "Have you remarked a very singular coincidence, monseigneur ?"

"No; what is it ?"

"The bad reception which his majesty, in appearance, gave the Comte de Guiche."

"In appearance ?"

"Yes, certainly ; since, in reality, he has restored him to favor."

"I did not notice it," said the prince.

"What, did you not remark, that, instead of ordering him to go away again into exile, as was natural, he encouraged him in his opposition by permitting him to resume his place in the ballet?"

"And you think the king was wrong, chevalier!" said the prince.

"Are not you of my opinion, prince?"

"Not altogether so, my dear chevalier ; and I think the king was quite right not to have made a disturbance against a poor fellow whose want of judgment is more to be complained of than his intention."

"Really," said the chevalier, "as far as I am concerned,

I confess that this magnanimity astonishes me to the highest degree."

"Why so ?" inquired Philip.

"Because I should have thought the king had been more jealous," replied the chevalier, spitefully. During the last few minutes Monsieur had felt there was something of an irritating nature concealed under his favorite's remarks ; this last word, however, ignited the powder.

"Jealous !" exclaimed the prince. "Jealous! what do you mean ? Jealous of what, if you please—or jealous of whom ?"

The chevalier perceived that he had allowed an excesssively mischievous remark to escape him, as he was in the habit of doing. He endeavored, therefore, apparently to recall it while it was still possible to do so. "Jealous of his authority," he said, with an assumed frankness ; "of what else would you have the king jealous ?"

"Ah!" said the prince, "that's very proper."

"Did your royal highness," continued the chevalier, "solicit dear De Guiche's pardon ?"

"No, indeed," said Monsieur. "De Guiche is an excellent fellow, and full of courage ; but as I do not approve of his conduct with Madame, I wish him neither harm nor good."

The chevalier had assumed a bitterness with regard to De Guiche, as he had attempted to do with regard to the king; but he thought he perceived that the time for indulgence, and even for the utmost indifference, had arrived, and that, in order to throw some light on the question, it might be necessary for him to put the lamp, as the saying is, beneath the husband's very nose.

"Very well, very well," said the chevalier to himself, "I must wait for De Wardes ; he will do more in one day than I in a month; for I verily believe he is even more envious than I am. Then, again, it is not De Wardes I

require so much as that some event or another should
happen; and in the whole of this affair I see none. That
De Guiche returned after he had been sent away is certainly serious enough, but all its seriousness disappears
when I learn that De Guiche has returned at the very
moment Madame troubles herself no longer about him.
Madame, in fact, is occupied with the king, that is clear;
but she will not be so much longer if, as is asserted,
the king has ceased to trouble his head about her. The
moral of the whole matter is, to remain perfectly neutral,
and await the arrival of some new caprice and let that
decide the whole affair." And the chevalier thereupon
settled himself resignedly in the arm-chair in which Monsieur permitted him to seat himself in his presence, and,
having no more spiteful or malicious remarks to make, the
consequence was that De Lorraine's wit seemed to have
deserted him. Most fortunately Monsieur was in high
good-humor, and he had enough for two, until the time
arrived for dismissing his servants and gentlemen of the
chamber, and he passed into his sleeping apartment.
As he withdrew, he desired the chevalier to present his
compliments to Madame, and say that, as the night was
cool, Monsieur, who was afraid of the toothache, would
not venture out again into the park during the remainder
of the evening. The chevalier entered the princess's apartments at the very moment she came in herself. He ac-
quitted himself faithfully of the commission intrusted to
him, and, in the first place, remarked the indifference and
annoyance with which Madame received her husband's
communication—a circumstance which appeared to him
fraught with something fresh. If Madame had been about
to leave her apartments with that strangeness of manner,
he would have followed her; but she was returning to
them; there was nothing to be done, therefore he turned
upon his heel like an unemployed heron, appearing to ques-

tion earth, air, and water about it; shook his head, and walked away mechanically in the direction of the gardens. He had hardly gone a hundred paces when he met two young men, walking arm-in-arm, with their heads bent down, and idly kicking the small stones out of their path as they walked on, plunged in thought. It was De Guiche and De Bragelonne, the sight of whom, as it always did, produced upon the chevalier, instinctively, a feeling of repugnance. He did not, however, the less, on that account, salute them with a very low bow, which they returned with interest. Then, observing that the park was nearly deserted, that the illuminations began to burn out, and that the morning breeze was setting in, he turned to the left, and entered the château again, by one of the smaller courtyards. The others turned aside to the right, and continued on their way towards the large park. As the chevalier was ascending the side staircase, which led to the private entrance, he saw a woman, followed by another, make her appearance under the arcade which led from the small to the large courtyard. The two women walked so fast that the rustling of their dresses could be distinguished through the silence of the night. The style of their mantles, their graceful figures, a mysterious yet haughty carriage which distinguished them both, especially the one who walked first, struck the chevalier.

"I certainly know those two," said he to himself, pausing upon the top step of the small staircase. Then, as with the instinct of a bloodhound he was about to follow them, one of the servants who had been running after him arrested his attention.

"Monsieur," he said, "the courier has arrived."

"Very well," said the chevalier, "there is time enough; to-morrow will do."

"There are some urgent letters which you would be glad to see, perhaps."

"Where from?" inquired the chevalier.

"One from England, and the other from Calais; the latter arrived by express, and seems of great importance."

"From Calais! Who the deuce can have to write to me from Calais?"

"I think I recognize the handwriting of Monsieur le Comte de Wardes."

"Oh!" cried the chevalier, forgetting his intention of acting the spy, "in that case I will come up at once." This he did, while the two unknown beings disappeared at the end of the court opposite to the one by which they had just entered. We shall now follow them, and leave the chevalier undisturbed to his correspondence. When they had arrived at the grove of trees, the foremost of the two halted, somewhat out of breath, and, cautiously raising her hood, said, "Are we still far from the tree?"

"Yes, madame, more than five hundred paces; but pray rest awhile, you will not be able to walk much longer at this rate."

"You are right," said the princess, for it was she; and she leaned against a tree. "And now," she resumed, after having recovered her breath, "tell me the whole truth, and conceal nothing from me."

"Oh, madame," cried the young girl, "you are already angry with me."

"No, my dear Athenaïs, reassure yourself, I am in no way angry with you. After all, these things do not concern me personally. You are anxious about what you may have said under the oak; you are afraid of having offended the king, and I wish to tranquillize you by ascertaining myself if it were possible you could have been overheard."

"Oh yes, madame, the king was close to us."

"Still, you were not speaking so loud that some of your remarks may not have been lost."

"We thought we were quite alone, madame."

"There were three of you, you say?"

"Yes; La Vallière, Montalais, and myself."

"And *you*, individually, spoke in a light manner of the king?"

"I am afraid so. Should such be the case, will your highness have the kindness to make my peace with his majesty?"

"If there should be any occasion for it, I promise you I will do so. However, as I have already told you, it will be better not to anticipate evil. The night is now very dark, and the darkness is still greater under trees. It is not likely you were recognized by the king. To inform him of it, by being the first to speak, is to denounce yourself."

"Oh, madame, madame! if Mademoiselle de la Vallière were recognized, I must have been recognized also. Besides, M. de Saint-Aignan left no doubt on the subject."

"Did you, then, say anything very disrespectful of the king?"

"Not at all; it was one of the others who made some very flattering speeches about the king: and my remarks must have been much in contrast with hers."

"Montalais is such a giddy girl," said Madame.

"It was not Montalais. Montalais said nothing; it was La Vallière."

Madame started as if she had not known it perfectly well already. "No, no," she said, "the king cannot have heard. Besides we will now try the experiment for which we came out. Show me the oak. Do you know where it is?" she continued.

"Alas! madame, yes."

"And you can find it again?"

"With my eyes shut."

"Very well; sit down on the bank where you were,

where La Vallière was, and speak in the same tone and to
the same effect as you did before; I will conceal myself
in the thicket, and if I can hear you, I will tell you so."

"Yes, madame."

"If, therefore, you really spoke loud enough for the king
to have heard you, in that case——"

Athenaïs seemed to await the conclusion of the sentence with some anxiety.

"In that case," said Madame, in a suffocated voice,
arising doubtless from her hurried progress; "in that
case, I forbid you——" And Madame again increased
her pace. Suddenly, however, she stopped. "An idea
occurs to me," she said.

"A good idea, no doubt, madame," replied Mademoiselle de Tonnay-Charente.

"Montalais must be as much embarrassed as La Vallière and yourself."

"Less so, for she is less compromised, having said
less."

"That does not matter; she will help you, I dare say,
by deviating a little from the exact truth."

"Especially if she knows that your highness is kind
enough to interest yourself about me."

"Very well, I think I have discovered what it is best
for you all to pretend."

"How delightful."

"You had better say that all three of you were perfectly well aware that the king was behind the tree, or
behind the thicket, whichever it might have been; and
that you knew M. de Saint-Aignan was there too."

"Yes, madame."

"For you cannot disguise it from yourself, Athenaïs,
Saint-Aignan takes advantage of some very flattering
remarks you made about him."

"Well, madame, you see very clearly that one can be

overheard," cried Athenaïs, "since M. de Saint-Aignan overheard us."

Madame bit her lips, for she had thoughtlessly committed herself. "Oh, you know Saint-Aignan's character very well," she said, "the favor the king shows him almost turns his brain, and he talks at random; not only so, he very often invents. That is not the question; the fact remains, Did or did not the king overhear?"

"Oh, yes, madame, he certainly did," said Athenaïs, in despair.

"In that case, do what I said: maintain boldly that all three of you knew—mind, all three of you, for if there is a doubt about any one of you, there will be a doubt about all,—persist, I say, that you knew that the king and M. de Saint-Aignan were there, and that you wished to amuse yourselves at the expense of those who were listening."

"Oh, madame, at the *king's* expense; we shall never dare say that!"

"It is a simple jest; an innocent deception readily permitted in young girls whom men wish to take by surprise. In this manner everything explains itself. What Montalais said of Malicorne, a mere jest; what you said of M. de Saint-Aignan, a mere jest too; and what La Vallière might have said of——"

"And which she would have given anything to recall."

"Are you sure of that?"

"Perfectly."

"Very well, an additional reason. Say the whole affair was a mere joke. M. de Malicorne will have no occasion to get out of temper; M. de Saint-Aignan will be completely put out of countenance; *he* will be laughed at instead of you; and lastly, the king will be punished for a curiosity unworthy of his rank. Let people laugh a little at the king in this affair, and I do not think he will complain of it."

"Oh, madame, you are indeed an angel of goodness and sense!"

"It is to my own advantage."

"In what way?"

"How can you ask me why it is to my advantage to spare my maids of honor the remarks, annoyances, perhaps even calumnies, that might follow? Alas! you well know that the court has no indulgence for this sort of peccadilloes. But we have now been walking for some time, shall we be long before we reach it?"

"About fifty or sixty paces further; turn to the left, madame, if you please."

"And so you are sure of Montalais?" said Madame.

"Oh, certainly."

"Will she do what you ask her?"

"Everything. She will be delighted."

"And La Vallière——" ventured the princess.

"Ah, there will be some difficulty with her, madame; she would scorn to tell a falsehood."

"Yet, when it is her interest to do so——"

"I am afraid that that would not make the slightest difference in her ideas."

"Yes, yes," said Madame, "I have been already told that; she is one of those over-nice and affectedly-particular people who place heaven in the foreground in order to conceal themselves behind it. But if she refuse to tell a falsehood,—as she will expose herself to the jests of the whole court, as she will have annoyed the king by a confession as ridiculous as it was immodest,—Mademoiselle Labaume le Blanc de la Vallière will think it but proper I should send her back again to her pigeons in the country, in order that, in Touraine yonder, or in le Blaisois—I know not where it may be, she may at her ease study sentiment and pastoral life combined.

These words were uttered with a vehemence and harsh-

ness that terrified Mademoiselle de Tonnay-Charente; and
the consequence was, that, as far as she was concerned,
she promised to tell as many falsehoods as might be necessary. It was in this frame of mind that Madame and her
companion reached the precincts of the royal oak.

"Here we are," said Tonnay-Charente.

"We shall soon learn if one can overhear," replied Madame.

"Hush!" whispered the young girl, holding Madame
back with a hurried gesture, entirely forgetful of her companion's rank. Madame stopped.

"You see that you can hear," said Athenaïs.

"How?"

"Listen."

Madame held her breath; and, in fact, the following
words, pronounced by a gentle and melancholy voice;
floated towards them.

"I tell you, vicomte, I tell you I love her madly; I tell
you, I love her to distraction."

Madame started at the voice; and, beneath her hood, a
bright joyous smile illumined her features. It was she
who now held back her companion, and with a light step
leading her some twenty paces away, that is to say, out of
the reach of the voice, she said, "Remain here, my dear
Athenaïs, and let no one surprise us. I think it must be
you they are conversing about."

"Me, Madame?"

"Yes, you—or rather your adventure. I will go and
listen; if we were both there, we should be discovered.
Or, stay!—go and fetch Montalais, and then return and
wait for me with her at the entrance of the forest." And
then, as Athenaïs hesitated, she again said "Go!" in a
voice which did not admit of reply. Athenaïs thereupon
arranged her dress so as to prevent its rustling being
heard; and, by a path beyond the group of trees, she re-

gained the flower-garden. As for Madame, she concealed herself in the thicket, leaning her back against a gigantic chestnut-tree, one of the branches of which had been cut in such a manner as to form a seat, and waited there, full of anxiety and apprehension. " Now," she said, " since one can hear from this place, let us listen to what M. de Bragelonne and that other madly-in-love fool, the Comte de Guiche, have to say about me."

CHAPTER X.

IN WHICH MADAME ACQUIRES A PROOF THAT LISTENERS HEAR WHAT IS SAID.

THERE was a moment's silence, as if the mysterious sounds of night were hushed to listen, at the same time as Madame, to the youthful passionate disclosures of De Guiche.

Raoul was about to speak. He leaned indolently against the trunk of the large oak, and replied in his sweet and musical voice, " Alas, my dear De Guiche, it is a great misfortune."

" Yes," cried the latter, " great indeed."

" You do not understand me, De Guiche. I say that it is a great misfortune for you, not merely loving, but not knowing how to conceal your love."

" What do you mean ? " said De Guiche.

" Yes, you do not perceive one thing ; namely, that it is no longer to the only friend you have,—in other words,— to a man who would rather die than betray you ; you do not perceive, I say, that it is no longer to your only friend that you confide your passion, but to the first person that approaches you."

" Are you mad, Bragelonne," exclaimed De Guiche, " to say such a thing to me ? "

" The fact stands thus, however."

" Impossible!   How, in what manner can I have ever been indiscreet to such an extent ? "

" I mean, that your eyes, your looks, your sighs, proclaim, in spite of yourself, that exaggerated feeling which leads and hurries a man beyond his own control.   In such a case he ceases to be master of himself; he is a prey to a mad passion, that makes him confide his grief to the trees, or to the air, from the very moment he has no longer any living being within reach of his voice.   Besides, remember this; it very rarely happens that there is not always some one present to hear, especially the very things which ought *not* to be heard."   De Guiche uttered a deep sigh. "Nay," continued Bragelonne, " you distress me; since your return here, you have a thousand times, and in a thousand different ways, confessed your love for her; and yet, had you not said one word your return would alone have been a terrible indiscretion.   I persist, then, in draw-ing this conclusion; that if you do not place a better watch over yourself than you have hitherto done, one day or other something will happen that will cause an explo-sion.   Who will save you then?   Answer me?   Who will save her? for, innocent as she will be of your affection, your affection will be an accusation against her in the hands of her enemies."

" Alas! " murmured De Guiche; and a deep sigh accom-panied the exclamation.

" That is not answering me, De Guiche."

"Yes, yes."

" Well, what reply have you to make ? "

" This, that when that day arrives I shall be no more a living being than I feel myself now."

" I do not understand you."

" So many vicissitudes have worn me out. At present, I am no more a thinking, acting being; at present, the most worthless of men is better than I am ; my remaining strength is exhausted, my latest-formed resolutions have vanished, and I abandon myself to my fate. When a man is out campaigning, as we have been together, and he sets off alone and unaccompanied for a skirmish, it sometimes happens that he may meet with a party of five or six foragers, and although alone, he defends himself ; afterwards, five or six others arrive unexpectedly, his anger is aroused and he persists ; but if six, eight, or ten others should still be met with, he either sets spurs to his horse, if he should still happen to retain one, or lets himself be slain to save an ignominious flight. Such, indeed, is my own case ; first, I had to struggle against myself ; afterwards, against Buckingham ; now since the king is in the field, I will not contend against the king, nor even against the nature of that woman. Still I do not deceive myself ; having devoted myself to the service of such a love, I will lose my life in it."

" It is not the lady you ought to reproach," replied Raoul ; " it is yourself."

" Why so ? "

" You know the princess's character,—somewhat giddy, easily captivated by novelty, susceptible to flattery, whether it come from a blind person or a child, and yet you allow your passion for her to eat your very life away. Look at her,—love her, if you will,—for no one whose heart is not engaged elsewhere can see her without loving her. Yet, while you love her, respect, in the first place, her husband's rank, then herself, and lastly, your own safety."

" Thanks, Raoul."

" What for ? "

" Because, seeing how much I suffer through this woman,

you endeavor to console me, because you tell me all the good of her you think, and perhaps even that which you do not think."

"Oh," said Raoul, "there you are wrong, comte; what I think I do not always say, but in that case I say nothing; but when I speak, I know not either how to feign or to deceive; and whoever listens to me may believe me."

During this conversation, Madame, her head stretched forward with eager ear and dilated glance, endeavoring to penetrate the obscurity, thirstily drank in the faintest sound of their voices.

"Oh, I know her better than you do, then!" exclaimed Guiche. "She is not merely giddy, but frivolous; she is not only attracted by novelty, she is utterly oblivious, and is without faith, she is not simply susceptible to flattery, she is a practiced and cruel coquette. A thorough coquette! yes, yes, I am sure of it. Believe me, Bragelonne, I am suffering all the torments of hell; brave, passionately fond of danger, I meet a danger greater than my strength and my courage. But, believe me, Raoul, I reserve for myself a victory which shall cost her floods of tears."

"A victory," he asked, "and of what kind?"

"Of what kind, you ask?"

"Yes."

"One day I will accost her, and will address her thus: 'I was young—madly in love, I possessed, however sufficient respect to throw myself at your feet, and to prostrate myself in the dust, if your looks had not raised me to your hand. I fancied I understood your looks, I rose, and then, without having done anything more towards you than love you yet more devotedly, if that were possible—you, a woman without heart, faith, or love, in very wantonness, dashed me down again from sheer caprice. You are unworthy, princess of the royal blood

though you may be, of the love of a man of honor; I offer
my life as a sacrifice for having loved you too tenderly, and
I die despising you.'"

"Oh!" cried Raoul, terrified at the accents of profound
truth which De Guiche's words betrayed, "I was right in
saying you were mad, Guiche."

"Yes, yes," exclaimed De Guiche, following out his own
idea; "since there are no wars here now, I will flee
yonder to the north, seek service in the Empire, where
some Hungarian, or Croat, or Turk, will perhaps kindly
put me out of my misery." De Guiche did not finish, or
rather as he finished, a sound made him start, and at the
same moment caused Raoul to leap to his feet. As for
De Guiche, buried in his own thoughts, he remained
seated, with his head tightly pressed between his hands.
The branches of the trees were pushed aside, and a woman,
pale and much agitated, appeared before the two young
men. With one hand she held back the branches, which
would have struck her face, and, with the other, she
raised the hood of the mantle which covered her shoulders.
By her clear and lustrous glance, by her lofty carriage,
by her haughty attitude, and, more than all, by the
throbbing of his own heart, De Guiche recognized Madame,
and, uttering a loud cry, he removed his hands from his
temples, and covered his eyes with them. Raoul, trembling and out of countenance, merely muttered a few
words of respect.

"Monsieur de Bragelonne," said the princess, "have
the goodness, I beg, to see if my attendants are not somewhere yonder, either in the walks or in the groves; and
you, M. de Guiche, remain here: I am tired, and you
will perhaps give me your arm."

Had a thunderbolt fallen at the feet of the unhappy
young man, he would have been less terrified than by her
cold and severe tone. However, as he himself had just

said, he was brave ; and as in the depths of his own heart
he had just decisively made up his mind, De Guiche arose,
and, observing Bragelonne's hesitation, he turned towards
him a glance full of resignation and grateful acknowledgment. Instead of immediately answering Madame, he even
advanced a step towards the vicomte, and holding out the
arm which the princess had just desired him to give her,
he pressed his friend's hand in his own with a sigh, in
which he seemed to give to friendship all the life that was
left in the depths of his heart.   Madame, who in her pride
had never known what it was to wait, now waited until
this mute colloquy was at an end.   Her royal hand remained suspended in the air, and, when Raoul had left, it
sank without anger, but not without emotion, in that of
De Guiche.   They were alone in the depths of the dark
and silent forest, and nothing could be heard but Raoul's
hastily retreating footsteps along the obscure paths.
Over their heads was extended the thick and fragrant
vault of branches, through the occasional openings of
which the stars could be seen glittering in their beauty.
Madame softly drew De Guiche about a hundred paces
away from that indiscreet tree which had heard, and had
allowed so many things to be heard, during the evening,
and, leading him to a neighboring glade, so that they
could see a certain distance around them, she said in a
trembling voice, "I have brought you here, because
yonder where you were, everything can be overheard."

"Everything can be overheard, did you say, madame ?"
replied the young man, mechanically.

"Yes."

"Which means——" murmured De Guiche.

"Which means that I have heard every syllable you
have said."

"Oh, Heaven! this only was wanting to destroy me,"
stammered De Guiche; and he bent down his head, like

an exhausted swimmer beneath the wave which engulfs him.

"And so," she said, "you judge me as you have said?" De Guiche grew pale, turned his head aside, and was silent. He felt almost on the point of fainting.

"I do not complain," continued the princess, in a tone of voice full of gentleness; "I prefer a frankness that wounds me, to flattery, which would deceive me. And so, according to your opinion, M. de Guiche, I am a coquette and a worthless creature."

"Worthless," cried the young man; "you worthless! Oh, no; most certainly I did not say, I could not have said, that that which was the most precious object in life for me could be worthless. No, no; I did not say that."

"A woman who sees a man perish, consumed by the fire she has kindled, and who does not allay that fire, is, in my opinion, a worthless woman."

"What can it matter to you what I said?" returned the comte. "What am I compared to you, and why should you even trouble yourself to know whether I exist or not?"

"Monsieur de Guiche, both you and I are human beings, and, knowing you as I do, I do not wish you to risk your life; with you I will change my conduct and character. I will be, not frank, for I am always so, but truthful. I implore you, therefore, to love me no more, and to forget utterly that I have ever addressed a word or a glance towards you."

De Guiche turned around, bending a look full of passionate devotion upon her. "You," he said; "*you* excuse yourself; *you* implore me?"

"Certainly; since I have done evil, I ought to repair the evil I have done. And so, comte, this is what we will agree to. You will forgive my frivolity and my coquetry. Nay, do not interrupt me. I will forgive you for having said I was frivolous and a coquette, or something worse, perhaps; and you will renounce your idea of dying, and will preserve for your family, for the king, and for our sex, a cavalier whom every one esteems, and whom many hold dear." Madame pronounced this last word in such an accent of frankness, and even of tenderness, that poor De Guiche's heart felt almost bursting.

"Oh! madame, madame!" he stammered out.

"Nay, listen further," she continued. "When you shall have renounced all thought of me forever, from necessity in the first place, and, next, because you will yield to my entreaty, then you will judge me more favorably, and I am convinced you will replace this love—forgive the frivolity of the expression—by a sincere friendship, which you will be ready to offer me, and which, I promise you, shall be cordially accepted."

De Guiche, his forehead bedewed with perspiration, a feeling of death in his heart, and a trembling agitation through his whole frame, bit his lip, stamped his foot on the ground, and, in a word, devoured the bitterness of his grief. "Madame," he said, "what you offer is impossible, and I cannot accept such conditions."

"What!" said Madame, "do you refuse my friendship, then?"

"No, no! I do not need your friendship, madame. I prefer to die from love, than to live for friendship."

"Comte!"

"Oh! madame," cried De Guiche, "the present is a moment for me, in which no other consideration and no other respect exist, than the consideration and respect of a man of honor towards the woman he worships. Drive me away, curse me, denounce me, you will be perfectly right. I have uttered complaints against you, but their bitterness has been owing to my passion for you; I have said I wish to die, and die I will. If I lived, you would forget me; but dead, you would never forget me, I am sure."

Henrietta, who was standing buried in thought, and nearly as agitated as De Guiche himself, turned aside her head as but a minute before he had turned aside his. Then, after a moment's pause, she said, "And you love me, then, very much?"

"Madly; madly enough to die from it, whether you drive me from you, or whether you listen to me still."

"It is a hopeless case," she said, in a playful manner; "a case which must be treated with soothing applications. Give me your hand. It is as cold as ice." De Guiche knelt down, and pressed to his lips, not one, but both of Madame's hands.

"Love me, then," said the princess, "since it cannot be otherwise." And almost imperceptibly she pressed his fingers, raising him thus, partly in the manner of a queen, and partly as a fond and affectionate woman would have done. De Guiche trembled from head to foot, and Madame, who felt how passion coursed through every fiber of his being, knew that he indeed loved truly. "Give me your arm, comte," she said, "and let us return."

"Ah! madame," said the comte, trembling and bewildered; you have discovered a third way of killing me."

"But, happily, it is the slowest, is it not?" she replied, as she led him towards the grove of trees they had so lately quitted.

CHAPTER XI.

ARAMIS'S CORRESPONDENCE.

WHILST De Guiche's affairs, which had been suddenly set to right without his having been able to guess the cause of their improvement, assumed the unexpected aspect we have seen, Raoul, in obedience to the request of the princess, had withdrawn in order not to interrupt an explanation, the results of which he was far from guessing; and he soon after joined the ladies of honor who were walking about in the flower gardens. During this time, the Chevalier de Lorraine, who had returned to his own room, read De Wardes' letter with surprise, for it informed him of the sword-thrust received at Calais, and of all the details of the adventure, and invited him to inform De Guiche and Monsieur, whatever there might be in the affair likely to be most disagreeable to both of them. De Wardes particularly endeavored to prove to the chevalier the violence of Madame's affection for Buckingham, and he finished his letter by declaring that he thought this feeling was returned. The chevalier shrugged his shoulders at the last paragraph, and, in fact, De Wardes was out of date, as we have seen. De Wardes was still only at Buckingham's affair. The chevalier threw the letter over his shoulders upon an adjoining table, and said in a disdainful tone, "It is really incredible; and yet poor De Wardes is not deficient in ability; but the truth is, it is not very apparent, so easy is it to grow rusty in the country. The deuce take the simpleton, who ought to have written to me about matters of importance, and yet he writes such silly stuff as that. If it had not been for that miserable letter, which has no meaning at all in it, I should have detected in the grove yonder a charming little intrigue, which would have compromised a woman, would have perhaps been as good as a sword thrust for a man, and have diverted Monsieur for many days to come."

He looked at his watch. "It is now too late," he said. "One o'clock in the morning; every one must have returned to the king's apartments, where the night is to be finished; well, the scent is lost, and unless some extraordinary chance——" And thus saying, as if to appeal to his good star, the chevalier, greatly out of temper, approached the window, which looked out upon a somewhat solitary part of the garden. Immediately, and as if some evil genius was at his orders, he perceived returning towards the château, accompanied by a man, a silk mantle of a dark color, and recognized the figure which had struck his attention half an hour previously.

"Admirable!" he thought, striking his hands together, "this is ·my providential mysterious affair." And he started out precipitately, along the staircase, hoping to reach the courtyard in time to recognize the woman in the mantle, and her companion. But as he arrived at the door of the little court, he nearly knocked against Madame, whose radiant face seemed full of charming revelations beneath the mantle which protected without concealing her. Uufortunately, Madame was alone. The chevalier knew that since he had seen her, not five minutes before, with a gentleman, the gentleman in question could not be far off. Consequently, he hardly took time to salute the princess as he drew up to allow her to pass; then when she had advanced a few steps, with the rapidity of a woman who fears recognition, and when the chevalier perceived that she was too much occupied with her own thoughts to trouble herself about him, he darted into the garden, looked hastily round on every side, and embraced within his glance as much of the horizon as he possibly could. He was just in time; the gentleman who had accompanied Madame was still in sight; only he was hurrying towards one of the wings of the château, behind which he was on the point of disappearing. There was not an instant to lose; the chevalier darted in pursuit of him, prepared to slacken his pace as he approached the unknown; but in spite of the diligence he used, the unknown had disappeared behind the flight of steps before he approached.

It was evident, however, that as the man pursued was walking quietly, in a pensive manner, with his head bent down, either beneath the weight of grief or happiness, when once the angle was passed, unless, indeed, he were to enter by some door or another, the chevalier could not fail to overtake him. And this, certainly, would have happened, if, at the very moment he turned the angle, the chevalier had not run against two persons, who were themselves wheeling in the opposite direction. The chevalier was ready to seek a quarrel with these two troublesome intruders, when looking up he recognized the superintendent. Fouquet was accompanied by a person whom the chevalier now saw for the first time. This stranger was the bishop of Vannes. Checked by the important character of the individual, and obliged out of politeness to make his own excuses when he expected to receive them, the chevalier stepped back a few paces; and as Monsieur Fouquet possessed, if not the friendship, at least the respect of every one; as the king himself, although he was rather his enemy than his friend, treated M. Fouquet as a man of great consideration, the chevalier did what the king himself would have done, namely, he bowed to M. Fouquet, who returned his salutation with kindly politeness, perceiving that the gentleman had run against him by mistake and without any intention of being rude. Then, almost immediately afterwards, having recognized the Chevalier de Lorraine, he made a few civil remarks, to which the chevalier was obliged to reply. Brief as the conversation was, De Lorraine saw, with the most unfeigned displeasure, the figure of his unknown becoming dimmer in the distance, and fast disappearing in the darkness. The chevalier resigned himself, and, once resigned, gave his entire attention to Fouquet :—" You arrive late, monsieur," he said. " Your absence has occasioned great surprise, and I heard Monsieur express himself as much astonished that, having been invited by the king, you had not come."

"It was impossible for me to do so; but I came as soon as I was free."

"Is Paris quiet?"

"Perfectly so. Paris has received the last tax very well."

"Ah! I understand you wished to assure yourself of this good feeling before you came to participate in our *fêtes*."

"I have arrived, however, somewhat late to enjoy them. I will ask you, therefore, to inform me if the king is in the château or not, if I am likely to be able to see him this evening, or if I shall have to wait until to-morrow."

"We have lost sight of his majesty during the last half hour nearly," said the chevalier.

"Perhaps he is in Madame's apartments?" inquired Fouquet.

"Not in Madame's apartments, I should think, for I just now met Madame as she was entering by the small staircase; and unless the gentleman whom you a moment ago encountered was the king himself——" and the chevalier paused, hoping that, in this manner, he might learn who it was he had been hurrying after. But Fouquet, whether he had or had not recognized De Guiche, simply replied, "No, monsieur, it was not the king."

The chevalier, disappointed in his expectation, saluted them; but as he did so, casting a parting glance around him, and perceiving M. Colbert in the center of a group, he said to the superintendent: "Stay, monsieur; there is some one under the trees yonder, who will be able to inform you better than myself."

"Who?" asked Fouquet, whose near-sightedness prevented him from seeing through the darkness.

"M. Colbert," returned the chevalier.

"Indeed! That person, then, who is speaking yonder

to those men with torches in their hands, is M. Colbert?"

"M. Colbert himself. He is giving his orders personally to the workmen who are arranging the lamps for the illuminations."

"Thank you," said Fouquet, with an inclination of the head, which indicated that he had obtained all the information he wished. The chevalier, on his side, having, on the contrary, learned nothing at all, withdrew with a profound salutation.

He had scarcely left when Fouquet, knitting his brows, fell into a deep reverie. Aramis looked at him for a moment with a mingled feeling of compassion and sadness. "What!" he said to him, "the fellow's name alone seemed to affect you. Is it possible, that, full of triumph and delight as you were just now, the sight merely of that man is capable of dispiriting you? Tell me, have you faith in your good star?"

"No," replied Fouquet, dejectedly.

"Why not?"

"Because I am too full of happiness at this present moment," he replied, in a trembling voice. "You, my dear D'Herblay, who are so learned, will remember the history of a certain tyrant of Samos. What can I throw into the sea to avert approaching evil? Yes! I repeat it once more, I am too full of happiness! so happy that I wish for nothing beyond what I have . . . . I have risen so high . . . . You know my motto: ' *Quia non ascendam?* ' I have risen so high that nothing is left me but to descend from my elevation. I cannot believe in the progress of a success already more than human."

Aramis smiled as he fixed his kind and penetrating glance upon him. "If I were aware of the cause of your happiness," he said, "I should probably fear for your disgrace; but you regard me in the light of a true friend; I mean, you turn to me in misfortune, nothing more. Even that is an immense and precious boon, I know; but the truth is, I have a just right to beg you to confide in me, from time to time, any fortunate circumstances that befall you, in which I should rejoice, you know, more than if they had befallen myself."

"My dear prelate," said Fouquet, laughing, "my secrets are of too profane a character to confide them to a bishop, however great a worldling he may be."

"Bah! in confession."

"Oh! I should blush too much if you were my confessor." And Fouquet began to sigh. Aramis again looked at him without further betrayal of his thoughts than a placid smile.

"Well," he said, "discretion is a great virtue."

"Silence," said Fouquet; "yonder venomous reptile has recognized us, and is crawling this way."

"Colbert?"

"Yes; leave me, D'Herblay; I do not wish that fellow to see you with me, or he will take an aversion to *you*."

Aramis pressed his hand, saying, "What need have I of his friendship, while you are here?"

"Yes, but I may not be always here," replied Fouquet, dejectedly.

"On that day, then, if that day should ever dawn," said Aramis, tranquilly, "we will think over a means of dispensing with the friendship, or of braving the dislike of M. Colbert. But tell me, my dear Fouquet, instead of conversing with this reptile, as you did him the honor of styling him, a conversation the need for which I do not perceive, why do you not pay a visit, if not to the king, at least to Madame?"

"To Madame," said the superintendent, his mind occupied by his *souvenirs*.

"Yes, certainly, to Madame."

"You remember," continued Aramis, "that we have

been told that Madame stands high in favor during the last two or three days. It enters into your policy, and forms part of our plans, that you should assiduously devote yourself to his majesty's friends. It is a means of counteracting the growing influence of M. Colbert. Present yourself, therefore, as soon as possible to Madame, and, for our sakes, treat this ally with consideration."

"But," said Fouquet, "are you quite sure that it is upon her the king has his eyes fixed at the present moment?"

"If the needle has turned, it must be since the morning. You know I have my police."

"Very well! I will go there at once, and, at all events, I shall have a means of introduction in the shape of a magnificent pair of antique cameos set with diamonds."

"I have seen them, and nothing could be more costly and regal."

At this moment they were interrupted by a servant followed by a courier. "For you, monseigneur," said the courier aloud, presenting a letter to Fouquet.

"For your grace," said the lackey in a low tone, handing Aramis a letter. And as the lackey carried a torch in his hand, he placed himself between the superintendent and the bishop of Vannes, so that both of them could read at the same time. As Fouquet looked at the fine and delicate writing on the envelope, he started with delight. Those who love, or who are beloved, will understand his anxiety in the first place, and his happiness in the next. He hastily tore open the letter, which, however, contained only these words: "It is but an hour since I quitted you, it is an age since I told you how much I love you." And that was all. Madame de Bellière had, in fact, left Fouquet about an hour previously, after having passed two days with him; and, apprehensive lest his remembrance of her might be effaced for too long a period from

the heart she regretted, she dispatched a courier to him
as the bearer of this important communication. Fouquet
kissed the letter, and rewarded the bearer with a hand-
ful of gold. As for Aramis, he, on his side, was engaged
in reading, but with more coolness and reflection, the following letter:

"The king has this evening been struck with a strange
fancy; a woman loves him. He learned it accidentally, as
he was listening to the conversation of this young girl
with her companions; and his majesty has entirely abandoned himself to his new caprice. The girl's name is
Mademoiselle de la Vallière, and she is sufficiently pretty
to warrant this caprice becoming a strong attachment.
Beware of Mademoiselle de la Vallière."

There was not a word about Madame. Aramis slowly
folded the letter and put it in his pocket. Fouquet was
still delightedly inhaling the perfume of his epistle.

"Monseigneur," said Aramis, touching Fouquet's arm.

"Yes, what is it?" he asked.

"An idea has just occurred to me. Are you acquainted
with a young girl of the name of La Vallière?"

"Not at all."

"Reflect a little."

"Ah! yes, I believe so; one of Madame's maids of
honor."

"That must be the one."

"Well, what then?"

"Well, monseigneur, it is to that young girl that you
must pay your visit this evening."

"Bah! why so?"

"Nay, more than that, it is to her you must present
your cameos."

"Nonsense."

"You know, monseigneur, that my advice is not to be regarded lightly."

"But this is unforeseen——"

"That is my affair. Pay your court in due form, and without loss of time, to Mademoiselle de la Vallière. I will be your guarantee with Madame de Bellière that your devotion is altogether politic."

"What do you mean, my dear D'Herblay, and whose name have you just pronounced?

"A name which ought to convince you that, as I am so well informed about yourself, I may possibly be just as well informed about others. Pay your court therefore to La Vallière."

"I will pay my court to whomsoever you like," replied Fouquet, his heart filled with happiness.

"Come, come, descend again to the earth, traveler in the seventh heaven," said Aramis; "M. de Colbert is approaching. He has been recruiting while we were reading; see, how he is surrounded, praised, congratulated; he is decidedly becoming powerful." In fact, Colbert was advancing, escorted by all the courtiers who remained in the gardens, every one of whom complimented him upon the arrangements of the *fête:* all of which so puffed him up that he could hardly contain himself.

"If La Fontaine were here," said Fouquet, smiling, "what an admirable opportunity for him to recite his fable of 'The Frog that wanted to make itself as big as the Ox.'"

Colbert arrived in the center of the circle blazing with light; Fouquet awaited his approach, unmoved and with a slightly mocking smile. Colbert smiled too; he had been observing his enemy during the last quarter of an hour, and had been approaching him gradually. Colbert's smile was a presage of hostility.

"Oh! oh!" said Aramis, in a low tone to the superintendent; "the scoundrel is going to ask you again for a few more millions to pay for his fireworks and his colored lamps." Colbert was the first to salute them, and with an air which he endeavored to render respectful. Fouquet hardly moved his head.

"Well, monseigneur, what do your eyes say? Have we shown our good taste?"

"Perfect taste," replied Fouquet, without permitting the slightest tone of raillery to be remarked in his words.

"Oh!" said Colbert, maliciously, "you are treating us with indulgence. We are poor, we servants of the king, and Fontainebleau is no way to be compared as a residence with Vaux."

"Quite true," replied Fouquet coolly.

"But what can we do, monseigneur?" continued Colbert, "we have done our best on slender resources."

Fouquet made a gesture of assent.

"But," pursued Colbert, "it would be only a proper display of your magnificence, monseigneur, if you were to offer to his majesty a *fête* in your wonderful gardens— in those gardens which have cost you sixty millions of francs."

"Seventy-two," said Fouquet.

"An additional reason," returned Colbert; "it would, indeed, be truly magnificent."

"But do you suppose, monsieur, that his majesty would deign to accept my invitation?"

"I have no doubt whatever of it," cried Colbert, hastily; "I will guarantee that he does."

"You are exceedingly kind," said Fouquet. "I may depend on it then?"

"Yes, monseigneur; yes, certainly."

"Then I will consider the matter," yawned Fouquet.

"Accept, accept," whispered Aramis, eagerly.

"You will consider?" repeated Colbert.

"Yes," replied Fouquet; "in order to know what day I shall submit my invitation to the king."

"This very evening, monseigneur, this very evening."

"Agreed," said the superintendent. "Gentlemen, I should wish to issue my invitations; but you know that, wherever the king goes, the king is in his own palace; it is by his majesty, therefore, that you must be invited." A murmur of delight immediately arose. Fouquet bowed and left.

"Proud and dauntless man," thought Colbert, "you accept and yet you know it will cost you ten millions."

"You have ruined me," whispered Fouquet, in a low tone to Aramis.

"I have saved you," replied the latter, whilst Fouquet ascended the flight of steps and inquired whether the king was still visible.

CHAPTER XII.

THE ORDERLY CLERK.

THE king, anxious to be again quite alone, in order to reflect well upon what was passing in his heart, had withdrawn to his own apartments, where M. de Saint-Aignan had, after his conversation with Madame, gone to meet him. This conversation has already been related. The favorite, vain of his twofold importance, and feeling that he had become, during the last two hours, the confidant of the king, began to treat the affairs of the court in a somewhat indifferent manner; and, from the position in which he had placed himself, or rather, where chance had placed him, he saw nothing but love and garlands of flowers around him. The king's love for Madame, that of Madame for the king, that of Guiche for Madame, that of La Vallière for the king, that of Malicorne for Montalais,

that of Mademoiselle de Tonnay-Charente for himself, was
not all this, truly, more than enough to turn the head of
any courtier? Besides, Saint-Aignan was the model of
courtiers, past, present and to come; and, moreover, showed
himself such an excellent narrator, and so discerningly
appreciative that the king listened to him with an appearance of great interest, particularly when he described the
excited manner with which Madame had sought for him
to converse about the affair of Mademoiselle de la Vallière.
While the king no longer experienced for Madame any
remains of the passion he had once felt for her, there was,
in this same eagerness of Madame to procure information
about him, great gratification for his vanity, from which
he could not free himself. He experienced this pleasure
then, but nothing more, and his heart was not, for a single
moment, alarmed at what Madame might, or might not,
think of his adventure.   When, however, Saint-Aignan had
finished, the king, while preparing to retire to rest asked,
" Now, Saint Aignan, you know what Mademoiselle de la
Vallière is, do you not?"

" Not only what she is, but what she will be."

" What do you mean?"

" I mean that she is everything that woman can wish
to be—that is to say, beloved by your majesty; I mean,
that she will be everything your majesty may wish her
to be."

" That is not what I am asking.   I do not wish to know
what she is to-day, or what she will be to-morrow ; as you
have remarked, that is my affair.   But tell me what others
say of her."

" They say she is well-conducted."

" Oh !" said the king, smiling, " that is mere report."

" But rare enough, at court, sire, to believe when it is
spread."

" Perhaps you are right.   Is she well-born ? "

"Excellently ; the daughter of the Marquis de la Vallière, and step-daughter of that good M. de Saint-Remy."

"Ah! yes, my aunt's major-domo ; I remember ; and I remember now that I saw her as I passed through Blois. She was presented to the queens. I have even to reproach myself that I did not on that occasion pay her the attention she deserved."

"Oh! sire, I trust that your majesty will now repair time lost."

"And the report—you tell me—is, that Mademoiselle de la Vallière never had a lover."

"In any case, I do not think your majesty would be much alarmed at the rivalry."

"Yet, stay," said the king, in a very serious tone of voice.

"Your majesty ? "

"I remember."

"Ah!"

"If she has no lover, she has, at least, a betrothed."

"A betrothed!"

"What! Count, do you not know that ? "

"No."

"You, the man who knows all the news ? "

"Your majesty will excuse me. You know this betrothed, then ? "

"Assuredly! his father came to ask me to sign the marriage contract : it is——" The king was about to pronounce the vicomte de Bragelonne's name, when he stopped, and knitted his brows.

"It is——" repeated Saint-Aignan, inquiringly.

"I don't remember now," replied Louis XIV., endeavoring to conceal an annoyance he had some trouble to disguise.

"Can I put your majesty in the way ? " inquired the Comte de Saint-Aignan.

"No : for I no longer remember to whom I intended to

refer; indeed, I only remember very indistinctly, that one of the maids of honor, was to marry——the name, however, has escaped me."

" Was it Mademoiselle de Tonnay-Charente he was going to marry ? " inquired Saint-Aignan.

" Very likely," said the king.

" In that case, the intended was M. de Montespan ; but Mademoiselle de Tonnay-Charente did not speak of it, it seemed to me, in such a manner as would frighten suitors away."

" At all events," said the king, " I know nothing, or almost nothing, about Mademoiselle de la Vallière.   Saint-Aignan, I rely upon you to procure me every information about her."

" Yes, sire, and when shall I have the honor of seeing your majesty again, to give you the latest news ? "

" Whenever you have procured it."

" I shall obtain it speedily, then, if the information can be as quickly obtained as my wish to see your majesty again."

" Well said, count !   By the by, has Madame displayed any ill-feeling against this poor girl ? "

" None, sire."

" Madame did not get angry, then ? "

" I do not know ; I only know that she laughed continually."

" That's well ; but I think I hear voices in the anterooms—no doubt a courier has just arrived.   Inquire, Saint-Aignan."   The count ran to the door and exchanged a few words with the usher; he returned to the king, saying, " Sire, it is M. Fouquet who has this moment arrived, by your majesty's orders, he says.   He presented himself, but, because of the lateness of the hour, he does not press for an audience this evening, and is satisfied to have his presence here formally announced."

"M. Fouquet! I wrote to him at three o'clock, inviting him to be at Fontainebleau the following day, and he arrives at Fontainebleau at two o'clock in the morning! This is, indeed, zeal!" exclaimed the king, delighted to see himself so promptly obeyed. "On the contrary, M. Fouquet shall have his audience. I summoned him, and will receive him. Let him be introduced. As for you, count, pursue your inquiries, and be here to-morrow."

The king placed his finger on his lips; and Saint-Aignan, his heart brimful of happiness, hastily withdrew, telling the usher to introduce M. Fouquet, who, thereupon, entered the king's apartment. Louis rose to receive him.

"Good-evening, M. Fouquet," he said, smiling graciously; "I congratulate you on your punctuality; and yet my message must have reached you late?"

"At nine in the evening, sire."

"You have been working very hard lately, M. Fouquet, for I have been informed that you have not left your rooms at Saint-Mandé during the last three or four days."

"It is perfectly true, your majesty, that I have kept myself shut up for the past three days," replied Fouquet.

"Do you know, M. Fouquet, that I had a great many things to say to you?" continued the king, with a most gracious air.

"Your majesty overwhelms me, and since you are so graciously disposed towards me, will you permit me to remind you of the promise made to grant an audience?"

"Ah! yes; some church dignitary, who thinks he has to thank me for something, is it not?"

"Precisely so, sire. The hour is, perhaps, badly chosen; but the time of the companion whom I have brought with me is valuable, and as Fontainebleau is on the way to his diocese——"

"Who is it, then?"

"The bishop of Vannes, whose appointment your majesty, at my recommendation, deigned, three months since, to sign."

"That is very possible," said the king, who had signed without reading; "and is he here?"

"Yes, sire; Vannes is an important diocese; the flock belonging to this pastor need his religious consolation; they are savages, whom it is necessary to polish, at the same time that he instructs them, and M. d'Herblay is unequalled in such kind of missions."

"M. d'Herblay!" said the king, musingly, as if his name, heard long since, was not, however, unknown to him.

"Oh!" said Fouquet, promptly, "your majesty is not acquainted with the obscure name of one of your most faithful and valuable servants?"

"No, I confess I am not. And so he wishes to set off again?"

"He has this very day received letters which will, perhaps, compel him to leave, so that, before setting off for that unknown region called Bretagne, he is desirous of paying his respects to your majesty."

"Is he waiting?"

"He is here, sire."

"Let him enter."

Fouquet made a sign to the usher in attendance, who was waiting behind the tapestry. The door opened, and Aramis entered. The king allowed him to finish the compliments which he addressed to him, and fixed a long look upon a countenance which no one could forget, after having once beheld it.

"Vannes!" he said: "you are bishop of Vannes, I believe?"

"Yes, sire."

"Vannes is in Bretagne, I think?" Aramis bowed.

"Near the coast?" Aramis again bowed.

"A few leagues from Belle-Isle, is it not?"

"Yes, sire," replied Aramis; "six leagues, I believe."

"Six leagues; a mere step, then," said Louis XIV.

"Not for us poor Bretons, sire," replied Aramis; "six leagues, on the contrary, is a great distance, if it be six leagues on land; and an immense distance, if it be leagues on the sea. Besides, I have the honor to mention to your majesty that there are six leagues of sea from the river to Belle-Isle."

"It is said that M. Fouquet has a very beautiful house there?" inquired the king.

"Yes, it is said so," replied Aramis, looking quietly at Fouquet.

"What do you mean by 'it is said so?'" exclaimed the king.

"He has, sire."

"Really, M. Fouquet, I must confess that one circumstance surprises me."

"What may that be, sire?"

"That you should have at the head of the diocese a man like M. d'Herblay, and yet should not have shown him Belle-Isle?"

"Oh, sire," replied the bishop, without giving Fouquet time to answer, "we poor Breton prelates seldom leave our residences."

"M. de Vannes," said the king, "I will punish M. Fouquet for his indifference."

"In what way, sire?"

"I will change your bishopric."

Fouquet bit his lips, but Aramis only smiled.

"What income does Vannes bring you in?" continued the king.

"Sixty thousand livres, sire," said Aramis.

"So trifling an amount as that; but you possess other property, Monsieur de Vannes?"

"I have nothing else, sire; only M. Fouquet pays me one thousand two hundred livres a year for his pew in the church."

"Well, M. d'Herblay, I promise you something better than that."

"Sire——"

"I will not forget you."

Aramis bowed, and the king also bowed to him in a respectful manner, as he was accustomed to do towards women and members of the Church. Aramis gathered that his audience was at an end; he took his leave of the king in the simple, unpretending language of a country pastor, and disappeared.

"His is, indeed, a remarkable face," said the king, following him with his eyes as long as he could see him, and even to a certain degree when he was no longer to be seen.

"Sire," replied Fouquet, "if that bishop had been educated early in life, no prelate in the kingdom would deserve the highest distinctions better than he."

"His learning is not extensive, then?"

"He changed the sword for the crucifix, and that rather late in life. But it matters little, if your majesty will permit me to speak of M. de Vannes again on another occasion——"

"I beg you to do so. But before speaking of him, let us speak of yourself, M. Fouquet."

"Of me, sire?"

"Yes, I have to pay you a thousand compliments."

"I cannot express to your majesty the delight with which you overwhelm me."

"I understand you, M. Fouquet. I confess, however, to have had certain prejudices against you."

"In that case, I was indeed unhappy, sire."

"But they exist no longer. Did you not perceive——"

"I did, indeed, sire; but I awaited with resignation the day when the truth would prevail; and it seems that that day has now arrived."

"Ah! you knew, then, you were in disgrace with me?"

"Alas! sire, I perceived it."

"And do you know the reason?"

"Perfectly well; your majesty thought that I had been wastefully lavish in expenditure."

"Not so; far from that."

"Or, rather an indifferent administrator. In a word, you thought that, as the people had no money, there would be none for your majesty either."

"Yes, I thought so; but I was deceived."

Fouquet bowed.

"And no disturbances, no complaints?"

"And money enough," said Fouquet.

"The fact is that you have been profuse with it during the last month."

"I have more, not only for all your majesty's requirements, but for all your caprices."

"I thank you, Monsieur Fouquet," replied the king, seriously. "I will not put you to the proof. For the next two months I do not intend to ask you for anything."

"I will avail myself of the interval to amass five or six millions, which will be serviceable as money in hand in case of war."

"Five or six millions!"

"For the expenses of your majesty's household only, be it understood."

"You think war probable, M. Fouquet?"

"I think that if heaven has bestowed on the eagle a

beak and claws, it is to enable him to show his royal character."

The king blushed with pleasure.

" We have spent a great deal of money these few days past, Monsieur Fouquet; will you not scold me for it ? "

" Sire, your majesty has still twenty years of youth to enjoy, and a thousand million francs to lavish in those twenty years."

" That is a great deal of money, M. Fouquet," said the king.

" I will economize, sire. Besides, your majesty has two valuable servants in M. Colbert and myself. The one will encourage you to be prodigal with your treasures—and this shall be myself, if my services should continue to be agreeable to your majesty ; and the other will economize money for you, and this will be M. Colbert's province."

" M. Colbert ? " returned the king, astonished.

" Certainly, sire; M. Colbert is an excellent accountant."

At this commendation, bestowed by the traduced on the traducer, the king felt himself penetrated with confidence and admiration. There was not, moreover, either in Fouquet's voice or look, anything which injuriously affected a single syllable of the remark he had made; he did not pass one eulogium, as it were, in order to acquire the right of making two reproaches. The king comprehended him, and yielding to so much generosity and address, he said, " You praise M. Colbert, then ? "

" Yes, sire, I praise him ; for, besides being a man of merit, I believe him to be devoted to your majesty's interests."

" Is that because he has often interfered with your own views ? " said the king, smiling.

" Exactly, sire."

" Explain yourself."

" It is simple enough. I am the man who is needed to

make the money come in; he the man who is needed to prevent it leaving."

"Nay, nay, monsieur le surintendant, you will presently say something which will correct this good opinion?"

"Do you mean as far as administrative abilities are concerned, sire?"

"Yes."

"Not in the slightest."

"Really?"

"Upon my honor, sire, I do not know throughout France a better clerk than M. Colbert."

This word "clerk" did not possess, in 1661, the somewhat subservient signification attached to it in the present day; but, as spoken by Fouquet, whom the king had addressed as the superintendent, it seemed to acquire an insignificant and petty character, that at this juncture served admirably to restore Fouquet to his place, and Colbert to his own.

"And yet," said Louis XIV., "it was Colbert, however, that notwithstanding his economy, had the arrangement of my *fêtes* here at Fontainebleau; and I assure you, Monsieur Fouquet, that in no way has he checked the expenditure of money." Fouquet bowed, but did not reply.

"Is it not your opinion too?" said the king.

"I think, sire," he replied, "that M. Colbert has done what he had to do in an exceedingly orderly manner, and that he deserves, in this respect, all the praise your majesty may bestow upon him."

The word "orderly" was a proper accompaniment for the word "clerk." The king possessed that extreme sensitiveness of organization, that delicacy of perception, which pierced through and detected the regular order of feelings and sensations, before the actual sensations themselves, and he therefore comprehended that the clerk had, in Fouquet's opinion, been too full of method and order in his arrangements; in other words, that the magnificent *fêtes* of Fontainebleau might have been rendered more magnificent still. The king consequently felt that there was something in the amusements he had provided with which some person or another might be able to find fault; he experienced a little of the annoyance felt by a person coming from the provinces to Paris, dressed out in the very best clothes which his wardrobe can furnish, only to find that the fashionably-dressed man there looks at him either too much or not enough. This part of the conversation, which Fouquet had carried on with so much moderation, yet with extreme tact, inspired the king with the highest esteem for the character of the man and the capacity of the minister. Fouquet took his leave at a quarter to three in the morning, and the king went to bed a little uneasy and confused at the indirect lesson he had received; and a good hour was employed by him in going over again in memory the embroideries, the tapestries, the bills of fare of the various banquets, the architecture of the triumphal arches, the arrangements for the illuminations and fireworks, all the offspring of the " Clerk Colbert's " invention. The result was, the king passed in review before him everything that had taken place during the last eight days, and decided that faults could be found in his *fêtes*. But Fouquet, by his politeness, his thoughtful consideration, and his generosity, had injured Colbert more deeply than the latter by his artifice, his ill-will, and his persevering hatred, had ever yet succeeded in hurting Fouquet.

CHAPTER XIII.

FONTAINEBLEAU AT TWO O'CLOCK IN THE MORNING.

As we have seen, Saint-Aignan had quitted the king's apartment at the very moment the superintendent entered it. Saint-Aignan was charged with a mission that required dispatch, and he was going to do his utmost to turn his time to the best advantage. He whom we have introduced as the king's friend was indeed an uncommon personage; he was one of those valuable courtiers whose vigilance and acuteness of perception threw all other favorites into the shade, and counterbalanced, by his close attention, the servility of Dangeau, who was not the favorite, but the toady of the king. M. de Saint-Aignan began to think what was to be done in the present position of affairs. He reflected that his first information ought to come from De Guiche. He therefore set out in search of him, but De Guiche, whom we saw disappear behind one of the wings, and who seemed to have returned to his own apartments, had not entered the château. Saint-Aignan therefore went in quest of him, and after having turned, and twisted, and searched in every direction, he perceived something like a human form leaning against a tree. This figure was as motionless as a statue, and seemed deeply engaged in looking at a window, although its curtains were closely drawn. As this window happened to be Madame's, Saint-Aignan concluded that the form in question must be that of De Guiche. He advanced cautiously, and found he was not mistaken. De Guiche had, after his conversation with Madame, carried away

such a weight of happiness, that all his strength of mind
was hardly sufficient to enable him to support it. On
his side, Saint-Aignan knew that De Guiche had had something to do with La Vallière's introduction to Madame's
household, for a courtier knows everything and forgets
nothing; but he had never learned under what title or
conditions De Guiche had conferred his protection upon
La Vallière. But, as in asking a great many questions it
is singular if a man does not learn something, Saint-
Aignan reckoned upon learning much or little, as the case
might be, if he questioned De Guiche with that extreme
tact, and, at the same time, with that persistence in at-
taining an object of which he was capable. Saint-Aignan's
plan was as follows :—If the information obtained was sat-
isfactory, he would inform the king, with alacrity, that
he had lighted upon a pearl, and claim the privilege of
setting the pearl in question in the royal crown. If the
information were unsatisfactory—which, after all, might be
possible,—he would examine how far the king cared about
La Vallière, and make use of his information in such a
manner as to get rid of the girl altogether, and thereby
obtain all the merit of her banishment with all the ladies
of the court who might have the least pretensions to the
king's heart, beginning with Madame and finishing with
the queen. In case the king should show himself obstinate in his fancy, then he would not produce the damaging information he had obtained, but would let La
Vallière know that this damaging information was carefully preserved in a secret drawer of her confidant's
memory. In this manner he would be able to air his
generosity before the poor girl's eyes, and so keep her,
in constant suspense between gratitude and apprehension,
to such an extent as to make her a friend at court, interested, as an accomplice, in trying to make his fortune,
while she was making her own. As far as concerned the

day when the bombshell of the past should burst, if ever
there were any occasion, Saint-Aignan promised himself
that he would by that time have taken all possible precautions, and would pretend an entire ignorance of the
matter to the king; while, with regard to La Vallière,
he would still have an opportunity of being considered
the personification of generosity.   It was with such ideas
as these, which the fire of covetousness had caused to
dawn in half an hour, that Saint-Aignan, the son of earth,
as La Fontaine would have said, determined to get De
Guiche into conversation : in other words, to trouble him
in his happiness—a happiness of which Saint-Aignan was
quite ignorant.   It was long past one o'clock in the morn-
ning when Saint-Aignan perceived De Guiche, standing,
motionless, leaning against the trunk of a tree, with his
eyes fastened upon the lighted window,—the sleepiest
hour of night-time, which painters crown with myrtles
and budding poppies, the hour when eyes are heavy,
hearts throb, and heads feel dull and languid—an hour
which casts upon the day which has passed away a look of
regret, while addressing a loving greeting to the dawning
light.   For De Guiche it was the dawn of unutterable happiness ; he would have bestowed a treasure upon a beggar,
had one stood before him, to secure him uninterrupted indulgence in his dreams.   It was precisely at this hour that
Saint-Aignan, badly advised,—selfishness always counsels
badly,—came and struck him on the shoulder, at the
very moment he was murmuring a word or rather a
name.

"Ah ! " he cried loudly, "I was looking for you."

"For me ? " said De Guiche, starting.

"Yes ; and I find you seemingly moon-struck.   Is it
likely, my dear comte, you have been attacked by a poetical malady, and are making verses ? "

The young man forced a smile upon his lips, while a

thousand conflicting sensations were muttering defiance of Saint-Aignan in the deep recesses of his heart. " Perhaps," he said. " But by what happy chance——"

" Ah! your remark shows that you did not hear what I said."

" How so ? "

" Why, I began by telling you I was looking for you."

" You were looking for me ? "

" Yes : and I find you now in the very act."

" Of doing what, I should like to know ? "

" Of singing the praises of Phyllis."

" Well, I do not deny it," said De Guiche, laughing. " Yes, my dear comte, I was celebrating Phyllis's praises."

" And you have acquired the right to do so."

" I ? "

" You ; no doubt of it.   You ; the intrepid protector of every beautiful and clever woman."

" In the name of goodness, what story have you got hold of now ? "

" Acknowledged truths, I am well aware. But stay a moment ; I am in love."

" You ? "

" Yes."

" So much the better, my dear comte ; tell me all about it."   And De Guiche, afraid that Saint-Aignan might perhaps presently observe the window, where the light was still burning, took the comte's arm and endeavored to lead him away.

" Oh! " said the latter, resisting, " do not take me towards those dark woods, it is too damp there. Let us stay in the moonlight."   And while he yielded to the pressure of De Guiche's arm, he remained in the flower-garden adjoining the château.

" Well," said De Guiche, resigning himself, " lead me where you like, and ask me what you please."

" It is impossible to be more agreeable than you are."
And then, after a moment's silence, Saint-Aignan continued, " I wish you to tell me something about a certain
person in whom you have interested yourself."

"And with whom you are in love ? "

"I will neither admit nor deny it. You understand
that a man does not very readily place his heart where
there is no hope of return, and that it is most essential he
should take measures of security in advance."

" You are right," said De Guiche with a sigh ; "a man's
heart is a very precious gift."

" Mine particularly is very tender, and in that light I
present it to you."

"Oh ! you are well known, comte. Well ? "

" It is simply a question of Mademoiselle de Tonnay-
Charente."

" Why, my dear Saint-Aignan, you are losing your
senses, I should think."

" Why so ? "

"I have never shown or taken any interest in Mademoiselle de Tonnay-Charente."

" Bah ! "

" Never."

" Did you not obtain admission for Mademoiselle de
Tonnay-Charente into Madame's household ? "

" Mademoiselle de Tonnay-Charente—and you ought to
know it better than any one else, my dear comte—is of a
sufficiently good family to make her presence here desirable, and her admittance very easy."

" You are jesting."

" No ; and upon my honor I do not know what you
mean."

" And you had nothing, then, to do with her admission ? "

" No."

"You do not know her?"

"I saw her for the first time the day she was presented to Madame. Therefore, as I have never taken any interest in her, as I do not know her, I am not able to give you the information you require." And De Guiche made a movement as though he were about to leave his questioner.

"Nay, nay, one moment, my dear comte," said Saint-Aignan; "you shall not escape me in this manner."

"Why, really, it seems to me that it is now time to return to our apartments."

"And yet you were not going in when I—did not meet, but, found you."

"Therefore, my dear comte," said De Guiche, "as long as you have anything to say to me, I place myself entirely at your service."

"And you are quite right in doing so. What matters half an hour more or less? Will you swear that you have no injurious communications to make to me about her, and that any injurious communications you might possibly have to make are not the cause of your silence?"

"Oh! I believe the poor child to be as pure as crystal."

"You overwhelm me with joy. And yet I do not wish to have towards you the appearance of a man so badly informed as I seem. It is quite certain that you supplied the princess's household with the ladies of honor. Nay, a song even has been written about it."

"Oh! songs are written about everything."

"Do you know it?"

"No: sing it to me and I shall make its acquaintance."

"I cannot tell you how it begins; I only remember how it ends."

"Very well, at all events that is something."

> "When Maids of Honor happen to run short,
> Lo!—Guiche will furnish the entire Court."

"The idea is weak, and the rhyme poor," said De Guiche.

"What can you expect, my dear fellow? it is not Racine's or Molière's, but La Feuillade's; and a great lord cannot rhyme like a beggarly poet."

"It is very unfortunate, though, that you only remember the termination."

"Stay, stay, I have just recollected the beginning of the second couplet.

> Why, there's the birdcage, with a pretty pair,
> The charming Montalais, and. . . .

"And La Vallière," exclaimed Guiche, impatiently, and completely ignorant besides of Saint-Aignan's object.

"Yes, yes, you have it. You have hit upon the word, 'La Vallière.'"

"A grand discovery indeed."

"Montalais and La Vallière, these, then, are the two young girls in whom you interest yourself," said Saint-Aignan laughing.

"And so, Mademoiselle de Tonnay-Charente's name is not to be met with in the song?"

"No, indeed."

"And you are satisfied, then?"

"Perfectly; but I find Montalais there," said Saint-Aignan, still laughing.

"Oh! you will find her everywhere. She is a singularly active young lady."

"You know her?"

"Indirectly. She was the *protégée* of a man named Malicorne, who is a *protégée* of Manicamp's; Manicamp asked me to get the situation of maid of honor for Montalais in Madame's household, and a situation for Malicorne, as an officer in Monsieur's household. Well, I asked for the appointments, for you know very well that I have a weakness for that droll fellow Manicamp."

" And you obtained what you sought? "

" For Montalais, yes : for Malicorne, yes and no ; for as yet he is only on trial. Do you wish to know anything else ? "

" The last word of the couplet still remains, La Vallière," said Saint-Aignan, resuming the smile that so tormented Guiche.

" Well," said the latter, " it is true that I obtained admission for her in Madame's household."

" Ah ! " said Saint-Aignan.

" But," continued Guiche, assuming a great coldness of manner, " you will oblige me, comte, not to jest about that name. Mademoiselle Labaume le Blanc de la Vallière is a young lady perfectly well-conducted."

" Perfectly well-conducted, do you say ? "

" Yes."

" Then you have not heard the last rumor ? " exclaimed Saint-Aignan.

" No, and you will do me a service, my dear comte, in keeping this report to yourself and to those who circulate it."

" Ah ! bah ! you take the matter up very seriously."

" Yes ; Mademoiselle de Vallière is beloved by one of my best friends."

Saint-Aignan started. " Aha ! " he said.

" Yes, comte," continued Guiche : " and consequently, you, the most distinguished man in France for polished courtesy of manner, will understand that I cannot allow my friend to be placed in a ridiculous position."

Saint-Aignan began to bite his nails, partially from vexation, and partially from disappointed curiosity. Guiche made him a very profound bow.

" You send me away," said Saint-Aignan, who was dying to know the name of the friend.

" I do not send you away, my dear fellow. I am going to finish my lines to Phyllis."

" And those lines——"

" Are a *quatrain*.   You understand, I trust, that a *quatrain* is a serious affair ? "

" Of course."

" And as, of these four lines, of which it is composed, I have yet three and a half to make, I need my undivided attention."

" I quite understand.   Adieu ! comte.   By the by——"

" What ? "

" Are you quick at making verses ? "

" Wonderfully so."

" Will you have quite finished the three lines and a half to-morrow morning ? "

" I *hope* so."

" Adieu, then, until to-morrow."

" Adieu, adieu ! "

Saint-Aignan was obliged to accept the notice to quit ; he accordingly did so, and disappeared behind the hedge. Their conversation had led Guiche and Saint-Aignan a good distance from the château.

Every mathematician, every poet, and every dreamer has his own subjects of interest.   Saint-Aignan on leaving Guiche, found himself at the extremity of the grove,—at the very spot where the outbuildings for the servants begin, and where, behind the thickets of acacias and chestnut-trees interlacing their branches, which were hidden by masses of clematis and young vines, the wall which separated the woods from the courtyard was erected.   Saint-Aignan, alone, took the path which led towards these buildings ; De Guiche going off in the opposite direction. The one proceeded to the flower-garden, while the other bent his steps toward the walls. Saint-Aignan walked on between rows of mountain-ash, lilac, and hawthorn, which formed an almost impenetrable roof above his head; his feet were buried in the soft gravel and thick moss. He was deliberating a means of taking his revenge which seemed difficult for him to carry out, and was vexed with himself for not having learned more about La Vallière, notwithstanding the ingenious measures he had resorted to in order to acquire more information about her, when suddenly the murmur of a human voice attracted his attention. He heard whispers, the complaining tones of a woman's voice mingled with entreaties, smothered laughter, sighs, and half-stifled exclamations of surprise; but above them all, the woman's voice prevailed. Saint-Aignan stopped to look about him; he perceived with the greatest surprise that the voices proceeded, not from the ground but from the branches of the trees. As he glided along under the covered walk, he raised his head, and observed at the top of the wall a woman perched upon a ladder, in eager conversation with a man seated on a branch of a chestnut-tree, whose head alone could be seen, the rest of his body being concealed in the thick covert of the chestnut.

CHAPTER XIV.

THE LABYRINTH.

SAINT-AIGNAN, who had only been seeking for information, had met with an adventure. This was indeed a piece of good luck. Curious to learn why, and particularly what about, this man and woman were conversing at such an hour and in such a singular position, Saint-Aignan made himself as small as he possibly could, and approached almost under the rounds of the ladder. And taking measures to make himself as comfortable as possible, he leaned his back against a tree and listened, and heard the following conversation. The woman was the first to speak.

"Really, Monsieur Manicamp," she said, in a voice which, notwithstanding the reproaches she addressed to him, preserved a marked tone of coquetry, " really your indiscretion is of a very dangerous character. We cannot talk long in this manner without being observed."

"That is very probable," said the man, in the calmest and coolest of tones.

"In that case, then, what would people say? Oh! if any one were to see me, I declare I should die of very shame."

"Oh! that would be very silly; I do not believe you would."

"It might have been different if there had been anything between us; but to injure myself gratuitously, is really very foolish of me; so, adieu, Monsieur Manicamp."

"So far so good; I know the man, and now let me see who the woman is," said Saint-Aignan, watching the rounds of the ladder, on which were standing two pretty little feet covered with blue satin shoes.

"Nay, nay, for pity's sake, my dear Montalais," cried Manicamp, "deuce take it, do not go away; I have a great many things to say to you, of the greatest importance still."

"Montalais," said Saint-Aignan to himself, " one of the three. Each of the three gossips had her adventure, only I imagined the hero of this one's adventure was Malicorne and not Manicamp."

At her companion's appeal, Montalais stopped in the middle of her descent, and Saint-Aignan could observe

the unfortunate Manicamp climb from one branch of the
chestnut-tree to another, either to improve his situation or
to overcome the fatigue consequent upon his inconvenient
position.

" Now, listen to me," said he ; " you quite understand,
I hope, that my intentions are perfectly innocent."

" Of course.   But why did you write me a letter stimu-
lating my gratitude towards you?   Why did you ask me
for an interview at such an hour and in such a place as
this? "

" I stimulated your gratitude in reminding you that it
was I who had been the means of your becoming attached
to Madame's household ; because most anxiously desirous
of obtaining the interview you have been kind enough to
grant me, I employed the means which appeared to me
most certain to insure it.   And my reason for soliciting
it, at such an hour and in such a locality, was, that the
hour seemed to me to be the most prudent and the locality the least open to observation.   Moreover, I had occasion to speak to you upon certain subjects which require
both prudence and solitude."

" Monsieur Manicamp ! "

" But everything I wish to say is perfectly honorable, I
assure you."

" I think, Monsieur Manicamp, it will be more becoming in me to take my leave."

" No, no !—listen to me, or I will jump from my perch
here to yours ; and be careful how you set me at defiance ;
for a branch of this chestnut tree causes me a good deal
of annoyance, and may provoke me to extreme measures.
Do not follow the example of this branch, then, but
listen to me."

" I am listening, and I agree to do so ; but be as brief
as possible, for if you have a branch of the chestnut-tree
which annoys you, I wish you to understand that one of

the rounds of the ladder is hurting the soles of my feet, and my shoes are being cut through."

" Do me the kindness to give me your hand."

" Why ? "

" Will you have the goodness to do so ? "

" There is my hand, then ; but what are you going to do ? "

" To draw you towards me."

" What for ? You surely do not wish me to join you in the tree ? "

" No ; but I wish you to sit down upon the wall ; there, that will do ; there is quite room enough, and I would give a great deal to be allowed to sit down beside you."

" No, no ; you are very well where you are ; we should be seen."

" Do you really think so ? " said Manicamp, in an insinuating voice ?

" I am sure of it."

" Very well, I remain in my tree, then, although I cannot be worse placed."

" Monsieur Manicamp, we are wandering away from the subject."

" You are right, we are so."

" You wrote me a letter ? "

" I did."

" Why did you write ? "

" Fancy, at two o'clock to-day, De Guiche left."

" What then ? "

" Seeing him set off, I followed him, as I usually do."

" Of course, I see that, since you are here now."

" Don't be in a hurry. You are aware, I suppose, that De Guiche is up to his very neck in disgrace ? "

" Alas ! yes."

" It was the very height of imprudence on his part,

then, to come to Fontainebleau to seek those who had
at Paris sent him away into exile, and particularly those
from whom he had been separated."

"Monsieur Manicamp, you reason like Pythagoras."

"Moreover, De Guiche is as obstinate as a man in love
can be, and he refused to listen to any of my remon-
strances. I begged, I implored him, but he would not listen
to anything. Oh! the deuce!"

"What's the matter?"

"I beg your pardon, Mademoiselle Montalais, but this
confounded branch, about which I have already had the
honor of speaking to you, has just torn a certain portion
of my dress."

"It is quite dark," replied Montalais, laughing; "so,
pray continue, M. Manicamp."

De Guiche set off on horseback as hard as he could, I
following him, at a slower pace. You quite understand
that to throw one's self into the water, for instance, with
a friend, at the same headlong rate as he himself would
do it, would be the act either of a fool or a madman. I
therefore allowed De Guiche to get in advance, and I
proceeded on my way with a commendable slowness of
pace, feeling quite sure that my unfortunate friend would
not be received, or, if he had been, that he would ride
off again at the very first cross, disagreeable answer; and
that I should see him returning much faster than he went,
without having, myself, gone farther than Ris or Melun
—and that even was a good distance you will admit, for it
is eleven leagues to get there and as many to return."

Montalais shrugged her shoulders.

"Laugh as much as you like; but if, instead of being
comfortably seated on the top of the wall as you are, you
were sitting on this branch as if you were on horseback,
you would, like Augustus, aspire to descend."

"Be patient, my dear M. Manicamp; a few minutes will

soon pass away; you were saying, I think, that you had gone beyond Ris and Melun."

" Yes, I went through Ris and Melun, and I continued to go on, more and more surprised that I did not see him returning; and here I am at Fontainebleau; I look for and inquire after De Guiche everywhere, but no one has seen him, no one in the town has spoken to him; he arrived riding at full gallop, he entered the château; and there he has disappeared. I have been here at Fontainebleau since eight o'clock this evening inquiring for De Guiche in every direction, but no De Guiche can be found. I am dying with uneasiness. You understand that I have not been running my head into the lion's den, in entering the château, as my imprudent friend has done; I came at once to the servants' offices, and I succeeded in getting a letter conveyed to you; and now, for Heaven's sake, my dear young lady, relieve me from my anxiety."

"There will be no difficulty in that, my dear M. Manicamp; your friend De Guiche has been admirably received."

"Bah!"

" The king made quite a fuss over him."

" The king, who exiled him!"

"Madame smiled upon him, and Monsieur appears to like him better than ever."

" Ah! ah!" said Manicamp, "that explains to me, then, why and how he has remained. And did he not say anything about me?"

"Not a word."

" That is very unkind. What is he doing now?"

"In all probability he is asleep, or, if not asleep, dreaming."

" And what have they been doing all the evening?"

" Dancing."

"The famous ballet? How did De Guiche look?"

"Superb?"

"Dear fellow! And now, pray forgive me, Mademoiselle Montalais; but all I now have to do is to pass from where I now am to your apartment."

"What do you mean?"

"I cannot suppose that the door of the château will be opened for me at this hour; and as for spending the night upon this branch, I possibly might not object to do so, but I declare it is impossible for any other animal than a boa-constrictor to do it."

"But, M. Manicamp, I cannot introduce a man over the wall in that manner."

"Two, if you please," said a second voice, but in so timid a tone that it seemed as if its owner felt the utter impropriety of such a request.

"Good gracious!" exclaimed Montalais, "who is that speaking to me?"

"Malicorne, Mademoiselle Montalais."

And as Malicorne spoke, he raised himself from the ground to the lowest branches, and thence to the height of the wall.

"Monsieur Malicorne! why, you are both mad!"

"How do you do, Mademoiselle Montalais?" inquired Malicorne.

"I needed but this!" said Montalais, in despair.

"Oh! Mademoiselle Montalais," murmured Malicorne; "do not be so severe, I beseech you."

"In fact," said Manicamp, "we are your friends, and you cannot possibly wish your friends to lose their lives; and to leave us to pass the night on these branches, is in fact, condemning us to death."

"Oh!" said Montalais, "Monsieur Malicorne is so robust that a night passed in the open air with the beautiful stars above him will not do him any harm, and it will be a just punishment for the trick he has played me."

"Be it so, then; let Malicorne arrange matters with you in the best way he can; I pass over," said Manicamp. And bending down the famous branch against which he had directed such bitter complaints, he succeeded, by the assistance of his hands and feet, in seating himself side by side with Montalais, who tried to push him back, while he endeavored to maintain his position, and, moreover, he succeeded. Having taken possession of the ladder, he stepped on it, and then gallantly offered his hand to his fair antagonist. While this was going on, Malicorne had installed himself in the chestnut-tree, in the very place Manicamp had just left, determining within himself to succeed him in the one which he now occupied. Manicamp and Montalais descended a few rounds of the ladder, Manicamp insisting, and Montalais laughing and objecting.

Suddenly Malicorne's voice was heard in tones of entreaty :—

"I entreat you, Mademoiselle Montalais, not to leave me here. My position is very insecure, and some accident will be certain to befall me, if I attempt unaided to reach the other side of the wall; it does not matter if Manicamp tears his clothes, for he can make use of M. de Guiche's wardrobe; but I shall not be able to use even those belonging to M. Manicamp, for they will be torn."

"My opinion," said Manicamp, without taking any notice of Malicorne's lamentations, "is that the best thing to be done is to go and look for De Guiche without delay, for, by and by, perhaps, I may not be able to get to his apartments."

"That is my own opinion too," replied Montalais: "so, go at once, Monsieur Manicamp."

"A thousand thanks. Adieu, Mademoiselle Montalais,"

said Manicamp, jumping to the ground; "your conde-
scension cannot be repaid."

"Farewell, M. Manicamp; I am now going to get rid
of M. Malicorne."

Malicorne sighed. Manicamp went away a few paces,
but returning to the foot of the ladder, he said, "By the
by, how do I get to M. de Guiche's apartments?"

"Nothing easier. You go along by the hedge until you
reach a place where the paths cross."

"Yes."

"You will see four paths."

"Exactly."

"One of which you will take."

"Which of them?"

"That to the right."

"To the right?"

"No, to the left."

"The deuce!"

"No, no, wait a minute——"

"You do not seem to be quite sure. Think again, I
beg."

"You take the middle path."

"But there are *four*."

"So there are. All that I know is, that one of the four
paths leads straight to Madame's apartments; and that
one I am well acquainted with."

"But M. de Guiche is not in Madame's apartments, I
suppose?"

"No, indeed."

"Well, then the path which leads to Madame's apartments is of no use to me, and I would willingly exchange
it for the one that leads to where M. de Guiche is lodging."

"Of course, and I know that as well; but as for indicating it from where we are, it is quite impossible."

" Well, let us suppose that I have succeeded in finding that fortunate path."

" In that case, you are almost there, for you have nothing else to do but to cross the labyrinth."

" *Nothing* more than that ? The deuce! so there is a labyrinth as well."

" Yes, and complicated enough too; even in daylight one may sometimes be deceived,—there are turnings and windings without end: in the first place, you must turn three times to the right, then twice to the left, then turn once—stay, is it once or twice, though? at all events, when you get clear of the labyrinth, you will see an avenue of sycamores, and this avenue leads straight to the pavilion in which M. de Guiche is lodging."

"Nothing could be more clearly indicated," said Manicamp; "and I have not the slightest doubt in the world that if I were to follow your directions, I should lose my way immediately. I have, therefore, a slight service to ask of you."

" What may that be ? "

"That you will offer me your arm and guide me yourself, like another—like another—I used to know mythology, but other important matters have made me forget it ; pray come with me, then ? "

" And am I to be abandoned, then ? " cried Malicorne.

" It is quite impossible, monsieur," said Montalais to Manicamp; "if I were to be seen with you at such an hour, what would be said of me ?"

" Your own conscience would acquit you," said Manicamp, sententiously.

" Impossible, monsieur, impossible."

" In that case, let me assist Malicorne to get down; he is a very intelligent fellow, and possesses a very keen scent; he will guide me, and if we lose ourselves, both of us will be lost, and the one will save the other. If we are

together, and should be met by any one, we shall look as
if we had some matter of business in hand; whilst alone
I should have the appearance either of a lover or a robber.
Come, Malicorne, here is the ladder."

Malicorne had already stretched out one of his legs
towards the top of the wall, when Manicamp said, in a
whisper, "Hush!"

"What's the matter?" inquired Montalais.

"I hear footsteps."

"Good heavens!"

In fact, the fancied footsteps soon became a reality;
the foliage was pushed aside, and Saint-Aignan appeared,
with a smile on his lips, and his hand stretched out
towards them, taking every one by surprise; that is to
say, Malicorne upon the tree with his head stretched out,
Montalais upon the rounds of the ladder and clinging to
it tightly, and Manicamp on the ground with his foot advanced ready to set off. "Good-evening, Manicamp," said
the comte, "I am glad to see you, my dear fellow; we
missed you this evening, and a good many inquiries have
been made about you. Mademoiselle de Montalais, your
most obedient servant."

Montalais blushed. "Good heavens!" she exclaimed,
hiding her face in both her hands.

"Pray reassure yourself; I know how perfectly innocent
you are, and I shall give a good account of you. Manicamp, do you follow me: the hedge, the cross-paths, and
labyrinth, I am well acquainted with them all; I will be
your Ariadne. There now, your mythological name is
found at last."

"Perfectly true, comte."

"And take M. Malicorne away with you at the same
time," said Montalais.

"No, indeed," said Malicorne; "M. Manicamp has
conversed with you as long as he liked, and now it is my

turn, if you please; I have a multitude of things to tell you about our future prospects."

"You hear," said the comte, laughing; "stay with him, Mademoiselle Montalais. This is, indeed, a night for secrets." And, taking Manicamp's arm, the comte led him rapidly away in the direction of the road Montalais knew so well, and indicated so badly. Montalais followed them with her eyes as long as she could perceive them.

CHAPTER XV.

HOW MALICORNE HAD BEEN TURNED OUT OF THE HOTEL OF THE BEAU PAON.

While Montalais was engaged in looking after the comte and Manicamp, Malicorne had taken advantage of the young girl's attention being drawn away to render his position somewhat more tolerable, and when she turned round, she immediately noticed the change which had taken place; for he had seated himself, like a monkey, upon the wall, with his feet resting upon the top rounds of the ladder, the foliage of the wild vine and honeysuckle curled round his head like a faun, while the twisted ivy branches represented tolerably enough his cloven feet. Montalais required nothing to make her resemblance to a dryad as complete as possible. "Well," she said, ascending another round of the ladder, "are you resolved to render me unhappy? have you not persecuted me enough, tyrant that you are?"

"I a tyrant?" said Malicorne.

"Yes, you are always compromising me, Monsieur Malicorne; you are a perfect monster of wickedness."

"I?"

"What have you to do with Fontainebleau? Is not Orleans your place of residence?"

"Do you ask me what I have to do here? I wanted to see you."

"Ah, great need of that."

"Not as far as concerns yourself, perhaps, but as far as I am concerned, Mademoiselle Montalais, you know very well that I have left my home, and that, for the future, I have no other place of residence than that which you may happen to have. As you, therefore, are staying at Fontainebleau at the present moment, I have come to Fontainebleau."

Montalais shrugged her shoulders. "You wished to see me, did you not?" she said.

"Of course."

"Very well, you have seen me,—you are satisfied; so now go away."

"Oh, no," said Malicorne; "I came to talk with you as well as to see you."

"Very well, we will talk by and by, and in another place than this."

"By and by! heaven only knows if shall meet you by and by in another place. We shall never find a more favorable one than this."

"But I cannot this evening, nor at the present moment."

"Why not?"

"Because a thousand things have happened to-night."

"Well, then, my affair will make a thousand and one."

"No no; Mademoiselle de Tonnay-Charente is waiting for me in our room to communicate something of the very greatest importance."

"How long has she been waiting?"

"For an hour at least."

"In that case," said Malicorne, tranquilly, "she can wait a few minutes longer."

"Monsieur Malicorne," said Montalais, "you are forgetting yourself."

"You should rather say that it is you who are forgetting me, and that I am getting impatient at the part you make me play here indeed! For the last week I have been prowling about among the company, and you have not once deigned to notice my presence."

"Have you been prowling about here for a week, M. Malicorne?"

"Like a wolf; sometimes I have been burnt by the fireworks, which have singed two of my wigs; at others, I have been completely drenched in the osiers by the evening damps, or the spray from the fountains,—half-famished, fatigued to death, with the view of a wall always before me, and the prospect of having to scale it perhaps. Upon my word, this is not the sort of life for any one to lead who is neither a squirrel, a salamander, nor an otter; and since you drive your inhumanity so far as to wish to make me renounce my condition as a man, I declare it openly. A man I am, indeed, and a man I will remain, unless by superior orders."

"Well, then, tell me, what do you wish,—what do you require,—what do you insist upon?" said Montalais, in a submissive tone.

"Do you mean to tell me that you did not know I was at Fontainebleau?"

"I!"

"Nay, be frank."

"I suspected so."

"Well, then, could you not have contrived during the last week to have seen me once a day, at least?"

"I have always been prevented, M. Malicorne."

"Fiddlesticks!"

" Ask my companion, if you do not believe me."

" I shall ask no one to explain matters, I know better than any one."

" Compose yourself, M. Malicorne ; things will change."

" They must indeed."

" You know that, whether I see you or not, I am think-ing of you," said Montalais, in a coaxing tone of voice.

" Oh, you are thinking of me, are you ? well, and is there anything new ? "

" What about ? "

" About my post in Monsieur's household."

" Ah, my dear Monsieur Malicorne, no one has ventured lately to approach his royal highness."

" Well, but now ? "

" Now, it is quite a different thing ; since yesterday he has left off being jealous."

" Bah ! how has his jealousy subsided ? "

" It has been diverted into another channel."

" Tell me all about it."

" A report was spread that the king had fallen in love with some one else, and Monsieur was tranquillized im-mediately."

" And who spread the report ? "

Montalais lowered her voice. " Between ourselves," she said, " I think that Madame and the king have come to a secret understanding about it."

" Ah ! " said Malicorne ; " that was the only way to manage it. But what about poor M. de Guiche ? "

" Oh, as for him, he is completely turned off."

" Have they been writing to each other ? "

" No, certainly not ; I have not seen a pen in either of their hands for the last week."

" On what terms are you with Madame ? "

" The very best."

" And with the king ? "

"The king always smiles at me whenever I pass him."

"Good. Now tell me whom have the two lovers selected to serve as their screen?"

"La Vallière."

"Oh, oh, poor girl! We must prevent that?"

"Why?"

"Because, if M. Raoul Bragelonne were to suspect it, he would either kill her or kill himself."

"Raoul, poor fellow! do you think so?"

"Women pretend to have a knowledge of the state of people's affections," said Malicorne, "and they do not even know how to read the thoughts of their own minds and hearts. Well, I can tell you, that M. de Bragelonne loves La Vallière to such a degree that, if she deceived him, he would, I repeat, either kill himself or kill her."

"But the king is there to defend her," said Montalais.

"The king!" exclaimed Malicorne; "Raoul would kill the king as he would a common thief."

"Good heavens!" said Montalais; "you are mad, M. Malicorne."

"Not in the least. Everything I have told you is, on the contrary, perfectly serious; and, for my own part, I know one thing."

"What is that?"

"That I shall quietly tell Raoul of the trick."

"Hush!" said Montalais, mounting another round of the ladder, so as to approach Malicorne more closely, "do not open your lips to poor Raoul."

"Why not?"

"Because, as yet you know nothing at all."

"What is the matter, then?"

"Why, this evening—but no one is listening, I hope?"

"No."

"This evening, then, beneath the royal oak, La Vallière said aloud, and innocently enough, 'I cannot conceive that

when one has once seen the king, one can ever love another
man.' "

Malicorne almost jumped off the wall.   " Unhappy girl!
did she really say that ? "

" Word for word."

" And she thinks so ? "

" La Vallière always thinks what she says."

" That positively cries aloud for vengeance.   Why,
women are the veriest serpents," said Malicorne,

" Compose yourself, my dear Malicorne, compose yourself."

" No, no ; let us take the evil in time, on the contrary.
There is time enough yet to tell Raoul of it."

" Blunderer, on the contrary, it is too late," replied Montalais.

" How so ? "

" La Vallière's remark, which was intended for the king,
reached its destination."

" The king knows it, then ?   The king was told of it, I
suppose ? "

" The king heard it."

" *Ohimé !* as the cardinal used to say."

" The king was hidden in the thicket close to the royal
oak."

" It follows, then," said Malicorne, " that for the future,
the plan which the king and Madame have arranged, will
go as easily as if it were on wheels, and will pass over
poor Bragelonne's body."

" Precisely so."

" Well," said Malicorne, after a moment's reflection, " do
not let us interpose our poor selves between a large oak-
tree and a great king, for we should certainly be ground
to pieces."

" The very thing I was going to say to you."

" Let us think of ourselves, then."

"My own idea."

"Open your beautiful eyes, then."

"And you your large ears."

"Approach your little mouth for a kiss."

"Here," said Montalais, who paid the debt immediately in ringing coin.

"Now let us consider. First, we have M. de Guiche, who is in love with Madame; then La Vallière, who is in love with the king; next, the king, who is in love both with Madame and La Vallière : lastly Monsieur, who loves no one but himself. Among all these loves, a noodle would make his fortune : a greater reason, therefore, for sensible people like ourselves to do so."

"There you are with your dreams again."

"Nay, rather with realities. Let me still lead you, darling. I do not think you have been very badly off hitherto."

"No."

"Well, the future is guaranteed by the past. Only, since all here think of themselves before anything else, let us do so too."

"Perfectly right."

"But of ourselves only."

"Be it so."

"An offensive and defensive alliance."

"I am ready to swear it."

"Put out your hand, then, and say, 'All for Malicorne.'"

"All for Malicorne."

"And I, 'All for Montalais,'" replied Malicorne, stretching out his hand in his turn.

"And now, what is to be done?"

"Keep your eyes and ears constantly open ; collect every means of attack which may be serviceable against others ; never let anything lie about which can be used against ourselves."

" Agreed."

" Decided."

" Sworn to. And now the agreement entered into,
good-bye."

" What do you mean by ' good-bye ? ' "

" Of course you can now return to your inn."

" To my inn ? "

" Yes ; are you not lodging at the sign of the Beau
Paon ? "

" Montalais, Montalais, you now betray that you were
aware of my being at Fontainebleau."

" Well ; and what does that prove, except that I occupied
myself about you more than you deserve ? "

" Hum ! "

" Go back, then, to the Beau Paon."

" That is now quite out of the question."

" Have you not a room there ? "

" I had, but have it no longer."

" Who has taken it from you, then ? "

" I will tell you. Some little time ago I was returning
there, after I had been running about after you ; and
having reached my hotel quite out of breath, I perceived
a litter, upon which four peasants were carrying a sick
monk."

" A monk ? "

" Yes, an old gray-bearded Franciscan. As I was looking at the monk, they entered the hotel ; and as they were
carrying him up the staircase, I followed, and as I reached
the top of the staircase I observed that they took him
into my room."

" Into your room ? "

" Yes, into my own apartment. Supposing it to be a mistake, I summoned the landlord, who said that the room
which had been let to me for the past eight days was let
to the Franciscan for the ninth."

" Oh, oh! "

"That was exactly what I said ; nay, I did even more, for I was inclined to get out of temper. I went up stairs again. I spoke to the Franciscan himself, and wished to prove to him the impropriety of the step ; when this monk, dying though he seemed to be, raised himself upon his arm, fixed a pair of blazing eyes upon me, and, in a voice which was admirably suited for commanding a charge of cavalry, said, ' Turn this fellow out of doors ; ' which was done immediately by the landlord and the four porters, who made me descend the staircase somewhat faster than was agreeable.   This is how it happens, dearest, that I have no lodging."

" Who can this Franciscan be? " said Montalais.   " Is he a general ? "

" That is exactly the very title that one of the bearers of the litter gave him as he spoke to him in a low tone."

" So that——" said Montalais.

" So that I have no room, no hotel, no lodging; and I am as determined as my friend Manicamp was just now, not to pass the night in the open air."

" What is to be done, then ? " said Montalais.

" Nothing easier," said a third voice ; whereupon Montalais and Malicorne uttered a simultaneous cry, and Saint-Aignan appeared.   " Dear Monsieur Malicorne," said Saint-Aignan, " a very lucky accident has brought me back to extricate you from your embarrassment. Come, I can offer you a room in my own apartments, which, I can assure you, no Franciscan will deprive you of. As for you, my dear young lady, rest easy. I already knew Mademoiselle de la Vallière's secret, and that of Mademoiselle de Tonnay-Charente ; your own you have just been kind enough to confide to me; for which I thank you. I can keep three quite as well as one." Malicorne and Montalais looked at each other, like children detected in a theft; but as Malicorne saw a great advantage in the proposition which had been made to him, he gave Montalais a sign of assent, which she returned. Malicorne then descended the ladder, round by round, reflecting at every step on the means of obtaining piecemeal from M. de Saint-Aignan all he might possibly know about the famous secret. Montalais had already darted away like a deer, and neither cross-road nor labyrinth was able to lead her wrong. As for Saint-Aignan, he carried off Malicorne with him to his apartments, showing him a thousand attentions, enchanted to have close at hand the very two men who, even supposing De Guiche were to remain silent, could give him the best information about the maids of honor.

CHAPTER XVI.

WHAT ACTUALLY OCCURRED AT THE INN CALLED THE BEAU PAON.

In the first place, let us supply our readers with a few details about the inn called the Beau Paon. It owed its name to its sign, which represented a peacock spreading its tail. But, in imitation of certain painters who bestowed the face of a handsome young man on the serpent which tempted Eve, the limner of this sign had conferred upon the peacock the features of a woman. This famous inn, an architectural epigram against that half of the human race which renders existence delightful, was situated at Fontainebleau, in the first turning on the left-hand side, which divides the road from Paris, the large artery that constitutes in itself alone the entire town of Fontainebleau. The side street in question was then known as the Rue de Lyon, doubtless because, geographically, it led in the

direction of the second capital of the kingdom. The
street itself was composed of two houses occupied by
persons of the class of tradespeople, the houses being separated by two large gardens bordered with hedges running
round them. Apparently, however, there were three
houses in the street. Let us explain, notwithstanding ap-
pearances, how there were in fact only two. The inn of
the Beau Paon had its principal front towards the main
street; but upon the Rue de Lyon there were two ranges
of buildings divided by courtyards, which comprised sets
of apartments for the reception of all classes of travelers,
whether on foot or on horseback, or even with their own
carriages; and in which could be supplied, not only
board and lodging, but also accommodation for exercise,
or opportunities of solitude for even the wealthiest courtiers, whenever, after having received some check at the
court, they wished to shut themselves up to their own
society, either to devour an affront, or to brood on revenge.
From the windows of this part of the building travelers
could perceive, in the first place, the street with the grass
growing between the stones, which were being gradually
loosened by it; next the beautiful hedges of elder and
thorn, which embraced, as though within two green and
flowery arms, the houses of which we have spoken; and
then, in the spaces between those houses, forming the
groundwork of the picture, and appearing an almost im-
passable barrier, a line of thick trees, the advanced senti-
nels of the vast forest which extends in front of Fontainebleau. It was therefore easy, provided one secured an
apartment at the angle of the building, to obtain, by the
main street from Paris, a view of, as well as to hear, the
passers-by and the *fêtes;* and, by the Rue de Lyon, to
look upon and to enjoy the calm of the country. And
this without reckoning that, in cases of urgent necessity,
at the very moment people might be knocking at the

principal door in the Rue de Paris, one could make one's escape by the little door in the Rue de Lyon, and, creeping along the gardens of the private houses, attain the outskirts of the forest. Malicorne, who, it will be remembered, was the first to speak about this inn, by way of deploring his being turned out of it, being then absorbed in his own affairs, had not told Montalais all that could be said about this curious inn; and we will try to repair the omission. With the exception of the few words he had said about the Franciscan friar, Malicorne had not given any particulars about the travelers who were staying in the inn. The manner in which they had arrived, the manner in which they lived, the difficulty which existed for every one but certain privileged travelers, of entering the hotel without a password, or living there without certain preparatory precautions, must have struck Malicorne; and, we will venture to say, really did so. But Malicorne, as we have already said, had personal matters of his own to occupy his attention, which prevented him from paying much attention to others. In fact, all the apartments of the hotel were engaged and retained by certain strangers, who never stirred out, who were incommunicative in their address, with countenances full of thoughtful preoccupation, and not one of whom was known to Malicorne. Every one of these travelers had reached the hotel after his own arrival there; each man had entered after having given a kind of password, which had at first attracted Malicorne's attention; but having inquired, in an indirect manner, about it, he had been informed that the host had given as a reason for this extreme vigilance, that, as the town was so full of wealthy noblemen, it must also be as full of clever and zealous pickpockets. The reputation of an honest inn like that of the Beau Paon was concerned in not allowing its visitors to be robbed. It occasionally

happened that Malicorne asked himself, as he thought
matters carefully over in his mind, and reflected upon his
own position in the inn, how it was that they had allowed
him to become an inmate of the hotel, when he had observed, since his residence there, admission refused to so
many. He asked himself, too, how it was that Manicamp,
who, in his opinion, must be a man to be looked upon
with veneration by everybody, having wished to bait his
horse at the Beau Paon, on arriving there, both horse and
rider had been incontinently turned away with a *nescio
vos* of the most positive character. All this for Malicorne, whose mind being fully occupied by his own love
affair and personal ambition, was a problem he had not
applied himself to solve. Had he wished to do so, we
should hardly venture, notwithstanding the intelligence
we have accorded as his due, to say he would have succeeded. A few words will prove to the reader that no one
but Œdipus in person could have solved the enigma in
question. During the week, seven travelers had taken up
their abode in the inn, all of them having arrived there
the day after the fortunate day on which Malicorne had
fixed his choice on the Beau Paon. These seven persons,
accompanied by a suitable retinue, were the following :—
    First of all, a brigadier in the German army, his secre-
tary, physician, three servants, and seven horses. The
brigadier's name was the Comte de Wostpur.—A Spanish
cardinal, with two nephews, two secretaries, an officer of
his household, and twelve horses. The cardinal's name was
Monseigneur Herrebia.—A rich merchant of Bremen, with
his man-servant and two horses. This merchant's name
was Meinheer Bonstett.—A Venetian senator, with his wife
and daughter, both extremely beautiful. The senator's
name was Signor Marini.—A Scotch laird, with seven
Highlanders of his clan, all on foot. The laird's name
was MacCumnor.—An Austrian from Vienna, without

title or coat-of-arms, who had arrived in a carriage; a good deal of the priest, and something of the soldier. He was called the Councilor.—And, finally, a Flemish lady, with a man-servant, a lady's maid, and a female companion, a large retinue of servants, great display, and immense horses. She was called the Flemish lady.

All these travelers had arrived on the same day, and yet their arrival had occasioned no confusion in the inn, no stoppage in the street; their apartments had been fixed upon beforehand, by their couriers or secretaries, who had arrived the previous evening or that very morning. Malicorne, who had arrived the previous day, riding an ill-conditioned horse, with a slender valise, had announced himself at the hotel of the Beau Paon as the friend of a nobleman desirous of witnessing the *fêtes*, and who would himself arrive almost immediately. The landlord, on hearing these words, had smiled as if he were perfectly well acquainted either with Malicorne or his friend the nobleman, and had said to him, "Since you are the first arrival, monsieur, choose what apartment you please." And this was said with that obsequiousness of manners, so full of meaning with landlords, which means, "Make yourself perfectly easy, monsieur: we know with whom we have to do, and you will be treated accordingly." These words, and their accompanying gesture, Malicorne had thought very friendly, but rather obscure. However, as he did not wish to be very extravagant in his expenses, and as he thought that if he were to ask for a small apartment he would doubtless have been refused, on account of his want of consequence, he hastened to close at once with the innkeeper's remark, and deceive him with a cunning equal to his own. So, smiling as a man would do for whom whatever might be done was but simply his due, he said, "My dear host, I shall take the best and the gayest room in the house."

"With a stable?"

"Yes, with a stable."

"And when will you take it?"

"Immediately, if it be possible."

"Quite so."

"But," said Malicorne, "I shall leave the large room unoccupied for the present."

"Very good!" said the landlord, with an air of intelligence.

"Certain reasons, which you will understand by and by, oblige me to take, at my own cost, this small room only."

"Yes, yes," said the host.

"When my friend arrives, he will occupy the large apartment: and, as a matter of course, as this larger apartment will be his own affair, he will settle for it himself."

"Certainly," said the landlord, "certainly; let it be understood in that manner."

"It is agreed, then, that such shall be the terms?"

"Word for word."

"It is extraordinary," said Malicorne to himself. "You quite understand, then?"

"Yes."

"There is nothing more to be said. Since you understand, for you do clearly understand, do you not?"

"Perfectly."

"Very well; and now show me to my room."

The landlord, cap in hand, preceded Malicorne, who installed himself in his room, and became more and more surprised to observe that the landlord, at every ascent or descent, looked and winked at him in a manner which indicated the best possible intelligence between them. There is some mistake here," said Malicorne to himself; "but until it is cleared up, I shall take advantage of it, which is the best thing I can possibly do." And he darted out of his room, like a hunting-dog following a scent, in search of all the news and curiosities of the court, getting himself burnt in one place and drowned in another, as he had told Mademoiselle de Montalais. The day after he had been installed in his room, he had noticed the seven travelers arrive successively, who speedily filled the whole hotel. When he saw this perfect multitude of people, of carriages, and retinue, Malicorne rubbed his hands delightedly, thinking that, one day later, he should not have found a bed to lie upon after his return from his exploring expeditions. When all the travelers were lodged, the landlord entered Malicorne's room, and with his accustomed courteousness, said to him, "You are aware, my dear monsieur, that the large room in the third detached building is still reserved for you?"

"Of course I am aware of it."

"I am really making you a present of it."

"Thank you."

"So that when your friend comes——"

"Well!"

"He will be satisfied with me, I hope: or, if he be not, he will be very difficult to please."

"Excuse me, but will you allow me to say a few words about my friend?"

"Of course, for you have a perfect right to do so."

"He intended to come, as you know."

"And he does so still."

"He may possibly have changed his opinion."

"No."

"You are quite sure, then?"

"Quite sure."

"But in case you should have some doubt."

"Well!"

"I can only say that I do not positively assure you that he will come."

"Yet he told you——"

"He certainly did tell me; but you know that man proposes and God disposes,—*verba volant, scripta manent.*"

"Which is as much as to say——"

"That what is spoken flies away, and what is written remains; and, as he did not write to me, but contented himself by saying to me, 'I will authorize you, yet without specially instructing you,' you must feel that it places me in a very embarrassing position."

"What do you authorize me to do, then?"

"Why, to let your rooms if you find a good tenant for them."

"I?"

"Yes, you."

"Never will I do such a thing, monsieur. If he has not written to you, he has written to me."

"Ah! what does he say? Let us see if his letter agrees with his words."

"These are almost his very words. "To the landlord of the Beau Paon Hotel,—You will have been informed of the meeting arranged to take place in your inn between some people of importance; I shall be one of those who will meet the others at Fontainebleau. Keep for me, then, a small room for a friend who will arrive either before or after me——' and you are the friend I suppose," said the landlord, interrupting his reading of the letter. Malicorne bowed modestly. The landlord continued: "And a large apartment for myself. The large apartment is my own affair, but I wish the price of the smaller room to be moderate, as it is destined for a fellow who is deucedly poor." It is still you he is speaking of, is he not?" said the host.

" Oh, certainly," said Malicorne.

" Then we are agreed ; your friend will settle for his apartment, and you for your own."

"May I be broken alive on the wheel," said Malicorne to himself, "if I understand anything at all about it," and then he said aloud, " Well, then, are you satisfied with the name?"

" With what name?"

" With the name at the end of the letter. Does it give you the guarantee you require?"

" I was going to ask you the name."

" What! was not the letter signed?"

" No," said the landlord, opening his eyes very wide, full of mystery and curiosity.

" In that case," replied Malicorne, imitating his gesture and his mysterious look, "if he has not given you his name, you understand, he must have his reasons for it."

" Oh, of course."

" And, therefore, I, his friend, his confidant, must not betray him."

" You are perfectly right, monsieur," said the landlord, " and I do not insist upon it."

" I appreciate your delicacy. As for myself, as my friend told you, my room is a separate affair, so let us come to terms about it. Short accounts make long friends. How much is it?"

" There is no hurry."

" Never mind, let us reckon it up all the same. Room, my own board, a place in the stable for my horse, and his feed. How much per day?"

" Four livres, monsieur."

" Which will make twelve livres for the three days I have been here ?"

" Yes, monsieur."

" Here are your twelve livres, then."

"But why settle now?"

"Because," said Malicorne, lowering his voice, and resorting to his former air of mystery, because he saw that the mysterious had succeeded, "because if I had to set off suddenly, to decamp at any moment, my account would be settled."

"You are right, monsieur."

"I may consider myself at home, then?"

"Perfectly."

"So far so well. Adieu!" And the landlord withdrew. Malicorne, left alone, reasoned with himself in the following manner:—"No one but De Guiche or Manicamp could have written to this fellow; De Guiche, because he wishes to secure a lodging for himself beyond the precincts of the court, in the event of his success or failure, as the case might be; Manicamp, because De Guiche must have intrusted him with his commission. And De Guiche or Manicamp will have argued in this manner. The large apartment would serve for the reception, in a befitting manner, of a lady thickly veiled, reserving to the lady in question a double means of exit, either in a street somewhat deserted, or closely adjoining the forest. The smaller room, might either shelter Manicamp for a time, who is De Guiche's confidant, and would be the vigilant keeper of the door, or De Guiche himself, acting, for greater safety, the part of master and confidant at the same time. Yet," he continued, "how about this meeting which is to take place, and which indeed has actually taken place, in this hotel? No doubt they are persons who are going to be presented to the king. And the 'poor devil,' for whom the smaller room is destined, is a trick, in order to better conceal De Guiche or Manicamp. If this be the case, as very likely it is, there is only half the mischief done, for there is simply the length of a purse string beween Manicamp and Malicorne."

After he had thus reasoned the matter out, Malicorne slept soundly, leaving the seven travelers to occupy, and in every sense of the word to walk up and down, their several lodgings in the hotel. Whenever there was nothing at court to put him out, when he had wearied himself with his excursions and investigations, tired of writing letters which he could never find an opportunity of delivering to the people they were intended for, he returned home to his comfortable little room, and leaning upon the balcony, which was filled with nasturtiums and white pinks, began to think over these strange travelers, for whom Fontainebleau seemed to possess no attractions with all its illuminations, amusements, and *fêtes*. Things went on in this manner until the seventh day, a day of which we have given such full details, with its night also, in the preceding chapters. On that night Malicorne was enjoying the fresh air, seated at his window, towards one o'clock in the morning, when Manicamp appeared on horseback, with a thoughtful and listless air.

"Good!" said Malicorne to himself, recognizing him at the first glance; "there's my friend, who is come to take possession of his apartment, that is to say, of my room." And he called to Manicamp, who looked up and immediately recognized Malicorne.

"Ah! by Jove!" said the former, his countenance clearing up, "glad to see you, Malicorne. I have been wandering about Fontainebleau, looking for three things I cannot find: De Guiche, a room, and a stable."

"Of M. de Guiche I cannot give you either good or bad news, for I have not seen him; but as far as concerns your room and a stable, that's another matter, for they have been retained here for you."

"Retained—and by whom?"

"By yourself, I presume."

"By *me?*"

"Do you mean to say you did not take lodgings here?"

"By no means," said Manicamp.

At this moment the landlord appeared on the threshold of the door.

"I want a room," said Manicamp.

"Did you engage one, monsieur?"

"No."

"Then I have no rooms to let."

"In that case, I have engaged a room," said Manicamp.

"A room simply, or lodgings?"

"Anything you please."

"By letter?" inquired the landlord.

Malicorne nodded affirmatively to Manicamp.

"Of course by letter," said Manicamp. "Did you not receive a letter from me?"

"What was the date of the letter?" inquired the host, in whom Manicamp's hesitation had aroused suspicion. Manicamp rubbed his ear, and looked up at Malicorne's window; but Malicorne had left his window and was coming down the stairs to his friend's assistance. At the very same moment, a traveler, wrapped in a large Spanish cloak, appeared at the porch, near enough to hear the conversation.

"I ask you what was the date of the letter you wrote to me to retain apartments here?" repeated the landlord, pressing the question.

"Last Wednesday was the date," said the mysterious stranger, in a soft and polished tone of voice, touching the landlord on the shoulder.

Manicamp drew back, and it was now Malicorne's turn, who appeared on the threshold, to scratch his ear. The landlord saluted the new arrival as a man who recognizes his true guest.

"Monsieur," he said to him, with civility, "your apartment is ready for you, and the stables too, only—" He looked round him and inquired, "Your horses?"

"My horses may or may not arrive. That, however, matters but little to you, provided you are paid for what has been engaged." The landlord bowed still lower.

"You have," continued the unknown traveler, "kept for me, in addition, the small room I asked for."

"Oh!" said Malicorne, endeavoring to hide himself.

"Your friend has occupied it during the last week," said the landlord, pointing to Malicorne, who was trying to make himself as small as possible. The traveler, drawing his cloak round him so as to cover the lower part of his face, cast a rapid glance at Malicorne, and said, "This gentleman is no friend of mine."

The landlord started violently.

"I am not acquainted with this gentleman," continued the traveler.

"What!" exclaimed the host, turning to Malicorne, "are you not this gentleman's friend, then?"

"What does it matter whether I am or not, provided you are paid?" said Malicorne, parodying the stranger's remark in a very majestic manner.

"It matters so far as this," said the landlord, who began to perceive that one person had been taken for another, "that I beg you, monsieur, to leave the rooms, which had been engaged beforehand, and by some one else instead of you."

"Still," said Malicorne, "this gentleman cannot require at the same time a room on the first floor and an apartment on the second. If this gentleman will take the room, I will take the apartment: if he prefers the apartment, I will be satisfied with the room."

"I am exceedingly distressed, monsieur," said the

traveler, in his soft voice, " but I need both the room and the apartment."

" At least, tell me for whom?" inquired Malicorne.

" The apartment I require for myself."

" Very well; but the room?"

" Look," said the traveler pointing towards a sort of procession which was approaching.

Malicorne looked in the direction indicated, and observed borne upon a litter, the arrival of the Franciscan, whose installation in his apartment he had, with a few details of his own, related to Montalais, and whom he had so uselessly endeavored to convert to humbler views. The result of the arrival of the stranger, and of the sick Franciscan, was Malicorne's expulsion, without any consideration for his feelings, from the inn, by the landlord and the peasants who had carried the Franciscan. The details have already been given of what followed this expulsion; of Manicamp's conversation with Montalais; how Manicamp, with greater cleverness than Malicorne had shown, had succeeded in obtaining news of De Guiche, of the subsequent conversation of Montalais with Malicorne, and, finally, of the billets with which the Comte de Saint-Aignan had furnished Manicamp and Malicorne. It remains for us to inform our readers who was the traveler in the cloak—the principal tenant of the double apartment, of which Malicorne had only occupied a portion ;—and the Franciscan, quite as mysterious a personage, whose arrival, together with that of the stranger, unfortunately upset the two friends' plans.

CHAPTER XVII.

A JESUIT OF THE ELEVENTH YEAR.

IN the first place, in order not to weary the reader's patience, we will hasten to answer the first question. The traveler with the cloak held over his face was Aramis, who, after he had left Fouquet, and taken from a portmanteau, which his servant had opened, a cavalier's complete costume, quitted the château, and went to the hotel of the Beau Paon, where, by letters, seven or eight days previously, he had, as the landlord had stated, directed a room and an apartment to be retained for him. Immediately after Malicorne and Manicamp had been turned out, Aramis approached the Franciscan, and asked him whether he would prefer the apartment or the room. The Franciscan inquired where they were both situated. He was told that the room was on the first, and the apartment on the second floor.

"The room, then," he said.

Aramis did not contradict him, but, with great submissiveness, said to the landlord: "The room." And bowing with respect, he withdrew into the apartment, and the Franciscan was accordingly carried at once into the room. Now, is it not extraordinary that this respect should be shown by a prelate of the church for a simple monk, for one, too, belonging to a mendicant order; to whom was given up, without a request for it even, a room which so many travelers were desirous of obtaining? How, too, explain the unexpected arrival of Aramis at the hotel—he who had entered the château with M. Fouquet, and could have remained at the château with M. Fouquet if he had liked? The Franciscan supported his removal up the staircase without uttering a complaint, although it was evident he suffered very much, and that every time the litter knocked against the wall or the railing of the staircase, he experienced a terrible shock throughout his frame. And finally, when he had arrived in the room, he said to those who carried him : "Help me to place myself in that arm-chair." The bearers of the litter placed it on the ground, and lifting the sick man up as gently as possible, carried him to the chair he had indicated, which was situated at the head of the bed. "Now," he added, with a marked benignity of gesture and tone, "desire the landlord to come."

They obeyed, and five minutes afterwards the landlord appeared at the door.

"Be kind enough," said the Franciscan to him, "to send these excellent fellows away; they are vassals of the Comte de Melun. They found me when I had fainted on the road overcome by the heat, and without thinking whether they would be paid for their trouble, they wished to carry me to their own homes. But I know at what cost to themselves is the hospitality which the poor extend to a sick man, and I preferred this hotel, where, moreover, I was expected."

The landlord looked at the Franciscan in amazement, but the latter, with his thumb, made the sign of the cross in a peculiar manner upon his breast. The host replied by making a similar sign on his left shoulder. "Yes indeed," he said, "we did expect you, but we hoped that you would arrive in a better state of health." And as the peasants were looking at the innkeeper, usually so supercilious, and saw how respectful he had become in the presence of a poor monk, the Franciscan drew from a deep pocket three or four pieces of gold, which he held out.

"My friends," said he, "here is something to repay you for the care you have taken of me. So make yourselves perfectly easy, and do not be afraid of leaving me here. The order to which I belong, and for which I am traveling, does not require me to beg; only, as the attention you have shown me deserves to be rewarded, take these two louis and depart in peace."

The peasants did not dare to take them; the landlord took the two louis out of the monk's hand and placed them in that of one of the peasants, all four of whom withdrew, opening their eyes wider than ever. The door was then closed; and, while the innkeeper stood respectfully near it, the Franciscan collected himself for a moment. He then passed across his sallow face a hand which seemed dried up by fever, and rubbed his nervous and agitated fingers across his beard. His large eyes, hollowed by sickness and inquietude, seemed to pursue in the vague distance a mournful and fixed idea.

"What physicians have you at Fontainebleau?" he inquired, after a long pause.

"We have three, holy father."

"What are their names?"

"Luiniguet first."

"The next one?"

"A brother of the Carmelite order, named Brother Hubert."

"The next?"

"A secular member, named Grisart."

"Ah! Grisart?" murmured the monk, "send for M. Grisart immediately."

The landlord moved in prompt obedience to the direction.

"Tell me what priests are there here?"

"What priests?"

"Yes; belonging to what orders?"

"There are Jesuits, Augustines, and Cordeliers; but the Jesuits are the closest at hand. Shall I send for a confessor belonging to the order of Jesuits?"

"Yes, immediately."

It will be imagined that, at the sign of the cross which they had exchanged, the landlord and the invalid monk had recognized each other as two affiliated members of the well-known Society of Jesus. Left to himself, the Franciscan drew from his pocket a bundle of papers, some of which he read over with the most careful attention. The violence of his disorder, however, overcame his courage; his eyes rolled in their sockets, a cold sweat poured down his face, and he nearly fainted, and lay with his head thrown backwards and his arms hanging down on both sides of his chair. For more than five minutes he remained without any movement, when the landlord returned, bringing with him the physician, whom he hardly allowed time to dress himself. The noise they made in entering the room, the current of air, which the opening of the door occasioned, restored the Franciscan to his senses. He hurriedly seized hold of the papers which were lying about, and with his long and bony hand concealed them under the cushions of the chair. The landlord went out of the room, leaving patient and physician together.

"Come here, Monsieur Grisart," said the Franciscan to the doctor; "approach closer, for there is no time to lose. Try, by touch and sound, and consider, and pronounce your sentence."

"The landlord," replied the doctor, "told me that I had the honor of attending an affiliated brother."

"Yes," replied the Franciscan, "it is so. Tell me the truth, then; I feel very ill, and I think I am about to die."

The physician took the monk's hand and felt his pulse. "Oh, oh," he said, "a dangerous fever."

"What do you call a dangerous fever?" inquired the Franciscan, with an imperious look.

"To an affiliated member of the first or second year," replied the physician, looking inquiringly at the monk, "I should say—a fever that may be cured."

"But to me?" said the Franciscan. The physician hesitated.

"Look at my gray hair, and my forehead, full of anxious thought," he continued: "look at the lines in my face, by which I reckon up the trials I have undergone; I am a Jesuit of the eleventh year, Monsieur Grisart." The physician started, for, in fact, a Jesuit of the eleventh year was one of those men who had been initiated in all the secrets of the order, one of those for whom science has no more secrets, the society no further barriers to present—temporal obedience, no more trammels.

"In that case," said Grisart, saluting him with respect, "I am in the presence of a master?"

"Yes; act, therefore, accordingly."

"And you wish to know?"

"My real state."

"Well," said the physician, "it is a brain fever, which has reached its highest degree of intensity."

"There is no hope, then?" inquired the Franciscan, in a quick tone of voice.

"I do not say that," replied the doctor; "yet, considering the disordered state of the brain, the hurried respiration, the rapidity of the pulse, and the burning nature of the fever which is devouring you——"

"And which has thrice prostrated me since this morning," said the monk.

"All things considered, I shall call it a terrible attack. But why did you not stop on your road?"

"I was expected here, and I was obliged to come."

"Even at the risk of your life?"

" Yes, at the risk of dying on the way."

" Very well. Considering all the symptoms of your case, I must tell you that your condition is almost desperate."

The Franciscan smiled in a strange manner.

" What you have just told me is, perhaps, sufficient for what is due to an affiliated member, even of the eleventh year ; but for what is due to me, Monsieur Grisart, it is too little, and I have a right to demand more. Come, then, let us be more candid still, and as frank as if you were making your own confession to Heaven. Besides I have already sent for a confessor."

"Oh ! I have hopes, however," murmured the doctor.

"Answer me," said the sick man, displaying with a dignified gesture a golden ring, the stone of which had, until that moment, been turned inside, and which bore engraved thereon the distinguishing mark of the Society of Jesus.

Grisart uttered a loud exclamation.   " The general ! " he cried.

" Silence," said the Franciscan, " you now understand that the whole truth is all important."

" Monseigneur, monseigneur," murmured Grisart, " send for the confessor, for in two hours, at the next seizure, you will be attacked by delirium, and will pass away in its course."

" Very well," said the patient, for a moment contracting his eyebrows, "I have still two hours to live then ?"

" Yes; particularly if you take the potion I will send you presently."

" And that will give me two hours of life ?"

" Two hours."

" I would take it, were it poison, for those two hours are necessary not only for myself, but for the glory of the order."

"What a loss, what a catastrophe for us all!" murmured the physician.

"It is the loss of one man—nothing more," replied the Franciscan, "for Heaven will enable the poor monk, who is about to leave you, to find a worthy successor. Adieu, Monsieur Grisart; already even, through the goodness of Heaven, I have met with you. A physician who had not been one of our holy order, would have left me in ignorance of my condition; and, confident that existence would be prolonged a few days further, I should not have taken the necessary precautions. You are a learned man, Monsieur Grisart, and that confers an honor upon us all; it would have been repugnant to my feelings to have found one of our order of little standing in his profession. Adieu, Monsieur Grisart; send me the cordial immediately."

"Give me your blessing, at least, monseigneur."

"In my mind, I do; go, go; in my mind, I do so, I tell you—*animo*, Maître Grisart, *viribus impossibile*." And he again fell back on the arm-chair, in an almost senseless state. M. Grisart hesitated, whether he should give him immediate assistance, or should run to prepare the cordial he had promised. He decided in favor of the cordial, for he darted out of the room and disappeared down the staircase.

CHAPTER XVIII.

THE STATE SECRET.

A FEW moments after the doctor's departure, the confessor arrived. He had hardly crossed the threshold of the door when the Franciscan fixed a penetrating look upon him, and, shaking his head, murmured—" A weak mind I see; may Heaven forgive me if I die without the help of this living piece of human infirmity." The confessor, on his side, regarded the dying man with astonishment, almost with terror. He had never beheld eyes so burningly bright at the very moment they were about to close, nor looks so terrible at the moment they were about to be quenched in death. The Franciscan made a rapid and imperious movement of his hand. " Sit down, there, my father," he said, " and listen to me." The Jesuit confessor, a good priest, a recently initiated member of the order, who had merely seen the beginning of its mysteries, yielded to the superiority assumed by the penitent.

" There are several persons staying in this hotel," continued the Franciscan.

"But," inquired the Jesuit, " I thought I had been summoned to listen to a confession. Is your remark, then, a confession ? "

" Why do you ask ? "

" In order to know whether I am to keep your words secret."

" My remarks are part of my confession ; I confide them to you in your character of a confessor."

" Very well," said the priest, seating himself on the chair which the Franciscan had, with great difficulty, just left, to lie down on the bed.

The Franciscan continued,—" I repeat, there are several persons staying in this inn."

" So I have heard."

" They ought to be eight in number."

The Jesuit made a sign that he understood him. " The first to whom I wish to speak," said the dying man, " is a German from Vienna, whose name is the Baron de Wostpur. Be kind enough to go to him, and tell him the person he expected has arrived." The confessor, astounded, looked at his penitent; the confession seemed a singular one.

"Obey," said the Franciscan, in a tone of command impossible to resist. The good Jesuit, completely subdued, rose and left the room. As soon as he had gone, the Franciscan again took up the papers which a crisis of the fever had already, once before, obliged him to put aside.

"The Baron de Wostpur? Good!" he said; "ambitious, a fool and straitened in means."

He folded up the papers, which he thrust under his pillow. Rapid footsteps were heard at the end of the corridor. The confessor returned, followed by the Baron de Wostpur, who walked along with his head raised, as if he were discussing with himself the possibility of touching the ceiling with the feather in his hat. Therefore, at the appearance of the Franciscan, at his melancholy look, and seeing the plainness of the room, he stopped, and inquired—"Who summoned me?"

"I," said the Franciscan, who turned towards the confessor, saying, "My good father, leave us for a moment together; when this gentleman leaves, you will return here." The Jesuit left the room, and, doubtless, availed himself of this momentary exile from the presence of the dying man to ask the host for some explanation about this strange penitent, who treated his confessor no better than he would a man servant. The baron approached the bed, and wished to speak, but the hand of the Franciscan imposed silence upon him.

" Every moment is precious," said the latter, hurriedly. "You have come here for the competition, have you not?"

"Yes, my father."

" You hope to be elected general of the order?"

"I hope so."

" You know on what conditions only you can possibly

attain this high position, which makes one man the master of monarchs, the equal of Popes?"

"Who are you," inquired the baron, "to subject me to these interrogatories?"

"I am he whom you expected."

"The elector-general?"

"I am the elected."

"You are——"

The Franciscan did not give him time to reply; he extended his shrunken hand, on which glittered the ring of the general of the order. The baron drew back in surprise; and then, immediately afterwards, bowing with the profoundest respect, he exclaimed—"Is it possible that you are here, monseigneur; you, in this wretched room; you, upon this miserable bed; you, in search of and selecting the future general, that is, your own successor?"

"Do not distress yourself about that, monsieur, but fulfil immediately the principal condition, of furnishing the order with a secret of importance, of such importance that one of the greatest courts of Europe will, by your instrumentality, forever be subjected to the order. Well! do you possess the secret which you promised, in your request, addressed to the grand council?"

"Monseigneur——"

"Let us proceed, however, in due order," said the monk. "You are the Baron de Wostpur?"

"Yes, monseigneur."

"And this letter is from you?"

The general of the Jesuits drew a paper from his bundle, and presented it to the baron, who glanced at it, and made a sign in the affirmative, saying, "Yes, monseigneur, this letter is mine."

"Can you show me the reply which the secretary of the grand council returned to you?"

"Here it is," said the baron, holding towards the Franciscan a letter bearing simply the address, "To his excellency the Baron de Wostpur," and containing only this phrase, "From the 15th to the 22nd May, Fontainebleau, the hotel of the Beau-Paon.—A.M.D.G." *

"Right," said the Franciscan, "and now speak."

"I have a body of troops, composed of 50,000 men; all the officers are gained over. I am encamped on the Danube. In four days I can overthrow the emperor, who is, as you are aware, opposed to the progress of our order, and can replace him by whichever of the princes of his family the order may determine upon." The Franciscan listened, unmoved.

"Is that all?" he said.

"A revolution throughout Europe is included in my plan," said the baron.

"Very well, Monsieur de Wostpur, you will receive a reply; return to your room, and leave Fontainebleau within a quarter of an hour." The baron withdrew backwards, as obsequiously as if he were taking leave of the emperor he was ready to betray.

"There is no secret there," murmured the Franciscan, "it is a plot. Besides," he added, after a moment's reflection, "the future of Europe is no longer in the hands of the House of Austria."

And with a pencil he held in his hand, he struck the Baron de Wostpur's name from the list.

"Now for the cardinal," he said; "we ought to get something more serious from the side of Spain."

Raising his head, he perceived the confessor, who was awaiting his orders as respectfully as a school-boy.

"Ah, ah!" he said, noticing his submissive air, "you have been talking with the landlord."

---

* Ad majorem Dei gloriam.

"Yes, monseigneur; and to the physician."

"To Grisart?"

"Yes."

"He is here, then?"

"He is waiting with the potion he promised."

"Very well; if I require him, I will call; you now understand the great importance of my confession, do you not?"

"Yes, monseigneur."

"Then go and fetch me the Spanish Cardinal Herrebia. Make haste. Only, as you now understand the matter in hand, you will remain near me, for I begin to feel faint."

"Shall I summon the physician?"

"Not yet, not yet . . . the Spanish cardinal no one else. Fly."

Five minutes afterwards, the cardinal, pale and disturbed, entered the little room.

"I am informed, monseigneur——" stammered the cardinal.

"To the point," said the Franciscan, in a faint voice, showing the cardinal a letter which he had written to the Grand Council. "Is that your handwriting?"

"Yes, but——"

"And your summons?"

The cardinal hesitated to answer. His purple revolted against the mean garb of the poor Franciscan, who stretched out his hand and displayed the ring, which produced its effect, greater in proportion to the greatness of the person over whom the Franciscan exercised his influence.

"Quick, the secret, the secret!" said the dying man, leaning upon his confessor.

"*Coram isto?*" inquired the Spanish cardinal.

"Speak in Spanish," said the Franciscan, showing the liveliest attention.

"You are aware, monseigneur," said the cardinal, continuing the conversation in Castilian, "that the condition of the marriage of the Infanta with the king of France was the absolute renunciation of the rights of the said Infanta, as well as of King Louis XIV., to all claim to the crown of Spain." The Franciscan made a sign in the affirmative.

"The consequence is," continued the cardinal, "that the peace and alliance between the two kingdoms depend upon the observance of that clause of the contract." A similar sign from the Franciscan. "Not only France and Spain," continued the cardinal, "but the whole of Europe even, would be violently rent asunder by the faithlessness of either party." Another movement of the dying man's head.

"It further results," continued the speaker, "that the man who might be able to foresee events, and to render certain that which is no more than a vague idea floating in the mind of man; that is to say, the idea of future good or evil, would preserve the world from a great catastrophe; and the event, which has no fixed certainty even in the brain of him who originated it, could be turned to the advantage of our order."

"Closer!" murmured the Franciscan, in Spanish, who suddenly became paler, and leaned upon the priest. The cardinal approached the ear of the dying man, and said, "Well, monseigneur, I know that the king of France has determined that, at the very first pretext, a death for instance, either that of the King of Spain or that of a brother of the Infanta, France will, arms in hand, claim the inheritance, and I have in my possession already prepared the plan of policy agreed upon by Louis XIV. for this occasion."

"And this plan?" said the Franciscan.

"Here it is," returned the cardinal.

"In whose handwriting is it?"

"My own."

"Have you anything further to say to me?"

"I think I have said a good deal, my lord," replied the cardinal.

"Yes, you have rendered the order a great service. But how did you procure the details, by the aid of which you have constructed your plan?"

"I have the under-servants of the king of France in my pay, and I obtain from them all the waste papers, which have been saved from being burnt."

"Very ingenious," murmured the Franciscan, endeavoring to smile; "you will leave this hotel, cardinal, in a quarter of an hour, and a reply shall be sent you." The cardinal withdrew.

"Call Grisart, and desire the Venetian Marini to come," said the sick man.

While the confessor obeyed, the Franciscan, instead of striking out the cardinal's name, as he had done the baron's, made a cross at the side of it. Then, exhausted by the effort, he fell back on his bed, murmuring the name of Dr. Grisart. When he returned to his senses, he had drunk about half of the potion, of which the remainder was left in the glass, and he found himself supported by the physician, while the Venetian and the confessor were standing close to the door. The Venetian submitted to the same formalities as his two predecessors, hesitated as they had done at the sight of the two strangers, but his confidence restored by the order of the general, he revealed that the pope, terrified at the power of the order, was weaving a plot for the general expulsion of the Jesuits, and was tampering with the different courts of Europe, in order to obtain their assistance. He described the pontiff's auxiliaries, his means of action, and indicated the particular locality in the

Archipelago, where, by a sudden surprise, two cardinals, adepts of the eleventh year, and, consequently, high in authority, were to be transported, together with thirty-two of the principal affiliated members of Rome. The Franciscan thanked the Signor Marini. It was by no means a slight service he had rendered the society by denouncing this pontifical project. The Venetian thereupon received directions to set off in a quarter of an hour, and left as radiant as if he already possessed the ring, the sign of the supreme authority of the society. As, however, he was departing, the Franciscan murmured to himself:—"All these men are either spies, or a sort of police, not one of them a general; they have all discovered a plot, but not one of them a secret. It is not by means of ruin, or war, or force, that the Society of Jesus is to be governed, but by that mysterious influence moral superiority alone confers. No, the man is not yet found, and to complete the misfortune, Heaven strikes me down, and I am dying. Oh! must the society indeed fall with me for want of a column to support it? Must death, which is waiting for me, swallow up with me the future of the order; that future which ten years more of my own life would have rendered eternal? for that future, with the reign of the new king, is opening radiant and full of splendor." These words, which had been half-reflected, half-pronounced aloud, were listened to by the Jesuit confessor with a terror similar to that with which one listens to the wanderings of a person attacked by fever, whilst Grisart, with a mind of a higher order, devoured them as the revelations of an unknown world, in which his looks were plunged without ability to comprehend. Suddenly the Franciscan recovered himself.

"Let us finish this," he said; "death is approaching. Oh! just now I was dying resignedly, for I hoped . . . while now I sink in despair, unless those who remain . . .

Grisart, Grisart, give me to live a single hour longer."

Grisart approached the dying monk, and made him swallow a few drops, not of the potion which was still left in the glass, but of the contents of a small bottle he had upon his person.

" Call the Scotchman ! " exclaimed the Franciscan ; "call the Bremen merchant. Call, call, quickly. I am dying. I am suffocated."

The confessor darted forward to seek assistance, as if there had been any human strength which could hold back the hand of death, which was weighing down the sick man ; but, at the threshold of the door, he found Aramis, who, with his finger on his lips, like the statue of Harpocrates, the god of silence, by a look motioned him back to the end of the apartment. The physician and the confessor, after having consulted each other by looks, made a movement as if to push Aramis aside, who, however, with two signs of the cross, each made in a different manner, transfixed them both in their places.

" A chief ! " they both murmured.

Aramis slowly advanced into the room where the dying man was struggling against the first attack of the agony which had seized him. As for the Franciscan, whether owing to the effect of the elixir, or whether the appearance of Aramis had restored his strength, he made a movement, and his eyes glaring, his mouth half open, and his hair damp with sweat, sat up upon the bed. Aramis felt that the air of the room was stifling ; the windows were closed ; the fire was burning upon the hearth; a pair of candles of yellow wax were guttering down in the copper candlesticks, and still further increased, by their thick smoke, the temperature of the room. Aramis opened the window, and fixing upon the dying man a look full of intelligence and respect, said to him : " Monseigneur, pray forgive my coming in this manner, before you summoned me, but your state alarms me, and I thought you might possibly die before you had seen me, for I am but the sixth upon your list."

The dying man started and looked at the list.

" You are, therefore, he who was formerly called Aramis, and since, the Chevalier d'Herblay ?   You are the bishop of Vannes ? "

" Yes, my lord."

" I know you, I have seen you."

" At the last jubilee, we were with the Holy Father together."

" Yes, yes, I remember; and you place yourself on the list of candidates ? "

" Monseigneur, I have heard it said that the order required to become possessed of a great state secret, and knowing that from modesty you had in anticipation resigned your functions in favor of the person who should be the depositary of such a secret, I wrote to say that I was ready to compete, possessing alone a secret I believe to be important."

" Speak," said the Franciscan; " I am ready to listen to you, and to judge of the importance of the secret."

" A secret of the value of that which I have the honor to confide to you cannot be communicated by word of mouth. Any idea which, when once expressed, has thereby lost its safeguard, and has become vulgarized by any manifestation or communication of it whatever, no longer is the property of him who gave it birth. My words may be overheard by some listener, or perhaps by an enemy; one ought not, therefore, to speak at random, for, in such a case, the secret would cease to be one."

" How do you propose, then, to convey your secret ?" inquired the dying monk.

With one hand Aramis signed to the physician and the confessor to withdraw, and with the other he handed to the Franciscan a paper enclosed in a double envelope. "Is not writing more dangerous still than language?"

"No, my lord," said Aramis, "for you will find within this envelope characters which you and I alone can understand." The Franciscan looked at Aramis with an astonishment which momentarily increased.

"It is a cipher," continued the latter, "which you used in 1655, and which your secretary, Ivan Injan, who is dead, could alone decipher, if he were restored to life."

"You knew this cipher, then?"

"It was I who taught it him," said Aramis, bowing with a gracefulness full of respect, and advancing towards the door as if to leave the room: but a gesture of the Franciscan, accompanied by a cry for him to remain, restrained him.

"_Ecce homo!_" he exclaimed; then reading the paper a second time, he called out, "Approach, approach quickly!"

Aramis returned to the side of the Franciscan, with the same calm countenance and the same respectful manner, unchanged. The Franciscan, extending his arm, burnt by the flame of the candle the paper which Aramis had handed him. Then, taking hold of Aramis's hand, he drew him towards him, and inquired:—" In what manner and by whose means could you possibly become acquainted with such a secret?"

"Through Madame de Chevreuse, the intimate friend and _confidante_ of the queen."

"And Madame de Chevreuse——"

"Is dead."

"Did any others know it?"

"A man and a woman only, and they of the lower classes."

"Who are they?"

"Persons who had brought him up."

"What has become of them?"

" Dead also.   This secret burns like vitriol."

" But you survive ? "

" No one is aware that I know it."

" And for what length of time have you possessed this secret ? "

" For the last fifteen years."

" And you have kept it ? "

" I wished to live."

" And you give it to the order without ambition, without acknowledgment ? "

" I give it to the order with ambition and with a hope of return," said Aramis ; " for if you live, my lord, you will make of me, now you know me, what I can and ought to be."

" And as I am dying," exclaimed the Franciscan, " I constitute you my successor . . . . Thus." And drawing off the ring, he passed it on Aramis's finger. Then, turning towards the two spectators of this scene, he said ; " Be ye witnesses of this, and testify, if need be, that, sick in body, but sound in mind, I have freely and voluntarily bestowed this ring, the token of supreme authority, upon Monseigneur d'Herblay, bishop of Vannes, whom I nominate my successor, and before whom I, an humble sinner, about to appear before Heaven, prostrate myself, as an example for all to follow." And the Franciscan bowed lowly and submissively, whilst the physician and the Jesuit fell on their knees. Aramis, even while he became paler than the dying man himself, bent his looks successively upon all the actors of this scene. Profoundly gratified ambition flowed with life-blood toward his heart.

" We must lose no time," said the Franciscan ; " what I had still to do on earth was urgent. I shall never succeed in carrying it out."

" I will do it," said Aramis.

" It is well," said the Franciscan, and then turning towards the Jesuit and the doctor, he added, " Leave us
alone," a direction they instantly obeyed.

" With this sign," he said, " you are the man needed to
shake the world from one end to the other ; with this sign
you will overthrow ; with this sign you will edify ; *in hoc
signo vinces !* "

" Close the door," continued the Franciscan after a
pause. Aramis shut and bolted the door, and returned
to the side of the Franciscan.

" The pope is conspiring against the order," said the
monk, " the pope must die."

" He shall die," said Aramis, quietly.

" Seven hundred thousand livres are owing to a Bremen merchant of the name of Bonstett, who came here to
get the guarantee of my signature."

" He shall be paid," said Aramis.

" Six knights of Malta, whose names are written here,
have discovered by the indiscretion of one of the affiliated
of the eleventh year, the three mysteries ; it must be ascertained what these men have done with the secret, to
get it back again and bury it."

" It shall be done."

" Three dangerous affiliated members must be sent
away into Thibet, there to perish ; they stand condemned.
Here are their names."

" I will see that the sentence be carried out."

" Lastly, there is a lady at Anvers, grand-niece of Ra-
vaillac ; she holds certain papers in her hands that compromise the order. There has been payable to the family
during the last fifty-one years a pension of fifty thousand
livres. The pension is a heavy one, and the order is not
wealthy. Redeem the papers for a sum of money paid
down, or in case of refusal, stop the pension—but run no
risk."

"I will quickly decide what is best to be done," said Aramis.

" A vessel chartered from Lima entered the port of Lisbon last week; ostensibly it is laden with chocolate, in reality with gold. Every ingot is concealed by a coating of chocolate. The vessel belongs to the order; it is worth seventeen millions of livres; you will see that it is claimed; here are the bills of lading."

" To what port shall I direct it to be taken?"·

" To Bayonne."

" Before three weeks are over it shall be there, wind and weather permitting. Is that all?" The Franciscan made a sign in the affirmative, for he could no longer speak; the blood rushed to his throat and his head, and gushed from his mouth, his nostrils, and his eyes. The dying man had barely time to press Aramis's hand, when he fell in convulsions from his bed upon the floor. Aramis placed his hand upon the Franciscan's heart, but it had ceased to beat. As he stooped down, Aramis observed that a fragment of the paper he had given the Franciscan had escaped being burnt. He picked it up, and burnt it to the last atom. Then, summoning the confessor and the physician, he said to the former :—" Your penitent is in heaven; he needs nothing more than prayers and the burials bestowed upon the pious dead. Go and prepare what is necessary for a simple interment, such as a poor monk only would require. Go."

The Jesuit left the room. Then, turning towards the physician, and observing his pale and anxious face, he said, in a low tone of voice :—" Monsieur Grisart, empty and clean this glass; *there is too much left in it of what the grand council desired you to put in.*"

Grizart amazed, overcome, completely astounded, almost fell backwards in his extreme terror. Aramis shrugged his shoulders in sign of pity, took the glass and poured out the contents among the ashes of the hearth. He then left the room, carrying the papers of the dead man with him.

CHAPTER XIX.

A MISSION.

THE next day, or rather the same day (for the events we have just described were concluded only at three o'clock in the morning), before breakfast was served, and as the king was preparing to go to mass with the two queens ; as Monsieur, with the Chevalier de Lorraine, and a few other intimate companions, was mounting his horse to set off for the river, to take one of those celebrated baths with which the ladies of the court were so infatuated, as, in fact, no one remained in the château, with the exception of Madame, who, under the pretext of indisposition, would not leave her room; Montalais was seen, or rather was not seen, to glide stealthily out of the room appropriated to the maids of honor, leading La Vallière after her, who tried to conceal herself as much as possible, and both of them, hurrying secretly through the gardens, succeeded, looking round them at every step they took, in reaching the thicket. The weather was cloudy, a warm breeze bowed the flowers and the shrubs, the burning dust, swept along in clouds by the wind, was whirled in eddies towards the trees. Montalais, who, during their progress, had discharged the functions of a clever scout, advanced a few steps further, and turning round again, to be quite sure that no one was either listening or approaching, said to her companion, " Thank goodness, we are quite alone! Since yesterday every one spies us here, and a circle seems to be drawn round us, as if

we were plague-stricken." La Vallière bent down her
head and sighed. " It is positively unheard of," continued
Montalais; " from M. Malicorne to M. de Saint-Aignan,
every one wishes to get hold of our secret. Come, Louise,
let us take counsel, you and I, together, in order that I
may know what to do."

La Vallière lifted towards her companion her beautiful
eyes, pure and deep as the azure of a spring sky, " And
I," she said, " will ask you why have we been summoned
to Madame's own room ? Why have we slept close to her
apartment, instead of sleeping as usual in our own?
Why did you return so late, and whence are these measures of strict supervision which have been adopted since
this morning, with respect to us both ?"

" My dear Louise, you answer my question by another,
or rather, by ten others, which is not answering me at all.
I will tell you all you want to know later, and as it is of
secondary importance, you can wait. What I ask you—
for everything will depend upon that—is, whether there
is or is not any secret ? "

" I do not know if there is any secret," said La Vallière ;
" but I do know, for my own part at least, that there
has been great imprudence committed. Since the foolish
remark I made, and my still more silly fainting yesterday, every one here is making remarks about us."

" Speak for yourself," said Montalais, laughing, " speak
for yourself and for Tonnay-Charente ; for both of you
made your declarations of love to the skies, which unfortunately were intercepted."

La Vallière hung down her head. " Really you over-
· whelm me," she said.

" I ? "

" Yes, you torture me with your jests."

" Listen to me, Louise. These are no jests, for nothing
is more serious ; on the contrary, I did not drag you out

of the château ; I did not miss attending mass ; I did not
pretend to have a cold, as Madame did, which she has no
more than I have ; and, lastly, I did not display ten times
more diplomacy than M. Colbert inherited from M. de
Mazarin, and makes use of with respect to M. Fouquet, in
order to find means of confiding my perplexities to you,
for the sole end and purpose that when, at last, we were
alone, with no one to listen to us, you should deal hypo-
critically with me. No, no; believe me, that when I ask you
a question, it is not from curiosity alone, but really because the position is a critical one. What you said yesterday is now known,—it is a text on which every one is
discoursing. Every one embellishes it to the utmost, and
according to his own fancy ; you had the honor last night,
and you have it still to-day, of occupying the whole court,
my dear Louise ; and the number of tender and witty remarks which have been ascribed to you, would make Mademoiselle de Scudery and her brother burst from very spite,
if they were faithfully reported."

"But, dearest Montalais," said the poor girl, "you know
better than any one exactly what I said, since you were
present when I said it."

"Yes, I know. But that is not the question. I have
not forgotten a single syllable you uttered, but did you
think what you were saying ? "

Louise became confused. "What," she exclaimed,
"more questions still ! Oh, heavens ! when I would give
the world to forget what I did say, how does it happen
that every one does all he possibly can to remind me of
it ? Oh, this is indeed terrible ! "

"What is ? "

"To have a friend who ought to spare me, who might
advise me and help me to save myself, and yet who is un-
doing me—is killing me."

"There, there, that will do," said Montalais ; "after

having said too little, you now say too much. No one thinks of killing you, nor even of robbing you, even of your secret ; I wish to have it voluntarily, and in no other way ; for the question does not concern your own affairs only, but ours also ; and Tonnay-Charente would tell you as I do, if she were here. For, the fact is, that last evening she wished to have some private conversation in our room, and I was going there after the Manicamp and Malicorne colloquies terminated, when I learned, on my return, rather late, it is true, that Madame had sequestered her maids of honor, and that we were to sleep in her apartments, instead of our own. Moreover, Madame has shut up her maids of honor in order that they should not have the time to concert any measures together, and this morning she was closeted with Tonnay-Charente with the same object. Tell me, then, to what extent Athenaïs and I can rely upon you, as we will tell you in what way you can rely upon us ? "

" I do not clearly understand the question you have put," said Louise, much agitated.

" Hum ! and yet, on the contrary, you seem to understand me very well. However, I will put my questions in a more precise manner, in order that you may not be able, in the slightest degree, to evade them. Listen to me : *Do you love M. de Bragelonne ?* That is plain enough, is it not ? "

At this question, which fell like the first bombshell of a besieging army into a doomed town, Louise started. " You ask me," she exclaimed, " if I love Raoul, the friend of my childhood,—my brother almost ? "

" No, no, no ! Again you evade me, or rather, you wish to escape me. I do not ask you if you love Raoul, your childhood's friend,—your brother; but I ask if you love the Vicomte de Bragelonne, your affianced husband ? "

"Good heavens! dear Montalais," said Louise, "how severe your tone is!"

" You deserve no indulgence,—I am neither more nor less severe than usual. I put a question to you, so answer it."

" You certainly do not," said Louise, in a choking voice, " speak to me like a friend; but I will answer you as a true friend."

" Well, do so."

" Very well; my heart is full of scruples and silly feelings of pride, with respect to everything that a woman ought to keep secret, and in this respect no one has ever read into the bottom of my soul."

"That I know very well. If I had read it, I should not interrogate you as I have done; I should simply say,—' My good Louise, you have the happiness of an acquaintance with M. de Bragelonne, who is an excellent young man, and an advantageous match for a girl without fortune. M. de la Fère will leave something like fifteen thousand livres a year to his son. At a future day, then, you, as this son's wife, will have fifteen thousand livres a year; which is not bad. Turn, then, neither to the right hand nor to the left, but go frankly to M. de Bragelonne; that is to say, to the altar to which he will lead you. Afterwards, why—afterwards, according to his disposition, you will be emancipated or enslaved; in other words, you will have a right to commit any piece of folly people commit who have either too much liberty or too little.' That is, my dear Louise, what I should have told you at first, if I had been able to read your heart."

"And I should have thanked you," stammered out Louise, " although the advice does not appear to me to be altogether sound."

" Wait, wait. But immediately after having given you that advice, I should have added :—' Louise, it is very dangerous to pass whole days with your head drooping, your hands unoccupied, your eyes restless and full of thought; it is dangerous to prefer the least frequented paths, and no longer to be amused with such diversions as gladden young girl's hearts ; it is dangerous, Louise, to scrawl with the point of your foot, as you do, upon the gravel, certain letters it is useless for you to efface, but which appear again under your heel, particularly when those letters rather resemble the letter L. than the letter B ; and, lastly, it is dangerous to allow the mind to dwell on a thousand wild fancies, the fruits of solitude and heart-ache; these fancies, while they sink into a young girl's mind, make her cheeks sink in also, so that it is not un-usual, on such occasions, to find the most delightful per-sons in the world become the most disagreeable, and the wittiest to become the dullest.' "

"I thank you, dearest Aure," replied La Vallière, gently; "it is like you to speak to me in this manner, and I thank you for it."

"It was only for the benefit of wild dreamers, such as I have just described, that I spoke; do not take any of my words, then, to yourself except such as you think you de-serve. Stay, I hardly know what story recurs to my memory of some silly or melancholy girl, who was grad-ually pining away because she fancied that the prince, or the king, or the emperor, whoever it was—and it does not much matter which—had fallen in love with her ; while on the contrary, the prince, or the king, or the emperor, whichever you please, was plainly in love with some one else, and—a singular circumstance, one, indeed, which she could not perceive, although every one around and about her perceived it clearly enough—made use of her as a screen for his own love affair. You laugh as I do, at this poor silly girl, do you not, Louise?"

"I?—oh! of course," stammered Louise, pale as death.

"And you are right, too, for the thing is amusing enough. The story, whether true or false, amused me, and so I remembered it and told it to you. Just imagine, then, my good Louise, the mischief that such a melancholy would create in anybody's brain,—a melancholy, I mean, of that kind. For my own part, I resolved to tell you the story; for if such a thing were to happen to either of *us*, it would be most essential to be assured of its truth; to-day it is a snare, to-morrow it would become a jest and mockery, the next day it would mean death itself." La Vallière started again, and became, if possible, still paler.

"Whenever a king takes notice of us," continued Montalais, "he lets us see it easily enough, and, if we happen to be the object he covets, he knows very well how to gain his object. You see, then, Louise, that, in such circumstances, between young girls exposed to such a danger as the one in question, the most perfect confidence should exist, in order that those hearts which are not disposed towards melancholy may watch over those likely to become so."

"Silence, silence!" said La Vallière; "some one approaches."

"Some one is approaching, in fact," said Montalais; "but who can it possibly be? Everybody is away, either at mass with the king, or bathing with Monsieur."

At the end of the walk the young girls perceived almost immediately, beneath the arching trees, the graceful carriage and noble stature of a young man, who, with his sword under his arm and a cloak thrown across his shoulders, booted and spurred besides, saluted them from the distance with a gentle smile. "Raoul!" exclaimed Montalais.

"M. de Bragelonne!" murmured Louise.

"A very proper judge to decide upon our difference of opinion," said Montalais.

" Oh! Montalais, Montalais, for pity's sake," exclaimed
La Vallière, "after having been so cruel, show me a little
mercy." These words, uttered with all the fervor of a
prayer, effaced all trace of irony, if not from Montalais's
heart, at least from her face.

" Why, you are as handsome as Amadis, Monsieur de
Bragelonne," she cried to Raoul, " and armed and booted
like him."

" A thousand compliments, young ladies," replied Raoul,
bowing.

" But why, I ask, are you booted in this manner ? " repeated Montalais, whilst La Vallière, although she looked
at Raoul with a surprise equal to that of her companion,
nevertheless uttered not a word.

" Why ? " inquired Raoul.

" Yes! " ventured Louise.

" Because I am about to set off," said Bragelonne, looking at Louise.

" The young girl seemed as though smitten by some superstitious feeling of terror, and tottered. " You are going
away, Raoul! " she cried ; " and where are you going ? "

" Dearest Louise," he replied, with that quiet, composed
manner which was natural to him, " I am going to England."

" What are you going to do in England ? "

" The king has sent me there."

" The king ! " exclaimed Louise and Aure together, involuntarily exchanging glances, the conversation which
had just been interrupted recurring to them both. Raoul
intercepted the glance, but could not understand its meaning, and, naturally enough, attributed it to the interest
both the young girls took in him.

" His Majesty," he said, " has been good enough to remember that the Comte de la Fère is high in favor with
King Charles II. This morning, as he was on his way to

attend mass, the king, seeing me as he passed, signed to me to approach, which I accordingly did. 'Monsieur de Bragelonne,' he said to me, 'you will call upon M. Fouquet, who has received from me letters for the king of Great Britain ; you will be the bearer of them.' I bowed. 'Ah!' His Majesty added, 'before you leave, you will be good enough to take any commissions which Madame may have for the king her brother."

"Gracious Heaven!" murmured Louise, much agitated, and yet full of thought at the same time.

"So quickly! You are desired to set off in such haste!" said Montalais, almost paralyzed by this unforeseen event.

"Properly to obey those whom we respect," said Raoul, "it is necessary to obey quickly. Within ten minutes after I had received the order, I was ready. Madame, already informed, is writing the letter which she is good enough to do me the honor of intrusting to me. In the meantime, learning from Mademoiselle de Tonnay-Charente that it was likely you would be in this direction, I came here, and am happy to find you both."

"And both of us very sad, as you see," said Montalais, going to Louise's assistance, whose countenance was visibly altered.

"Suffering?" responded Raoul, pressing Louise's hand with a tender curiosity. "Your hand is like ice."

"It is nothing."

"This coldness does not reach your heart, Louise, does it?" inquired the young man, with a tender smile. Louise raised her head hastily, as if this question had been inspired by some suspicion, and had aroused a feeling of remorse.

"Oh! you know," she said, with an effort, "that my heart will never be cold towards a friend like yourself, Monsieur de Bragelonne."

"Thank you, Louise. I know both your heart and your

mind; it is not by the touch of the hand that one can judge of an affection like yours. You know, Louise, how devotedly I love you, with what perfect and unreserved confidence I reserve my life for you; will you not forgive me, then, for speaking to you with something like the frankness of a child?"

"Speak, Monsieur Raoul," said Louise, trembling painfully, "I am listening."

"I cannot part from you, carrying away with me a thought that tortures me; absurd I know it to be, and yet one which rends my very heart."

"Are you going away, then, for any length of time?" inquired La Vallière, with faltering utterance, while Montalais turned her head aside.

"No; probably I shall not be absent more than a fortnight." La Vallière pressed her hand upon her heart, which felt as though it was breaking.

"It is strange," pursued Raoul, looking at the young girl with a melancholy expression; "I have often left you when setting off on adventures fraught with danger. Then I started joyously enough—my heart free, my mind intoxicated by thoughts of happiness in store for me, hopes of which the future was full; and yet I was about to face the Spanish cannon, or the halberds of the Walloons. To-day, without the existence of any danger or uneasiness, and by the sunniest path in the world, I am going in search of a glorious recompense, which this mark of the king's favor seems to indicate, for I am, perhaps, going to win *you*, Louise. What other favor, more precious than yourself, could the king confer upon me? Yet, Louise, in very truth I know not how or why, but this happiness and this future seem to vanish before my very eyes like mist—like an idle dream; and I feel here, here at the very bottom of my heart, a deep-seated grief, a dejection I cannot overcome—something heavy, passionless, death-like,—resem-

bling a corpse. Oh! Louise, too well do I know why; it is because I have never loved you so truly as now. God help me! "

At this last exclamation, which issued as it were from a broken heart, Louise burst into tears, and threw herself into Montalais's arms. The latter, although she was not easily moved, felt the tears rush to her eyes. Raoul noted only the tears Louise shed; his look, however, did not penetrate—nay, sought not to penetrate—beyond those tears. He bent his knee before her, and tenderly kissed her hand; and it was evident that in that kiss he poured out his whole heart.

"Rise, rise," said Montalais to him, ready to cry, "for Athenaïs is coming."

Raoul rose, brushed his knee with the back of his hand, smiled again upon Louise, whose eyes were fixed on the ground, and, having pressed Montalais's hand gratefully, he turned round to salute Mademoiselle de Tonnay-Char-ente, the sound of whose silken robe was already heard upon the gravel walk. "Has Madame finished her letter?" he inquired, when the young girl came within reach of his voice.

"Yes, the letter is finished, sealed, and her royal high-ness is ready to receive you."

Raoul, at this remark, hardly gave himself time to sa-lute Athenaïs, cast one last look at Louise, bowed to Mon-talais, and withdrew in the direction of the château. As he withdrew he again turned round, but at last, at the end of the grand walk, it was useless to do so again, as he could no longer see them. The three young girls, on their side, had, with widely different feelings, watched him dis-appear.

"At last," said Athenaïs, the first to interrupt the silence, "at last we are alone, free to talk of yesterday's great af-fair, and to come to an understanding upon the conduct it

is advisable for us to pursue. Besides, if you will listen
to me," she continued, looking round on all sides, " I will
explain to you, as briefly as possible, in the first place, our
own duty, such as I imagine it to be, and, if you do ·not
understand a hint, what is Madame's desire on the subject.
And Mademoiselle de Tonnay-Charente pronounced these
words in such a tone, as to leave no doubt, in her companion's minds, upon the official character with which she
was invested.

"Madame's desire!" exclaimed Montalais and La Vallière
together.

"Her *ultimatum*," replied Mademoiselle de Tonnay-
Charente, diplomatically.

"But," murmured La Vallière, "does Madame know,
then——"

"Madame knows more about the matter than we said,
even," said Athenaïs, in a formal, precise manner. "Therefore, let us come to a proper understanding."

"Yes, indeed," said Montalais, "and I am listening in
breathless attention."

"Gracious Heavens!" murmured Louise, trembling,
"shall I ever survive this cruel evening?"

"Oh! do not frighten yourself in that manner," said
Athenaïs; "we have found a remedy. So, seating herself between her two companions, and taking each of them
by the hand, which she held in her own, she began. The
first words were hardly spoken, when they heard a horse
galloping away over the stones of the public high-road,
outside the gates of the château.

CHAPTER XX.

HAPPY AS A PRINCE.

At the very moment he was about entering the château, Bragelonne met De Guiche. But before having been met by Raoul, De Guiche had met Manicamp, who had met Malicorne. How was it that Malicorne had met Manicamp? Nothing more simple, for he had awaited his return from mass, where he had accompanied M. de Saint-Aignan. When they met, they congratulated each other upon their good fortune, and Manicamp availed himself of the circumstance to ask his friend if he had not a few crowns still remaining at the bottom of his pocket. The latter, without expressing any surprise at the question, which he perhaps expected, answered that every pocket, which is always being drawn upon without anything ever being put in it, resembles those wells which supply water during the winter, but which gardeners render useless by exhausting during the summer; that his, Malicorne's, pocket certainly was deep, and that there would be a pleasure in drawing on it in times of plenty, but that, unhappily, abuse had produced barrenness. To this remark, Manicamp, deep in thought, had replied, " Quite true ! "

"The question, then, is how to fill it?" Malicorne added.

"Of course; but in what way?"

" Nothing easier, my dear Monsieur Manicamp."

" So much the better. How?"

" A post in Monsieur's household, and the pocket is full again."

"You have the post?"

"That is, I have the promise of being nominated."

"Well!"

"Yes; but the promise of nomination, without the post itself, is like a purse with no money in it."

"Quite true," Manicamp replied a second time.

"Let us try for the post, then," the candidate had persisted.

"My dear fellow," sighed Manicamp, "an appointment in his royal highness's household is one of the gravest difficulties of our position."

"Oh! oh!"

"There is no question that, at the present moment, we cannot ask Monsieur for anything."

"Why so?"

"Because we are not on good terms with him."

"A great absurdity, too," said Malicorne, promptly.

"Bah! and if we were to show Madame any attention," said Manicamp, "frankly speaking, do you think we should please Monsieur?"

"Precisely; if we show Madame any attention, and do it adroitly, Monsieur ought to adore us."

"Hum!"

"Either that or we are great fools. Make haste, therefore, M. Manicamp, you who are so able a politician, and make M. de Guiche and his royal highness friendly again."

"Tell me, what did M. de Saint-Aignan tell you, Malicorne?"

"Tell me? nothing; he asked me several questions, and that was all."

"Well, he was less discreet, then, with me."

"What did he tell you?"

"That the king is passionately in love with Mademoiselle de la Vallière."

"We knew that already," replied Malicorne, ironically;

and everybody talks about it loud enough for all to know it; but in the meantime, do what I advise you; speak to M. de Guiche, and endeavor to get him to make advances to Monsieur. Deuce take it! he owes his royal highness that, at least."

" But we must see De Guiche, then ? "

" There does not seem to be any great difficulty in that; try to see him in the same way I tried to see you; wait for him; you know that he is naturally very fond of walking."

" Yes; but whereabouts does he walk ? "

" What a question to ask! Do you not know that he is in love with Madame ? "

" So it is said."

" Very well; you will find him walking about on the side of the château where her apartments are."

" Stay, my dear Malicorne, you were not mistaken, for here he is coming."

" Why should I be mistaken? Have you ever noticed that I am in the habit of making a mistake? Come, we only need to understand each other. Are you in want of money ? "

" Ah! " exclaimed Manicamp, mournfully.

" Well, I want my appointment. Let Malicorne have the appointment, and Manicamp, shall have the money. There is no greater difficulty in the way than that."

" Very well; in that case make yourself easy. I will do my best."

" Do."

De Guiche approached, Malicorne stepped aside, and Manicamp caught hold of De Guiche, who was thoughtful and melancholy. " Tell me, my dear comte, what rhyme you were trying to find," said Manicamp. " I have an excellent one to match yours, particularly if yours ends in âme."

De Guiche shook his head, and recognizing a friend, he took him by the arm. "My dear Manicamp," he said, "I am in search of something very different from a rhyme."

"What is it you are looking for."

"You will help me to find what I am in search of," continued the comte: "you who are such an idle fellow, in other words, a man with a mind full of ingenious devices?"

"I am getting my ingenuity ready, then, my dear comte."

"This is the state of the case, then: I wish to approach a particular house, where I have some business."

"You must get near the house, then," said Manicamp.

"Very good; but in this house dwells a husband who happens to be jealous."

"Is he more jealous than the dog Cerberus?"

"Not more, but quite as much so."

"Has he three mouths, as that obdurate guardian of the infernal regions had? Do not shrug your shoulders, my dear comte: I put the question to you with an excellent reason, since poets pretend that, in order to soften Monsieur Cerberus, the visitor must take something enticing with him—a cake, for instance. Therefore, I, who view the matter in a prosaic light, that is to say, in the light of reality, I say: one cake is very little for three mouths. If your jealous husband has three mouths, comte, get three cakes."

"Manicamp, I can get such advice as that from M. de Beautru."

"In order to get better advice," said Manicamp, with a comical seriousness of expression, "you will be obliged to adopt a more precise formula than you have used towards me."

"If Raoul were here," said De Guiche, "he would be sure to understand me."

"So I think, particularly if you said to him: 'I should very much like to see Madame, a little nearer, but I fear Monsieur, because he is jealous.'"

"Manicamp!" cried the comte, angrily, and endeavoring to overwhelm his tormentor by a look, who did not, however, appear to be in the slightest degree disturbed by it.

"What is the matter now, my dear comte?" inquired Manicamp.

"What! is it thus that you blaspheme the most sacred of names?"

"What names?"

"Monsieur! Madame! the highest names in the kingdom."

"You are very strangely mistaken, my dear comte. I never mentioned the highest names in the kingdom. I merely answered you in reference to the subject of a jealous husband, whose name you did not tell me, and who as a matter of course, has a wife. I therefore replied to you, in order to see Madame, you must get a little more intimate with Monsieur."

"Double-dealer, that you are," said the comte, smiling; "was that what you said?"

"Nothing else."

"Very good; what then?"

"Now," added Manicamp, "let the question be regarding the Duchess —— or the Duke ——; very well, I shall say: Let us get into the house in some way or other, for that is a tactic which cannot in any case be unfavorable to your love-affair."

"Ah! Manicamp, if you could but find me a pretext, a good pretext."

"A pretext; I can find you a hundred, nay, a thousand. If Malicorne were here, he would have already hit upon a thousand excellent pretexts."

" Who is Malicorne ? " replied De Guiche, half-shutting his eyes like a person reflecting, " I seem to know the name."

" Know him! I should think so: you owe his father thirty thousand crowns."

" Ah, indeed! so it's that worthy fellow from Orleans."

" Whom you promised an appointment in Monsieur's household; not the jealous husband, but the other."

" Well, then, since your friend Malicorne is such an inventive genius, let him find me a means of being adored by Monsieur, and a pretext to make my peace with him."

" Very good: I'll talk to him about it."

" But who is that coming?"

"The Vicomte de Bragelonne."

" Raoul! yes, it is he," said De Guiche, as he hastened forward to meet him. " You here, Raoul?" said De Guiche.

" Yes: I was looking for you, to say farewell," replied Raoul, warmly, pressing the comte's hand. " How do you do, Monsieur Manicamp?"

" How is this, vicomte, you are leaving us?"

" Yes, a mission from the king."

" Where are you going?"

" To London. On leaving you, I am going to Madame; she has a letter to give me for his majesty Charles II."

" You will find her alone, for Monsieur has gone out; gone to bathe, in fact."

" In that case, you, who are one of Monsieur's gentlemen in waiting, will undertake to make my excuses to him. I would have waited in order to receive any directions he might have to give me, if the desire for my immediate departure had not been intimated to me by M. Fouquet on behalf of his majesty."

Manicamp touched De Guiche's elbow, saying, " There's a pretext for you."

" What ? "

" M. de Bragelonne's excuses."

" A weak pretext," said De Guiche.

" An excellent one, if Monsieur is not angry with you ; but a paltry one if he bears you ill-will."

"You are right, Manicamp; a pretext, however poor it may be, is all I require. And so, a pleasant journey to you, Raoul!" And the two friends took a warm leave of each other.

Five minutes afterwards Raoul entered Madame's apartments, as Mademoiselle de Montalais had begged him to do. Madame was still seated at the table where she had written her letter. Before her was still burning the rose-colored taper she had used to seal it. Only in her deep reflection, for Madame seemed to be buried in thought, she had forgotten to extinguish the light. Bragelonne was a very model of elegance in every way; it was impossible to see him once without always remembering him; and, not only had Madame seen him once, but it will not be forgotten he was one of the very first who had gone to meet her, and had accompanied her from Havre to Paris. Madame preserved therefore an excellent recollection of him.

" Ah! M. 'de Bragelonne," she said to him, "you are going to see my brother, who will be delighted to pay to the son a portion of the debt of gratitude he contracted with the father."

"The Comte de la Fère, Madame, has been abundantly recompensed for the little service he had the happiness to render the king, by the kindness manifested towards him, and it is I who will have to convey to his majesty the assurance of the respect, devotion, and gratitude of both father and son."

"Do you know my brother?"

" No, your highness ; I shall have the honor of seeing his majesty for the first time."

" You require no recommendation to him. At all events, however, if you have any doubt about your personal merit, take me unhesitatingly for your surety."

Your royal highness overwhelms me with kindness."

" No ! M. de Bragelonne, I well remember that we were fellow-travelers once, and that I remarked your extreme prudence in the midst of the extravagant absurdities committed, on both sides, by two of the greatest simpletons in the world, — M de Guiche and the Duke of Buckingham. Let us not speak of them, however ; but of yourself. Are you going to England to remain there permanently ? Forgive my inquiry : it is not curiosity, but a desire to be of service to you in anything I can."

" No, madame ; I am going to England to fulfil a mission which his majesty has been kind enough to confide to me —nothing more."

" And you propose to return to France ? "

" As soon as I have accomplished my mission ; unless, indeed, his majesty King Charles II. should have other orders for me."

" He will beg you, at the very least, I am sure, to remain near him as long as possible."

" In that case, as I shall not know how to refuse, I will now beforehand entreat your royal highness to have the goodness to remind the King of France that one of his devoted servants is far away from him."

" Take care that when you *are* recalled, you do not consider his command as an abuse of power."

" I do not understand you, madame."

" The court of France is not easily matched, I am aware, but yet we have some pretty women at the court of England also."

Raoul smiled.

"Oh!" said Madame, "yours is a smile which portends no good to my countrywomen. It is as though you were telling them, Monsieur de Bragelonne: 'I visit you, but I leave my heart on the other side of the Channel.' Did not your smile indicate that?"

"Your highness is gifted with the power of reading the inmost depths of the soul, and you will understand, therefore, why, at present, any prolonged residence at the court of England would be a matter of the deepest regret."

"And I need not inquire if so gallant a knight is recompensed in return?"

"I have been brought up, Madame, with her whom I love, and I believe our affection is mutual."

"In that case, do not delay your departure, Monsieur de Bragelonne, and delay not your return, for on your return we shall see two persons happy; for I hope no obstacle exists to your felicity."

"There is a great obstacle, madame."

"Indeed! what is it?"

"The king's wishes on the subject."

"The king opposes your marriage?"

"He postpones it, at least. I solicited His Majesty's consent through the Comte de la Fère, and, without absolutely refusing it, he positively said it must be deferred."

"Is the young lady whom you love unworthy of you, then?"

"She is worthy of a king's affection, madame."

"I mean, she is not, perhaps, of birth equal to your own."

"Her family is excellent."

"Is she young, beautiful?"

"She is seventeen, and, in my opinion, exceedingly beautiful."

"Is she in the country, or at Paris?"

"She is here at Fontainebleau, madame."

" At the court ? "

" Yes."

" Do I know her ? "

" She has the honor to form one of your highness's household."

" Her name ? " inquired the princess, anxiously ; " if indeed," she added hastily, " her name is not a secret ? "

" No, madame, my affection is too pure for me to make a secret of it to any one, and with still greater reason to your royal highness, whose kindness towards me has been so extreme. It is Mademoiselle Louise de la Vallière."

Madame could not restrain an exclamation, in which a feeling stronger than surprise might have been detected. " Ah ! " she said, " La Vallière—she who yesterday——" she paused and then continued, " she who was taken ill, I believe."

" Yes, madame ; it was only this morning that I heard of the accident that had befallen her."

" Did you see her before you came to me ? "

" I had the honor of taking leave of her."

" And you say," resumed Madame, making a powerful effort over herself, " that the king has—deferred your marriage with this young girl."

" Yes, madame, deferred it."

" Did he assign any reason for this postponement ? "

" None."

" How long is it since the Comte de la Fère preferred his request to the king ? "

" More than a month, madame."

" It is very singular," said the princess, as something like a film clouded her eyes.

" A month ? " she repeated.

" About a month."

" You are right, vicomte," said the princess, with a smile, in which De Bragelonne might have remarked a kind of restraint, " my brother must not keep you too long in England; set off at once, and in the first letter I write to England, I will claim you in the king's name." And Madame rose to place her letter in Bragelonne's hands. Raoul understood that his audience was at an end; he took the letter, bowed lowly to the princess, and left the room.

" A month!" murmured the princess; "could I have been blind, then, to so great an extent, and could he have loved her for this last month?" And as Madame had nothing to do, she sat down to begin a letter to her brother, the postscript of which was a summons for Bragelonne to return.

The Comte de Guiche, as we have seen, had yielded to the pressing persuasions of Manicamp, and allowed himself to be led to the stables, where they desired their horses to be got ready for them; then, by one of the side paths, a description of which has already been given, they advanced to meet Monsieur, who, having just finished bathing, was returning towards the château, wearing a woman's veil to protect his face from getting burnt by the sun, which was shining very brightly. Monsieur was in one of those fits of good humor to which the admiration of his own good looks sometimes gave occasion. As he was bathing he had been able to compare the whiteness of his body with that of his courtiers, and, thanks to the care which his royal highness took of himself, no one, not even the Chevalier de Lorraine, was able to stand the comparison. Monsieur, moreover, had been tolerably successful in swimming, and his muscles having been exercised by the healthy immersion in the cool water, he was in a light and cheerful state of mind and body. So that, at the sight of Guiche, who advanced to meet him at a hand gallop, mounted upon a magnificent white horse, the prince could not restrain an exclamation of delight.

" I think matters look well," said Manicamp, who

fancied he could read this friendly disposition upon his
royal highness's countenance.

"Good-day, De Guiche, good-day," exclaimed the prince.

"Long life to your royal highness!" replied De Guiche,
encouraged by the tone of Philip's voice; "health, joy,
happiness, and prosperity to your highness."

"Welcome, De Guiche, come on my right side, but keep
your horse in hand, for I wish to return at a walking pace
under the cool shade of these trees."

"As you please, monseigneur," said De Guiche, taking
his place on the prince's right as he had been invited to
do.

"Now, my dear De Guiche," said the prince, "give me
a little news of that De Guiche whom I used to know
formerly, and who used to pay attentions to my wife."

Guiche blushed to the very whites of his eyes, while
Monsieur burst out laughing, as though he had made the
wittiest remark in the world. The few privileged courtiers
who surrounded Monsieur thought it their duty to follow
his example, although they had not heard the remark,
and a noisy burst of laughter immediately followed, beginning with the first courtier, passing on through the whole
company, and only terminating with the last. De Guiche,
although blushing scarlet, put a good countenance on the
matter; Manicamp looked at him.

"Ah! monseigneur," replied De Guiche, "show a little
charity towards such a miserable fellow as I am; do not
hold me up to the ridicule of the Chevalier de Lorraine."

"How do you mean?"

"If he hears you ridicule me, he will go beyond your
highness, and will show no pity."

"About your passion and the princess, do you mean?"

"For mercy's sake, monseigneur."

"Come, come, De Guiche, confess that you *did* get a
little sweet upon Madame."

"I will never confess such a thing, monseigneur."

"Out of respect for me, I suppose; but I release you from your respect, De Guiche. Confess, as if it were simply a question about Mademoiselle de Chalais or Mademoiselle de la Vallière."

Then breaking off, he said, beginning to laugh again. "Come, that wasn't at all bad!—a remark like a sword, which cuts two ways at once. I hit you and my brother at the same time, Chalais and La Vallière, your affianced bride and his future lady-love."

"Really, monseigneur," said the comte, "you are in a most brilliant humor to-day."

"The fact is, I feel well, and then I am pleased to see you again. But you were angry with me, were you not?"

"I, monseigneur? Why should I have been so?"

"Because I interfered with your sarabands and your other Spanish amusements. Nay, do not deny it. On that day you left the princess's apartments with your eyes full of fury; that brought you ill-luck, for you danced in the ballet yesterday in a most wretched manner. Now don't get sulky, De Guiche, for it does you no good, but makes you look like a tame bear. If the princess did look at you attentively yesterday, I am quite sure of one thing."

"What is that, monseigneur? Your highness alarms me."

"She has quite forsworn you now," said the prince, with a burst of loud laughter.

"Decidedly," thought Manicamp, "rank has nothing to do with it, and all men are alike."

The prince continued: "At all events, you have now returned, and it is to be hoped that the chevalier will become amiable again.

"How so, monseigneur: and by what miracle can I exercise such an influence over M. de Lorraine?"

"The matter is very simple, he is jealous of you."

"Bah! it is not possible."

"It is the case, though."

"He does me too much honor."

"The fact is, that when you are here, he is full of kindness and attention, but when you are gone he makes me suffer a perfect martyrdom. I am like a see-saw. Besides, you do not know the idea that has struck me?"

"I do not even suspect it."

"Well, then; when you were in exile, for you really were exiled, my poor De Guiche——"

"I should think so, indeed; but whose fault was it?" said De Guiche, pretending to speak in an angry tone.

"Not mine, certainly, my dear comte," replied his royal highness, "upon my honor, I did not ask the king to exile you——"

"No, not you, monseigneur, I am well aware; but——"

"But Madame; well, as far as that goes, I do not say it was not the case. Why, what the deuce did you do or say to Madame?"

"Really, monseigneur——"

"Women, I know, have their grudges, and my wife is not free from caprices of that nature. But if she were the cause of your being exiled I bear you no ill-will."

"In that case, monseigneur," said De Guiche. "I am not altogether unhappy."

Manicamp, who was following closely behind De Guiche, and who did not lose a word of what the prince was saying, bent down to his very shoulders over his horse's neck, in order to conceal the laughter he could not repress.

"Besides, your exile started a project in my head."

"Good."

"When the chevalier—finding you were no longer here, and sure of reigning undisturbed—began to bully

me, I, observing that my wife, in the most perfect contrast to him, was most kind and amiable towards me who
had neglected her so much, the idea occurred to me of
becoming a model husband—a rarity, a curiosity, at the
court; and I had an idea of getting very fond of my
wife."

De Guiche looked at the prince with a stupefied expression of countenance, which was not assumed.

" Oh! monseigneur," De Guiche stammered out;
" surely, that never seriously occurred to you."

" Indeed it did. I have some property that my brother
gave me on my marriage; she has some money of her
own, and not a little either, for she gets money from her
brother and brother-in-law of England and France at the
same time. Well! we should have left the court. I
should have retired to my château at Villers-Cotterets,
situated in the middle of a forest, in which we should
have led a most sentimental life in the very same spot
where my grandfather, Henry IV., sojourned with La
Belle Gabrielle. What do you think of that idea, De
Guiche! "

" Why, it is enough to make one shiver, monseigneur,"
replied De Guiche, who shuddered in reality.

" Ah! I see you would never be able to endure being
exiled a second time."

" I, monseigneur ? "

" I will not carry you off with us, as I had at first intended."

" What, with you, monseigneur ? "

" Yes; if the idea should occur to me again of taking a
dislike to the court."

" Oh! do not let that make any difference, monseigneur;
I would follow your highness to the end of the world."

" Clumsy fellow, that you are! " said Manicamp, grum-
blingly, pushing his horse towards De Guiche, so as al-

most to unseat him, and then, as he passed close to him as if he had lost command over the horse, he whispered, "For goodness' sake, think what you are saying."

"Well, it is agreed, then," said the prince; "since you are so devoted to me, I shall take you with me."

"Anywhere, monseigneur," replied De Guiche in a joyous tone, "whenever you like, and at once, too. Are you ready?"

And De Guiche, laughingly, gave his horse the rein, and galloped forward a few yards.

"One moment," said the prince. "Let us go to the château first."

"What for?"

"Why, to take my wife, of course."

"What for?" asked De Guiche.

"Why, since I tell you that it is a project of conjugal affection, it is necessary I should take my wife with me."

"In that case, monseigneur," replied the comte, "I am greatly concerned, but no De Guiche for you."

"Bah!"

"Yes.—Why do you take Madame with you?"

"Because I begin to fancy I love her," said the prince.

De Guiche turned slightly pale, but endeavored to preserve his seeming cheerfulness.

"If you love Madame, monseigneur," he said, "that ought to be quite enough for you, and you have no further need of your friends."

"Not bad, not bad," murmured Manicamp.

"There, your fear of Madame has begun again," replied the prince.

"Why, monseigneur, I have experienced that to my cost; a woman who was the cause of my being exiled!"

"What a revengeful disposition you have, De Guiche, how virulently you bear malice."

"I should like the case to be your own, monseigneur."

"Decidedly, then, that was the reason why you danced so badly yesterday; you wished to revenge yourself, I suppose, by trying to make Madame make a mistake in her dancing; ah! that is very paltry, De Guiche, and I will tell Madame of it."

"You may tell her whatever you please, monseigneur, for Her Highness cannot hate me more than she does."

"Nonsense, you are exaggerating; and this because merely of the fortnight's sojourn in the country she imposed on you."

"Monseigneur, a fortnight is a fortnight; and when the time is passed in getting sick and tired of everything, a fortnight is an eternity."

"So that you will not forgive her?"

"Never!"

"Come, come, De Guiche, be a better disposed fellow than that. I wish to make your peace with her; you will find, in conversing with her, that she has no malice or unkindness in her nature, and that she is very talented."

"Monseigneur——"

"You will see, that she can receive her friends like a princess, and laugh like a citizen's wife; you will see that, when she pleases, she can make the pleasant hours pass like minutes. Come, De Guiche, you must really make up your differences with my wife."

"Upon my word," said Manicamp to himself, "the prince is a husband whose wife's name will bring him ill-luck, and King Candaules, of old, was a tiger beside his royal highness."

"At all events," added the prince, "I am sure you will make it up with my wife: I guarantee you will do so. Only, I must show you the way now. There is nothing commonplace about her : it is not every one who takes her fancy."

"Monseigneur——"

"No resistance, De Guiche, or I shall get out of temper," replied the prince.

"Well, since he will have it so," murmured Manicamp, in Guiche's ear, "do as he wants you to do."

"Well, monseigneur," said the comte, "I obey."

"And to begin," resumed the prince, "there will be cards, this evening, in Madame's apartment; you will dine with me, and I will take you there with me."

"Oh! as for that, monseigneur," objected De Guiche, "you will allow me to object."

"What, again! this is positive rebellion."

"Madame received me too indifferently, yesterday, before the whole court."

"Really!" said the prince, laughing.

"Nay, so much so, indeed, that she did not even answer me when I addressed her; it may be a good thing to have no self-respect at all, but to have too little is not enough, as the saying is."

"Comte! after dinner, you will go to your own apartments, and dress yourself, and then you will come to fetch me. I shall wait for you."

"Since your highness absolutely commands it."

"Positively."

"He will not loose his hold," said Manicamp; "these are the things to which husbands cling most obstinately. Ah! what a pity M. Molière could not have heard this man; he would have turned him into verse if he had."

The prince and his court, chatting in this manner, returned to the coolest apartments of the château.

"By the by," said De Guiche, as they were standing by the door, "I had a commission for your Royal Highness."

"Execute it, then."

"M. de Bragelonne has, by the king's order, set off for

London, and he charged me with his respects for you, monseigneur."

"A pleasant journey to the vicomte, whom I like very much. Go and dress yourself, De Guiche, and come back for me. If you don't come back——"

"What will happen, monseigneur?"

"I will have you sent to the Bastile."

"Well," said De Guiche, laughing, "his royal highness, Monseigneur, is decidedly the counterpart of Her royal highness, Madame. Madame gets me sent into exile, because she does not care for me sufficiently; and Monseigneur gets me imprisoned, because he cares for me too much. I thank Monseigneur, and I thank Madame."

"Come, come," said the prince, "you are a delightful companion, and you know I cannot do without you. Return as soon as you can."

"Very well; but I am in the humor to prove myself difficult to be pleased, in *my* turn, monseigneur."

"Bah!"

"So, I will not return to your royal highness, except upon one condition."

"Name it."

"I want to oblige the friend of one of my friends."

"What's his name?"

"Malicorne."

"An ugly name."

"But very well borne, monseigneur."

"That may be. Well?"

"Well, I owe M. Malicorne a place in your household, monseigneur."

"What kind of a place?"

"Any kind of place; a supervision of some sort or another, for instance."

"That happens very fortunately, for yesterday I dismissed my chief usher of the apartments."

" That will do admirably.   What are his duties ? "

" Nothing, except to look about and make his report."

" A sort of interior police ? "

" Exactly."

" Ah, how excellently that will suit Malicorne," Mani-camp ventured to say.

" You know the person we are speaking of, M. Mani-camp ? " inquired the prince.

" Intimately, monseigneur.   He is a friend of mine."

" And your opinion is ? "

" That   your   highness   could   never   get   a   better usher of the apartments than he will make."

" How much does the appointment bring in ? " inquired the comte of the prince.

" I don't know at all, only I have always been told that he could make as much as he pleased when he was thor-oughly in earnest."

" What do you call being thoroughly in earnest, prince ? "

" It means, of course, when the functionary in question is a man who has his wits about him."

" In that case I think your highness will be content, for Malicorne is as sharp as the devil himself."

" Good ! the appointment will be an expensive one for me, in that case," replied the prince, laughing.   " You are making me a positive present, comte."

" I believe so, monseigneur."

" Well, go and announce to your M. Mélicorne——"

" Malicorne, monseigneur."

" I shall never get hold of that name."

" You say Manicamp very well, monseigneur."

" Oh, I ought to say Malicorne very well, too.   The allit-eration will help me."

" Say what you like, monseigneur, I can promise you your inspector of apartments will not be annoyed ; he has the very happiest disposition that can be met with."

"Well, then, my dear De Guiche, inform him of his nomination. But, stay——"

"What is it, monseigneur?"

"I wish to see him beforehand; if he be as ugly as his name, I retract every word I have said."

"Your highness knows him, for you have already seen him at the Palais-Royal; nay, indeed, it was I who presented him to you."

"Ah, I remember now—not a bad-looking fellow."

"I know you must have noticed him, monseigneur."

"Yes, yes, yes. You see, De Guiche, I do not wish that either my wife or myself should have ugly faces before our eyes. My wife will have all her maids of honor pretty; I, all the gentlemen about me good-looking. In this way, De Guiche, you see, that any children we may have will run a good chance of being pretty, if my wife and myself have handsome models before us."

"Most magnificently argued, monseigneur," said Manicamp showing his approval by look and voice at the same time.

As for De Guiche, he very probably did not find the argument so convincing, for he merely signified his opinion by a gesture, which, moreover, exhibited in a marked manner some indecision of mind on the subject. Manicamp went off to inform Malicorne of the good news he had just learned. De Guiche seemed very unwilling to take his departure for the purpose of dressing himself. Monsieur, singing, laughing and admiring himself, passed away the time until the dinner-hour, in a frame of mind that justified the proverb of "Happy as a prince."

CHAPTER XXI.

STORY OF A DRYAD AND A NAIAD.

EVERY one had partaken of the banquet at the château, and afterwards assumed their full court dresses. The usual hour for the repast was five o'clock. If we say, then, that the repast occupied an hour, and the toilette two hours, everybody was ready about eight o'clock in the evening. Towards eight o'clock, then, the guests began to arrive at Madame's, for we have already intimated that it was Madame who " received " that evening. And at Madame's *soirées* no one failed to be present; for the evenings passed in her apartments had aways that perfect charm about them which the queen, that pious and excellent princess, had not been able to confer upon her *réunions*. For, unfortunately, one of the advantages of goodness of disposition is that it is far less amusing than wit of an ill-natured character. And yet, let us hasten to add, that such a style of wit could not be assigned to Madame, for her disposition of mind, naturally of the very highest order, comprised too much true generosity, too many noble impulses and high-souled thoughts to warrant her being termed ill-natured. But Madame was endowed with a spirit of resistance—a gift frequently fatal to its possessor, for it breaks where another disposition would have bent; the result was that blows did not become deadened upon her as upon what might be termed the cotton-wadded feelings of Maria-Theresa. Her heart rebounded at each attack, and therefore, whenever she was attacked, even in a manner that almost stunned her, she returned blow for blow to any one imprudent enough to tilt against her.

Was this really maliciousness of disposition or simply waywardness of character? We regard those rich and powerful natures as like the tree of knowledge, producing good and evil at the same time; a double branch, always blooming and fruitful, of which those who wish to eat know how to detect the good fruit, and from which the worthless and frivolous die who have eaten of it—a circumstance which is by no means to be regarded as a great misfortune. Madame, therefore, who had a well-digested plan in her mind of constituting herself the second, if not even the principal, queen of the court, rendered her receptions delightful to all, from the conversation, the opportunities of meeting, and the perfect liberty she allowed every one of making any remark he pleased, on the condition, however, that the remark was amusing or sensible. And it will hardly be believed, that, by that means, there was less talking among the society Madame assembled together than elsewhere. Madame hated people who talked much, and took a remarkably cruel revenge upon them, for she allowed them to talk. She disliked pretension, too, and never overlooked that defect, even in the king himself. It was more than a weakness of Monsieur, and the princess had undertaken the amazing task of curing him of it. As for the rest, poets, wits, beautiful women, all were received by her with the air of a mistress superior to her slaves. Sufficiently meditative in her liveliest humors to make even poets meditate; sufficiently pretty to dazzle by her attractions, even among the prettiest; sufficiently witty for the most distinguished persons who were present, to be listened to with pleasure— it will easily be believed that the *réunions* held in Madame's apartment must naturally have proved very attractive. All who were young flocked there, and when the king himself happens to be young, everybody at court is so too. And so, the older ladies of the court, the strong-minded women of the regency, or of the last reign, pouted and sulked at their ease; but others only laughed at the fits of sulkiness in which these venerable individuals indulged, who had carried the love of authority so far as even to take command of bodies of soldiers in the wars of the Fronde, in order, as Madame asserted, not to lose their influence over men altogether. As eight o'clock struck her royal highness entered the great drawing-room, accompanied by her ladies in attendance, and found several gentlemen belonging to the court already there, having been waiting for some minutes. Among those who had arrived before the hour fixed for the reception she looked round for the one who, she thought, ought to have been first in attendance, but he was not there. However, almost at the very moment she completed her investigation, Monsieur was announced. Monsieur looked splendid. All the precious stones and jewels of Cardinal Mazarin, which of course that minister could not do otherwise than leave; all the queen-mother's jewels as well as a few belonging to his wife—Monsieur wore them all, and he was as dazzling as the rising sun. Behind him followed De Guiche, with hesitating steps and an air of contrition admirably assumed; De Guiche wore a costume of French-gray velvet, embroidered with silver, and trimmed with blue ribbons : he wore also Mechlin lace, as rare and beautiful in its own way as the jewels of Monsieur in theirs. The plume in his hat was red. Madame, too, wore several colors, and preferred red for embroidery, gray for dress, and blue for flowers. M. de Guiche, dressed as we have described, looked so handsome that he excited every one's observation. An interesting pallor of complexion, a languid expression of the eyes, his white hands seen through the masses of lace that covered them, the melan-

GASTON DE FRANCE,

DUC D'ORLEANS.

choly expression of his mouth—it was only necessary, indeed, to see M. de Guiche to admit that few men at the court of France could hope to equal him. The consequence was that Monsieur, who was pretentious enough to fancy he could eclipse a star even, if a star had adorned itself in a similar manner to himself, was, on the contrary, completely eclipsed in all imaginations, which are silent judges certainly, but very positive and firm in their convictions. Madame looked at De Guiche lightly, but light as her look had been, it brought a delightful color to his face. In fact, Madame found De Guiche so handsome and so admirably dressed, that she almost ceased regretting the royal conquest she felt was on the point of escaping her. Her heart, therefore, sent the blood to her face. Monsieur approached her. He had not noticed the princess's blush, or if he had seen it, he was far from attributing it to its true cause.

" Madame," he said, kissing his wife's hand, " there is some one present here, who has fallen into disgrace, an unhappy exile whom I venture to recommend to your kindness. Do not forget, I beg, that he is one of my best friends, and that a gentle reception of him will please me greatly."

" What exile ? what disgraced person are you speaking of?" inquired Madame, looking all round, and not permitting her glance to rest more on the count than on the others.

This was the moment to present De Guiche, and the prince drew aside and let De Guiche pass him, who, with a tolerably well-assumed awkwardness of manner, approached Madame and made his reverence to her.

" What ! " exclaimed Madame, as if she were greatly surprised, " is M. de Guiche the disgraced individual you speak of, the exile in question ?"

" Yes, certainly," returned the duke.

"Indeed," said Madame, " he seems almost the only person here! "

" You are unjust, Madame," said the prince.

" I ? "

" Certainly. Come, forgive the poor fellow."

" Forgive him what? What have I to forgive M. de Guiche ? "

" Come, explain yourself, De Guiche. What do you wish to be forgiven? " inquired the prince.

" Alas! her royal highness knows very well what it is," replied the latter, in a hypocritical tone.

" Come, come, give him your hand, Madame," said Philip.

" If it will give you any pleasure, Monsieur," and, with a movement of her eyes and shoulders, which it would be impossible to describe, Madame extended towards the young man her beautiful and perfumed hand, upon which he pressed his lips. It was evident that he did so for some little time, and that Madame did not withdraw her hand too quickly, for the duke added :—

" De Guiche is not wickedly disposed, Madame; so do not be afraid, he will not bite you."

A pretext was given in the gallery by the duke's remark, which was not perhaps, very laughable, for every one to laugh excessively. The situation was odd enough, and some kindly disposed persons had observed it. Monsieur was still enjoying the effect of his remark, when the king was announced. The appearance of the room at that moment was as follows :—in the center, before the fireplace, which was filled with flowers, Madame was standing up, with her maids of honor formed in two wings, on either side of her; around whom the butterflies of the court were fluttering. Several other groups were formed in the recesses of the windows, like soldiers stationed in their different towers who belong to the same garrison. From their respective places they could pick up the remarks which fell from the principal group. From one of these groups, the nearest to the fireplace, Malicorne, who had been at once raised to the dignity, through Manicamp and De Guiche, of the post of master of the apartments, and whose official costume had been ready for the last two months, was brilliant with gold lace, and shone upon Montalais, standing on Madame's extreme left, with all the fire of his eyes and splendor of his velvet. Madame was conversing with Mademoiselle de Chatillon and Mademoiselle de Créquy, who were next to her, and addressed a few words to Monsieur, who drew aside as soon as the king was announced. Mademoiselle de la Vallière, like Montalais, was on Madame's left hand, and the last but one on the line, Mademoiselle de Tonnay-Charente being on her right. She was stationed as certain bodies of troops are, whose weakness is suspected, and who are placed between two experienced regiments. Guarded in this manner by the companions who had shared her adventure, La Vallière, whether from regret at Raoul's departure, or still suffering from the emotion caused by recent events, which had begun to render her name familiar on the lips of the courtiers, La Vallière, we repeat, hid her eyes, red with weeping, behind her fan, and seemed to give the greatest attention to the remarks which Montalais and Athenaïs, alternately, whispered to her from time to time. As soon as the king's name was announced a general movement took place in the apartment. Madame, in her character as hostess, rose to receive the royal visitor; but as she rose, notwithstanding her preoccupation of mind, she glanced hastily towards her right; her glance, which the presumptuous De Guiche regarded as intended for himself, rested, as it swept over the whole circle, upon La Vallière, whose warm blush and restless emotion it instantly perceived.

The king advanced to the middle of the group, which had now become a general one, by a movement which took place from the circumference to the center. Every head bowed low before his majesty, the ladies bending like frail, magnificent lilies before king Aquilo. There was nothing very severe, we will even say, nothing very royal that evening about the king, except youth and good looks. He wore an air of animated joyousness and good-humor which set all imaginations at work, and, thereupon, all present promised themselves a delightful evening, for no other reason than from having remarked the desire his majesty had to amuse himself in Madame's apartments. If there was any one in particular whose high spirits and good-humor equaled the king's, it was M. de Saint-Aignan, who was dressed in a rose-colored costume, with face and ribbons of the same color, and, in addition, particularly rose-colored in his ideas, for that evening M. de Saint-Aignan was prolific in jests. The circumstance which had given a new expansion to the numerous ideas germinating in his fertile brain was, that he had just perceived that Mademoiselle de Tonnay-Charente was, like himself, dressed in rose-color. We would not wish to say, however, that the wily courtier had not known beforehand that the beautiful Athenaïs was to wear that particular color; for he very well knew the art of unlocking the lips of a dressmaker or a ladies'-maid as to her mistress's intentions. He cast as many killing glances at Mademoiselle Athenaïs as he had bows of ribbon on his stockings and doublet; in other words, he discharged a prodigious number. The king having paid Madame the customary compliments, and Madame having requested him to be seated, the circle was immediately formed. Louis inquired of Monsieur the particulars of the day's bathing; and stated, looking at the ladies present while he spoke, that certain poets were engaged

turning into verse the enchanting diversion of the baths
of Valvins, and that one of them particularly, M. Loret,
seemed to have been intrusted with the confidence of
some water-nymph, as he had in his verses recounted
many circumstances that were actually true—at which
remark more than one lady present felt herself bound to
blush. The king at this moment took the opportunity of
looking round him at more leisure; Montalais was the
only one who did not blush sufficiently to prevent her
looking at the king, and she saw him fix his eyes devour-
ingly on Mademoiselle de la Vallière. This undaunted
maid of honor, Mademoiselle de Montalais, be it understood, forced the king to lower his gaze, and so saved
Louise de la Vallière from a sympathetic warmth of feeling this gaze might possibly have conveyed. Louis was
appropriated by Madame, who overwhelmed him with
inquiries, and no one in the world knew how to ask questions better than she did. He tried, however, to render
the conversation general, and, with the view of effecting
this, he redoubled his attention and devotion to her. Madame coveted complimentary remarks, and, determined
to procure them at any cost, she addressed herself to the
king, saying:

"Sire, your majesty, who is aware of everything which
occurs in your kingdom, ought to know beforehand the
verses confided to M. Loret by this nymph; will your
majesty kindly communicate them to us?"

"Madame," replied the king, with perfect grace of
manner, "I dare not—you, personally, might be in no
little degree confused at having to listen to certain details
—but Saint-Aignan tells a story well, and has a perfect
recollection of the verses. If he does not remember them,
he will invent. I can certify he is almost a poet himself."
Saint-Aignan, thus brought prominently forward, was
compelled to introduce himself as advantageously as pos-

sible. Unfortunately, however, for Madame, he thought of his own personal affairs only; in other words, instead of paying Madame the compliments she so much desired and relished, his mind was fixed upon making as much display as possible of his own good fortune. Again glancing, therefore, for the hundredth time, at the beautiful Athenaïs, who carried into practice her previous evening's theory of not even deigning to look at her adorer, he said :—

" Your majesty will perhaps pardon me for having too indifferently remembered the verses which the nymph dictated to Loret; but if the king has not retained any recollection of them, how could I possibly remember? "

Madame did not receive this shortcoming of the courtier very favorably.

" Ah! madame," added Saint-Aignan, " at present it is no longer a question what the water-nymphs have to say; and one would almost be tempted to believe that nothing of any interest now occurs in those liquid realms. It is upon earth madame, important events happen. Ah! madame, upon the earth, how many tales are there full of——"

" Well," said Madame, " and what is taking place upon the earth ? "

" That question must be asked of the Dryads," replied the comte; " the Dryads inhabit the forest, as your royal highness is aware."

" I am aware, also, that they are naturally very talkative, Monsieur de Saint-Aignan."

" Such is the case, madame ; but when they say such delightful things, it would be ungracious to accuse them of being too talkative."

"Do they talk so delightfully, then?" inquired the princess, indifferently. "Really, Monsieur de Saint-Aignan, you excite my curiosity; and, if I were the king

I would require you immediately to tell us what the delightful things are these Dryads have been saying since you alone seem to understand their language."

" I am at his majesty's orders, madame, in that respect," replied the comte, quickly.

" What a fortunate fellow this Saint-Aignan is to understand the language of the Dryads," said Monsieur.

"I understand it perfectly, monseigneur, as I do my own language."

"Tell us all about them, then," said Madame.

The king felt embarrassed, for his confidant was, in all probability, about to embark in a difficult matter. He felt that it would be so, from the general attention excited by Saint-Aignan's preamble, and aroused too by Madame's peculiar manner. The most reserved of those who were present seemed ready to devour every syllable the comte was about to pronounce. They coughed, drew closer together, looked curiously at some of the maids of honor, who, in order to support with greater propriety, or with more steadiness, the fixity of the inquisitorial looks bent upon them, adjusted their fans accordingly, and assumed the bearing of a duelist about to be exposed to his adversary's fire. At this epoch, the fashion of ingeniously-constructed conversations, and hazardously-dangerous recitals, so prevailed, that, where, in modern times, a whole company assembled in a drawing-room would begin to suspect some scandal, or disclosure, or tragic event, and would hurry away in dismay, Madame's guests quietly settled themselves in their places, in order not to lose a word or gesture of the comedy composed by Monsieur de Saint-Aignan for their benefit, and the termination of which, whatever the style and the plot might be, must, as a matter of course, be marked by the most perfect propriety. The comte was known as a man of extreme refinement, and an admirable narrator. He courageously began, then, amidst a profound silence, which would have been formidable to any one but himself :—" Madame, by the king's permission, I address myself, in the first place, to your royal highness, since you admit yourself to be the person present possessing the greatest curiosity. I have the honor, therefore, to inform your royal highness that the Dryad more particularly inhabits the hollows of oaks; and, as Dryads are mythological creatures of great beauty, they inhabit the most beautiful trees, in other words, the largest to be found."

At this exordium, which recalled, under a transparent veil, the celebrated story of the royal oak, which had played so important a part in the last evening, so many hearts began to beat, both from joy and uneasiness, that, if Saint-Aignan had not had a good and sonorous voice, their throbbings might have been heard above the sound of his voice.

"There must surely be Dryads at Fontainebleau, then," said Madame, in a perfectly calm voice; "for I have never, in all my life, seen finer oaks than in the royal park." And as she spoke, she directed towards De Guiche a look of which he had no reason to complain, as he had of the one that preceded it; which, as we have already mentioned, had reserved a certain amount of indefiniteness most painful for so loving a heart as his.

" Precisely, madame, it is of Fontainebleau I was about to speak to your royal highness," said Saint-Aignan; " for the Dryad whose story is engaging our attention, lives in the park belonging to the château of his majesty."

The affair was fairly embarked on; the action was begun, and it was no longer possible for auditory or narrator to draw back.

" It will be worth listening to," said Madame; "for the story not only appears to me to have all the interest of a

national incident, but still more, seems to be a circumstance of very recent occurrence."

"I ought to begin at the beginning," said the comte.
"In the first place, then, there lived at Fontainebleau,
in a cottage of modest and unassuming appearance, two
shepherds. The one was the shepherd Tyrcis, the owner
of extensive domains transmitted to him from his parents,
by right of inheritance. Tyrcis was young and handsome, and, from his many qualifications, he might be
pronounced to be the first and foremost among the shepherds in the whole country ; one might even boldly say he
was the king of shepherds." A subdued murmur of approbation encouraged the narrator, who continued :—
"His strength equals his courage ; no one displays greater
address in hunting wild beasts, nor greater wisdom in
matters where judgment is required. Whenever he
mounts and exercises his horse in the beautiful plains of
his inheritance, or whenever he joins with the shepherds
who owe him allegiance, in different games of skill and
strength, one might say that it is the god Mars hurling
his lance on the plains of Thrace, or, even better, that it
was Apollo himself, the god of day, radiant upon earth,
bearing his flaming darts in his hand." Every one understood that this allegorical portrait of the king was not
the worst exordium the narrator could have chosen ; and,
consequently it did not fail to produce its effect, either
upon those who, from duty or inclination, applauded it to
the very echo, or on the king himself, to whom flattery
was very agreeable when delicately conveyed, and whom,
indeed, it did not always displease, even when it was
a little too broad. Saint-Aignan then continued :—" It
is not in games of glory only, ladies, that the shepherd
Tyrcis had acquired that reputation by which he was
regarded as the king of shepherds."

"Of the shepherds of Fontainebleau," said the king, smilingly, to Madame.

"Oh!" exclaimed Madame, "Fontainebleau is selected arbitrarily by the poet; but I should say, of the shepherds of the whole world." The king forgot his part of a passive auditor, and bowed.

"It is," pursued Saint-Aignan, amidst a flattering murmur of applause, "it is with ladies fair especially that the qualities of this king of the shepherds are most prominently displayed. He is a shepherd with a mind as refined as his heart is pure; he can pay a compliment with a charm of manner whose fascination it is impossible to resist; and in his attachments he is so discreet, that beautiful and happy conquests may regard their lot as more than enviable. Never a syllable of disclosure, never a moment's forgetfulness. Whoever has seen and heard Tyrcis must love him; whoever loves and is beloved by him, has indeed found happiness." Saint-Aignan here paused; he was enjoying the pleasure of all these compliments; and the portrait he had drawn, however grotesquely inflated it might be, had found favor in certain ears, in which the perfections of the shepherd did not seem to have been exaggerated. Madame begged the orator to continue. "Tyrcis," said the comte, "had a faithful companion, or rather a devoted servant, whose name was—Amyntas."

"Ah!" said Madame, archly, "now for the portrait of Amyntas; you are such an excellent painter, Monsieur de Saint-Aignan."

"Madame——"

"Oh! comte, do not, I entreat you, sacrifice poor Amyntas; I should never forgive you."

"Madame, Amyntas is of too humble a position, particularly beside Tyrcis, for his person to be honored by a parallel. There are certain friends who resemble those

followers of ancient times, who caused themselves to be
buried alive at their masters' feet. Amyntas's place, too,
is at the feet of Tyrcis; he cares for no other; and if,
sometimes, the illustrious hero——"

"Illustrious shepherd, you mean?" said Madame, pretending to correct M. de Saint-Aignan.

"Your royal highness is right; I was mistaken," returned the courtier; "if, I say, the shepherd Tyrcis
deigns occasionally to call Amyntas his friend, and to open
his heart to him, it is an unparalleled favor, which the
latter regards as the most unbounded felicity."

"All that you say," interrupted Madame, "establishes
the extreme devotion of Amyntas to Tyrcis, but does not
furnish us with the portrait of Amyntas. Comte, do not
flatter him, if you like; but describe him to us. I will
have Amyntas's portrait." Saint-Aignan obeyed, after
having bowed profoundly towards his majesty's sister-in-
law.

"Amyntas," he said, "is somewhat older than Tyrcis;
he is not an ill-favored shepherd; it is even said that the
muses condescended to smile upon him at his birth, even
as Hebe smiled upon youth. He is not ambitious of display, but he is ambitious of being loved; and he might
not, perhaps, be found unworthy of it, if he were only
sufficiently well-known."

This latter paragraph, strengthened by a killing glance,
was directed straight to Mademoiselle de Tonnay-
Charente, who received them both unmoved. But the
modesty and tact of the allusion had produced a good
effect; Amyntas reaped the benefit of it in the applause
bestowed on him: Tyrcis's head even gave the signal for
it by a consenting bow, full of good feeling.

"One evening," continued Saint-Aignan, "Tyrcis and
Amyntas were walking together in the forest, talking of
their love disappointments. Do not forget, ladies, that

the story of the Dryad is now beginning, otherwise it would be easy to tell you what Tyrcis and Amyntas, the two most discreet shepherds of the whole earth, were talking about. They reached the thickest part of the forest, for the purpose of being quite alone, and of confiding their troubles more freely to each other, when suddenly the sound of voices struck upon their ears."

"Ah, ah!" said those who surrounded the narrator. "Nothing can be more interesting."

At this point, Madame, like a vigilant general inspecting his army, glanced at Montalais and Tonnay-Charente, who could not help wincing as they drew themselves up.

"These harmonious voices, resumed Saint-Aignan, "were those of certain shepherdesses, who had been likewise desirous of enjoying the coolness of the shade, and who, knowing the isolated and almost unapproachable situation of the place, had betaken themselves there to interchange their ideas upon——" A loud burst of laughter occasioned by this remark of Saint-Aignan, and an imperceptible smile of the king, as he looked at Tonnay-Charente, followed this sally.

"The Dryad affirms positively," continued Saint-Aignan, "that the shepherdesses were three in number, and that all three were young and beautiful."

"What were their names?" said Madame, quietly.

"Their names?." said Saint-Aignan, who hesitated from fear of committing an indiscretion.

"Of course; you called your shepherds Tyrcis and Amyntas; give your shepherdesses names in a similar manner."

"Oh! Madame, I am not an inventor; I relate simply what took place as the Dryad related it to me."

"What did your Dryad, then, call these shepherdesses? You have a very treacherous memory, I fear. This Dryad must have fallen out with the goddess Mnemosyne."

"These shepherdesses, Madame? Pray remember that it is a crime to betray a woman's name."

"From which a woman absolves you, comte, on condition that you will reveal the names of the shepherdesses."

"Their names were Phyllis, Amaryllis, and Galatea."

"Exceedingly well!—they have not lost by the delay," said Madame, "and now we have three charming names. But now for their portraits."

Saint-Aignan again made a slight movement.

"Nay, comte, let us proceed in due order," returned Madame. "Ought we not, sire, to have the portraits of the shepherdesses?"

The king, who expected this determined perseverance, and who began to feel some uneasiness, did not think it safe to provoke so dangerous an interrogator. He thought, too, that Saint-Aignan, in drawing the portraits, would find a means of insinuating some flattering allusions which would be agreeable to the ears of one his majesty was interested in pleasing. It was with this hope and with this fear that Louis authorized Saint-Aignan to sketch the portraits of the shepherdesses, Phillis, Amaryllis, and Galatea.

"Very well, then; be it so," said Saint-Aignan, like a man who has made up his mind, and he began.

CHAPTER XXII.

CONCLUSION OF THE STORY OF A NAIAD AND OF A DRYAD.

"PHYLLIS," said Saint-Aignan, with a glance of defiance at Montalais, such as a fencing-master would give who invites an antagonist worthy of him to place himself on guard, "Phyllis is neither fair nor dark, neither tall nor

short, neither too grave or too gay ; though but a shepherdess, she is as witty as a princess, and as coquettish as
the most finished flirt that ever lived. Nothing can equal
her excellent vision. Her heart yearns for everything her
gaze embraces. She is like a bird, which, always warbling,
at one moment skims the ground, at the next rises fluttering in pursuit of a butterfly, then rests itself upon the
topmost branch of a tree where it defies the bird-catchers
either to come and seize it or to entrap it in their nets."
The portrait bore such a strong resemblance to Montalais,
that all eyes were directed towards her ; she, however,
with her head raised, and with a steady, unmoved look,
listened to Saint-Aignan, as if he were speaking of an
utter stranger.

" Is that all, Monsieur de Saint-Aignan ? " inquired the
princess.

"Oh ! your royal highness, the portrait is a mere sketch,
and many more additions could be made, but I fear to
weary your patience, or offend the modesty of the shepherdess, and I shall therefore pass on to her companion,
Amaryllis."

" Very well," said Madame, " pass on to Amaryllis,
Monsieur de Saint-Aignan, we are all attention."

" Amaryllis is the eldest of the three, and yet," Saint-
Aignan hastened to add, " this advanced age does not
reach twenty years."

Mademoiselle de Tonnay-Charente, who had slightly
knitted her brows at the commencement of the description,
unbent them with a smile.

" She is tall, with an astonishing abundance of beautiful
hair, which she fastens in the manner of the Grecian
statues ; her walk is full of majesty, her attitude haughty ;
she has the air, therefore, rather of a goddess than a mere
mortal, and among the goddesses, she most resembles
Diana the huntress ; with this sole difference, however,

that the cruel shepherdess, having stolen the quiver of young love, while poor Cupid was sleeping in a thicket of roses, instead of directing her arrows against the inhabitants of the forest, discharges them pitilessly against all poor shepherds who pass within reach of her bow and of her eyes."

" Oh ! what a wicked shepherdess ! " said Madame. " She may some day wound herself with one of those arrows she discharges, as you say, so mercilessly on all sides."

" It is the hope of shepherds, one and all ! " said Saint-Aignan.

" And that of the shepherd Amyntas in particular, I suppose ? " said Madame.

" The shepherd Amyntas is so timid," said Saint-Aignan, with the most modest air he could assume, that if he cherishes such a hope as that, no one has ever known anything about it, for he conceals it in the very depths of his heart." A flattering murmur of applause greeted this profession of faith on behalf of the shepherd.

" And Galatea ? " inquired Madame. " I am impatient to see a hand so skillful as yours continue the portrait where Virgil left it, and finish it before our eyes."

" Madame," said Saint-Aignan, " I am indeed a poor dumb post beside the mighty Virgil. Still, encouraged by your desire, I will do my best."

Saint-Aignan extended his foot and hand, and thus began :—" White as milk, she casts upon the breeze the perfume of her fair hair tinged with golden hues, as are the ears of corn. One is tempted to inquire if she is not the beautiful Europa, who inspired Jupiter with a tender passion as she played with her companions in the flower-spangled meadows. From her exquisite eyes, blue as azure heaven on the clearest summer day, emanates a tender light, which reverie nurtures, and love dispenses.

When she frowns, or bends her looks toward the ground, the sun is veiled in token of mourning. When she smiles, on the contrary, nature resumes her jollity, and the birds, for a brief moment silenced, recommence their songs amid the leafy covert of the trees. Galatea," said Saint-Aignan, in conclusion, " is worthy of the admiration of the whole world; and if she should ever bestow her heart upon another, happy will that man be to whom she consecrates her first affections."

Madame, who had attentively listened to the portrait Saint-Aignan had drawn, as, indeed, had all the others, contented herself with accentuating her approbation of the most poetic passage by occasional inclinations of her head; but it was impossible to say if these marks of assent were accorded to the ability of the narrator or the resemblance of the portrait. The consequence, therefore, was, that as Madame did not openly exhibit any approbation, no one felt authorized to applaud, not even Monsieur, who secretly thought that Saint-Aignan dwelt too much upon the portraits of the shepherdesses, and had somewhat slightingly passed over the portraits of the shepherds. The whole assembly seemed suddenly chilled. Saint-Aignan, who had exhausted his rhetorical skill and his palate of artistic tints in sketching the portrait of Galatea, and who, after the favor with which his other descriptions had been received, already imagined he could hear the loudest applause allotted to this last one, was himself more disappointed than the king and rest of the company. A moment's silence followed, which was last broken by Madame.

" Well, sir," she inquired, " what is your majesty's opinion of these three portraits ? "

The king, who wished to relieve Saint-Aignan's embarrassment without compromising himself, replied, " Why, Amaryllis, in my opinion, is beautiful."

" For my part," said Monsieur, "I prefer Phyllis ; she is a capital girl, or rather a good-sort-of-fellow of a nymph."

A gentle laugh followed, and this time the looks were so direct, that Montalais felt herself blushing almost scarlet.

" Well," resumed Madame, " what were those shepherdesses saying to each other ? "

Saint-Aignan, however, whose vanity had been wounded, did not feel himself in a position to sustain an attack of new and refreshed troops, and merely said, " Madame, the shepherdesses were confiding to one another their little preferences."

" Nay, nay ! Monsieur de Saint-Aignan, you are a perfect stream of pastoral poesy," said Madame, with an amiable smile, which somewhat comforted the narrator.

" They confessed that love is a mighty peril, but that the absence of love is the heart's sentence of death."

" What was the conclusion they came to ? " inquired Madame.

" They came to the conclusion that love was necessary."

" Very good !   Did they lay down any conditions ? "

"That of choice, simply," said Saint-Aignan.   " I ought even to add,—remember it is the Dryad who is speaking,—that one of the shepherdesses, Amaryllis, I believe, was completely opposed to the necessity of loving, and yet she did not positively deny that she had allowed the image of a certain shepherd to take refuge in her heart."

" Was it Amyntas or Tyrcis ? "

" Amyntas, Madame," said Saint-Aignan, modestly. " But Galatea, the gentle and soft-eyed Galatea, immediately replied, that neither Amyntas, nor Alphesibœus, nor Tityrus, nor indeed any of the handsomest shepherds of the country, were to be compared to Tyrcis ; that Tyrcis was as superior to all other men, as the oak to all other trees, as the lily in its majesty to all other flowers. She drew even such a portrait of Tyrcis that Tyrcis himself, who was listening, must have felt truly flattered at it, notwithstanding his rank as a shepherd. Thus Tyrcis and Amyntas had been distinguished by Phillis and Galatea; and thus had the secrets of two hearts revealed beneath the shades of evening, and amid the recesses of the woods. Such, madame, is what the Dryad related to me; she who knows all that takes place in the hollows of oaks and grassy dells; she who knows the loves of the birds, and all they wish to convey by their songs; she who understands, in fact, the language of the wind among the branches, the humming of the insect with its gold and emerald wings in the corolla of the wild-flowers; it was she who related the particulars to me, and I have repeated them."

"And now you have finished, Monsieur de Saint-Aignan, have you not?" said Madame, with a smile that made the king tremble.

"Quite finished," replied Saint-Aignan, "and but too happy if I have been able to amuse your royal highness for a few moments."

"Moments which have been too brief," replied the princess, "for you have related most admirably all you know; but, my dear Monsieur de Saint-Aignan, you have been unfortunate enough to obtain your information from one Dryad only, I believe?"

"Yes, Madame, only from one, I confess."

"The fact was, that you passed by a little Naiad, who pretended to know nothing at all, and yet knew a great deal more than your Dryad, my dear comte."

"A Naiad!" repeated several voices, who began to suspect that the story had a continuation.

"Of course close beside the oak you are speaking of,

which, if I am not mistaken, is called the royal oak—is it not so, Monsieur de Saint-Aignan?"

Saint-Aignan and the king exchanged glances.

"Yes, Madame," the former replied.

"Well, close beside the oak there is a pretty little spring, which runs murmuringly over the pebbles between banks of forget-me-nots and daffodils."

"I believe you are correct," said the king, with some uneasiness, and listening with some anxiety to his sister-in-law's narrative.

"Oh! there is one, I can assure you," said Madame; "and the proof of it is, that the Naiad who resides in that little stream, stopped me as I was about to cross."

"Ah?" said Saint-Aignan.

"Yes, indeed," continued the princess, "and she did so in order to communicate to me many particulars Monsieur de Saint-Aignan has omitted in his recital."

"Pray relate them yourself," said Monsieur, "you can relate stories in such a charming manner." The princess bowed at the conjugal compliment paid her.

"I do not possess the poetical powers of the comte, nor his ability to bring to light the smallest details."

"You will not be listened to with less interest on that account," said the king, who already perceived that something hostile was intended in his sister-in-law's story.

"I speak, too," continued Madame, "in the name of that poor little Naiad, who is indeed the most charming creature I ever met. Moreover, she laughed so heartily while she was telling me her story, that, in pursuance of that medical axiom that laughter is the finest physic in the world, I ask permission to laugh a little myself when I recollect her words."

The king and Saint-Aignan, who noticed spreading over many of the faces present a distant and prophetic ripple of the laughter Madame announced, finished by looking at each other, as if asking themselves whether there was not some little conspiracy concealed beneath these words. But Madame was determined to turn the knife in the wound over and over again; she therefore resumed with an air of the most perfect candor, in other words, with the most dangerous of all her airs :—"Well, then, I passed that way," she said, "and as I found beneath my steps many fresh flowers newly blown, no doubt Phyllis, Amaryllis, Galatea, and all your shepherdesses had passed the same way before me."

The king bit his lips, for the recital was becoming more and more threatening. "My little Naiad," continued Madame, "was cooing out her quaint song in the bed of the rivulet; as I perceived that she accosted me by touching the hem of my dress, I could not think of receiving her advances ungraciously, and more particularly so, since, after all, a divinity even though she be of a second grade, is always of greater importance than a mortal, though a princess. I thereupon accosted the Naiad, and bursting into laughter, this is what she said to me:

" 'Fancy, princess . . . .' You understand, sire, it is the Naiad who is speaking ? "

The king bowed assentingly; and Madame continued ; —" 'Fancy, princess, the banks of my little stream have just witnessed a most amusing scene. Two shepherds, full of curiosity, even indiscreetly so, have allowed themselves to be mystified in a most amusing manner by three nymphs, or three shepherdesses,—I beg your pardon, but I do not now remember if it was nymphs or shepherdesses she said; but it does not much matter, so we will continue."

The king, at this opening, colored visibly, and Saint-Aignan, completely losing countenance, began to open his eyes in the greatest possible anxiety.

" ' The two shepherds,' pursued my nymph, still laughing, ' followed in the wake of the three young ladies,'—
no, I mean, of the three nymphs ; forgive me, I ought
to say, of the three shepherdesses.   It is not always wise
to do that, for it may be awkward for those who are
followed.   I appeal to all the ladies present, and not one
of them, I am sure, will contradict me."

The king, who was much disturbed by what he suspected was about to follow, signified his assent by a gesture.

" ' But,' continued the Naiad, ' the shepherdesses had
noticed Tyrcis and Amyntas gliding into the wood, and, by
the light of the moon, they had recognized them through
the grove of trees.' Ah, you laugh ! " interrupted
Madame ; " wait, wait, you are not yet at the end."

The king turned pale ; Saint-Aignan wiped his forehead, now dewed with perspiration.   Among the groups
of ladies present could be heard smothered laughter and
stealthy whispers.

" ' The shepherdesses, I was saying, noticing how indiscreet the two shepherds were, proceeded to sit down
at the foot of the royal oak ; and, when they perceived
that their over-curious listeners were sufficiently near, so
that not a syllable of what they might say could be lost,
they addressed towards them very innocently, in the most
artless manner in the world indeed, a passionate declara-
tion, which from the vanity natural to all men, and even
to the most sentimental of shepherds, seemed to the two
listeners as sweet as honey.' "

The king, at these words, which the assembly was unable to hear without laughing, could not restrain a flash
of anger darting from his eyes.   As for Saint-Aignan, he
let his head fall upon his breast, and concealed, under a
silly laugh, the extreme annoyance he felt.

" Oh," said the king, drawing himself up to his full

height, " upon my word, that is a most amusing jest
certainly ; but, really and truly, are you sure you quite
understood the language of the Naiads ? "

" The comte, sire, pretends to have perfectly understood that of the Dryads," retorted Madame icily.

" No doubt," said the king ; " but you know the comte
has the weakness to aspire to become a member of the
Academy, so that, with this object in view, he has learnt
all sorts of things of which very happily you are ignorant ;
and it might possibly happen that the language of the
Nymph of the Waters might be among the number of
things you have not studied."

" Of course, sire," replied Madame, " for facts of that
nature one does not altogether rely upon one's self alone ; a
woman's ear is not infallible, so says Saint Augustine ; and
I, therefore, wished to satisfy myself by other opinions
besides my own, and as my Naiad, who, in her character
of a goddess, is polyglot,—is not that the expression,
M. de Saint-Aignan ? "

" I believe so," said the latter, quite out of countenance.

" Well," continued the princess, " as my Naiad, who, in
her character of a goddess, had, at first, spoken to me in
English, I feared, as you suggest, that I might have
misunderstood her, and I requested Mesdemoiselles de
Montalais, de Tonnay-Charente and de La Vallière, to
come to me, begging my Naiad to repeat to me in the
French language the recital she had already communicated
to me in English."

" And did she do so ? " inquired the king.

" Oh, she is the most polite divinity it is possible to
imagine ! Yes, sire, she did so ; so that no doubt whatever remains on the subject. Is it not so, young ladies ? "
said the princess, turning towards the left of her army ;
" did not the Naiad say precisely what I have related, and
have I, in any one particular, exceeded the truth, Phyllis ?

I beg your pardon, I mean Mademoiselle Aure de Montalais?"

"Precisely as you have stated, Madame," articulated Mademoiselle de Montalais, very distinctly.

"Is it true, Mademoiselle de Tonnay-Charente?"

"The perfect truth," replied Athenaïs, in a voice quite as firm, but yet not so distinct."

"And you, La Vallière?" asked Madame.

The poor girl felt the king's ardent look fixed upon her, —she dared not deny—she dared not tell a falsehood; she merely bowed her head; and everybody took it for a token of assent. Her head, however, was not raised again, chilled as she was by a coldness more bitter than that of death. This triple testimony overwhelmed the king. As for Saint-Aignan, he did not even attempt to dissemble his despair, and, hardly knowing what he said, he stammered out, "An excellent jest! admirably played!"

"A just punishment for curiosity," said the king, in a hoarse voice. "Oh! who would think, after the chastisement that Tyrcis and Amyntas had suffered, of endeavoring to surprise what is passing in the heart of shepherdesses? Assuredly I shall not, for one; and, you, gentlemen?"

"Nor I! nor I!" repeated, in a chorus, the group of courtiers.

Madame was filled with triumph at the king's annoyance; and was full of delight, thinking that her story had been, or was to be, the termination of the whole affair. As for Monsieur, who had laughed at the two stories without comprehending anything about them, he turned towards De Guiche, and said to him, "Well, comte, you say nothing; can you not find something to say? Do you pity M. Tyrcis and M. Amyntas, for instance?"

"I pity them with all my soul," replied De Guiche; "for, in very truth, love is so sweet a fancy, that to lose

it, fancy though it may be, is to lose more than life itself,
If, therefore, these two shepherds thought themselves
beloved,—if they were happy in that idea, and if instead
of that happiness, they meet not only that empty void
which resembles death, but jeers and jests at love itself
which is worse than a thousand deaths,—in that case, I
say that Tyrcis and Amyntas are the two most unhappy
men I know."

"And you are right, too, Monsieur de Guiche," said the
king; "for, in fact, the injury in question is a very hard
return for a little harmless curiosity."

"That is as much as to say, then, that the story of my
Naiad has displeased the king?" asked Madame, innocently.

"Nay, madame, undeceive yourself," said Louis, taking
the princess by the hand; "your Naiad, on the contrary,
has pleased me, and the more so, because she was so
truthful, and because her tale, I ought to add, is confirmed by the testimony of unimpeachable witnesses."

These words fell upon La Vallière, accompanied by a
look that no one, from Socrates to Montaigne, could have
exactly defined. The look and the king's remark succeeded
in overpowering the unhappy girl, who, with her head
upon Montalais's shoulder, seemed to have fainted away.
The king rose, without remarking this circumstance, of
which no one, moreover, took any notice, and, contrary to
his usual custom, for generally he remained late in Madame's apartments, he took his leave, and retired to his
own side of the palace. Saint-Aignan followed him, leaving the rooms in as much despair as he had entered them
with delight. Mademoiselle de Tonnay-Charente, less
sensitive than La Vallière, was not much frightened, and
did not faint. However, it may be that the last look of
Saint-Aignan had hardly been so majestic as the king's.

CHAPTER XXIII.

ROYAL PSYCHOLOGY.

THE king returned to his apartments with hurried steps. The reason he walked as fast as he did was probably to avoid tottering in his gait. He seemed to leave behind him as he went along a trace of a mysterious sorrow. That gayety of manner, which every one had remarked in him on his arrival, and which they had been delighted to perceive, had not perhaps been understood in its true sense : but his stormy departure, his disordered countenance, all knew, or at least thought they could tell the reason of. Madame's levity of manner, her somewhat bitter jests,—bitter for persons of a sensitive disposition, and particularly for one of the king's character ; the great resemblance which naturally existed between the king and an ordinary mortal, were among the reasons assigned for the precipitate and unexpected departure of his majesty. Madame, keen-sighted enough in other respects, did not, however, at first see anything extraordinary in it. It was quite sufficient for her to have inflicted some slight wound upon the vanity or self-esteem of one who, so soon forgetting the engagements he had contracted, seemed to have undertaken to disdain, without cause, the noblest and highest prize in France. It was not an unimportant matter for Madame, in the present position of affairs, to let the king perceive the difference which existed between the bestowal of his affections on one in a high station, and the running after each passing fancy, like a youth fresh from the provinces. With regard to those

higher placed affections, recognizing their dignity and
their illimitable influence, acknowledging in them a certain etiquette and display—a monarch, not only did not
act in a manner derogatory to his high position, but found
even repose, security, mystery, and general respect there-
in. On the contrary, in the debasement of a common or
humble attachment, he would encounter, even among his
meanest subjects, carping and sarcastic remarks; he
would forfeit his character of infallibility and inviola-
bility. Having descended to the region of petty human
miseries, he would be subjected to paltry contentions. In
one word, to convert the royal divinity into a mere mortal
by striking at his heart, or rather even at his face, like
the meanest of his subjects, was to inflict a terrible blow
upon the pride of that generous nature. Louis was more
easily captivated by vanity than affection. Madame had
wisely calculated her vengeance, and, it has been seen,
also, in what manner she carried it out. Let it not be
supposed, however, that Madame possessed such terrible
passions as the heroines of the middle ages, or that she
regarded things from a pessimistic point of view ; on the
contrary, Madame, young, amiable, of cultivated intellect,
coquettish, loving in her nature, but rather from fancy,
or imagination, or ambition, than from her heart—Madame, we say, on the contrary, inaugurated that epoch of
light and fleeting amusements, which distinguished the
hundred and twenty years that intervened between the
middle of the seventeenth century, and the last quarter
of the eighteenth. Madame saw, therefore, or rather
fancied she saw, things under their true aspect; she
knew that the king, her august brother-in-law, had been
the first to ridicule the humble La Vallière, and that, in
accordance with his usual custom, it was hardly probable
he would ever love the person who had excited his laughter, even had it been only for a moment. Moreover, was

not her vanity ever present, that evil influence which
plays so important a part in that comedy of dramatic incidents called the life of a woman? Did not her vanity tell
her, aloud, in a subdued voice, in a whisper, in every
variety of tone, that she could not, in reality, she a princess, young, beautiful and rich, be compared to the poor
La Vallière, as youthful as herself it is true, but far less
pretty certainly, and utterly without money, protectors
or position? And surprise need not be excited with
respect to Madame; for it is known that the greatest
characters are those who flatter themselves the most in
the comparisons they draw between themselves and
others, between others and themselves. It may perhaps
be asked what was Madame's motive for an attack so
skillfully conceived and executed. Why was there such
a display of forces, if it were not seriously her intention
to dislodge the king from a heart that had never been
occupied before, in which he seemed disposed to take
refuge? Was there any necessity, then, for Madame to
attach so great an importance to La Vallière, if she did
not fear her? Yet, Madame did not fear La Vallière in
that direction in which an historian, who knows everything, sees into the future, or rather, the past. Madame
was neither a prophetess nor a sibyl; nor could she, any
more than another, read what was written in that terrible
and fatal book of the future, which records in its most
secret pages the most serious events. No, Madame
desired simply to punish the king for having availed himself of secret means altogether feminine in their nature;
she wished to prove to him that if he made use of offensive weapons of that nature, she, a woman of ready wit
and high descent, would assuredly discover in the arsenal
of her imagination defensive weapons proof even against
the thrusts of a monarch. Moreover, she wished him to
learn that, in a war of that description, kings are held of

no account, or, at all events, that kings who fight on their
own behalf, like ordinary individuals, may witness the
fall of their crown in the first encounter ; and that, in
fact, if he had expected to be adored by all the ladies of
the court from the very first, from a confident reliance on
his mere appearance, it was a pretension which was most
preposterous and insulting even, for certain persons who
filled a higher position than others, and that a lesson
taught in season to this royal personage, who assumed
too high and haughty a carriage, would be rendering him
a great service.   Such, indeed, were Madame's reflections
with respect to the king.   The sequel itself was not
thought of.   And in this manner, it will be seen that she
had exercised her influence over the minds of her maids
of honor, and with all its accompanying details, had arranged the comedy which had just been acted.   The king
was completely bewildered by it ; for the first time since
he had escaped from the trammels of M. de Mazarin, he
found himself treated as a man.   Similar severity from
any of his subjects would have been at once resisted by
him.   Strength comes with battle.   But to match one's
self with women, to be attacked by them, to have been
imposed upon by mere girls from the country, who had
come from Blois expressly for that purpose ; it was the
depth of dishonor for a young sovereign full of the pride
his personal advantages and his royal power inspired him
with.   There was nothing he could do—neither reproaches, nor exile—nor could he even show the annoyance
he felt.   To manifest vexation would have been to admit
that he had been touched, like Hamlet, by a sword
from which the button had been removed—the sword
of ridicule.   To show animosity against women—humilia-
tion ! especially when the women in question have laughter on their side, as a means of vengeance.   If, instead of
leaving all the responsibility of the affair to these women,

one of the courtiers had had anything to do with the intrigue, how delightedly would Louis have seized the opportunity of turning the Bastile to personal account. But there, again, the king's anger paused, checked by reason. To be the master of armies, of prisons, of an almost divine authority, and to exert such majesty and might in the service of a petty grudge, would be unworthy not only of a monarch, but even of a man. It was necessary, therefore, simply to swallow the affront in silence, and to wear his usual gentleness and graciousness of expression. It was essential to treat Madame as a friend. As a friend!— Well, and why not? Either Madame had been the instigator of the affair, or the affair itself had found her passive. If she had been the instigator of it, it certainly was a bold measure on her part, but at all events, it was but natural in her. Who was it that had sought her in the earliest moments of her married life to whisper words of love in her ear? Who was it that had dared to calculate the possibility of committing a crime against the marriage vow—a crime, too, still more deplorable on account of the relationship between them? Who was it that, shielded behind his royal authority, had said to this young creature: be not afraid, love but the king of France, who is above all, and a movement of whose sceptered hand will protect you against all attacks, even from your own remorse? And she had listened to and obeyed the royal voice, had been influenced by his ensnaring tones; and when, morally speaking, she had sacrificed her honor in listening to him, she saw herself repaid for her sacrifice by an infidelity the more humiliating, since it was occasioned by a woman far beneath her in the world.

Had Madame, therefore, been the instigator of the revenge, she would have been right. If, on the contrary, she had remained passive in the whole affair, what grounds

had the king to be angry with her on that account?
Was it for her to restrain, or rather could she restrain,
the chattering of a few country girls? and was it for her,
by an excess of zeal that might have been misinterpreted,
to check, at the risk of increasing it, the impertinence of
their conduct? All these various reasonings were like so
many actual stings to the king's pride; but when he had
carefully, in his own mind, gone over all the various
causes of complaint, Louis was surprised, upon due reflection—in other words, after the wound has been dressed
—to find that there were other causes of suffering, secret
unendurable, and unrevealed. There was one circumstance he dared not confess, even to himself; namely, that
the acute pain from which he was suffering had its seat
in his heart. The fact is, he had permitted his heart to
be gratified by La Vallière's innocent confusion. He had
dreamed of a pure affection—of an affection for Louis the
man, and not the sovereign—of an affection free from all
self-interest; and his heart, simpler and more youthful than
he had imagined it to be, had to meet that other heart that
had revealed itself to him by its aspirations. The commonest thing in the complicated history of love, is the
double inoculation of love to which any two hearts are
subjected; the one loves nearly always before the other,
in the same way that the latter finishes nearly always by
loving after the other. In this way, the electric current
is established, in proportion to the intensity of the passion which is first kindled. The more Mademoiselle de
la Vallière showed her affection, the more the king's
affection had increased. And it was precisely that which
had annoyed his majesty. For it was now fairly demon-
strated to him, that no sympathetic current had been the
means of hurrying his heart away in its course, because
there had been no confession of love in the case—because
the confession was, in fact, an insult towards the man and

towards the sovereign; and finally, because—and the word, too, burnt like a hot iron—because, in fact, it was nothing but a mystification after all. This girl, therefore, who, in strictness, could not lay claim to beauty, or birth, or great intelligence—who had been selected by Madame herself, on account of her unpretending position, had not only aroused the king's regard, but had, moreover, treated him with disdain—he, the king, a man who, like an eastern potentate, had but to bestow a glance, to indicate with his finger, to throw his handkerchief. And, since the previous evening, his mind had been so absorbed with this girl that he could think and dream of nothing else. Since the previous evening his imagination had been occupied clothing her image with charms to which she could not lay claim. In very truth, he whom such vast interests summoned, and whom so many women smiled upon invitingly, had, since the previous evening, consecrated every moment of his time, every throb of his heart, to this sole dream. It was, indeed, either too much, or not sufficient. The indignation of the king, making him forget everything, and among others, that Saint-Aignan was present, was poured out in the most violent imprecations. True it is, that Saint-Aignan had taken refuge in a corner of the room; and from his corner, regarded the tempest passing over. His own personal disappointment seemed contemptible, in comparison with the anger of the king. He compared with his own petty vanity the prodigious pride of offended majesty; and, being well read in the hearts of kings in general, and in those of powerful kings in particular, he began to ask himself if this weight of anger, as yet held in suspense, would not soon terminate by falling upon his own head, for the very reason that others were guilty, and he innocent. In point of fact, the king, all at once, did arrest his hurried pace; and, fixing

a look full of anger upon Saint-Aignan, suddenly cried
out : "And you, Saint-Aignan?"

Saint-Aignan made a sign which was intended to
signify. "Well, sire?"

"Yes; you have been as silly as myself, I think."

"Sire," stammered out Saint-Aignan.

"You permitted us to be deceived by this shameless
trick."

"Sire," said Saint-Aignan, whose agitation was such
as to make him tremble in every limb, "let me entreat
your majesty not to exasperate yourself. Women, you
know, are characters full of imperfections, created for the
misfortune of mankind: to expect anything good from
them is to require them to perform impossibilities."

The king, who had the greatest consideration for himself, and who had begun to acquire over his emotions that
command which he preserved over them all his life, perceived that he was doing an outrage to his own dignity
in displaying so much animosity about so trifling an
object. "No," he said, hastily; "you are mistaken,
Saint-Aignan; I am not angry; I can only wonder that
we should have been turned into ridicule so cleverly and
with such audacity by these young girls. I am particularly surprised that, although we might have informed
ourselves accurately on the subject, we were silly enough
to leave the matter for our own hearts to decide."

"The heart, sire, is an organ which requires positively
to be reduced to its material functions, but which, for the
sake of humanity's peace of mind, should be deprived
of all its metaphysical inclinations. For my own part, I
confess, that when I saw that your majesty's heart was so
taken up by this little——"

"My heart taken up! I! My mind might, perhaps,
have been so; but as for my heart, it was——" Louis
again perceived that, in order to fill one gulf, he was

about to dig another. "Besides," he added, "I have no fault to find with the girl. I was quite aware that she was in love with some one else."

"The Vicomte de Bragelonne. I informed your majesty of the circumstance."

"You did so; but you were not the first who told me. The Comte de la Fère had solicited from me Mademoiselle de la Vallière's hand for his son. And, on his return from England, the marriage shall be celebrated, since they love each other."

"I recognize your majesty's great generosity of disposition in that act."

"So, Saint-Aignan, we will cease to occupy ourselves with these matters any longer," said Louis.

"Yes, we will digest the affront, sire," replied the courtier, with resignation.

"Besides, it will be an easy matter to do so," said the king, checking a sigh.

"And, by way of a beginning, I will set about the composition of an epigram upon all three of them. I will call it 'The Naiad and Dryad,' which will please Madame."

"Do so, Saint-Aignan, do so," said the king, indifferently. "You shall read me your verses; they will amuse me. Ah! it does not signify, Saint-Aignan," added the king, like a man breathing with difficulty, "the blow requires more than human strength to support in a dignified manner." As the king thus spoke, assuming an air of the most angelic patience, one of the servants in attendance knocked gently at the door. Saint-Aignan drew aside, out of respect.

"Come in," said the king. The servant partially opened the door. "What is it?" inquired Louis.

The servant held out a letter of a triangular shape. "For your majesty," he said.

"From whom?"

"I do not know. One of the officers on duty gave it me."

The valet, in obedience to a gesture of the king, handed him the letter. The king advanced towards the candles, opened the note, read the signature, and uttered a loud cry. Saint-Aignan was sufficiently respectful not to look on ; but, without looking on, he saw and heard all, ran towards the king, who with a gesture dismissed the servant.

"Oh, Heavens!" said the king, as he read the note.

"Is your majesty unwell?" inquired Saint-Aignan, stretching forward his arms.

"No, no, Saint-Aignan—read!" and he handed him the note.

Saint-Aignan's eyes fell upon the signature. "La Vallière!" he exclaimed. "Oh, sire!"

"Read, *read!*"

And Saint-Aignan read :—

"Forgive my importunity, sire ; and forgive, also, the absence of the formalities which may be wanting in this letter. A note seems to be more speedy and more urgent than a dispatch. I venture, therefore, to address this note to your majesty. I have retired to my own room, overcome with grief and fatigue, sire ; and I implore your majesty to grant me the favor of an audience which will enable me to confess the *truth* to my sovereign.

"LOUISE DE LA VALLIERE."

"Well?" asked the king, taking the letter from Saint-Aignan's hands, who was completely bewildered by what he had just read.

"Well!" repeated Saint-Aignan.

"What do you think of it?"

"I hardly know."

"Still, what is your opinion?"

"Sire, the young lady must have heard the muttering of the thunder, and has got frightened."

"Frightened at what?" asked Louis with dignity.

"Why, your majesty has a thousand reasons to be angry with the author or authors of so hazardous a joke; and, if your majesty's memory were to be awakened in a disagreeable sense, it would be a perpetual menace hanging over the head of this imprudent girl."

"Saint-Aignan, I do not think as you do."

"Your majesty doubtless sees more clearly than myself."

"Well! I see affliction and restraint in these lines; more particularly since I recall some of the details of the scene which took place this evening in Madame's apartments——" The king suddenly stopped, leaving his meaning unexpressed.

"In fact," resumed Saint-Aignan, "your majesty will grant an audience; nothing is clearer than that."

"I will do better, Saint-Aignan."

"What is that, sire?"

"Put on your cloak."

"But, sire——"

"You know the suite of rooms where Madame's maids of honor are lodged?"

"Certainly."

"You know some means of obtaining an entrance there."

"As far as that is concerned, I do not."

"At all events, you must be acquainted with some one there."

"Really, your majesty is the source of every good idea."

"You do know some one, then. Who is it?"

"I know a certain gentleman, who is on very good terms with a certain young lady there."

"One of the maids of honor?"

"Yes, sire."

"With Mademoiselle de Tonnay-Charente, I suppose?" said the king, laughing.

"Fortunately, no, sire; with Montalais."

"What is his name?"

"Malicorne."

"And you can depend on him?"

"I believe so, sire. He ought to have a key of some sort in his possession; and if he should happen to have one, as I have done him a service, why, he will let us have it."

"Nothing could be better. Let us set off, immediately."

The king threw his cloak over Saint-Aignan's shoulders, asked him for his, and both went out into the vestibule.

CHAPTER XXIV.

SOMETHING THAT NEITHER NAIAD NOR DRYAD FORESAW.

SAINT-AIGNAN stopped at the foot of the staircase leading to the *entresol*, where the maids of honor were lodged, and to the first floor, where Madame's apartments were situated. Then, by means of one of the servants who was passing, he sent to apprise Malicorne, who was still with Monsieur. After having waited ten minutes, Malicorne arrived, full of self-importance. The king drew back towards the darkest part of the vestibule. Saint-Aignan, on the contrary, advanced to meet him, but at the first words, indicating his wish, Malicorne drew back abruptly.

"Oh! oh!" he said, "you want me to introduce you into the rooms of the maids of honor?"

"Yes."

"You know very well that I cannot do anything of the kind, without being made acquainted with your object."

"Unfortunately, my dear Monsieur Malicorne, it is quite impossible for me to give you any explanation; you must therefore confide in me as in a friend who got you out of a great difficulty yesterday, and who now begs you to draw him out of one to-day."

"Yet I told you, monsieur, what my object was; which was, not to sleep out in the open air, and any man might express the same wish, whilst you, however, admit nothing."

"Believe me, my dear Monsieur Malicorne," Saint-Aignan persisted, "that if I were permitted to explain myself, I would do so."

"In that case, my dear monsieur, it is impossible for me to allow you to enter Mademoiselle de Montalais's apartment."

"Why so?"

"You know why, better than any one else, since you caught me on the wall paying my addresses to Mademoiselle de Montalais; it would, therefore, be an excess of kindness on my part, you will admit, since I am paying my attentions to her, to open the door of her room to you."

"But who told you it was on her account I asked you for the key?"

"For whom, then?"

"She does not lodge there alone, I suppose?"

"No, certainly; for Mademoiselle de la Vallière shares her rooms with her; but, really, you have nothing more to do with Mademoiselle de la Vallière than with Mademoiselle de Montalais, and there are only two men to whom I would give this key; to M. de Bragelonne, if he

begged me to give it to him, and to the king, if he commanded me."

"In that case, give me the key, monsieur: I order you
to do so," said the king, advancing from the obscurity,
and partially opening his cloak. "Mademoiselle de Montalais will step down to talk with you, while we go upstairs to Mademoiselle de la Vallière, for, in fact, it is she
only whom we desire to see."

"The king!" exclaimed Malicorne, bowing to the very
ground.

"Yes, the king," said Louis, smiling: "the king, who
is as pleased with your resistance as with your capitula-
tion. Rise, monsieur, and render us the service we request of you."

"I obey, your majesty," said Malicorne, leading the way
up the staircase.

"Get Mademoiselle de Montalais to come down," said
the king, "and do not breathe a word to her of my visit."

Malicorne bowed in token of obedience, and proceeded
up the staircase. But the king, after a hasty reflection,
followed him, and that, too, with such rapidity, that,
although Malicorne was already more than half-way up
the staircase, the king reached the room at the same moment. He then observed, by the door which remained
half-opened behind Malicorne, La Vallière, sitting in an
arm-chair with her head thrown back, and in the opposite
corner Montalais, who, in her dressing-gown, was standing before a looking-glass, engaged in arranging her hair,
and parleying the while with Malicorne. The king hurriedly opened the door and entered the room. Montalais
called out at the noise made by the opening of the door,
and, recognizing the king, made her escape. La Vallière
rose from her seat, like a dead person galvanized, and then
fell back in her arm-chair. The king advanced slowly
towards her.

" You wished for an audience, I believe," he said coldly.
" I am ready to hear you.   Speak."

Saint-Aignan, faithful to his character of being deaf,
blind, and dumb, had stationed himself in a corner of the
door, upon a stool which by chance he found there.
Concealed by the tapestry which covered the door way,
and leaning his back against the wall, he could thus listen
without being seen ; resigning himself to the post of
a good watch-dog, who patiently waits and watches without ever getting in his master's way.

La Vallière, terror-stricken at the king's irritated
aspect, rose a second time, and assuming a posture full
of humility and entreaty, murmured, "Forgive me,
sire."

" What need is there for my forgiveness ? " asked
Louis.

" Sire, I have been guilty of a great fault ; nay, more
than a great fault, a great crime."

" You ? "

" Sire, I have offended your majesty."

" Not the slightest degree in the world," replied Louis
XIV.

" I implore you, sire, not to maintain towards me that
terrible seriousness of manner which reveals your majesty's just anger.   I feel I have offended you, sire; but
I wish to explain to you how it was that I have not
offended you of my own accord."

" In the first place," said the king, " in what way can
you possibly have offended me ?   I cannot perceive how.
Surely not on account of a young girl's harmless and very
innocent jest ?   You turned the credulity of a young man
into ridicule—it was very natural to do so : any other
woman in your place would have done the same."

" Oh ! your majesty overwhelms me by your remark."

" Why so ? "

"Because, if I had been the author of the jest, it would not have been innocent."

"Well, is that all you had to say to me in soliciting an audience?" said the king, as though about to turn away.

Thereupon La Vallière, in an abrupt and broken voice, her eyes dried up by the fire of her tears, made a step towards the king, and said, "Did your majesty hear everything?"

"Everything, what?"

"Everything I said beneath the royal oak."

"I did not lose a syllable."

"And now, after your majesty really heard all, are you able to think I abused your credulity?"

"Credulity; yes, indeed you have selected the very word."

"And your majesty did not suppose that a poor girl like myself might possibly be compelled to submit to the will of others?"

"Forgive me," returned the king; "but I shall never be able to understand that she, who of her own free will could express herself so unreservedly beneath the royal oak, would allow herself to be influenced to such an extent by the direction of others."

"But the threat held out against me, sire."

"Threat! who threatened you—who dared to threaten you?"

"Those who have the right to do so, sire."

"I do not recognize any one as possessing the right to threaten the humblest of my subjects."

"Forgive me, sire, but near your majesty even, there are persons sufficiently high in position to have, or to believe that they possess, the right of injuring a young girl, without fortune, and possessing only her reputation."

"In what way injure her?"

"In depriving her of her reputation, by disgracefully expelling her from the court."

"Oh! Mademoiselle de la Vallière," said the king bitterly, "I prefer those persons who exculpate themselves without incriminating others."

"Sire!"

"Yes; and I confess that I greatly regret to perceive, that an easy justification, as your own would have been, is now complicated in my presence by a tissue of reproaches and imputations against others."

"And which you do not believe?" exclaimed La Vallière. The king remained silent.

"Nay, but tell me!" repeated La Vallière, vehemently.

"I regret to confess it," repeated the king, bowing coldly.

The young girl uttered a deep groan, striking her hands together in despair. "You do not believe me, then," she said to the king, who still remained silent, while poor La Vallière's features became visibly changed at his continued silence. "Therefore, you believe," she said, "that I prearranged this ridiculous, this infamous plot, of trifling, in so shameless a manner, with your majesty."

"Nay," said the king, "it was neither ridiculous nor infamous; it was not even a plot; merely a jest, more or less amusing, and nothing more."

"Oh!" murmured the young girl, "the king does not, and will not believe me, then?"

"No, indeed, I will not believe you," said the king. "Besides, in point of fact, what can be more natural? The king, you argue, follows me, listens to me, watches me; the king wishes perhaps to amuse himself at my expense, I will amuse myself at his, and as the king is very tender-hearted, I will take his heart by storm."

La Vallière hid her face in her hands, as she stifled

her sobs.   The king continued pitilessly ; he was revenging himself upon the poor victim before him for all he had himself suffered.

"Let us invent, then, this story of my loving him and preferring him to others.   The king is so simple and so conceited that he will believe me; and then we can go and tell others how credulous the king is, and can enjoy a laugh at his expense."

"Oh!" exclaimed La Vallière, ' you think that you believe that !—it is frightful."

"And," pursued the king, "that is not all ; if this self-conceited prince take our jest seriously, if he should be imprudent enough to exhibit before others anything like delight at it, well, in that case, the king will be humiliated before the whole court ; and what a delightful story it will be, too, for him to whom I am really attached, in fact part of my dowry for my husband, to have the adventure to relate of the monarch who was so amusingly deceived by a young girl."

"Sire!" exclaimed La Vallière, her mind bewildered, almost wandering, indeed, " not another word, I implore you ; do you not see that you are killing me ?"

"A jest, nothing but a jest," murmured the king, who however, began to be somewhat affected.

La Vallière fell upon her knees, and that so violently, that the sound could be heard upon the hard floor.   " Sire," she said, "I prefer shame to disloyalty."

"What do you mean?" inquired the king, without moving a step to raise the young girl from her knees.

"Sire, when I shall have sacrificed my honor and my reason both to you, you will perhaps believe in my loyalty. The tale which was related to you in Madame's apartments, and by Madame herself, is utterly false; and that which I said beneath the great oak——"

"Well!"

"That only is the truth."

"What!" exclaimed the king.

"Sire," exclaimed La Vallière, hurried away by the violence of her emotions, "were I to die of shame on the very spot where my knees are fixed, I would repeat it until my latest breath; I said that I loved you, and it is true; I do love you."

"You!"

"I have loved you, sire, from the very first day I ever saw you; from the moment when at Blois, where I was pining away my existence, your royal looks, full of light and life, were first bent upon me. I love you still, sire; it is a crime of high treason, I know, that a poor girl like myself should love her sovereign, and should presume to tell him so. Punish me for my audacity, despise me for my shameless immodesty; but do not ever say, do not ever think, that I have jested with or deceived you. I belong to a family whose loyalty has been proved, sire, and I, too, love my king."

Suddenly her strength, voice and respiration ceased, and she fell forward, like the flower Virgil alludes to, which the scythe of the reaper severed in the midst of the grass. The king, at these words, at this vehement entreaty, no longer retained either ill-will or doubt in his mind: his whole heart seemed to expand at the glowing breath of an affection which proclaimed itself in such noble and courageous language. When, therefore, he heard the passionate confession of that young girl's affection, his strength seemed to fail him, and he hid his face in his hands. But when he felt La Vallière's hands clinging to his own, when their warm pressure fired his blood, he bent forward, and passing his arm round La Vallière's waist, he raised her from the ground and pressed her against his heart. But she, her drooping head fallen forward on her bosom, seemed to have ceased to live. The king, terrified, called out for Saint-Aignan. Saint-Aignan, who had carried his discretion so far as to remain without stirring in his corner, pretending to wipe away a tear, ran forward at the king's summons. He then assisted Louis to seat the young girl upon a couch, slapped her hands, sprinkled some Hungary water over her face, calling out all the while, "Come, come, it is all over; the king believes you, and forgives you. There, there now! take care, or you will agitate his majesty too much; his majesty is so sensitive, so tender-hearted. Now, really, Mademoiselle de la Vallière, you must pay attention, for the king is very pale."

The fact was, the king was visibly losing color. But La Vallière did not move.

"Do pray recover," continued Saint-Aignan. "I beg, I implore you; it is really time you should; think only of one thing, that if the king should become unwell, I should be obliged to summon his physician. What a state of things that would be! So do pray rouse yourself; make an effort, pray do, and do so at once, my dear."

It was difficult to display more persuasive eloquence than Saint-Aignan did, but something still more powerful, and of a more energetic nature than this eloquence, aroused La Vallière. The king, who was kneeling before her, covered the palms of her hands with those burning kisses which are to the hands what a kiss upon the lips is to the face. La Vallière's senses returned to her; she languidly opened her eyes, and with a dying look, murmured, "Oh! sire, has your majesty pardoned me, then?"

The king did not reply, for he was still too much overcome. Saint-Aignan thought it his duty again to retire, for he observed the passionate devotion which was displayed in the king's gaze. La Vallière rose.

" And now, sire, that I have justified myself, at least I trust so, in your majesty's eyes, grant me leave to retire into a convent. I shall bless your majesty all my life, and I shall die there thanking and loving Heaven for having granted me one hour of perfect happiness."

"No, no," replied the king, "you will live here blessing Heaven, on the contrary, but loving Louis, who will make your existence one of perfect felicity—Louis who loves you—Louis who swears it."

"Oh! sire, sire!"

And upon this doubt of La Vallière, the king's kisses became so warm that Saint-Aignan thought it his duty to retire behind the tapestry. These kisses, however, which she had not had the strength at first to resist, began to intimidate the young girl.

"Oh! sire," she exclaimed, "do not make me repent my loyalty, for this would show me that your majesty despises me still."

"Mademoiselle de la Vallière," said the king suddenly, drawing back with an air full of respect, "there is nothing in the world that I love and honor more than yourself, and nothing in my court, I call Heaven to witness, shall be so highly regarded as you shall be henceforward. I entreat your forgiveness for my transport; it arose from an excess of affection, but I can prove to you that I love you more than ever by respecting you as much as you can possibly desire or deserve." Then bending before her, and taking her by the hand, he said to her, "Will you honor me by accepting the kiss I press upon your hand?" And the king's lips were pressed respectfully and lightly upon the young girl's trembling hand. "Henceforth," added Louis, rising and bending his glance upon La Vallière, "henceforth you are under my safeguard. Do not speak to any one of the injury I have done you, forgive others that which they may have attempted. For the future, you shall be so far above all those, that, far from inspiring you with fear, they shall be even beneath your pity." And he bowed as reverently as though he were leaving a place of worship. Then calling to Saint-Aignan, who approached with great humility, he said, " I hope, comte, that Mademoiselle de la Vallière will kindly confer a little of her friendship upon you, in return for that which I have vowed to her eternally."

Saint-Aignan bent his knee before La Vallière, saying, " How happy, indeed, would such an honor make me! "

" I will send your companion back to you," said the king. " Farewell! or, rather, adieu till we meet again ; do not forget me in your prayers, I entreat."

" Oh! " cried La Vallière, " be assured that you and Heaven are in my heart together."

These words of Louise elated the king, who, full of happiness, hurried Saint-Aignan down the stairs. Madame had not anticipated this *dénouement ;* and neither the Naiad nor the Dryad had breathed a word about it.

CHAPTER XXV.

THE NEW GENERAL OF THE JESUITS.

WHILE La Vallière and the king were mingling, in their first confession of love, all the bitterness of the past, the happiness of the present, and hopes of the future, Fouquet had retired to the apartments which had been assigned to him in the château, and was conversing with Aramis precisely upon the very subjects which the king at that moment was forgetting.

" Now tell me," began Fouquet, after having installed his guest in an arm-chair and seated himself by his side, " tell me, Monsieur d'Herblay, what is our position with regard to the Belle-Isle affair, and whether you have received any news about it."

" Everything is going on in that direction as we wish," replied Aramis; "the expenses have been paid, and nothing has transpired of our designs."

" But what about the soldiers the king wished to send there ? "

" I have received news this morning that they arrived there fifteen days ago."

" And how have they been treated ? "

" In the best manner possible."

" What has become of the former garrison? "

"The soldiers were landed at Sarzeau, and then transferred immediately to Quimper."

" And the new garrison ? "

" Belongs to us from this very moment."

" Are you sure of what you say, my dear Monsieur de Vannes ? "

" Quite sure, and, moreover, you will see by and by how matters have turned out."

" Still you are very well aware that, of all the garrison towns, Belle-Isle is precisely the very worst."

" I know it, and have acted accordingly; no space to move about, no gayety, no cheerful society, no gambling permitted: well, it is a great pity," added Aramis, with one of those smiles so peculiar to him, "to see how much young people at the present day seek amusement, and how much, consequently, they incline to the man who procures and pays for their favorite pastimes."

" But if they amuse themselves at Belle-Isle ? "

" If they amuse themselves through the king's means, they will attach themselves to the king; but if they get bored to death through the king's means, and amuse themselves through M. Fouquet, they will attach themselves to M. Fouquet."

"And you informed my intendant, of course?—so that immediately on their arrival—— "

"By no means; they were left alone a whole week, to weary themselves at their ease; but, at the end of the week, they cried out, saying that former officers amused themselves much better. Whereupon they were told that the old officers had been able to make a friend of M. Fouquet, and that M. Fouquet, knowing them to be friends of his, had from that moment done all he possibly could to prevent their getting wearied or bored upon his estates. Upon this they began to reflect. Immediately afterwards, however, the intendant added, that without anticipating M. Fouquet's orders, he knew his master sufficiently well to be aware that he took an interest in every gentleman in the king's service, and that, although he did not know the new-comers, he would do as much for them as he had done for the others."

"Excellent! and I trust that the promises were followed up; I desire, as you know, that no promise should ever be made in my name without being kept."

"Without a moment's loss of time, our two privateers, and your own horses, were placed at the disposal of the officers; the keys of the principal mansion were handed over to them, so that they made up hunting-parties, and walking-excursions with such ladies as are to be found in Belle-Isle; and such other as they are enabled to enlist from the neighborhood, who have no fear of sea-sickness."

"And there is a fair sprinkling to be met with at Sarzeau and Vannes, I believe, your eminence?"

"Yes; in fact all along the coast," said Aramis, quietly.

"And now, how about the soldiers?"

"Everything precisely the same, in a relative degree, you understand; the soldiers have plenty of wine, excellent provisions, and good pay."

"Very good; so that——"

"So that this garrison can be depended upon, and it is a better one than the last."

"Good."

"The result is, if Fortune favors us, so that the garrisons are changed in this manner, only every two months, that, at the end of every three years, the whole army will, in its turn, have been there; and, therefore, instead of having one regiment in our favor, we shall have fifty thousand men."

"Yes, yes; I knew perfectly well," said Fouquet, "that no friend could be more incomparable and invaluable than yourself, my dear Monsieur d'Herblay; but," he added, laughing, "all this time we are forgetting our friend, Du Vallon; what has become of him? During the three days I spent at Saint-Mandé, I confess I have forgotten him completely."

"I do not forget him, however," returned Aramis. "Porthos is at Saint-Mandé; his joints are kept well greased, the greatest care is being taken of him with regard to the food he eats, and the wines he drinks; I advise him to take daily airings in the small park, which you have kept for your own use, and he makes use of it accordingly. He begins to walk again, he exercises his muscular powers by bending down young elm trees, or making the old oaks fly into splinters, as Milo of Crotona used to do; and, as there are no lions in the park, it is not unlikely we shall find him alive. Porthos is a brave fellow."

"Yes, but in the mean time he will get bored to death."

"Oh no; he never does that."

"He will be asking questions?"

"He sees no one."

"At all events, he is looking or hoping for something or another."

"I have inspired in him a hope which we will realize some fine morning, and on that he subsists."

"What is it?"

"That of being presented to the king."

"Oh! in what character?"

"As the engineer of Belle-Isle, of course."

"Is it possible?"

"Quite true."

"Shall we not be obliged then, to send him back to Belle-Isle?"

"Most certainly; I am even thinking of sending him as soon as possible. Porthos is very fond of display; he is a man whose weaknesses D'Artagnan, Athos, and myself are alone acquainted with; he never commits himself in any way; he is dignity itself; to the officers there, he would seem like a Paladin of the time of the Crusades. He would make the whole staff drunk, without getting tipsy in the least himself, and every one will regard him with admiration and sympathy; if, therefore, it should happen that we have any orders requiring to be carried out, Porthos is an incarnation of the order itself, and whatever he chose to do others would find themselves obliged to submit to."

"Send him back then."

"That is what I intend to do; but only in a few days; for I must not omit to tell you one thing."

"What is it?"

"I begin to mistrust D'Artagnan. He is not at Fontainebleau, as you may have noticed, and D'Artagnan is never absent, or apparently idle, without some object in view. And now that my own affairs are settled, I am going to try and ascertain what the affairs are in which D'Artagnan is engaged."

"Your own affairs are settled, you say?"

"Yes."

" You are very fortunate in that case, then, and I should like to be able to say the same."

" I hope you do not make yourself uneasy."

" Hum ! "

" Nothing could be better than the king's reception of you."

" True."

" And Colbert leaves you in peace."

"Nearly so."

" In that case," said Aramis, with that connection of ideas which marked him, " in that case, then, we can bestow a thought upon the young girl I was speaking to you about yesterday."

" Whom do you mean ? "

" What, have you forgotten already ? I mean La Vallière."

" Ah! of course, of course."

"Do you object then to try and make a conquest of her ? "

" In one respect only, my heart is engaged in another direction ; and I positively do not care about the girl in the least."

" Oh! oh ! " said Aramis, " your heart is engaged, you say. The deuce ! we must take care of that."

" Why ? "

" Because it is terrible to have the heart occupied, when others, beside yourself, have so much need of the head."

" You are right. So you see, at your first summons, I left everything. But to return to this girl. What good do you see in my troubling myself about her ? "

"This.—The king, it is said, has taken a fancy to her ; at least, so it is supposed."

"But you, who know everything, know very differently."

" I know that the king is greatly and suddenly changed,

that the day before yesterday he was crazy over Madame; that a few days ago, Monsieur complained of it, even to the queen-mother; and that some conjugal misunderstandings and maternal scoldings were the consequence."

"How do you know all that?"

"I do know it; at all events, since these misunderstandings and scoldings, the king has not addressed a word, has not paid the slightest attention, to her royal highness."

"Well, what next?"

"Since then, he has been taken up with Mademoiselle de la Vallière. Now, Mademoiselle de la Vallière is one of Madame's maids of honor. You happen to know, I suppose, what is called a *chaperon* in matters of love. Well, then, Mademoiselle de la Vallière is Madame's *chaperon*. It is for you to take advantage of this state of things. You have no occasion for me to tell you that. But, at all events, wounded vanity will render the conquest an easier one; the girl will get hold of the king, and Madame's secret, and you can scarcely predict what a man of intelligence can do with a secret."

"But how to get at her?"

"Nay, you, of all men, to ask me such a question!" said Aramis.

"Very true. I shall not have any time to take any notice of her."

"She is poor and unassuming, you will create a position for her, and whether she tames the king as his lady confessor, or his sweetheart, you will have enlisted a new and valuable ally."

"Very good," said Fouquet. "What is to be done, then, with regard to this girl?"

"Whenever you have taken a fancy to any lady, Monsieur Fouquet, what course have you generally pursued."

"I have written to her, protesting my devotion to her.

I have added, how happy I should be to render her any service in my power, and have signed 'Fouquet,' at the end of the letter."

"And has any one offered any resistance?"

"One person only," replied Fouquet. "But, four days ago, she yielded, as the others had done."

"Will you take the trouble to write?" said Aramis, holding a pen towards him, which Fouquet took, saying:

"I will write at your dictation. My head is so taken up in another direction, that I should not be able to write a couple of lines."

"Very well," said Aramis, "write."

And he dictated, as follows: "Mademoiselle—I have seen you—and you will not be surprised to learn, I think you very beautiful. But, for want of the position you merit at court, your presence there is a waste of time. The devotion of a man of honor, should ambition of any kind inspire you, might possibly serve as a means of display for your talents and beauty. I place my devotion at your feet; but, as an affection, however reserved and unpresuming it may be, might possibly, compromise the object of its worship, it would ill become a person of your merit running the risk of being compromised, without her future being assured. If you would deign to accept, and reply to my affection, my affection shall prove its gratitude to you in making you free and independent forever."

Having finished writing, Fouquet looked at Aramis.

"Sign it," said the latter.

"Is it absolutely necessary?"

"Your signature at the foot of that letter is worth a million; you forget that." Fouquet signed.

"Now, by whom do you intend to send this letter?" asked Aramis.

"By an excellent servant of mine."

" Can you rely on him ? "

" He is a man who has been with me all my life."

" Very well.   Besides, in this case, we are not playing for very heavy stakes."

" How so ?   For if what you say be true of the accommodating disposition of this girl for the king and Madame, the king will give her all the money she can ask for."

" The king has money, then ? " asked Aramis.

" I suppose so, for he has not asked me for any more."

" Be easy, he will ask for some, soon."

" Nay, more than that, I had thought he would have spoken to me about the *fête* at Vaux, but he never said a word about it."

" He will be sure to do so, though."

" You must think the king's disposition a very cruel one, Monsieur d'Herblay ?"

" It is not he who is so."

" He is young, and therefore his disposition is a kind one."

" He is young, and either he is weak, or his passions are strong ; and Monsieur Colbert holds his weaknesses and his passions in his villainous grasp."

" You admit that you fear him ? "

" I do not deny it."

" In that case I am lost."

" Why so ? "

" My only influence with the king has been through the money I commanded, and now I am a ruined man."

" Not so."

" What do you mean by ' not so ? '   Do you know my affairs better than myself ? "

" That is not unlikely."

" If he were to request this *fête* to be given ? "

" You would give it, of course."

" But where is the money to come from ? "

" Have you ever been in want of any ? "

" Oh ! if you only knew at what a cost I procured the last supply ? "

" The next shall cost you nothing."

" But who will give it me ? "

" I will."

" What, give me six millions ? "

" Ten, if necessary."

" Upon my word, D'Herblay," said Fouquet, " your confidence alarms me more than the king's displeasure. Who can you possibly be after all ? "

" You know me well enough, I should think."

" Of course ; but what is it you are aiming at ? "

" I wish to see upon the throne of France a king devoted to Monsieur Fouquet, and I wish Monsieur Fouquet to be devoted to me."

" Oh ! " exclaimed Fouquet, pressing his hand,—" as for being devoted to you, I am yours, entirely ; but believe me, my dear D'Herblay, you are deceiving yourself."

" In what respect ? "

" The king will never become devoted to me."

" I do not remember to have said that King Louis would ever become devoted to you."

" Why, on the contrary, you have this moment said so."

" I did not say *the* king ; I said *a* king."

" Is it not all the same ? "

" No, on the contrary, it is altogether different."

" I do not understand you."

" You will do so, shortly, then ; suppose, for instance, the king in question were to be a very different person to Louis XIV."

" Another person."

" Yes, who is indebted for everything to you."

" Impossible."

" His very throne, even."

"You are mad, D'Herblay. There is no man living besides Louis XIV. who can sit on the throne of France. I know of none, not one."

" *But* I know one."

" Unless it be Monsieur," said Fouquet, looking at Aramis uneasily ; " yet Monsieur——"

" It is *not* Monsieur."

" But how can it be, that a prince not of the royal line, that a prince without any right——"

" My king, or rather your king will be everything that is necessary, be assured of that."

" Be careful, Monsieur d'Herblay, you make my blood run cold, and my head swim."

Aramis smiled. " There is but little occasion for that," he replied.

" Again, I repeat, you terrify me," said Fouquet. Aramis smiled.

" You laugh," said Fouquet.

" The day will come when you will laugh too; only at the present moment I must laugh alone."

" But explain yourself."

" When the proper time comes, I will explain all. Fear nothing. Have faith in me, and doubt nothing."

" The fact is, I cannot but doubt, because I do not see clearly, or even at all."

" That is because of your blindness ; but a day will come when you will be enlightened."

" Oh ! " said Fouquet, " how willingly would I believe."

" You, without belief ! you, who, through my means, have ten times crossed the abyss yawning at your feet, and in which, had you been alone, you would have been irretrievably swallowed; you, without belief ; you, who from procureur-general attained the rank of intendant, from the rank of intendant that of the first minister of the crown, and who from the rank of first minister will pass to that of mayor of the palace. But no," he said, with the same unaltered smile, "no, no, you cannot see, and consequently cannot believe—what I tell you." And Aramis rose to withdraw.

" One word more," said Fouquet, "you have never yet spoken to me in this manner, you have never yet shown yourself so confident, I should rather say so daring."

" Because, it is necessary in order to speak confidently to have the lips unfettered."

" And that is now your case?"

"Yes."

" Since a very short time, then?"

"Since yesterday, only."

" Oh! Monsieur d'Herblay, take care, your confidence is becoming audacity."

" One can well be audacious when one is powerful."

" And you are powerful?"

" I have already offered you ten millions; I repeat the offer."

Fouquet rose, profoundly agitated.

" Come," he said, "come; you spoke of overthrowing kings and replacing them by others. If, indeed, I am not really out of my senses, is or is not that what you said just now?"

" You are by no means out of your senses, for it is perfectly true I did say all that just now."

" And why did you say so?"

" Because it is easy to speak in this manner of thrones being cast down, and kings being raised up, when one is, one's self, far above all kings and thrones, of this world at least."

" Your power is infinite, then?" cried Fouquet.

" I have told you so already, and I repeat it," replied Aramis, with glistening eyes and trembling lips.

Fouquet threw himself back in his chair, and buried his

face in his hands. Aramis looked at him for a moment, as the angel of human destinies might have looked upon a simple mortal.

"Adieu," he said to him, "sleep undisturbed, and send your letter to La Vallière. To morrow we shall see each other again."

"Yes, to-morrow," said Fouquet, shaking his hand like a man returning to his senses. "But where shall we see each other?"

"At the king's promenade, if you like."

"Agreed." And they separated.

CHAPTER XXVI.

THE STORM.

THE dawn of the following day was dark and gloomy, and as every one knew that the promenade was down in the royal programme, every one's gaze, as his eyes were opened, was directed towards the sky. Just above the tops of the trees a thick, suffocating vapor seemed to remain suspended, with barely sufficient power to rise thirty feet above the ground under the influence of the sun's rays, which was scarcely visible as a faint spot of lesser darkness through the veil of heavy mist. No dew had fallen in the morning; the turf was dried up for want of moisture, the flowers withered. The birds sang less inspiringly than usual upon the boughs, which remained motionless as the limbs of corpses. The strange confused and animated murmurs, which seemed born and to exist in virtue of the sun, that respiration of nature which is unceasingly heard amidst all other sounds, could not be heard now, and never had the silence been so profound.

The king had noticed the cheerless aspect of the heavens

as he approached the window immediately on rising. But as all the necessary directions had been given respecting the promenade, and every preparation had been made accordingly, and as, which was far more imperious than anything else, Louis relied upon this promenade to satisfy the cravings of his imagination, and we will even already say, the clamorous desires of his heart—the king unhesitatingly decided that the appearance of the heavens had nothing whatever to do with the matter; that the promenade was arranged, and that, whatever the state of the weather, the promenade should take place. Besides, there are certain terrestrial sovereigns who seem to have accorded them privileged existences, and there are certain times when it might almost be supposed that the expressed wish of an earthly monarch has its influence over the Divine will. It was Virgil who observed of Augustus : *Nocte placet tota redeunt spectacula mâne.* Louis attended mass as usual, but it was evident that his attention was somewhat distracted from the presence of the Creator by the remembrance of the creature. His mind was occupied during the service in reckoning more than once the number of minutes, then of seconds, which separated him from the blissful moment when the promenade would begin, that is to say, the moment when Madame would set out with her maids of honor. Besides, as a matter of course, everybody at the château was ignorant of the interview which had taken place between La Vallière and the king. Montalais, perhaps, with her usual chattering propensity, might have been disposed to talk about it ; but Montalais on this occasion was held in check by Malicorne, who had securely fastened on her pretty lips the golden padlock of mutual interest. As for Louis XIV., his happiness was so extreme that he had forgiven Madame, or nearly so, her little piece of malice of the previous evening. In fact, he had occasion to congratulate himself rather than to complain of

it. Had it not been for her ill-natured action, he would not
have received the letter from La Vallière; had it not been
for the letter, he would have had no interview; and had
it not been for the interview he would have remained
undecided. His heart was filled with too much happiness
for any ill-feeling to remain in it, at that moment at least.
Instead, therefore, of knitting his brows into a frown
when he perceived his sister-in-law, Louis resolved to
receive her in a more friendly and gracious manner than
usual. But on one condition only, that she would be
ready to set out early. Such was the nature of Louis's
thoughts during mass; which made him during the ceremony, forget matters, which, in his character of Most
Christian King and of the eldest son of the Church, ought
to have occupied his attention. He returned to the
château, and as the promenade was fixed for midday, and
it was at present just ten o'clock, he set to work des-
perately with Colbert and Lyonne. But even while he
worked Louis went from the table to the window, inasmuch as the window looked out upon Madame's pavilion :
he could see M. Fouquet in the courtyard, to whom the
courtiers, since the favor shown towards him on the previous evening, paid greater attention than ever. The
king, instinctively, on noticing Fouquet, turned towards
Colbert, who was smiling, and seemed full of benevolence
and delight, a state of feeling which had arisen from the
very moment one of his secretaries had entered and handed
him a pocket-book, which he had put unopened into his
pocket. But, as there was always something sinister at
the bottom of any delight expressed by Colbert, Louis
preferred, of the smiles of the two men, that of Fouquet.
He beckoned to the superintendent to come up, and then
turning towards Lyonne and Colbert he said :—" Finish
this matter, place it on my desk, and I will read it at my
leisure." And he left the room. At the sign the king

had made to him, Fouquet had hastened up the staircase, while Aramis, who was with the superintendent, quietly retired among the group of courtiers, and disappeared without having been even observed by the king. The king and Fouquet met at the top of the staircase.

"Sire," said Fouquet, remarking the gracious manner in which Louis was about to receive him, "Your majesty has overwhelmed me with kindness during the last few days. It is not a youthful monarch, but a being of a higher order, who reigns over France, one whom pleasure, happiness, and love acknowledge as their master." The king colored. The compliment, although flattering, was not the less somewhat pointed. Louis conducted Fouquet to a small room that divided his study from his sleeping apartment.

"Do you know why I summoned you?" said the king as he seated himself upon the edge of the window, so as not to lose anything that might be passing in the gardens which fronted the opposite entrance to Madame's pavilion.

"No, sire," replied Fouquet, "but I am sure for something agreeable, if I am to judge from your majesty's gracious smile."

"You are mistaken then."

"I, sire?"

"For I summoned you, on the contrary, to pick a quarrel with you."

"With me, sire?"

"Yes : and that a serious one."

"Your majesty alarms me—and yet I was most confident in your justice and goodness."

"Do you know I am told, Monsieur Fouquet, that you are preparing a grand *fête* at Vaux."

Fouquet smiled, as a sick man would do at the first shiver of a fever which has left him but returns again.

"And that you have not invited me!" continued the king.

"Sire," replied Fouquet, "I have not even thought of the *fête* you speak of, and it was only yesterday evening that one of my *friends*," Fouquet laid a stress upon the word, "was kind enough to make me think of it."

"Yet I saw you yesterday evening, Monsieur Fouquet, and you said nothing to me about it."

"How dared I hope that your majesty would so greatly descend from your own exalted station as to honor my dwelling with your royal presence?"

"Excuse me, Monsieur Fouquet, you did not speak to me about your *fête*."

"I did not allude to the *fête* to your majesty, I repeat, in the first place, because nothing had been decided with regard to it, and, secondly, because I feared a refusal."

"And something made you fear a refusal, Monsieur Fouquet? You see I am determined to push you hard."

"The profound wish I had that your majesty should accept my invitation——"

"Well, Monsieur Fouquet, nothing is easier, I perceive, than our coming to an understanding. Your wish is to invite me to your *fête*, my own is to be present at it; invite me and I will go."

"Is it possible that your majesty will deign to accept?" murmured the superintendent.

"Why, really, monsieur," said the king, laughing; "I think I do more than accept; I rather fancy I am inviting myself."

"Your majesty overwhelms me with honor and delight," exclaimed Fouquet, "but I shall be obliged to repeat what M. Vieuville said to your ancestor, Henry the Fourth, *Domine, non sum dignus*."

"To which I reply, Monsieur Fouquet, that if you give a *fête*, I will go, whether I am invited or not."

"I thank your majesty deeply," said Fouquet, as he

raised his head beneath this favor, which he was convinced would be his ruin.

"But how could your majesty have been informed of it ?"

"By public rumor, Monsieur Fouquet, which says such wonderful things of yourself and of the marvels of your house. Would you become proud, Monsieur Fouquet, if the king were to be jealous of you? "

"I should be the happiest man in the world, sire, since the very day on which your majesty were to be jealous of Vaux, I should possess something worthy of being offered to you."

"Very well, Monsieur Fouquet, prepare your *fête*, and open the doors of your house as wide as possible."

"It is for your majesty to fix the day."

"This day month, then."

"Has your majesty any further commands ?"

"Nothing, Monsieur Fouquet, except from the present moment until then to have you near me as much as possible."

"I have the honor to form one of your majesty's party for the promenade."

"Very good; indeed I am now setting out; for there are the ladies, I see, who are going to start."

With this remark, the king, with all the eagerness, not only of a young man, but of a young man in love, withdrew from the window, in order to take his gloves and cane, which his valet held ready for him. The neighing of the horses and the crunching of the wheels on the gravel of the courtyard could be distinctly heard. The king descended the stairs, and at the moment he appeared upon the flight of steps, every one stopped. The king walked straight up to the young queen. The queen-mother, who was still suffering more than ever from the illness with which she was afflicted, did not wish to go out. Maria

Theresa accompanied Madame in her carriage, and asked
the king in what direction he wished the promenade to drive.
The king, who had just seen La Vallière, still pale from
the events of the previous evening, get into a carriage with
three of her companions, told the queen that he had no
preference, and wherever she would like to go, there would
he be with her. The queen then desired that the outriders should proceed in the direction of Apremont. The
outriders set off accordingly before the others. The king
rode on horseback, and for a few minutes accompanied
the carriage of the queen and Madame. The weather had
cleared up a little, but a kind of veil of dust, like a thick
gauze, was still spread over the surface of the heavens,
and the sun made every atom glisten within the circuit
of its rays. The heat was stifling; but, as the king did
not seem to pay any attention to the appearance of the
heavens, no one made himself uneasy about it, and the
promenade, in obedience to the orders given by the queen,
took its course in the direction of Apremont. The courtiers who followed were in the very highest spirits; it was
evident that every one tried to forget, and to make others
forget, the bitter discussions of the previous evening.
Madame, particularly, was delightful. In fact, seeing the
king at the door of her carriage, as she did not suppose
he would be there for the queen's sake, she hoped that her
prince had returned to her. Hardly, however, had they
proceeded a quarter of a mile on the road, when the king,
with a gracious smile, saluted them and drew up his horse,
leaving the queen's carriage to pass on, then that of the
principal ladies of honor, and then all the others in suc-
cession, who, seeing the king stop, wished in their turn to
stop too; but the king made a sign to them to continue
their progress. When La Vallière's carriage passed, the
king approached it, saluted the ladies who were inside,
and was preparing to accompany the carriage containing

the maids of honor, in the same way he had followed that in which Madame was, when suddenly the whole file of carriages stopped. It was probable that Madame, uneasy at the king having left her, had just given directions for the performance of this maneuver, the direction in which the promenade was to take place having been left to her. The king having sent to inquire what her object was in stopping the cavalcade was informed in reply, that she wished to walk. She most likely hoped that the king, who was following the carriages of the maids of honor on horseback, would not venture to follow the maids of honor themselves on foot. They had arrived in the middle of the forest.

The promenade, in fact, was not ill-timed, especially for those who were dreamers or lovers. From the little open space where the halt had taken place, three beautiful long walks, shady and undulating, stretched out before them. These walks were covered with moss or with leaves that formed a carpet from the loom of nature; and each walk had its horizon in the distance, consisting of about a handbreadth of sky, apparent through the interlacing of the branches of the trees. At the end of almost every walk, evidently in great tribulation and uneasiness, the startled deer were seen hurrying to and fro, first stopping for a moment in the middle of the path, and then raising their heads they fled with the speed of an arrow or bounded into the depths of the forest, where they disappeared from view; now and then a rabbit, of philosophical mien, might be noticed quietly sitting upright, rubbing his muzzle with his fore paws, and looking about inquiringly, as though wondering whether all these people, who were approaching in his direction, and who had just disturbed him in his meditations and his meal were not followed by their dogs, or had not their guns under their arms. All alighted from their carriages as soon as they observed that the queen was doing so. Maria Theresa took the arm of one of her

ladies of honor, and, with a side glance towards the king,
who did not perceive that he was in the slightest degree
the object of the queen's attention, entered the forest by
the first path before her. Two of the outriders preceded
her majesty with long poles, which they used for the purpose of putting the branches of the trees aside, or remov-
ing the bushes that might impede her progress. As soon
as Madame alighted, she found the Comte de Guiche at
her side, who bowed and placed himself at her disposal.
Monsieur, delighted with his bath of the two previous days,
had announced his preference for the river, and, having
given De Guiche leave of absence, remained at the château
with the Chevalier de Lorraine and Manicamp. He was
not in the slightest degree jealous. He had been looked
for to no purpose among those present; but as Monsieur
was a man who thought a great deal of himself, and
usually added very little to the general pleasure, his absence was rather a subject of satisfaction than regret.
Every one had followed the example which the queen and
Madame had set, doing just as they pleased, according as
chance or fancy influenced them. The king, we have already observed, remained near La Vallière, and, throwing
himself off his horse at the moment the door of her carriage
was opened, he offered her his hand to alight. Montalais
and Tonnay-Charente immediately drew back and kept
at a distance; the former from calculated, the latter from
natural, motives. There was this difference, however,
between the two, that the one had withdrawn from a wish
to please the king, the other for a very opposite reason.
During the last half-hour the weather also had undergone
a change; the veil which had been spread over the sky, as
if driven by a blast of heated air had become massed together in the western part of the heavens; and afterwards,
as if driven by a current of air from the opposite direction,
was now advancing slowly and heavily towards them.

The approach of the storm could be felt, but as the king did not perceive it, no one thought it proper to do so. The promenade was therefore continued ; some of the company, with minds ill at ease on the subject, raised their eyes from time to time towards the sky ; others, even more timid still, walked about without wandering too far from the carriages, where they relied upon taking shelter in case the storm burst. The greater number of these, however, observing that the king fearlessly entered the wood with La Vallière, followed his majesty. The king noticing this, took La Vallière's hand, and led her to a lateral forest-alley ; where no one this time ventured to follow him.

CHAPTER XXVII.

THE SHOWER OF RAIN.

AT this moment, and in the same direction, too, that the king and La Vallière had taken, except that they were in the wood itself instead of following the path, two men were walking together, utterly indifferent to the appearance of the heavens. Their heads were bent down in the manner of people occupied with matters of great moment. They had not observed either De Guiche or Madame, the king or La Vallière. Suddenly something fell through the air like a colossal sheet of flame, followed by a loud but distant rumbling noise.

" Ah ! " said one of them, raising his head, " here comes the storm. Let us reach our carriages, my dear D'Herblay."

Aramis looked inquiringly at the heavens. " There is no occasion to hurry yet," he said ; and then resuming the conversation where it had doubtless been interrupted, he said, " You were observing that the letter we wrote last evening must by this time have reached its destination ? "

" I was saying that she certainly has it."

" Whom did you send it by ? "

" By my own servant, as I have already told you."

" Did he bring back an answer ? "

" I have not seen him since; the young girl was probably in attendance on Madame, or was in her own room dressing, and he may have had to wait. Our time for leaving arrived, and we set off, of course; I cannot, therefore, know what is going on yonder."

" Did you see the king before leaving ? "

" Yes."

" How did he seem ? "

" Nothing could have passed off better, or worse; according as he be sincere or hypocritical."

" And the *fête* ? "

" Will take place in a month."

" He invited himself, you say ? "

" With a pertinacity in which I detected Colbert's influence. But has not last night removed your illusions ? "

" What illusions ? "

" With respect to the assistance you may be able to give me under these circumstances."

" No; I have passed the night writing, and all my orders are given."

" Do not conceal it from yourself, D'Herblay, but the *fête* will cost some millions."

" I will supply six; do you on your side get two or three."

" You are a wonderful man, my dear D'Herblay."

Aramis smiled.

" But," inquired Fouquet, with some remaining uneasiness, " how is it that while now you are squandering millions in this manner, a few days ago you did not pay the fifty thousand francs to Baisemeaux out of your own pocket?"

" Because a few days ago I was as poor as Job."

"And to-day?"

" To-day I am wealthier than the king himself."

" Very well," said Fouquet; " I understand men pretty well; I know you are incapable of forfeiting your word; I do not wish to wrest your secret from you, and so let us talk no more about it."

At this moment a dull, heavy rumbling was heard, which suddenly developed into a violent clap of thunder.

"Oh, oh!" said Fouquet, "I was quite right in what I said."

" Come," said Aramis, " let us rejoin the carriages."

" We shall not have time," said Fouquet, "for here comes the rain."

In fact, as he spoke, and as if the heavens were opened, a shower of large drops of rain was suddenly heard pattering on the leaves about them.

" We shall have time," said Aramis, " to reach the carriage before the foliage becomes saturated."

" It will be better," said Fouquet, " to take shelter somewhere—in a grotto, for instance."

" Yes, but where are we to find a grotto?" inquired Aramis.

" I know one," said Fouquet, smiling, " not ten paces from here." Then looking round him, he added: " Yes, we are quite right."

" You are very fortunate to have so good a memory," said Aramis, smiling in his turn, " but are you not afraid that your coachman, finding we do not return, will suppose we have taken another road back, and that he will not follow the carriages belonging to the court?"

" Oh, there is no fear of that," said Fouquet; "whenever I place my coachman and my carriage in any partic-

ular spot, nothing but an express order from the king
could stir them; and more than that, too, it seems that
we are not the only ones who have come so far, for I hear
footsteps and the sound of voices."

As he spoke, Fouquet turned round, and opened with
his cane a mass of foliage which hid the path from his
view. Aramis's glance as well as his own plunged at the
same moment through the aperture he had made.

"A woman," said Aramis.

"And a man," said Fouquet.

"It is La Vallière and the king," they both exclaimed
together.

"Oh, oh!" said Aramis, "is his majesty aware of your
cavern as well? I should not be astonished if he were,
for he seems to be on very good terms with the dryads of
Fontainebleau."

"Never mind," said Fouquet; "let us get there. If he
is not aware of it, we shall see what he will do if he should
know it, as it has two entrances, so that whilst he enters
by one, we can leave by the other."

"Is it far?" asked Aramis, "for the rain is beginning to
penetrate."

"We are there now," said Fouquet, as he pushed aside
a few branches, and an excavation in the solid rock could
be observed, hitherto concealed by heaths, ivy, and a thick
covert of small shrubs.

Fouquet led the way, followed by Aramis; but as the
latter entered the grotto, he turned round saying: "Yes,
they are entering the wood; and, see, they are bending
their steps this way."

"Very well; let us make room for them," said Fouquet,
smiling and pulling Aramis by his cloak; "but I do not
think the king knows of my grotto."

"Yes," said Aramis, "they are looking about them, but
it is only for a thicker tree."

Aramis was not mistaken, the king's looks were directed upward, and not around him. He held La Vallière's arm within his own, and held her hand in his. La Vallière's feet began to slip on the damp grass. Louis again looked round him with greater attention than before, and perceiving an enormous oak with wide-spreading branches, he hurriedly drew La Vallière beneath its protecting shelter. The poor girl looked round her on all sides, and seemed half afraid, half desirous of being followed. The king made her lean her back against the trunk of the tree, whose vast circumference, protected by the thickness of the foliage, was as dry as if at that moment the rain had not been falling in torrents. He himself remained standing before her with his head uncovered. After a few minutes, however, some drops of rain penetrated through the branches of the tree and fell on the king's forehead, who did not pay any attention to them.

" Oh, sire ! " murmured La Vallière, pushing the king's hat toward him. But the king simply bowed, and determinedly refused to cover his head.

" Now or never is the time to offer your place," said Fouquet in Aramis's ear.

" Now or never is the time to listen, and not lose a syllable of what they may have to say to each other," replied Aramis in Fouquet's ear.

In fact they both remained perfectly silent, and the king's voice reached them where they were.

" Believe me," said the king, " I perceive, or rather I can imagine your uneasiness ; believe me I sincerely regret having isolated you from the rest of the company, and brought you, also, to a spot where you will be inconvenienced by the rain. You are wet already, and perhaps cold too ? "

" No, sire."

" And yet you tremble ? "

"I am afraid, sire, that my absence may be misinterpreted; at a moment, too, when all the others are reunited."

"I would not hesitate to propose returning to the carriages, Mademoiselle de la Vallière, but pray look and listen, and tell me if it be possible to attempt to make the slightest progress at present?"

In fact the thunder was still rolling, and the rain continued to fall in torrents.

"Besides," continued the king, "no possible interpretation can be made which would be to your discredit. Are you not with the King of France; in other words, with the first gentleman of the kingdom?"

"Certainly, sire," replied La Vallière, "and it is a very distinguished honor for me; it is not, therefore, for myself that I fear any interpretations that may be made."

"For whom, then?"

"For you, sire."

"For *me*?" said the king, smiling, "I do not understand you."

"Has your majesty already forgotten what took place yesterday evening in her royal highness's apartments?"

"Oh! forget that, I beg, or allow me to remember it for no other purpose than to thank you once more for your letter, and——"

"Sire," interrupted La Vallière, "the rain is falling, and your majesty's head is uncovered."

"I entreat you not to think of anything but yourself."

"Oh! I," said La Vallière, smiling, "I am a country girl, accustomed to roaming through the meadows of the Loire and the gardens of Blois, whatever the weather may be. And, as for my clothes," she added, looking at her simple muslin dress, "your majesty sees there is but little room for injury."

"Indeed, I have already noticed, more than once, that

you owed nearly everything to yourself and nothing to your toilette. Your freedom from coquetry is one of your greatest charms in my eyes."

" Sire, do not make me out better than I am, and say merely, ' You cannot possibly be a coquette.' "

" Why so?"

" Because," said La Vallière, smiling, " I am not rich."

" You admit, then," said the king, quickly, " that you have a love for beautiful things."

" Sire, I only regard those things as beautiful which are within my reach. Everything which is too highly placed for me——"

" You are indifferent to?"

" Is foreign to me, as being prohibited."

" And I," said the king, " do not find that you are at my court on the footing you should be. The services of your family have not been sufficiently brought under my notice. The advancement of your family was cruelly neglected by my uncle."

"On the contrary, sire. His royal highness, the Duke of Orleans, was always exceedingly kind towards M. de Saint-Remy, my father-in-law. The services rendered were humble, and, properly speaking, our services have been adequately recognized. It is not every one who is happy enough to find opportunities of serving his sovereign with distinction. I have no doubt at all, that, if ever opportunities had been met with, my family's actions would have been as lofty as their loyalty was firm : but that happiness was never ours."

" In that case, Mademoiselle de la Vallière, it belongs to kings to repair the want of opportunity, and most delightedly do I undertake to repair, in your instance, and with the least possible delay, the wrongs of fortune towards you."

"Nay, sire," cried La Vallière, eagerly; "leave things, I beg, as they now are."

"Is it possible! you refuse what I ought, and what I wish to do for you?"

"All I desired has been granted me, when the honor was conferred upon me of forming one of Madame's household."

"But if you refuse for yourself, at least accept for your family."

"Your generous intentions, sire, bewilder me and make me apprehensive, for, in doing for my family what your kindness urges you to do, your majesty will raise up enemies for us, and enemies for yourself, too. Leave me in the ranks of middle-life, sire; of all the feelings and sentiments I experience, leave me to enjoy the pleasing instinct of disinterestedness."

"The sentiments you express," said the king, "are indeed admirable."

"Quite true," murmured Aramis in Fouquet's ear, "and he cannot be accustomed to them."

"But," replied Fouquet, "suppose she were to make a similar reply to my letter."

"True!" said Aramis, "let us not anticipate, but wait the conclusion."

"And then, dear Monsieur d'Herblay," added the superintendent, hardly able to appreciate the sentiments which La Vallière had just expressed, "it is very often sound calculation to seem disinterested with monarchs."

"Exactly what I was thinking this very minute," said Aramis. "Let us listen."

The king approached nearer to La Vallière, and as the rain dripped more and more through the foliage of the oak, he held his hat over the head of the young girl, who raised her beautiful blue eyes towards the royal hat which sheltered her, and shook her head, sighing deeply as she did so.

"What melancholy thought," said the king, "can possibly reach your heart when I place mine as a rampart
before it?"

"I will tell you, sire. I had already once before broached
this question, which is so difficult for a young girl of my
age to discuss, but your majesty imposed silence on me.
Your majesty belongs not to yourself alone: you are married; and every sentiment which would separate your
majesty from the queen, in leading you to take notice of
me, will be a source of the profoundest sorrow for the
queen." The king endeavored to interrupt the young girl,
but she continued with a suppliant gesture. "The Queen
Maria, with an attachment which can be well understood,
follows with her eyes every step of your majesty which
separates you from her. Happy enough in having had
her fate united to your own, she weepingly implores
Heaven to preserve you to her, and is jealous of the
faintest throb of your heart bestowed elsewhere." The
king again seemed anxious to speak, but again did La
Vallière venture to prevent him.—"Would it not, therefore, be a most blamable action," she continued, "if your
majesty, a witness of this anxious and disinterested affection, gave the queen any cause for jealousy? Forgive me,
sire, for the expressions I have used. I well know it is
impossible, or rather that it would be impossible, that the
greatest queen of the whole world could be jealous of a
poor girl like myself. But though a queen, she is still a
woman, and her heart, like that of the rest of her sex,
cannot close itself against the suspicions which such as
are evil disposed, insinuate. For heaven's sake, sire, think
no more of me: I am unworthy of your regard."

"Do you not know that in speaking as you have done
you change my esteem for you into the profoundest admiration?"

"Sire, you assume my words to be contrary to the

truth; you suppose me to be better than I really am, and attach a greater merit to me than God ever intended should be the case. Spare me, sire; for, did I not know that your majesty was the most generous man in your kingdom, I should believe you were jesting."

"You do not, I know, fear such a thing; I am quite sure of that," exclaimed Louis.

"I shall be obliged to believe it, if your majesty continues to hold such language towards me."

"I am most unhappy, then," said the king, in a tone of regret which was not assumed; "I am the unhappiest prince in the Christian world, since I am powerless to induce belief in my words, in one whom I love the best in the wide world, and who almost breaks my heart by refusing to credit my regard for her."

"Oh, sire!" said La Vallière, gently putting the king aside, who had approached nearer to her, "I think the storm has passed away now, and the rain has ceased." At the very moment, however, as the poor girl, fleeing as it were, from her own heart, which doubtless throbbed but too well in unison with the king's, uttered these words, the storm undertook to contradict her. A dead-white flash of lightning illumined the forest with a weird glare, and a peal of thunder, like a discharge of artillery, burst over their heads, as if the height of the oak that sheltered them had attracted the storm. The young girl could not repress a cry of terror. The king with one hand drew her towards his heart, and stretched the other above her head, as though to shield her from the lightning. A moment's silence ensued, as the group, delightful as everything young and loving is delightful, remained motionless, while Fouquet and Aramis contemplated it in attitudes as motionless as La Vallière and the king. "Oh, sire!" murmured La Vallière, "do you hear?" and her head fell upon his shoulder.

" Yes," said the king. " You see, the storm has not passed away."

" *It is a warning, sire.*" The king smiled. " Sire, it is the voice of Heaven in anger."

" Be it so," said the king. " I agree to accept that peal of thunder as a warning, and even as a menace, if, in five minutes from the present moment, it is renewed with equal violence ; but if not, permit me to think that the storm is a storm simply, and nothing more." And the king, at the same moment, raised his head, as if to interrogate the heavens. But, as if the remark had been heard and accepted, during the five minutes which elapsed after the burst of thunder which had alarmed them, no renewed peal was heard ; and, when the thunder was again heard, it was passing away as plainly as if, during those same five minutes, the storm, put to flight, had traversed the heavens with the wings of the wind. " Well, Louise," said the king, in a low tone of voice, " do you still threaten me with the anger of Heaven ? and, since you wished to regard the storm as a warning, do you still believe it bodes misfortune ? "

The young girl looked up, and saw that while they had been talking, the rain had penetrated the foliage above them, and was trickling down the king's face. " Oh, sire, sire ! " she exclaimed, in accents of eager apprehension, which greatly agitated the king. " Is it for me," she murmured, " that the king remains thus uncovered, and exposed to the rain ? What am I, then ? "

" You are, you perceive," said the king, " the divinity who dissipates the storm, and brings back fine weather." In fact, even as the king spoke, a ray of sunlight streamed through the forest, and caused the rain-drops which rested upon the leaves, or fell vertically among the openings in the branches of the trees, to glisten like diamonds.

" Sire," said La Vallière, almost overcome, but making

a powerful effort over herself, " think of the anxieties your majesty will have to submit to on my account. At this very moment, they are seeking you in every direction. The queen must be full of uneasiness ; and Madame—oh, Madame ! " the young girl exclaimed, with an expression almost resembling terror.

This name had a certain effect upon the king. He started, and disengaged himself from La Vallière, whom he had, till that moment, held pressed against his heart. He then advanced towards the path, in order to look round, and returned, somewhat thoughtfully, to La Vallière. " Madame, did you say ? " he remarked.

" Yes, Madame ; she, too, is jealous," said La Vallière, with a marked tone of voice; and her eyes, so timorous in their expression, and so modestly fugitive in their glance, for a moment, ventured to look inquiringly into the king's.

" Still," returned Louis, making an effort over himself, " it seems to me that Madame has no reason, no right to be jealous of me."

" Alas ! " murmured La Vallière.

" Are you, too," said the king, almost in a tone of reproach, " are you among those who think the sister has a right to be jealous of the brother ? "

" It is not for me, sire, to seek to penetrate your majesty's secrets."

" You *do* believe it, then ? " exclaimed the king.

" I believe Madame is jealous, sire," La Vallière replied, firmly.

" Is it possible," said the king, with some anxiety, " that you have perceived it, then, from her conduct towards you ? Have her manners in any way been such towards you, that you can attribute them to the jealousy you speak of ? "

" Not at all, sire ; I am of so little importance."

"Oh! if it were really the case——" exclaimed Louis, violently.

"Sire," interrupted the young girl, "it has ceased raining; some one is coming, I think." And, forgetful of all etiquette, she had seized the king by the arm.

"Well," replied the king, "let them come. Who is there who would venture to think I had done wrong in remaining alone with Mademoiselle de la Vallière?"

"For pity's sake, sire! they will think it strange to see you wet through, in this manner, and that you should have run such risk for me."

"I have simply done my duty as a gentleman," said Louis; "and woe to him who may fail in his, in criticising his sovereign's conduct." In fact, at this moment, a few eager and curious faces were seen in the walk, as if engaged in a search. Catching glimpses at last of the king and La Vallière, they seemed to have found what they were seeking. They were some of the courtiers who had been sent by the queen and Madame, and uncovered themselves, in token of having perceived his majesty. But Louis, notwithstanding La Vallière's confusion, did not quit his respectful and tender attitude. Then, when all the courtiers were assembled in the walk—when every one had been able to perceive the extraordinary mark of deference with which he had treated the young girl, by remaining standing and bare-headed during the storm— he offered her his arm, led her towards the group who were waiting, recognized by an inclination of the head the respectful salutations which were paid him on all sides; and, still holding his hat in his hand, he conducted her to her carriage. And, as a few sparse drops of rain continued to fall—a last adieu of the vanishing storm—the other ladies, whom respect had prevented getting into their carriages before the king, remained altogether unprotected by hood or cloak, exposed to the rain from which the king was protecting, as well as he was able, the humblest among them. The queen and Madame must, like the others, have witnessed this exaggerated courtesy of the king. Madame was so disconcerted at it, that she touched the queen with her elbow, saying at the same time, " Look there, look there."

The queen closed her eyes as if she had been suddenly seized with a fainting-spell. She lifted her hand to her face and entered her carriage, Madame following her. The king again mounted his horse, and without showing a preference for any particular carriage door, he returned to Fontainebleau, the reins hanging over his horse's neck, absorbed in thought. As soon as the crowd had disappeared, and the sound of the horses and carriages grew fainter in the distance, and when they were certain, in fact, that no one could see them, Aramis and Fouquet came out of their grotto, and both of them in silence passed slowly on towards the walk. Aramis looked most narrowly not only at the whole extent of the open space stretching out before and behind him, but even into the very depth of the wood.

" Monsieur Fouquet," he said, when he had quite satisfied himself that they were alone, " we must get back, at any cost, the letter you wrote to La Vallière."

" That will be easy enough," said Fouquet, " if my servant has not given it to her."

" In any case it must be had, do you understand?"

" Yes. The king is in love with this girl, you mean?"

" Deeply, and what is worse is, that on her side, the girl is passionately attached to him."

" As much as to say that we must change our tactics, I suppose?"

" Not a doubt of it; you have no time to lose. You must see La Vallière, and, without thinking any more of becoming her lover, which is out of the question, must declare yourself her most devoted friend and her most humble servant."

" I will do so," replied Fouquet, " and without the slightest feeling of disinclination, for she seems a good-hearted girl."

" Or a very clever one," said Aramis; "but in that case, all the greater reason." Then he added, after a moment's pause, " If I am not mistaken, that girl will become the strongest passion of the king's life. Let us return to our carriage, and, as fast as possible, to the château."

CHAPTER XXVIII.

TOBY.

Two hours after the superintendent's carriage had set off by Aramis's directions, conveying them both towards Fontainebleau with the fleetness of the clouds the last breath of the tempest was hurrying across the face of heaven, La Vallière was closeted in her own apartment, with a simple muslin wrapper round her, having just finished a slight repast, which was placed upon a marble table. Suddenly the door was opened, and a servant entered to announce M. Fouquet, who had called to request permission to pay his respects to her. She made him repeat the message twice over, for the poor girl only knew M. Fouquet by name, and could not conceive what business she could possibly have with a superintendent of finances. However, as he might represent the king—and, after the conversation we have recorded it was very likely—she glanced at her mirror, drew out still more the ringlets of her hair, and desired him to be admitted. La Vallière could not, however, refrain from a certain feeling of un-

easiness. A visit from the superintendent was not an ordinary event in the life of any woman attached to the court.
Fouquet, so notorious for his generosity, his gallantry,
and his sensitive delicacy of feeling with regard to women
generally, had received more invitations than he had requested audiences. In many houses, the presence of the
superintendent had been significant of fortune; in many
hearts, of love. Fouquet entered the apartment with a
manner full of respect, presenting himself with that ease
and gracefulness of manner which was the distinctive
characteristic of the men of eminence of that period, and
which at the present day seems no longer to be understood, even through the interpretation of the portraits of
the period, in which the painter has endeavored to recall
them to being. La Vallière acknowledged the ceremonious
salutation which Fouquet addressed to her by a gentle
inclination of the head, and motioned him to a seat. But
Fouquet, with a bow, said, " I will not sit down until you
have pardoned me."

" I ?" asked La Vallière, " pardon what ? "

Fouquet fixed a most piercing look upon the young girl,
and fancied he could perceive in her face nothing but the
most unaffected surprise. " I observe," he said, " that
you have as much generosity as intelligence, and I read
in your eyes the forgiveness I solicit. A pardon pronounced by your lips is insufficient for me, and I need the
forgiveness of your heart and mind."

" Upon my honor, monsieur," said La Vallière, " I assure you most positively I do not understand your meaning."

" Again, that is a delicacy on your part which charms
me," replied Fouquet, " and I see you do not wish me to
blush before you."

" Blush! blush before *me!* Why should you blush ? "

" Can I have deceived myself," said Fouquet; " and

can I have been happy enough not to have offended you by my conduct towards you?"

"Really, monsieur," said La Vallière, shrugging her shoulders, "you speak in enigmas, and I suppose I am too ignorant to understand you."

"Be it so," said Fouquet; "I will not insist. Tell me only, I entreat you, that I may rely upon your full and complete forgiveness."

"I have but only one reply to make to you, monsieur," said La Vallière, somewhat impatiently, "and I hope that will satisfy you. If I knew the wrong you have done me, I would forgive you, and I now do so with still greater reason since I am ignorant of the wrong you allude to."

Fouquet bit his lips, as Aramis would have done. "In that case," he said, "I may hope, that, notwithstanding what has happened, our good understanding will remain undisturbed, and that you will kindly confer the favor upon me of believing in my respectful friendship."

La Vallière fancied that she now began to understand, and said to herself, "I should not have believed M. Fouquet so eager to seek the source of a favor so very recent," and then added aloud, "Your friendship, monsieur! you offer me your friendship. The honor, on the contrary, is mine, and I feel overpowered by it."

"I am aware," replied Fouquet, "that the friendship of the master may appear more brilliant and desirable than that of the servant; but I assure you the latter will be quite as devoted, quite as faithful, and altogether disinterested."

La Vallière bowed, for, in fact, the voice of the superintendent seemed to convey both conviction and real devotion in its tone, and she held out her hand to him, saying, "I believe you."

Fouquet eagerly took hold of the young girl's hand.

"You see no difficulty, therefore," he added, "in restoring me that unhappy letter."

"What letter?" inquired La Vallière.

Fouquet interrogated her with his most searching gaze, as he had already done before, but the same ingenuous expression, the same transparently candid look met his. "I am obliged to confess," he said, after this denial, "that your heart is the most delicate in the world, and I should not feel I was a man of honor and uprightness if I were to suspect anything from a woman so generous as yourself."

"Really, Monsieur Fouquet," replied La Vallière, "it is with profound regret I am obliged to repeat that I absolutely understand nothing of what you refer to."

"In fact, then, upon your honor, mademoiselle, you have not received any letter from me?"

"Upon my honor, none," replied La Vallière, firmly.

"Very well, that is quite sufficient; permit me, then, to renew the assurance of my utmost esteem and respect," said Fouquet. Then, bowing, he left the room to seek Aramis, who was waiting for him in his own apartment, and leaving La Vallière to ask herself whether the superintendent had not lost his senses.

"Well!" inquired Aramis, who was impatiently waiting Fouquet's return, "are you satisfied with the favorite?"

"Enchanted," replied Fouquet; "she is a woman full of intelligence and fine feeling."

"She did not get angry, then?"

"Far from that—she did not even seem to understand."

"To understand what?"

"To understand that I had written to her."

"She must, however, have understood you sufficiently to give the letter back to you, for I presume she returned it."

"Not at all."

" At least, you satisfied yourself that she had burnt it."

" My dear Monsieur d'Herblay, I have been playing at cross-purposes for more than an hour, and, however amusing it may be, I begin to have had enough of this game. So understand me thoroughly : the girl pretended not to understand what I was saying to her; she denied having received any letter ; therefore, having positively denied its receipt, she was unable either to return or burn it."

" Oh! oh!" said Aramis, with uneasiness, "what is this you tell me?"

" I say that she swore most positively she had not received any letter."

" That is too much.   And did you not insist?"

" On the contrary, I did insist, almost impertinently even."

" And she persisted in her denial ? "

" Unhesitatingly."

" And she did not contradict herself once ? "

" Not once."

" But, in that case, then, you have left our letter in her hands ? "

" How could I do otherwise."

" Oh! it was a great mistake."

" What the deuce would you have done in my place? "

" One could not force her, certainly, but it is very embarrassing ; such a letter ought not to remain in existence against us."

" Oh! the young girl's disposition is generosity itself ; I looked at her eyes, and I can read eyes well."

" You think she can be relied upon ? "

" From my heart I do."

" Well, I think we are mistaken."

" In what way ?"

" I think that, in point of fact, as she herself told you, she did not receive the letter."

"What! do you suppose——"

"I suppose that, from some motive, of which we know nothing, your man did not deliver the letter to her."

Fouquet rang the bell. A servant appeared. "Send Toby here," he said. A moment afterwards a man made his appearance, with an anxious, restless look, shrewd expression of the mouth, with short arms, and his back somewhat bent. Aramis fixed a penetrating look upon him.

"Will you allow me to interrogate him myself?" inquired Aramis.

"Do so," said Fouquet.

Aramis was about to say something to the lackey, when he paused. "No," he said; "he would see that we attach too much importance to his answer; therefore question him yourself; I will pretend to be writing." Aramis accordingly placed himself at a table, his back turned towards the old attendant, whose every gesture and look he watched in a looking-glass opposite to him.

"Come here, Toby," said Fouquet to the valet, who approached with a tolerably firm step. "How did you execute my commission?" inquired Fouquet.

"In the usual way, monseigneur," replied the man.

"But how, tell me?"

"I succeeded in penetrating as far as Mademoiselle de la Vallière's apartment; but she was at mass, and so I placed the note on her toilette-table. Is not that what you told me to do?"

"Precisely; and is that all?"

"Absolutely all, monseigneur."

"No one was there?"

"No one."

"Did you conceal yourself as I told you?"

"Yes."

"And she returned?"

"Ten minutes afterwards."

" And no one could have taken the letter ? "

" No one ; for no one had entered the room."

" From the outside, but from the interior ? "

" From the place where I was secreted, I could see to the very end of the room."

" Now listen to me," said Fouquet, looking fixedly at the lackey; " if this letter did not reach its proper destination, confess it ; for, if a mistake has been made, your head shall be the forfeit."

Toby started, but immediately recovered himself. " Monseigneur," he said, " I placed the letter on the very place I told you : and I ask only half an hour to prove to you that the letter is in Mademoiselle de la Vallière's hand, or to bring you back the letter itself."

Aramis looked at the valet scrutinizingly. Fouquet was ready in placing confidence in people, and for twenty years this man had served him faithfully. " Go," he said ; " but bring me the proof you speak of." The lackey quitted the room.

" Well, what do you think of it ? " inquired Fouquet of Aramis.

" I think that you must, by some means or another, assure yourself of the truth, either that the letter has or has not, reached La Vallière; that, in the first case, La Vallière must return it to you, or satisfy you by burning it in your presence ; that, in the second, you must have the letter back again, even were it to cost you a million. Come, is not that your opinion ? "

" Yes ; but still, my dear bishop, I believe you are exaggerating the importance of the affair."

" Blind, how blind you are ! " murmured Aramis.

" La Vallière," returned Fouquet, " whom we assume to be a schemer of the first ability, is simply nothing more than a coquette, who hopes that I shall pay my court to her, because I have already done so, and who, now that she has received a confirmation of the king's regard, hopes to keep me in leading strings with the letter. It is natural enough."

Aramis shook his head.

" Is not that your opinion?" said Fouquet.

" She is not a coquette," he replied.

" Allow me to tell you——"

"Oh! I am well enough acquainted with women who are coquettes," said Aramis.

" My dear friend!"

"It is a long time ago since I finished my education, you mean. But women are the same, throughout the centuries."

" True; but men change, and you at the present day are far more suspicious than you formerly were." And then, beginning to laugh, he added, " Come, if La Vallière is willing to love me only to the extent of a third, and the king two-thirds, do you think the condition acceptable?"

Aramis rose impatiently. " La Vallière," he said " has never loved, and never will love, any one but the king."

"At all events," said Fouquet, " what would you do?"

" Ask me rather what I would have done?"

" Well! what would you have done?"

" In the first place, I should not have allowed that man to depart."

" Toby?"

"Yes; Toby is a traitor. Nay, I am sure of it, and I would not have let him go until he had told me the truth."

"There is still time. I will recall him, and do you question him in your turn."

" Agreed."

"But I assure you it is useless. He has been with me

for twenty years, and has never made the slightest mistake, and yet," added Fouquet, laughing, "it would have been easy enough for him to have done so."

"Still, call him back. This morning I fancy I saw that face, in earnest conversation with one of M. Colbert's men."

"Where was that?"

"Opposite the stables."

"Bah! all my people are at daggers drawn with that fellow."

"I saw him, I tell you, and his face, which should have been unknown to me when he entered just now, struck me as disagreeably familiar."

"Why did you not say something, then, while he was here?"

"Because it is only at this very minute that my memory is clear upon the subject."

"Really," said Fouquet, "you alarm me." And he again rang the bell.

"Provided that it is not already too late," said Aramis.

Fouquet once more rang impatiently. The valet usually in attendance appeared. "Toby!" said Fouquet, "send Toby." The valet again shut the door.

"You leave me at perfect liberty, I suppose?"

"Entirely so."

"I may employ all means, then to ascertain the truth."

"All."

"Intimidation, even?"

"I constitute you public prosecutor in my place."

They waited ten minutes longer, but uselessly, and Fouquet, thoroughly out of patience, again rang loudly.

"Toby!" he exclaimed.

"Monseigneur," said the valet, "they are looking for him."

" He cannot be far distant, I have not given him any commission to execute."

" I will go and see, monseigneur," replied the valet, as he closed the door.   Aramis, during this interview, walked impatiently but without a syllable, up and down the cabinet.   They waited a further ten minutes.   Fouquet rang in a manner to alarm the very dead.   The valet again presented himself, trembling in a way to induce a belief that he was the bearer of bad news.

" Monseigneur is mistaken," he said, before even Fouquet could interrogate him, " you must have given Toby some commission, for he has been to the stables and taken your lordship's swiftest horse, and saddled it himself."

" Well ? "

" And he has gone off."

" Gone ! " exclaimed Fouquet.   " Let him be pursued. let him be captured."

" Nay, nay," whispered Aramis, taking him by the hand, " be calm, the evil is done."

The valet quietly went out.

" The evil is done, you say ? "

" No doubt ; I was sure of it.   And now, let us give no cause for suspicion ; we must calculate the result of the blow and ward it off, if possible."

" After all," said Fouquet, " the evil is not great."

" You think so ? "   said Aramis.

" Of course.   Surely a man is allowed to write a love-letter to a woman."

" A man, certainly ; a subject, no: especially, too, when the woman in question is one with whom the king is in love."

" But the king was not in love with La Vallière a week ago! he was not in love with her yesterday, and the letter is dated yesterday ; I could not guess the king was in

love, when the king's affection was not even yet in existence."

"As you please," replied Aramis ; "but unfortunately
the letter is not dated, and it is that circumstance particularly which annoys me. If it had only been dated
yesterday, I should not have the slightest shadow of uneasiness on your account."

Fouquet shrugged his shoulders.

"Am I not my own master," he said, "and is the king,
then, king of my brain and of my flesh ? "

"You are right," replied Aramis, "do not let us attach
greater importance to matters than is necessary ; and
besides. . . . Well! if we are menaced, we have means of
defense."

"Oh! menaced!" said Fouquet, "you do not place
this gnat bite as it were, among the number of menaces
which may compromise my fortune and my life, do
you? "

"Do not forget, Monsieur Fouquet, that the bite of an
insect can kill a giant, if the insect be venomous."

"But has this sovereign power you were speaking of,
already vanished? "

"I am all-powerful, it is true, but I am not immortal."

"Come, then, the most pressing matter is to find Toby
again, I suppose. Is not that your opinion? "

"Oh! as for that, you will not find him again," said
Aramis, "and if he were of any great value to you, you
must give him up for lost."

"At all events he is somewhere or another in the
world," said Fouquet.

"You're right, let me act," replied Aramis.

CHAPTER XXIX.

MADAME'S FOUR CHANCES.

ANNE of Austria had begged the young queen to pay her a visit. For some time past suffering most acutely, and losing both her youth and beauty with that rapidity which signalizes the decline of women for whom life has been one long contest, Anne of Austria had, in addition to her physical sufferings, to experience the bitterness of being no longer held in any esteem, except as a surviving remembrance of the past, amidst the youthful beauties, wits, and influential forces of her court. Her physician's opinions, her mirror also, grieved her far less than the inexorable warnings which the society of the courtiers afforded, who, like rats in a ship, abandon the hold into which on the very next voyage the water will infallibly penetrate, owing to the ravages of decay. Anne of Austria did not feel satisfied with the time her eldest son devoted to her. The king, a good son, more from affectation than from affection, had at first been in the habit of passing an hour in the morning and one in the evening with his mother; but, since he had himself undertaken the conduct of state affairs, the duration of the morning and evening's visit had been reduced one half; and then, by degrees, the morning visit had been suppressed altogether. They met at mass; the evening visit was replaced by a meeting, either at the king's assembly or at Madame's, which the queen attended obligingly enough, out of regard to her two sons.

The result of this was, that Madame gradually acquired an immense influence over the court, which made her apartments the true royal place of meeting. This, Anne of Austria perceived; knowing herself to be very ill, and condemned by her sufferings to frequent retirement, she was distressed at the idea that the greater part of her future days and evenings would pass away solitary, useless, and in despondency. She recalled with terror the isolation in which Cardinal Richelieu had formerly left her, those dreaded and insupportable evenings, during which, however, she had both youth and beauty, which are ever accompanied by hope, to console her. She next formed the project of transporting the court to her own apartments, and of attracting Madame, with her brilliant escort, to her gloomy and already sorrowful abode, where the widow of a king of France, and the mother of a king of France, was reduced to console, in her artificial widowhood, the weeping wife of a king of France.

Anne began to reflect. She had intrigued a good deal in her life. In the good times past, when her youthful mind nursed projects that were, ultimately, invariably successful, she had by her side to stimulate her ambition and her love, a friend of her own sex, more eager, more ambitious than herself,—a friend who had loved her, a rare circumstance at court, and whom some petty considerations had removed from her forever. But for many years past—except Madame de Motteville, and La Molena, her Spanish nurse, a *confidante* in her character of countrywoman and woman too—who could boast of having given good advice to the queen? Who, too, among all the youthful heads there, could recall the past for her,—that past in which alone she lived? Anne of Austria remembered Madame de Chevreuse, in the first place exiled rather by her wish than the king's, and then dying in exile, the wife of a gentleman of obscure birth and position. She asked herself what Madame de Chevreuse would have advised her to do in similar circumstances; and after serious reflection, it seemed as if the clever, subtile mind of her friend, full of experience

and sound judgment, answered her in the well remembered
ironical tones : " All the insignificant young people are
poor and greedy of gain.   They require gold and in-
comes to supply means of amusement ; it is by interest
you must   gain them over."   And Anne of Austria
adopted this plan.   Her purse was well filled, and she had
at her disposal a considerable sum of money, which had
been amassed by Mazarin for her, and lodged in a place of
safety.   She possessed the most magnificent jewels in
France, and especially pearls of a size so large that they
made the king sigh every time he saw them, because the
pearls of his crown were like millet seed compared to
them.   Anne of Austria had neither beauty nor charms
any longer at her disposal.   She gave out, therefore, that
her wealth was great, and as an inducement for others to
visit her apartments she let it be known that there were
good gold crowns to be won at play, or that handsome
presents were likely to be made on days when all went
well with her ; or windfalls, in the shape of annuities which
she had wrung from the king by entreaty, and thus she
determined to maintain her credit.   In the first place, she
tried these means upon Madame; because, to gain her
consent was of more importance than anything else.
Madame, notwithstanding the bold confidence with which
her wit and beauty inspired her, blindly ran head foremost into the net thus stretched out to catch her.   En-
riched by degrees by these presents and transfers of property, she took a fancy to inheritances by anticipation.
Anne of Austria adopted the same means towards
Monsieur, and even towards the king himself.   She instituted lotteries in her apartments.   The day on which the
present chapter opens, invitations had been issued for a
late supper in the queen-mother's apartments, as she intended that two beautiful diamond bracelets of exquisite
workmanship should be put into a lottery.   The medal-

lions were antique cameos of the greatest value; the diamonds, in point of intrinsic value, did not represent a
very considerable amount, but the originality and rarity of
the workmanship were such, that every one at court not
only wished to possess the bracelets, but even to see the
queen herself wear them; for, on the days she wore them,
it was considered as a favor to be admitted to admire
them in kissing her hands. The courtiers had, even with
regard to this subject, adopted various expressions of gallantry to establish the aphorism, that the bracelets would
have been priceless in value if they had not been unfortunate enough to be placed in contact with arms as beautiful as the queen's. This compliment had been honored
by a translation into all the languages of Europe, and
numerous verses in Latin and French had been circulated
on the subject. The day that Anne of Austria had
selected for the lottery was a decisive moment; the king
had not been near his mother for a couple of days; Madame,
after the great scene of the Dryads and Naiads, was sulk-
ing by herself. It is true, the king's fit of resentment was
over, but his mind was absorbingly occupied by a circumstance that raised him above the stormy disputes and
giddy pleasures of the court.

Anne of Austria affected a diversion by the announcement of the famous lottery to take place in her apartments
on the following evening. With this object in view she
saw the young queen, whom, as we have already seen, she
had invited to pay her a visit in the morning. "I have
good news to tell you," she said to her; "the king has
been saying the most tender things about you. He is
young, you know, and easily drawn away; but so long as
you keep near me, he will not venture to keep away from
you, to whom, besides, he is most warmly and affection-
ately attached. I intend to have a lottery this evening
and shall expect to see you."

"I have heard," said the young queen, with a sort of timid reproach, "that your majesty intends to put in the lottery those lovely bracelets whose rarity is so great that we ought not to allow them to pass out of the custody of the crown, even were there no other reason than that they had once belonged to you."

"My daughter," said Anne of Austria, who read the young queen's thoughts, and wished to console her for not having received the bracelets as a present, "it is positively necessary that I should induce Madame to pass her time in my apartments."

"Madame!" said the young queen, blushing.

"Of course: would you not prefer to have a rival near you, whom you could watch and influence, to knowing that the king is with her always as ready to flirt as to be flirted with by her. The lottery I have proposed is my means of attraction for that purpose; do you blame me?"

"Oh no!" returned Maria Thérèsa, clapping her hands with a child-like expression of delight.

"And you no longer regret, then, that I did not give you these bracelets, as I at first intended to do?"

"Oh, no, no!"

"Very well; make yourself look as beautiful as possible, that our supper may be very brilliant; the gayer you seem, the more charming you appear, and you will eclipse all the ladies present as much by your brilliancy as by your rank."

Maria Theresa left full of delight. An hour afterwards, Anne of Austria received a visit from Madame, whom she covered with caresses, saying, "Excellent news! the king is charmed with my lottery."

"But I," replied Madame, "am not quite so greatly charmed; to see such beautiful bracelets on any one's arms but yours or mine, is what I cannot reconcile myself to."

"Well, well," said Anne of Austria, concealing by a smile a violent pang she had just experienced, "do not look at things in the worst light immediately."

"Ah, madame, fortune is blind, and I am told there are two hundred tickets."

"Quite as many as that; but you cannot surely forget that there can only be one winner."

"No doubt. But who will that be? Can you tell?" said Madame, in despair.

"You remind me that I had a dream last night; my dreams are always good,—I sleep so little."

"What was your dream?—but are you suffering?"

"No," said the queen, stifling with wonderful command the torture of a renewed attack of shooting pains in her bosom; "I dreamed that the king won the bracelets."

"The king!"

"You are going to ask me, I think, what the king could possibly do with the bracelets?"

"Yes."

"And you would not add, perhaps, that it would be very fortunate if the king were really to win, for he would be obliged to give the bracelets to some one else."

"To restore them to you, for instance."

"In which case I should immediately give them away; for you do not think, I suppose," said the queen, laughing, "that I have put these bracelets up to a lottery from necessity. My object was to give them without arousing any one's jealousy; but if fortune will not get me out of my difficulty—well, I will teach fortune a lesson—and I know very well to whom I intend to offer the bracelets." These words were accompanied by so expressive a smile, that Madame could not resist paying her by a grateful kiss.

"But," added Anne of Austria, "do you not know, as well as I do, that if the king were to win the bracelets, he would not restore them to me?"

"You mean he would give them to the queen?"

"No; and for the very same reason, that he would not give them back again to me; since, if I had wished to make the queen a present of them, I had no need of him for that purpose."

Madame cast a side glance upon the bracelets, which, in their casket, were dazzlingly exposed to view upon a table close beside her.

"How beautiful they are," she said, sighing. "But stay," Madame continued, "we are quite forgetting that your majesty's dream was nothing but a dream."

"I should be very much surprised," returned Anne of Austria, "if my dream were to deceive me; that has happened to me very seldom."

"We may look upon you as a prophetess, then."

"I have already said, that I dream but very rarely; but the coincidence of my dream about this matter, with my own ideas, is extraordinary! it agrees so wonderfully with my own views and arrangements."

"What arrangements do you allude to?"

"That you will get the bracelets, for instance."

"In that case, it will not be the king."

"Oh!" said Anne of Austria, "there is not such a very great distance between his majesty's heart and your own; for, are not you his sister, for whom he has a great regard? There is not, I repeat, so very wide a distance, that my dream can be pronounced false on that account. Come, let us reckon up the chances in its favor."

"I will count them."

"In the first place, we will begin with the dream. If the king wins, he is sure to give you the bracelets."

"I admit that is one."

"If you win them, they are yours."

"Naturally; that may be admitted also."

"Lastly;—if Monsieur were to win them!"

"Oh!" said Madame, laughing heartily, "he would give them to the Chevalier de Lorraine."

Anne of Austria laughed as heartily as her daughter-in-law; so, much so indeed, that her sufferings again returned, and made her turn suddenly pale in the very midst of her enjoyment.

"What is the matter?" inquired Madame, terrified.

"Nothing, nothing; a pain in my side. I have been laughing too much. We were at the fourth chance, I think."

"I cannot see a fourth."

"I beg your pardon; I am not excluded from the chance of winning, and if I be the winner, you are sure of me."

"Oh! thank you, thank you!" exclaimed Madame.

"I hope you look upon yourself as one whose chances are good, and that my dream now begins to assume the solid outlines of reality."

"Yes, indeed: you give me both hope and confidence," said Madame, "and the bracelets, won in this manner, will be a hundred times more precious to me."

"Well! then, good-bye, until this evening." And the two princesses separated. Anne of Austria, after her daughter-in-law had left her, said to herself, as she examined the bracelets, "They are, indeed, precious; since, by their means, this evening, I shall have won over a heart to my side, and, at the same time, fathomed an important secret."

"Then turning towards the deserted recess in her room, she said, addressing vacancy—"Is it not thus that you would have acted, my poor Chevreuse? Yes, yes; I know it is."

And, like a perfume of other, fairer days, her youth, her imagination, and her happiness, seemed to be wafted towards the echo of this invocation.

CHAPTER XXX.

THE LOTTERY.

By eight o'clock in the evening, every one had assembled in the queen-mother's apartments. Anne of Austria, in full dress, beautiful still, from former loveliness, and from all the resources coquetry can command at the hands of clever assistants, concealed, or rather pretended to conceal, from the crowd of courtiers who surrounded her, and who still admired her, thanks to the combination of circumstances which we have indicated in the preceding chapter, the ravages, which were already visible, of the acute suffering to which she finally yielded a few years later. Madame, almost as great a coquette as Anne of Austria, and the queen, simple and natural as usual, were seated beside her, each contending for her good graces. The ladies of honor, united in a body, in order to resist with greater effect and consequently with more success, the witty and lively conversations which the young men held about them, were enabled, like a battalion formed in square, to offer each other the means of attack and defense which were thus at their command. Montalais, learned in that species of warfare which consists of sustained skirmishing, protected the whole line by a sort of rolling fire she directed against the enemy. Saint-Aignan, in utter despair at the rigor, which became almost insulting, from the very fact of her persisting in it, Mademoiselle de Tonnay-Charente displayed, tried to turn his back upon her; but, overcome by the irresistible brilliancy of her eyes, he, every moment, returned to consecrate his defeat by new submissions, to which Mademoiselle de Tonnay-Charente did not fail to reply by fresh acts of impertinence. Saint-Aignan did not know which way to turn. La Vallière had about her, not exactly a court, but sprinklings of courtiers. Saint-Aignan, hoping by this maneuver to attract Athenaïs's attention towards him, approached the young girl, and saluted her with a respect that induced some to believe that he wished to balance Athenaïs by Louise. But these were persons who had neither been witnesses of the scene during the shower, nor had heard it spoken of. As the majority was already informed, and well informed too, on the matter, the acknowledged favor with which she was regarded had attracted to her side some of the most astute, as well as the least sensible, members of the court. The former, because they said with Montaigne, "How do I know?" and the latter, who said with Rabelais, "Perhaps." The greatest number had followed in the wake of the latter, just as in hunting five or six of the best hounds alone follow the scent of the animal hunted, whilst the remainder of the pack follow only the scent of the hounds. The two queens and Madame examined with particular attention the toilettes of their ladies and maids of honor; and they condescended to forget they were queens in recollecting that they were women. In other words, they pitilessly picked to pieces every person present who wore a petticoat. The looks of both princesses simultaneously fell upon La Vallière, who, as we have just said, was completely surrounded at that moment. Madame knew not what pity was, and said to the queen-mother, as she turned towards her, "If fortune were just, she would favor that poor La Vallière."

"That is not possible," said the queen-mother, smiling.

"Why not?"

"There are only two hundred tickets, so that it was not possible to inscribe every one's name on the list."

"And hers is not there, then?"

" No!"

" What a pity! she might have won them, and then sold them."

" Sold them! " exclaimed the queen.

" Yes; it would have been a dowry for her, and she would not have been obliged to marry without her *trousseau*, as will probably be the case."

" Really," answered the queen-mother, " poor little thing: has she no dresses, then?"

And she pronounced these words like a woman who has never been able to understand the inconveniences of a slenderly-filled purse.

" Stay, look at her. Heaven forgive me, if she is not wearing the very same petticoat this evening that she had on this morning during the promenade, and which she managed to keep clean, thanks to the care the king took of her, in sheltering her from the rain."

At the very moment Madame uttered these words the king entered the room. The two queens would not perhaps have observed his arrival, so completely were they occupied in their ill-natured remarks, had not Madame noticed that, all at once, La Vallière, who was standing up facing the gallery, exhibited certain signs of confusion, and then said a few words to the courtiers who surrounded her, who immediately dispersed. This movement induced Madame to look towards the door, and at that moment, the captain of the guards announced the king. At this moment La Vallière, who had hitherto kept her eyes fixed upon the gallery, suddenly cast them down as the king entered. His majesty was dressed magnificently and in the most perfect taste; he was conversing with Monsieur and the Duc de Roquelaure, Monsieur on his right and the Duc de Roquelaure on his left. The king advanced, in the first place, towards the queens, to whom he bowed with an air full of graceful respect. He took his mother's hand and kissed it, addressed a few compliments to Madame upon the beauty of her toilette, and then began to make the round of the assembly. La Vallière was saluted in the same manner as the others, but with neither more nor less attention. His majesty then returned to his mother and his wife. When the courtiers noticed that the king had only addressed some ordinary remark to the young girl who had been so particularly noticed in the morning, they immediately drew their own conclusion to account for this coldness of manner; this conclusion being, that although the king may have taken a sudden fancy to her, that fancy had already disappeared. One thing, however, must be remarked, that close beside La Vallière, among the number of the courtiers, M. Fouquet was to be seen; and his respectfully attentive manner served to sustain the young girl in the midst of the varied emotions that visibly agitated her.

M. Fouquet was just on the point, moreover, of speaking in a more friendly manner with Mademoiselle de la Vallière, when M. de Colbert approached, and after having bowed to Fouquet with all the formality of respectful politeness, he seemed to take up a post beside La Vallière, for the purpose of entering into conversation with her. Fouquet immediately quitted his place. These proceedings were eagerly devoured by the eyes of Montalais and Malicorne, who mutually exchanged their observations on the subject. De Guiche, standing within the embrasure of one of the windows, saw no one but Madame. But as Madame, on her side, frequently glanced at La Vallière, De Guiche's eyes following Madame's were from time to time cast upon the young girl. La Vallière instinctively felt herself sinking beneath the weight of all these different looks, inspired, some by interest, others by envy. She had nothing to compensate her for her sufferings, not a kind word from her companions, nor a look of affection

from the king.   No one could possibly express the misery
the poor girl was suffering.   The queen-mother next
directed the small table to be brought forward, on which
the lottery-tickets were placed, two hundred in number,
and begged Madame de Motteville to read the list of the
names.   It was a matter of course that this list had been
drawn out in strict accordance with the laws of etiquette.
The king's name was first on the list, next the queen-
mother, then the queen, Monsieur, Madame, and so on.   All
hearts throbbed anxiously as the list was read out; more
than three hundred persons had been invited, and each of
them was anxious to learn whether his or her name was
to be found in the number of privileged names.   The
king listened with as much attention as the others, and
when the last name had been pronounced, he noticed that
La Vallière had been omitted from the list.   Every one,
of course, remarked this omission.   The king flushed as
if much annoyed; but La Vallière, gentle, and resigned,
as usual, exhibited nothing of the sort.   While the list
was being read, the king had not taken his eyes off the
young girl, who seemed to expand, as it were, beneath the
happy influence she felt was shed around her, and who
was delighted and too pure in spirit for any other thought
than that of love to find an entrance either to her mind
or her heart.   Acknowledging this touching self-denial
by the fixity of his attention, the king showed La Vallière how much he appreciated its delicacy.   When the
list was finished, the different faces of those who had
been omitted or forgotten, fully expressed their disappointment.   Malicorne also was left out from amongst the men;
and the grimace he made plainly said to Montalais, who
was also forgotten, "Cannot we contrive to arrange
matters with fortune in such a manner that she shall not
forget us?" to which a smile full of intelligence from
Mademoiselle Aure, replied: "Certainly we can."

The tickets were distributed to each according to the number listed. The king received his first, next the queen-mother, then Monsieur, then the queen and Madame, and so on. After this, Anne of Austria opened a small Spanish leather bag, containing two hundred numbers engraved upon small balls of mother-of-pearl, and presented the open sack to the youngest of her maids of honor, for the purpose of taking one of the balls out of it. The eager expectation of the throng, amidst all the tediously slow preparations, was rather that of cupidity than curiosity. Saint-Aignan bent towards Mademoiselle de Tonnay-Charente to whisper to her, "Since we have each a number, let us unite our two chances. The bracelet shall be yours if I win, and if you are successful, deign to give me but one look of your beautiful eye."

" No," said Athenaïs, "if you win the bracelet keep it; every one for himself."

" You are without any pity," said Saint-Aignan, "and I will punish you by a quatrain :—

> " 'Beautiful Iris, to my vow
> You are too opposed——'"

" Silence," said Athenaïs, " you will prevent me hearing the winning number."

" Number one," said the young girl who had drawn the mother-of-pearl from the Spanish leather bag.

" The king!" exclaimed the queen-mother.

" The king has won," repeated the queen, delightedly.

"Oh! the king! your dream!" said Madame, joyously, in the ear of Anne of Austria.

The king was the only one who did not exhibit any satisfaction. He merely thanked Fortune for what she had done for him, in addressing a slight salutation to the young girl who had been chosen as her proxy. Then receiving from the hands of Anne of Austria, amid the eager desire of the whole assembly, the casket inclosing the bracelets, he said, " Are these bracelets really beautiful, then ? "

" Look at them," said Anne of Austria, " and judge for yourself."

The king looked at them, and said, " Yes, indeed, an admirable medallion. What perfect finish ! "

" What perfect finish ! " repeated Madame.

Queen Maria Theresa easily saw, and that, too, at the very first glance, that the king would not offer the bracelets to her ; but, as he did not seem the least degree in the world disposed to offer them to Madame, she felt almost satisfied, or nearly so. The king sat down. The most intimate among the courtiers approached, one by one, for the purpose of admiring more closely the beautiful piece of workmanship, which soon, with the king's permission, was handed about from person to person. Immediately, every one, connoisseurs or not, uttered various exclamations of surprise, and overwhelmed the king with congratulations. There was, in fact, something for everybody to admire—the brilliants for some, and the cutting for others. The ladies present visibly displayed their impatience to see such a treasure monopolized by the gentlemen.

" Gentlemen, gentlemen," said the king, whom nothing escaped, " one would almost think that you wore bracelets as the Sabines used to do; hand them round for a while for the inspection of the ladies, who seem to me to have, and with far greater right, an excuse for understanding such matters ! "

These words appeared to Madame the commencement of a decision she expected. She gathered, besides, this happy belief from the glances of the queen-mother. The courtier who held them at the moment the king made this remark, amidst the general agitation, hastened to place the bracelets in the hands of the queen, Maria Theresa, who, knowing too well, poor woman, that they were not designed for her, hardly looked at them, and almost immediately passed them on to Madame. The latter, and even more minutely, Monsieur, gave the bracelets a long look of anxious and almost covetous desire. She then handed the jewels to those ladies who were near her, pronouncing this single word, but with an accent which was worth a long phrase, " Magnificent ! "

The ladies who had received the bracelets from Madame's hands looked at them as long as they chose to examine them, and then made them circulate by passing them on towards the right. During this time the king was tranquilly conversing with De Guiche and Fouquet, rather passively letting them talk than himself listening. Accustomed to the set form of ordinary phrases, his ear, like that of all men who exercise an incontestable superiority over others, merely selected from the conversations held in various directions, the indispensable word which requires reply. His attention, however, was now elsewhere, for it wandered as his eyes did.

Mademoiselle de Tonnay-Charente was the last of the ladies inscribed for tickets ; and, as if she had ranked according to her name upon the list, she only had Montalais and La Vallière near her. When the bracelets reached these two latter no one appeared to take any further notice of them. The humble hands which for a moment touched these jewels, deprived them for the time, of their importance—a circumstance which did not, however, prevent Montalais from starting with joy, envy, and covetous desire, at the sight of the beautiful stones still more than at their magnificent workmanship. It is evident that if she were compelled to decide between the pecuniary value and the artistic beauty, Montalais would unhesitatingly have preferred diamonds to cameos, and her disinclination, therefore, to pass them to her companion, La Vallière, was very great. La Vallière fixed a look almost of indifference upon the jewels.

"Oh, how beautiful, how magnificent these bracelets are!" exclaimed Montalais; "and yet you do not go into ecstasies about them, Louise! You are no true woman, I am sure."

"Yes, I am indeed," replied the young girl, with an accent of the most charming melancholy; "but why desire that which can never, by any possibility, be ours?"

The king, his head bent forward, was listening to what Louise was saying. Hardly had the vibration of her voice reached his ear than he rose, radiant with delight, and passing across the whole assembly, from the place where he stood, to La Vallière, "You are mistaken, mademoiselle," be said, "you are a woman, and every woman has a right to wear jewels, which are a woman's appurtenance."

"Oh, sire!" said La Vallière, "your majesty will not absolutely believe in my modesty?"

"I believe you possess every virtue, mademoiselle; frankness as well as every other; I entreat you, therefore, to say frankly what you think of these bracelets?"

"That they are beautiful, sire, and cannot be offered to any other than a queen."

"I am delighted that such is your opinion, mademoiselle; the bracelets are yours, and the king begs your acceptance of them."

And as, with a movement almost resembling terror, La Vallière eagerly held out the casket to the king, the king gently pushed back her trembling hand.

A silence of astonishment, more profound than that of death, reigned in the assembly.

And yet, from the side where the queens were, no one had heard what he had said, nor understood what he had done. A charitable friend, however, took upon herself to spread the news; it was Tonnay-Charente, to whom Madame had made a sign to approach.

" Good heavens ! " explained Tonnay-Charente, " how happy that La Vallière is ! the king has just given her the bracelets."

Madame bit her lips to such a degree that the blood appeared upon the surface of the skin. The young queen looked first at La Vallière and then at Madame, and began to laugh. Anne of Austria rested her chin upon her beautiful white hand, and remained for a long time absorbed by a presentiment that disturbed her mind, and by a terrible pang which stung her heart. De Guiche, observing Madame turn pale, and guessing the cause of her change of color, abruptly quitted the assembly and disappeared. Malicorne was then able to approach Montalais very quietly, and under cover of the general din of conversation, said to her :

" Aure, your fortune and our future are standing at your elbow."

" Yes," was her reply, as she tenderly embraced La Vallière, whom, inwardly, she was tempted to strangle.

CHAPTER XXXI.

MALAGA.

DURING all these long and noisy debates between the opposite ambitions of politics and love, one of our characters, perhaps the one least deserving of neglect, was, however, very much neglected, very much forgotten, and exceedingly unhappy. In fact, D'Artagnan,—D'Artagnan we say, for we must call him by his name, to remind our readers of his existence—D'Artagnan, we repeat, had absolutely nothing whatever to do, amidst these brilliant butterflies of fashion.   After following the king during two whole days at Fontainebleau, and critically observing the various pastoral fancies and heroi-comic transformations of his sovereign, the musketeer felt that he needed something more than this to satisfy the cravings of his nature.   At every moment assailed by people asking him, "How do you think this costume suits me, Monsieur d'Artagnan?" he would reply to them in quiet, sarcastic tones, "Why, I think you are quite as well-dressed as the best-dressed monkey to be found in the fair at Saint Laurent."   It was just such a compliment D'Artagnan would choose where he did not feel disposed to pay any other: and, whether agreeable or not, the inquirer was obliged to be satisfied with it.   Whenever any one asked him, "How do you intend to dress yourself this evening?" he replied, "I shall undress myself;" at which the ladies all laughed, and a few of them blushed.   But after a couple of days passed in this manner, the musketeer, perceiving that nothing serious was likely to arise which would concern him, and that the king had completely, or, at least, appeared to have completely, forgotten Paris, Saint Mandé, and Belle-Isle—that M. Colbert's mind was occupied with illuminations and fireworks—that for the next month, at least, the ladies had plenty of glances to bestow, and also to receive in exchange—D'Artagnan asked the king for leave of absence for a matter of private business.   At the moment D'Artagnan made his request, his majesty was on the point of going to bed, quite exhausted from dancing.

"You wish to leave me, Monsieur d'Artagnan?" inquired the king, with an air of astonishment; for Louis XIV. could never understand that any one who had the distinguished honor of being near him, could wish to leave him.

"Sire," said D'Artagnan, "I leave you simply because I am not of the slightest service to you in anything.   Ah!

if I could only hold the balancing-pole while you were dancing, it would be a very different affair."

"But, my dear Monsieur d'Artagnan," said the king, gravely, "people dance without balancing-poles."

"Ah! indeed," said the musketeer, continuing his imperceptible tone of irony, "I had no idea such a thing was possible."

"You have not seen me dance, then?" inquired the king.

"Yes; but I always thought dancers went from easy to difficult acrobatic feats. I was mistaken; all the more greater reason, therefore, that I should leave for a time. Sire, I repeat, you have no present occasion for my services; besides, if your majesty should have any need of me, you would know where to find me."

"Very well," said the king, and he granted him leave of absence.

We shall not look for D'Artagnan, therefore, at Fontainebleau, for to do so would be useless; but, with the permission of our readers, follow him to the Rue des Lombards, where he was located at the sign of the Pilon d'Or, in the house of our old friend Planchet. It was about eight o'clock in the evening, and the weather was exceedingly warm; there was only one window open, and that one belonging to a room on the *entresol*. A perfume of spices, mingled with another perfume less exotic, but more penetrating, namely, that which arose from the street, ascended to salute the nostrils of the musketeer. D'Artagnan, reclining in an immense straight-backed chair, with his legs not stretched out, but simply placed upon a stool, formed an angle of the most obtuse form that could possibly be seen. Both his arms were crossed over his head, his head reclining upon his left shoulder, like Alexander the Great. His eyes, usually so quick and intelligent in their expression, were now half-closed, and seemed fastened, as it were, upon a small corner of blue sky, that was visible behind the opening of the chimneys ; there was just enough blue, and no more, to fill one of the sacks of lentils, or haricots, which formed the principal furniture of the shop on the ground floor.   Thus extended at his ease, and sheltered in his place of observation behind the window, D'Artagnan seemed as if he had ceased to be a soldier, as if he were no longer an officer belonging to the palace, but was, on the contrary, a quiet, easy-going citizen in a state of stagnation between his dinner and supper, or between his supper and his bed ; one of those strong, ossified brains, which have no more room for a single idea, so fiercely does animal matter keep watch at the doors of intelligence, narrowly inspecting the contraband trade which might result from the introduction into the brain of a symptom of thought.   We have already said night was closing in, the shops were being lighted, while the windows of the upper apartments were being closed, and the rhythmic steps of a patrol of soldiers forming the night watch could be heard retreating.   D'Artagnan continued, however, to think of nothing, except the blue corner of the sky.   A few paces from him, completely in the shade, lying on his stomach, upon a sack of Indian corn, was Planchet, with both his arms under his chin, and his eyes fixed on D'Artagnan, who was either thinking, dreaming, or sleeping, with his eyes open. Planchet had been watching him for a tolerably long time, and, by way of interruption, he began by exclaiming, " Hum! hum ! "   But D'Artagnan did not stir.   Planchet then saw that it was necessary to have recourse to more effectual means still : after a prolonged reflection on the subject, the most ingenious means that suggested itself to him under present circumstances, was to let himself roll off the sack on to the floor, murmuring, at the same time, against himself, the word "stupid."   But, notwithstanding the noise produced by Planchet's fall, D'Artagnan, who had in the course of his existence heard many other, and very different falls, did not appear to pay the least attention to the present one. Besides, an enormous cart, laden with stones, passing from the Rue Saint-Médéric, absorbed, in the noise of its wheels, the noise of Planchet's tumble. And yet Planchet fancied that, in token of tacit approval, he saw him imperceptibly smile at the word "stupid." This emboldened him to say, "Are you asleep, Monsieur d'Artagnan?"

"No, Planchet, I am not *even* asleep," replied the musketeer.

"I am in despair," said Planchet, "to hear such a word as *even*."

"Well, and why not; is it not a grammatical word, Monsieur Planchet?"

"Of course, Monsieur d'Artagnan."

"Well!"

"Well, then, the word distresses me beyond measure."

"Tell me why you are distressed, Planchet," said D'Artagnan.

"If you say that you are not *even* asleep, it is as much as to say that you have not even the consolation of being able to sleep; or, better still, it is precisely the same as telling me that you are getting bored to death."

"Planchet, you know I am never bored."

"Except to-day, and the day before yesterday."

"Bah!"

"Monsieur d'Artagnan, it is a week since you returned here from Fontainebleau; in other words, you have no longer your orders to issue, or your men to review and maneuver. You need the sound of guns, drums, and all that din and confusion; I who have myself carried a musket, can easily believe that."

"Planchet," replied D'Artagnan, "I assure you I am not bored the least in the world."

"In that case, what are you doing, lying there, as if you were dead?"

"My dear Planchet, there was, once upon a time, at the siege of Rochelle, when I was there, when you were there, when we both were there, a certain Arab, who was celebrated for the manner in which he adjusted culverins. He was a clever fellow, although of a very odd complexion, which was the same color as your olives. Well, this Arab, whenever he had done eating or working, used to sit down to rest himself, as I am resting myself now, and smoked I cannot tell you what sort of magical leaves, in a large amber-mouthed tube; and if any officers, happening to pass, reproached him for being always asleep, he used quietly to reply: 'Better to sit down than to stand up, to lie down than to sit down, to be dead than to lie down.' He was an acutely melancholy Arab, and I remember him perfectly well, from the color of his skin, and the style of his conversation. He used to cut off the heads of Protestants with the most singular gusto!"

"Precisely; and then used to embalm them, when they were worth the trouble; and when he was thus engaged with his herbs and plants about him, he looked like a basket-maker making baskets."

"You are quite right, Planchet, he did."

"Oh! I can remember things very well, at times!"

"I have no doubt of it; but what do you think of his mode of reasoning?"

"I think it good in one sense, but very stupid in another."

"Expound your meaning, M. Planchet."

"Well, monsieur, in point of fact then, 'better to sit down than to stand up,' is plain enough, especially when one may be fatigued," and Planchet smiled in a roguish way; " as for ' better to be lying down,' let that pass, but as for the last proposition, that it is ' better to be dead than alive,' it is, in my opinion, very absurd, my own undoubted preference being for my bed; and if you are not of my opinion, it is simply, as I have already had the honor of telling you, because you are boring yourself to death."

" Planchet, do you know M. La Fontaine? "

" The chemist at the corner of the Rue Saint-Médéric? "

" No, the writer of fables."

"Oh! *Maître Corbeau!* "

"Exactly; well, then, I am like his hare."

" He has got a hare also, then? "

" He has all sorts of animals."

" Well, what does his hare do, then? "

" M. La Fontaine's hare thinks."

" Ah, ha! "

" Planchet, I am like that hare—I am thinking."

" You are thinking, you say? " said Planchet, uneasily.

"Yes; your house is dull enough to drive people to think; you will admit that, I hope."

" And yet, monsieur, you have a look-out upon the street."

" Yes; and wonderfully interesting that is, of course."

" But it is no less true, monsieur, that, if you were living at the back of the house, you would bore yourself—I mean, you would think—more than ever."

" Upon my word, Planchet, I hardly know that."

" Still," said the grocer, "if your reflections are at all like those which led you to restore King Charles II.; " and Planchet finished by a little laugh which was not without its meaning.

" Ah! Planchet, my friend," returned D'Artagnan, "you are getting ambitious."

"Is there no other king to be restored, M. d'Artagnan —no second Monk to be packed up, like a salted hog, in a deal box?"

"No, my dear Planchet; all the kings are seated on their respective thrones; less comfortably so, perhaps, than I am upon this chair; but, at all events, there they are." And D'Artagnan sighed deeply.

"Monsieur d'Artagnan," said Planchet, "you are making me very uneasy."

"You are very good, Planchet."

"I begin to suspect something."

"What is it?"

"Monsieur d'Artagnan, you are getting thin."

"Oh!" said D'Artagnan, striking his chest, which sounded like an empty cuirass; "it is impossible, Planchet."

"Ah!" said Planchet, slightly overcome; "if you were to get thin in my house——"

"Well?"

"I should do something rash."

"What would you do? Tell me."

"I should look out for the man who was the cause of all your anxieties."

"Ah! according to your account, I am anxious now."

"Yes, you are anxious; and you are getting thin, visibly getting thin. *Malaga!* if you go on getting thin in this way, I will take my sword in my hand, and go straight to M. d'Herblay, and have it out with him."

"What!" said M. d'Artagnan, starting in his chair; "what's that you say? And what has M. d'Herblay's name to do with your groceries?"

"Just as you please. Get angry if you like, or call me names, if you prefer it; but, the deuce is in it. *I know what I know.*"

D'Artagnan had, during this second outburst of Planchet's, so placed himself as not to lose a single look of his face; that is, he sat with both his hands resting on both his knees, and his head stretched out towards the grocer. " Come, explain yourself," he said, " and tell me how you could possibly utter such a blasphemy. M. d'Herblay, your old master, my friend, an ecclesiastic, a musketeer turnéd bishop—do you mean to say you would raise your sword against him, Planchet?"

" I could raise my sword against my own father, when I see you in such a state as you are now."

"M. d'Herblay, a gentleman! "

" It's all the same to me whether he's a gentleman or not. He gives you the blue devils, that is all I know. And the blue devils make people get thin. *Malaga!* I have no notion of M. D'Artagnan leaving my house thinner than when he entered it."

" How does he give me the blue devils, as you call it? Come, explain, explain."

" You have had the nightmare during the last three nights."

" I?"

" Yes, you; and in your nightmare you called out, several times, ' Aramis, deceitful Aramis!' "

" Ah! I said that, did I?" murmured D'Artagnan uneasily.

" Yes, those very words, upon my honor."

" Well, what else? You know the saying, Planchet, 'dreams go by contraries.' "

"Not so; for, every time during the last three days, when you went out, you have not once failed to ask me, on your return, ' Have you seen M. d'Herblay?' or else ' Have you received any letters for me from M. d'Herblay?' "

" Well, it is very natural I should take an interest in my old friend," said D'Artagnan.

"Of course; but not to such an extent as to get thin on that account."

"Planchet, I'll get fatter; I give you my word of honor I will."

"Very well, monsieur, I accept it; for I know that when you give your word of honor, it is sacred."

"I will not dream of Aramis any more; and I will never ask you again if there are any letters from M. d'Herblay; but on condition that you explain one thing to me."

"Tell me what it is, monsieur."

"I am a great observer; and just now, you made use of a very singular oath, which is unusual for you."

"You mean *Malaga!* I suppose?"

"Precisely."

"It is the oath I have used ever since I have been a grocer."

"Very proper, too, it is the name of a dried grape, or raisin, I believe?"

"It is my most ferocious oath; when I have once said *Malaga!* I am a man no longer."

"Still, I never knew you use that oath before."

"Very likely not, monsieur. I had a present made me of it," said Planchet; and, as he pronounced these words, he winked his eye with a cunning expression, which thoroughly awakened D'Artagnan's attention.

"Come, come, M. Planchet."

"Why, I am not like you, monsieur," said Planchet. "I don't pass my life in thinking."

"You do wrong, then."

"I mean in boring myself to death. We have but a very short time to live—why not make the best of it?"

"You are an Epicurean philosopher, I begin to think, Planchet."

"Why not? My hand is still as steady as ever; I can

write, and can weigh out my sugar and spices; my foot is firm; I can dance and walk about; my stomach has its teeth still, for I eat and digest well; my heart is not quite hardened. Well, monsieur?"

"Well, what, Planchet?"

"Why, you see——" said the grocer, rubbing his hands together.

D'Artagnan crossed one leg over the other, and said, "Planchet, my friend, I am unnerved with extreme surprise; for you are revealing yourself to me under a perfectly new light."

Planchet, flattered in the highest degree by this remark, continued to rub his hands very hard together. "Ah, ah," he said, "because I happen to be only slow, you think me, perhaps, a positive fool."

"Very good, Planchet; very well reasoned."

"Follow my idea, monsieur, if you please. I said to myself," continued Planchet, "that, without enjoyment, there is no happiness on this earth."

"Quite true, what you say, Planchet," interrupted D'Artagnan.

"At all events, if we cannot obtain pleasure—for pleasure is not so common a thing, after all—let us, at least, get consolations of some kind or other."

"And so you console yourself?"

"Exactly so."

"Tell me how you console yourself."

"I put on a buckler for the purpose of confronting *ennui*. I place my time at the direction of patience; and on the very eve of feeling I am going to get bored, I amuse myself."

"And you don't find any difficulty in that?"

"None."

"And you found it out quite by yourself?"

"Quite so."

" It is miraculous."

" What do you say ? "

"I say, that your philosophy is not to be matched in the Christian or pagan world, in modern days or in antiquity ! "

" You think so?—follow my example, then."

" It is a very tempting one."

" Do as I do."

"I could not wish for anything better; but all minds are not of the same stamp ; and it might possibly happen that if I were required to amuse myself in the manner you do, I should bore myself horribly."

"Bah! at least try first."

" Well, tell me what you do."

" Have you observed that I leave home occasionally ? "

" Yes."

" In any particular way ? "

"Periodically."

" That's the very thing.   You have noticed it, then ? "

" My dear Planchet, you must understand that when people see each other every day, and one of the two absents himself, the other misses him.   Do not you feel the want of my society when I am in the country ? "

" Prodigiously ; that is to say, I feel like a body without a soul."

" That being understood, then, proceed."

" What are the periods when I absent myself ? "

" On the fifteenth and thirtieth of every month."

"And I remain away ? "

" Sometimes two, sometimes three, and sometimes four days at a time."

" Have you ever given it a thought, why I was absent? "

" To look after your debts, I suppose."

" And when I returned, how did you think I looked, as far as my face was concerned ? "

" Exceedingly self-satisfied."

" You admit, you say, that I always look satisfied. And what have you attributed my satisfaction to ? "

" That your business was going on very well ; that your purchases of rice, prunes, raw sugar, dried apples, pears, and treacle, were advantageous. You were always very picturesque in your notions and ideas, Planchet; and I was not in the slightest degree surprised to find you had selected grocery as an occupation, which is of all trades the most varied, and the very pleasantest, as far as character is concerned; inasmuch as one handles so many natural and perfumed productions."

" Perfectly true, monsieur ; but you are very greatly mistaken."

" In what way ? "

" In thinking that I leave here every fortnight, to collect my money, or to make purchases. Ho, ho ! how could you possibly have thought such a thing? Ho, ho, ho ! " And Planchet began to laugh in a manner that inspired D'Artagnan with very serious misgivings as to his sanity.

" I confess," said the musketeer, " that I do not precisely catch your meaning."

" Very true, monsieur."

" What do you mean by ' very true' ? "

" It must be true, since you say it; but pray, be assured that it in no way lessens my opinion of you."

" Ah, that is lucky."

" No ; you are a man of genius ; and whenever the question happens to be of war, tactics, surprises, or good honest blows to be dealt, why, kings are marionettes, compared to you. But for the consolations of the mind, the proper care of the body, the agreeable things of life, if one may say so—ah! monsieur don't talk to me about men of genius ; they are nothing short of executioners."

"Good," said D'Artagnan, really fidgety with curiosity, "upon my word you interest me in the highest degree."

"You feel already less bored than you did just now, do you not?"

"I was not bored; yet since you have been talking to me, I feel more animated."

"Very good, then; that is not a bad beginning. I will cure you, rely upon that."

"There is nothing I should like better."

"Will you let me try, then?"

"Immediately, if you like."

"Very well. Have you any horses here?"

"Yes; ten, twenty, thirty."

"Oh, there is no occasion for so many as that, two will be quite sufficient."

"They are quite at your disposal, Planchet."

"Very good; then I shall carry you off with me."

"When?"

"To-morrow."

"Where?"

"Ah, you are asking me too much."

"You will admit, however, that it is important I should know where I am going."

"Do you like the country?"

"Only moderately, Planchet."

"In that case, you like town better?"

"That is as may be."

"Very well; I am going to take you to a place, half town and half country."

"Good."

"To a place where I am sure you will amuse yourself."

"Is it possible?"

"Yes; and more wonderful still, to a place from which you have just returned, for the purpose only, it would seem, of getting bored here."

"It is to Fontainebleau you are going, then?"

"Exactly; to Fontainebleau."

"And, in heaven's name, what are you going to do at Fontainebleau?"

Planchet answered D'Artagnan by a wink full of sly humor.

"You have some property there, you rascal."

"Oh, a very paltry affair; a little bit of a house—nothing more."

"I understand you."

"But it is tolerable enough, after all."

"I am going to Planchet's country-seat!" exclaimed D'Artagnan.

"Whenever you like."

"Did we not fix to-morrow?"

"Let us say to-morrow, if you like; and then, besides, to-morrow is the 14th, that is to say, the day before the one when I am afraid of getting bored; so we will look upon it as an understood thing."

"Agreed, by all means."

"You will lend me one of your horses?"

"The best I have."

"No; I prefer the gentlest of all; I never was a very good rider, as you know, and in my grocery business I have got more awkward than ever; besides——"

"Besides what?"

"Why," added Planchet, "I do not wish to fatigue myself."

"Why so?" D'Artagnan ventured to ask.

"Because I should lose half the pleasure I expect to enjoy," replied Planchet. And thereupon he rose from his sack of Indian corn, stretching himself, and making all his bones crack, one after the other, with a sort of harmony.

"Planchet! Planchet!" exclaimed D'Artagnan, "I do

declare that there is no sybarite upon the whole face of the globe who can for a moment be compared to you. Oh, Planchet, it is very clear that we have never yet eaten a ton of salt together."

" Why so, monsieur ? "

"Because, even now I can scarcely say I know you," said D'Artagnan, "and because, in point of fact, I return to the opinion which, for a moment, I had formed of you that day at Boulogne, when you strangled, or did so as nearly as possible, M. de Wardes's valet, Lubin; in plain language, Planchet, that you are a man of great resources.

Planchet began to laugh with a laugh full of self-conceit; bade the musketeer good-night, and went down to his back shop, which he used as a bedroom. D'Artagnan resumed his original position upon his chair, and his brow, which had been unruffled for a moment, became more pensive than ever. He had already forgotten the whims and dreams of Planchet. " Yes," said he, taking up again the thread of his thoughts, which had been broken by the whimsical conversation in which we have just permitted our readers to participate. " Yes, yes, those three points include everything : First, to ascertain what Baisemeaux wanted with Aramis ; secondly, to learn why Aramis does not let me hear from him ; and thirdly, to ascertain where Porthos is. The whole mystery lies in these three points. Since, therefore," continued D'Artagnan, " our friends tell us nothing, we must have recourse to our own poor intelligence. I must do what I can, *mordioux*, or rather *Malaga*, as Planchet would say."

CHAPTER XXXII.

A LETTER FROM M. BAISEMEAUX.

D'ARTAGNAN, faithful to his plan, went the very next morning to pay a visit to M. de Baisemeaux. It was cleaning up or tidying day at the Bastile; the cannons were furbished up, the staircases scraped and cleaned; and the jailers seemed to be carefully engaged in polishing the very keys. As for the soldiers belonging to the garrison, they were walking about in different courtyards, under the pretense that they were clean enough. The governor, Baisemeaux, received D'Artagnan with more than ordinary politeness, but he behaved towards him with so marked a reserve of manner, that all D'Artagnan's tact and cleverness could not get a syllable out of him. The more he kept himself within bounds, the more D'Artagnan's suspicion increased. The latter even fancied he remarked that the governor was acting under the influence of a recent recommendation. Baisemeaux had not been at the Palais-Royal with D'Artagnan the same cold and impenetrable man which the latter now found in the Baisemeaux of the Bastile. When D'Artagnan wished to make him talk about the urgent money matters which had brought Baisemeaux in search of D'Artagnan, and had rendered him expansive, notwithstanding what had passed on that evening, Baisemeaux pretended that he had some orders to give in the prison, and left D'Artagnan so long alone, waiting for him, that our musketeer, feeling sure that he should not get another syllable out of him, left the Bastile without waiting until Baisemeaux returned from his inspection. But D'Artagnan's suspicions were aroused, and when once that was the case, D'Artagnan could not sleep or remain quiet for a moment. He was among men what the cat is among quadrupeds, the emblem of anxiety and impatience, at the same moment. A restless cat can no more remain in the same place than a silk thread wafted idly to and fro with every breath of air. A cat on the watch is as motionless as death stationed at its place of observation, and neither hunger nor thirst can draw it from its meditations. D'Artagnan, who was burning with impatience, suddenly threw aside the feeling, like a cloak which he felt too heavy on his shoulders, and said to himself that that which they were concealing from him, was the very thing it was important he should know; and, consequently, he reasoned that Baisemeaux would not fail to put Aramis on his guard, if Aramis had given him any particular recommendation, and this was, in fact, the very thing that happened.

Baisemeaux had hardly had time to return from the donjon, than D'Artagnan placed himself in ambuscade close to the Rue du Petit-Muse, so as to see every one who might leave the gates of the Bastile. After he had spent an hour on the look-out from the "Golden Portcullis," under the pent-house of which he could keep himself a little in the shade, D'Artagnan observed a soldier leave the Bastile. This was, indeed, the surest indication he could possibly have wished for, as every jailer or warder has certain days, and even certain hours, for leaving the Bastile, since all are alike prohibited from having either wives or lodgings in the castle, and can accordingly leave without exciting any curiosity; but a soldier once in barracks is kept there for four-and-twenty hours when on duty,—and no one knew this better than D'Artagnan. The guardsman in question, therefore, was not likely to leave in his regimentals, except on an express and urgent order. The soldier, we were saying, left the

Bastile at a slow and lounging pace, like a happy mortal, in fact, who, instead of mounting sentry before a wearisome guard-house, or upon a bastion no less wearisome, has the good luck to get a little liberty, in addition to a walk,—both pleasures being luckily reckoned as part of his time on duty. He bent his steps towards the Faubourg Saint-Antoine, enjoying the fresh air and the warmth of the sun, and looking at all the pretty faces he passed. D'Artagnan followed him at a distance; he had not yet arranged his ideas as to what was to be done. "I must, first of all," he thought, "see the fellow's face. A man seen is a man judged." D'Artagnan increased his pace, and, which was not very difficult, by the by, soon got in advance of the soldier. Not only did he observe that his face showed a tolerable amount of intelligence and resolution, but he noticed also that his nose was a little red. "He has a weakness for brandy, I see," said D'Artagnan to himself. At the same moment that he remarked his red nose, he saw that the soldier had a white paper in his belt.

"Good, he has a letter," added D'Artagnan. The only difficulty was to get hold of the letter. But a common soldier would, of course, be only too delighted at having been selected by M. de Baisemeaux as a special messenger, and would not be likely to sell his message. As D'Artagnan was biting his nails, the soldier continued to advance more and more into the Faubourg Saint-Antoine. "He is certainly going to Saint-Mandé," he said to himself, "and I shall not be able to learn what the letter contains." It was enough to drive him wild. "If I were in uniform," said D'Artagnan to himself, "I would have this fellow seized, and his letter with him. I could easily get assistance at the very first guard-house; but the devil take me if I mention my name in an affair of this kind. If I were to treat him to something to drink, his suspicions

would be roused; and besides, he might drink me drunk.
Mordioux! my wits seem to have left me," said D'Artagnan; "it is all over with me. Yet, supposing I were
to attack this poor devil, make him draw his sword
and kill him for the sake of his letter? No harm in that,
if it were a question of a letter from a queen to a nobleman, or a letter from a cardinal to a queen; but what
miserable intrigues are those of Messieurs Aramis and
Fouquet with M. Colbert. A man's life for that? No, no,
indeed; not even ten crowns." As he philosophized in
this manner, biting, first his nails, and then his mustaches,
he perceived a group of archers and a commissary of the
police engaged in carrying away a man of very gentle-
manly exterior, who was struggling with all his might
against them. The archers had torn his clothes, and were
dragging him roughly away. He begged they would
lead him along more respectfully, asserting that he was a
gentleman and a soldier. And observing our soldier
walking in the street, he called out, "Help, comrade."

The soldier walked on with the same step towards the
man who had called out to him, followed by the crowd.
An idea suddenly occurred to D'Artagnan; it was his first
one, and we shall find it was not a bad one either. During
the time the gentleman was relating to the soldier that
he had just been seized in a house as a thief, when the
truth was he was only there as a lover; and while the
soldier was pitying him, and offering him consolation and
advice with that gravity which a French soldier has always ready whenever his vanity or his *esprit de corps* is
concerned, D'Artagnan glided behind the soldier, who was
closely hemmed in by the crowd, and with a rapid sweep,
like a sabre slash, snatched the letter from his belt. As
at this moment the gentleman with the torn clothes was
pulling about the soldier, to show how the commissary of
police had pulled him about, D'Artagnan effected his

pillage of the letter without the slightest interference.
He stationed himself about ten paces distant, behind the
pillar of an adjoining house, and read on the address, "To
Monsieur du Vallon, at Monsieur Fouquet's Saint-Mandé."

"Good!" he said, and then he unsealed, without tearing the letter, drew out the paper, which was folded in
four, from the inside; which contained only these
words:—

"DEAR MONSIEUR DU VALLON—Will you be good
enough to tell Monsieur d'Herblay that *he* has been to the
Bastile, and has been making inquiries.

"Your devoted
"DE BAISEMEAUX."

"Very good! all right!" exclaimed D'Artagnan; "it is
clear enough now. Porthos is engaged in it." Being now
satisfied of what he wished to know: "*Mordioux!*"
thought the musketeer, "what is to be done with that poor
devil of a soldier? That hot-headed, cunning fellow, De
Baisemeaux, will make him pay dearly for my trick,—if
he returns without the letter, what will they do to him?
Besides, I don't want the letter; when the egg has been
sucked, what is the good of the shell?" D'Artagnan
perceived that the commissary and the archers had
succeeded in convincing the soldier, and went on their
way with the prisoner, the latter being still surrounded
by the crowd, and continuing his complaints. D'Artagnan advanced into the very middle of the crowd, let the
letter fall, without any one having observed him, and
then retreated rapidly. The soldier resumed his route towards Saint-Mandé, his mind occupied with the gentleman who had implored his protection. Suddenly he
thought of his letter, and, looking at his belt, saw that it
was no longer there. D'Artagnan derived no little satisfaction from his sudden terrified cry. The poor soldier

in the greatest anguish of mind looked round him on every side, and at last, about twenty paces behind him, he perceived the lucky envelope. He pounced on it like a falcon on its prey. The envelope was certainly a little dirty, and rather crumpled, but at all events the letter itself was found. D'Artagnan observed that the broken seal attracted the soldier's attention a good deal, but he finished apparently by consoling himself, and returned the letter to his belt. "Go on," said D'Artagnan, "I have plenty of time before me, so you may precede me. It appears that Aramis is not in Paris, since Baisemeaux writes to Porthos. Dear Porthos, how delighted I shall be to see him again, and to have some conversation with him!" said the Gascon. And, regulating his pace according to that of the soldier, he promised himself to arrive a quarter of an hour after him at M. Fouquet's.

CHAPTER XXXIII.

IN WHICH THE READER WILL BE DELIGHTED TO FIND THAT PORTHOS HAS LOST NOTHING OF HIS MUSCULARITY.

D'ARTAGNAN had, according to his usual style, calculated that every hour is worth sixty minutes, and every minute worth sixty seconds. Thanks to this perfectly exact calculation of minutes and seconds, he reached the superintendent's door at the very moment the soldier was leaving it with his belt empty. D'Artagnan presented himself at the door, which a porter with a profusely embroidered livery held half opened for him. D'Artagnan would very much have liked to enter without giving his name, but this was impossible, and so he gave it. Notwithstanding this concession, which ought to have removed every difficulty in the way, at least D'Artagnan thought so, the *concierge* hesitated ; however, at the second repetition of the title, captain of the king's guards, the *concierge*, without quite leaving the passage clear for him, ceased to bar it completely. D'Artagnan understood that orders of the most positive character had been given. He decided, therefore, to tell a falsehood,—a circumstance, moreover, which did not very seriously affect his peace of mind, when he saw that beyond the falsehood the safety of the state itself, or even purely and simply his own individual personal interest, might be at stake. He moreover added to the declarations he had already made, that the soldier sent to M. du Vallon was his own messenger, and that the only object that letter had in view was to announce his intended arrival. From that moment, no one opposed D'Artagnan's entrance any further, and he entered accordingly. A valet wished to accompany him, but he answered that it was useless to take that trouble on his account, inasmuch as he knew perfectly well where M. du Vallon was. There was nothing, of course, to say to a man so thoroughly and completely informed on all points, and D'Artagnan was permitted therefore to do as he liked. The terraces, the magnificent apartments, the gardens, were all reviewed and narrowly inspected by the musketeer. He walked for a quarter of an hour in this more than royal residence, which included as many wonders as articles of furniture, and as many servants as there were columns and doors. " Decidedly," he said to himself, " this mansion has no other limits than the pillars of the habitable world. Is it probable Porthos has taken it into his head to go back to Pierrefonds without even leaving M. Fouquet's house ? " He finally reached a remote part of the château inclosed by a stone wall, which was covered with a profusion of thick plants, luxuriant in blossoms as large and solid as fruit. At equal distances on the top of this wall were placed vari-

ous statues in timid or mysterious attitudes. These were
vestals hidden beneath the long Greek peplum, with its
thick sinuous folds : agile nymphs, covered with their
marble veils, and guarding the palace with their furtive
glances. A statue of Hermes, with his finger on his lips ;
one of Iris, with extended wings; another of Night,
sprinkled all over with poppies, dominated the gardens
and outbuildings, which could be seen through the trees.
All these statues threw in white relief their profiles upon
the dark ground of the tall cypresses, which darted their
somber summits towards the sky. Around these cypresses were entwined climbing roses, whose flowering
rings were fastened to every fork of the branches, and
spread over the lower boughs and the various statues
showers of flowers of the rarest fragrance. These en-
chantments seemed to the musketeer the result of the
greatest efforts of the human mind. He felt in a dreamy,
almost poetical, frame of mind. The idea that Porthos
was living in so perfect an Eden gave him a higher idea
of Porthos, showing how tremendously true it is, that
even the very highest orders of minds are not quite ex-
empt from the influence of surroundings. D'Artagnan
found the door, and on, or rather in the door a kind of
spring which he detected ; having touched it, the door
flew open. D'Artagnan entered, closed the door behind
him, and advanced into a pavilion built in a circular
form, in which no other sound could be heard but cas-
cades and the songs of birds. At the door of the pavilion he met a lackey.

"It is here, I believe," said D'Artagnan, without hesitation, "that M. le Baron du Vallon is staying?"

"Yes, monsieur," answered the lackey.

"Have the goodness to tell him that M. le Chevalier
d'Artagnan, captain of the king's musketeers, is waiting
to see him."

D'Artagnan was introduced into the *salon*, and had not long to remain in expectation: a well-remembered step shook the floor of the adjoining room, a door opened, or rather flew open, and Porthos appeared and threw himself into his friend's arms with a sort of embarrassment which did not ill become him. "You here?" he exclaimed.

"And you?" replied D'Artagnan. "Ah, you sly fellow!"

"Yes," said Porthos, with a somewhat embarrassed smile; "yes, you see I am staying in M. Fouquet's house, at which you are not a little surprised, I suppose?"

"Not at all; why should you not be one of M. Fouquet's friends? M. Fouquet has a very large number, particularly among clever men."

Porthos had the modesty not to take the compliment to himself. "Besides," he added, "you saw me at Belle-Isle."

"A greater reason for my believing you to be one of M. Fouquet's friends."

"The fact is, I am acquainted with him," said Porthos, with a certain embarrassment of manner.

"Ah, friend Porthos," said D'Artagnan, "how treacherously you have behaved towards me."

"In what way?" exclaimed Porthos.

"What! you complete so admirable a work as the fortifications of Belle-Isle, and you did not tell me of it!" Porthos colored. "Nay, more than that," continued D'Artagnan, "you saw me out yonder, you know I am in the king's service, and yet you could not guess that the king, jealously desirous of learning the name of the man whose abilities had wrought a work of which he heard the most wonderful accounts,—you could not guess, I say, that the king sent me to learn who this man was?"

"What! the king sent you to learn——"

"Of course; but don't let us speak of that any more."

"Not speak of it!" said Porthos; "on the contrary, we will speak of it; and so the king knew that we were fortifying Belle-Isle?"

"Of course; does not the king know everything?"

"But he did not know who was fortifying it?"

"No, he only suspected from what he had been told of the nature of the works, that it was some celebrated soldier or another."

"The devil!" said Porthos, "if I had only known that!"

"You would not have run away from Vannes as you did perhaps?"

"No; what did you say when you couldn't find me?"

"My dear fellow, I reflected."

"Ah, indeed; you reflect, do you? Well, and what did that reflection lead to?"

"It led me to guess the whole truth."

"Come, then, tell me what did you guess after all?" said Porthos, settling himself into an arm-chair, and assuming the airs of a sphinx.

"I guessed, in the first place, that you were fortifying Belle-Isle."

"There was no great difficulty in that, for you saw me at work."

"Wait a minute, I also guessed something else,—that you were fortifying Belle-Isle by M. Fouquet's orders."

"That's true."

"But even that is not all. Whenever I feel myself in trim for guessing, I do not stop on my road; and so I guessed that M. Fouquet wished to preserve the most absolute secrecy respecting these fortifications."

"I believe that was his intention, in fact," said Porthos.

"Yes; but do you know why he wished to keep it secret?"

"In order it should not become known, perhaps," said Porthos.

"That was his principal reason. But his wish was subservient to a bit of generosity——"

"In fact," said Porthos, "I have heard it said that M. Fouquet was a very generous man."

"To a bit of generosity he wished to exhibit towards the king."

"Oh, oh!"

"You seem surprised at that?"

"Yes."

"And you didn't guess?"

"No."

"Well, I know it, then."

"You are a wizard."

"Not at all, I assure you!"

"How do you know it, then?"

"By a very simple means. I heard M. Fouquet himself say so to the king."

"Say what to the king?"

"That he fortified Belle-Isle on his majesty's account, and that he had made him a present of Belle-Isle."

"And you heard M. Fouquet say that to the king?"

"In those very words. He even added: 'Belle-Isle has been fortified by an engineer, one of my friends, a man of a great deal of merit, whom I shall ask your majesty's permission to present to you.'

"'What is his name?' said the king.

"'The Baron du Vallon,' M. Fouquet replied.

"'Very well,' returned his majesty, 'you will present him to me.'"

"The king said that?"

"Upon the word of a D'Artagnan!"

"Oh, oh!" said Porthos. "Why have I not been presented, then?"

"Have they not spoken to you about this presentation ?"

"Yes, certainly; but I am always kept waiting for it."

"Be easy, it will be sure to come."

"Humph! humph!" grumbled Porthos, which D'Artagnan pretended not to hear; and, changing the conversation, he said, "You seem to be living in a very solitary place here, my dear fellow ?"

"I always preferred retirement. I am of a melancholy disposition," replied Porthos, with a sigh.

"Really, that is odd," said D'Artagnan, "I never remarked that before."

"It is only since I have taken to reading," said Porthos, with a thoughtful air.

"But the labors of the mind have not affected the health of the body, I trust ?"

"Not in the slightest degree."

"Your strength is as great as ever ?"

"Too great, my friend, too great."

"Ah! I had heard that, for a short time after your arrival——"

"That I could hardly move a limb, I suppose ?"

"How was it?" said D'Artagnan, smiling, "and why was it you could not move ?"

Porthos, perceiving that he had made a mistake, wished to correct it. "Yes, I came from Belle-Isle here upon very hard horses," he said, "and that fatigued me."

"I am no longer astonished, then, since I, who followed you, found seven or eight lying dead on the road."

"I am very heavy, you know," said Porthos.

"So that you were bruised all over."

"My marrow melted, and that made me very ill."

"Poor Porthos! But how did Aramis act towards you under those circumstances?"

"Very well, indeed. He had me attended to by M. Fouquet's own doctor. But just imagine, at the end of a week I could not breathe any longer."

"What do you mean?"

"The room was too small, I had absorbed every atom of air."

"Indeed?"

"I was told so, at least; and so I was removed into another apartment."

"Where you were able to breathe, I hope and trust?"

"Yes, more freely; but no exercise—nothing to do. The doctor pretended that I was not to stir; I, on the contrary, felt that I was stronger than ever; that was the cause of a very serious accident."

"What accident?"

"Fancy, my dear fellow, that I revolted against the directions of that ass of a doctor, and I resolved to go out, whether it suited him or not: and, consequently, I told the valet who waited on me to bring me my clothes."

"You were quite naked, then?"

"Oh, no! on the contrary, I had a magnificent dressing-gown to wear. The lackey obeyed; I dressed myself in my own clothes, which had become too large for me; but a strange circumstance had happened,—my feet had become too large."

"Yes, I quite understand."

"And my boots too small."

"You mean your feet were still swollen."

"Exactly; you have hit it."

"*Pardieu!* And is that the accident you were going to tell me about?"

"Oh, yes; I did not make the same reflection you have done. I said to myself: 'Since my feet have entered my boots ten times, there is no reason why they should not go in the eleventh.'"

"Allow me to tell you, my dear Porthos, that, on this occasion, you failed in your logic."

"In short, then, they placed me opposite to a part of the room which was partitioned; I tried to get my boot on; I pulled it with my hands, I pushed with all the strength of the muscles of my leg, making the most unheard-of efforts, when suddenly, the two tags of my boots remained in my hands, and my foot struck out like a ballista."

"How learned you are in fortification, dear Porthos."

"My foot darted out like a ballista, and came against the partition, which it broke in; I really thought that, like Samson, I had demolished the temple. And the number of pictures, the quantity of china, vases of flowers, carpets, and window-panes that fell down were really wonderful."

"Indeed!"

"Without reckoning that, on the other side of the partition was a small table laden with porcelain——"

"Which you knocked over?"

"Which I dashed to the other side of the room," said Porthos, laughing.

"Upon my word it is, as you say, astonishing," replied D'Artagnan, beginning to laugh also; whereupon Porthos laughed louder than ever.

"I broke," said Porthos, in a voice half-choked from his increasing mirth, "more than three thousand francs worth of china—ha, ha, ha!"

"Good!" said D'Artagnan.

"I smashed more than four thousand francs worth of glass!—ho, ho, ho!"

"Excellent."

"Without counting a luster, which fell on my head and was broken into a thousand pieces—ha, ha, ha!"

"Upon your head?" said D'Artagnan, holding his sides.

"On top."

"But your head was broken, I suppose?"

"No, since I tell you, on the contrary, my dear fellow, that it was the luster which was broken, like glass, which, in point of fact, it was."

"Ah! the luster was glass, you say."

"Venetian glass! a perfect curiosity, quite matchless, indeed, and weighed two hundred pounds."

"And it fell upon your head!"

"Upon my head. Just imagine, a globe of crystal, gilded all over, the lower part beautifully encrusted, perfumes burning at the top, with jets from which flame issued when they were lighted."

"I quite understand, but they were not lighted at the time, I suppose?"

"Happily not, or I should have been grilled prematurely."

"And you were only knocked down flat, instead?"

"Not at all."

"How, 'not at all'?"

"Why the luster fell on my skull. It appears that we have upon the top of our heads an exceedingly thick crust."

"Who told you that, Porthos?"

"The doctor. A sort of dome which would bear Nôtre-Dame."

"Bah!"

"Yes, it seems that our skulls are made in that manner."

"Speak for yourself, my dear fellow, it is your own skull that is made in that manner, and not the skulls of other people."

"Well, that may be so," said Porthos, conceitedly, "so much, however, was that the case, in my instance, that no sooner did the luster fall upon the dome which we have at the top of our head, than there was a report like a cannon, the crystal was broken to pieces, and I fell, covered from head to foot."

"With blood, poor Porthos!"

"Not at all; with perfumes, which smelt like rich creams; it was delicious, but the odor was too strong, and I felt quite giddy from it; perhaps you have experienced it sometimes yourself, D'Artagnan?"

"Yes, in inhaling the scent of the lily of the valley; so that, my poor friend, you were knocked over by the shock and overpowered by the perfumes?"

"Yes; but what is very remarkable, for the doctor told me he had never seen anything like it——"

"You had a bump on your head I suppose?" interrupted D'Artagnan.

"I had five."

"Why five?"

"I will tell you; the luster had, at its lower extremity five gilt ornaments, excessively sharp."

"Oh!"

"Well, these five ornaments penetrated my hair, which, as you see, I wear very thick."

"Fortunately so."

"And they made a mark on my skin. But just notice the singularity of it, these things seem really only to happen to me! Instead of making indentations, they made bumps. The doctor could never succeed in explaining that to me satisfactorily."

"Well, then, I will explain it to you."

"You will do me a great service if you will," said Porthos, winking his eyes which, with him, was a sign of the profoundest attention.

"Since you have been employing your brain in studies of an exalted character, in important calculations, and so on, the head has gained a certain advantage, so that your head is now too full of science."

"Do you think so?"

"I am sure of it. The result is, that, instead of allowing any foreign matter to penetrate the interior of the head, your bony box or skull, which is already too full, avails itself of the openings which are made in it allowing this excess to escape."

"Ah!" said Porthos, to whom this explanation appeared clearer than that of the doctor.

"The five protuberances, caused by the five ornaments of the luster, must certainly have been scientific globules, brought to the surface by the force of circumstances."

"In fact," said Porthos, "the real truth is, that I felt far worse outside my head than inside. I will even confess, that when I put my hat upon my head, clapping it on my head with that graceful energy which we gentlemen of the sword possess, if my fist was not very gently applied, I experienced the most painful sensations."

"I quite believe you, Porthos."

"Therefore, my friend," said the giant, "M. Fouquet decided, seeing how slightly-built the house was, to give me another lodging, and so they brought me here."

"It is the private park, I think, is it not?"

"Yes."

"Where the rendezvous are made; that park, indeed, which is so celebrated in some of those mysterious stories about the superintendent?"

"I don't know; I have had no rendezvous or heard mysterious stories myself, but they have authorized me to exercise my muscles, and I take advantage of the permission by rooting up some of the trees."

"What for?"

"To keep my hand in, and also to take some birds' nests; I find it more convenient than climbing."

"You are as pastoral as Tyrcis, my dear Porthos."

"Yes, I like the small eggs; I like them very much.

better than larger ones. You have no idea how delicate
an *omelette* is, if made of four or five hundred eggs of
linnets, chaffinches, starlings, blackbirds and thrushes."

"But five hundred eggs is perfectly monstrous!"

"A salad-bowl will hold them easily enough," said
Porthos.

D'Artagnan looked at Porthos admiringly for full five
minutes, as if he had seen him for the first time, while
Porthos spread his chest out joyously and proudly. They
remained in this state several minutes, Porthos smiling,
and D'Artagnan looking at him. D'Artagnan was evidently trying to give the conversation a new turn. "Do
you amuse yourself much here, Porthos?" he asked at
last, very likely after he had found out what he was
searching for.

"Not always."

"I can imagine that; but when you get thoroughly
bored, by and by, what do you intend to do?"

"Oh! I shall not be here for any length of time.
Aramis is waiting until the last bump on my head disappears, in order, to present me to the king, who I am told
cannot endure the sight of a bump."

"Aramis is still in Paris, then?"

"No."

"Whereabouts is he, then?"

"At Fontainebleau."

"Alone?"

"With M. Fouquet."

"Very good. But do you happen to know one thing?"

"No, tell it me, and then I shall know."

"Well, then, I think that Aramis is forgetting you."

"Do you really think so?"

"Yes; for at Fontainebleau yonder, you must know,
they are laughing, dancing, banqueting, and drawing the
corks of M. de Mazarin's wine in fine style. Are you

aware that they have a ballet every evening there?"

"The deuce they have!"

"I assure you that your dear Aramis is forgetting you."

"Well, that is not at all unlikely, and I have myself thought so.sometimes."

"Unless he is playing you a trick, the sly fellow!"

"Oh!"

"You know that Aramis is as sly as a fox."

"Yes, but to play *me* a trick——"

"Listen : in the first place, he puts you under a sort of sequestration."

"He sequestrates me!   Do you mean to say I am sequestrated?"

"I think so."

"I wish you would have the goodness to prove that to me."

"Nothing easier.   Do you ever go out ?"

"Never."

"Do you ever ride on horseback?"

"Never."

"Are your friends allowed to come and see you?"

"Never."

"Very well, then; never to go out, never to ride on horseback, never to be allowed to see your friends, that is called being sequestrated."

"But why should Aramis sequestrate me?" inquired Porthos.

"Come," said D'Artagnan, "be frank, Porthos."

"As gold."

"It was Aramis who drew the plan of the fortifications at Belle-Isle, was it not?"

Porthos colored as he said, "Yes ; but that was all he did."

"Exactly, and my own opinion is that it was no very great affair after all."

"That is mine, too."

"Very good; I am delighted we are ot the same opinion."

"He never even came to Belle-Isle," said Porthos.

"There now, you see."

"It was I who went to Vannes, as you may have seen."

"Say, rather, as I did see. Well, that is precisely the state of the case, my dear Porthos. Aramis, who only drew the plans, wishes to pass himself off as the engineer, whilst you, who, stone by stone, built the wall, the citadel, and the bastions, he wishes to reduce to the rank of a mere builder."

"By builders, you mean mason, perhaps?"

"Mason; the very word."

"Plasterer, in fact?"

"Precisely."

"Hodman?"

"Exactly."

"Oh! oh! my dear Aramis, you seem to think you are only five-and-twenty years of age still."

"Yes, and that is not all, for he believes you are fifty."

"I should have amazingly liked to have seen him at work."

"Yes, indeed."

"A fellow who has got the gout?"

"Yes."

"Who has lost three of his teeth?"

"Four."

"While I, look at mine." And Porthos, opening his large mouth very wide, displayed two rows of teeth not quite as white as snow, but even, hard, and sound as ivory.

"You can hardly believe, Porthos," said D'Artagnan, "what a fancy the king has for good teeth. Yours decide me; I will present you to the king myself."

"You?"

"Why not?   Do you think I have less credit at court than Aramis?"

"Oh, no!"

"Do you think that I have the slightest pretensions upon the fortifications at Belle-Isle?"

"Certainly not."

"It is your own interest alone which would induce me to do it."

"I don't doubt it in the least."

"Well, I am the intimate friend of the king; and a proof of that is, that whenever there is anything disagreeable to tell him, it is I who have to do it."

"But, dear D'Artagnan, "if you present me——"

"Well!"

"Aramis will be angry."

"With me?"

"No, with *me*."

"Bah! whether he or I present you, since you are to be presented, what does it matter?"

"They were going to get me some clothes made."

"Your own are splendid."

"Oh! those I had ordered were far more beautiful."

"Take care: the king likes simplicity."

"In that case, I will be simple.   But what will M. Fouquet say, when he learns that I have left?"

"Are you a prisoner, then, on parole?"

"No, not quite that.   But I promised him I would not leave without letting him know."

"Wait a minute, we shall return to that presently. Have you anything to do here?"

"I, nothing: nothing of any importance, at least."

"Unless, indeed, you are Aramis's representative for something of importance."

"By no means."

" What I tell you—pray understand that—is out of interest for you. I suppose, for instance, that you are com-
missioned to send messages and letters to him?"

" Ah! letters—yes. I send certain letters to him."

" Where?"

" To Fontainebleau."

" Have you any letters, then?"

" But——"

" Nay, let me speak. Have you any letters, I say?"

" I have just received one for him."

" Interesting?"

" I suppose so."

" You do not read them, then?"

" I am not at all curious," said Porthos, as he drew out
of his pocket the soldier's letter which Porthos had not
read, but D'Artagnan had.

" Do you know what to do with it?" said D'Artagnan.

" Of course; do as I always do, send it to him."

" Not so."

" Why not? Keep it, then?"

" Did they not tell you that this letter was important?"

" Very important."

" Well you must take it yourself to Fontainebleau."

" To Aramis?"

" Yes."

" Very good."

" And since the king is there——"

" You will profit by that."

" I shall profit by the opportunity to present you to
the king."

" Ah! D'Artagnan, there is no one like you for expedi-
ents."

" Therefore, instead of forwarding to our friend any

messages, which may or may not be faithfully delivered, we will ourselves be the bearers of the letter."

" I had never even thought of that, and yet it is simple enough."

" And therefore, because it is urgent, Porthos, we ought to set off at once."

" In fact," said Porthos, " the sooner we set off the less chance there is of Aramis's letter being delayed."

"Porthos, your reasoning is always accurate, and, in your case, logic seems to serve as an auxiliary to the imagination."

" Do you think so?" said Porthos.

"It is the result of your hard reading," replied D'Artagnan.   " So come along, let us be off."

" But," said Porthos, "my promise to M. Fouquet?"

" Which?"

" Not to leave St. Mandé without telling him of it."

" Ah! Porthos," said D'Artagnan, " how very young you still are."

" In what way?"

" You are going to Fontainebleau, are you not, where you will find M. Fouquet?"

" Yes."

" Probably in the king's palace?"

" Yes," repeated Porthos, with an air full of majesty.

" Well, you will accost him with these words : ' M. Fouquet, I have the honor to inform you that I have just left St. Mandé.' "

" And," said Porthos, with the same majestic mien, " seeing me at Fontainebleau at the king's, M. Fouquet will not be able to tell me I am not speaking the truth."

" My dear Porthos, I was just on the point of opening my lips to make the same remark, but you anticipate me in everything.   Oh! Porthos, how fortunately you are gifted! Years have made not the slightest impression on you."

"Not over-much, certainly."

"Then there is nothing more to say?"

"I think not."

"All your scruples are removed?"

"Quite so."

"In that case I shall carry you off with me."

"Exactly; and I will go and get my horse saddled."

"You have horses here, then?"

"I have five."

"You had them sent from Pierrefonds, I suppose?"

"No, M. Fouquet gave them to me."

"My dear Porthos, we shall not want five horses for two persons; besides, I have already three in Paris, which would make eight, and that will be too many."

"It would not be too many if I had some of my servants here; but, alas! I have not got them."

"Do you regret them, then?"

"I regret Mousqueton; I miss Mousqueton."

"What a good-hearted fellow you are, Porthos," said D'Artagnan; "but the best thing you can do is to leave your horses here, as you have left Mousqueton out yonder."

"Why so?"

"Because, by and by, it might turn out a very good thing if M. Fouquet had never given you anything at all."

"I don't understand you," said Porthos.

"It is not necessary you should understand."

"But yet——"

"I will explain to you later, Porthos."

"I'll wager it is some piece of policy or other."

"And of the most subtle character," returned D'Artagnan.

Porthos nodded his head at this word policy; then,

after a moment's reflection, he added, " I confess, D'Artagnan, that I am no politician."

" I know that well."

" Oh ! no one knows what you told me yourself, you, the bravest of the brave."

" What did I tell you, Porthos ? "

" That every man has his day. You told me so, and I have experienced it myself. There are certain days when one feels less pleasure than others in exposing one's self to a bullet or a sword-thrust."

" Exactly my own idea."

" And mine, too, although I can hardly believe in blows or thrusts that kill outright."

" The deuce ! and yet you have killed a few in your time."

" Yes ; but I have never been killed."

" Your reason is a very good one."

" Therefore, I do not believe I shall ever die from a thrust of a sword or a gun-shot."

" In that case, then, you are afraid of nothing. Ah ! water perhaps ? "

" Oh ! I swim like an otter."

" Of a quartan fever, then ? "

" I never had one yet, and I don't believe I ever shall ; but there is one thing I will admit," and Porthos dropped his voice.

" What is that ? " asked D'Artagnan, adopting the same tone of voice as Porthos.

" I must confess," repeated Porthos, " that I am horribly afraid of politics."

" Ah ! bah ! " exclaimed D'Artagnan.

" Upon my word, it's true," said Porthos, in a stentorian voice. " I have seen his eminence Monsieur le Cardinal de Richelieu, and his eminence Monsieur le Cardinal de Mazarin ; the one was a red politician, the other a black politician ; I never felt very much more satisfied with the

one than with the other; the first struck off the heads of
M. de Marillac, M. de Thou, M. de Cinq-Mars, M. Châlais,
M. de Boutteville, and M. de Montmorency; the second
got a whole crowd of Frondeurs cut in pieces, and we belonged to them."

"On the contrary, we did not belong to them," said
D'Artagnan.

"Oh! indeed, yes; for, if I unsheathed my sword for
the cardinal, I struck for the king."

"My good Porthos!"

"Well, I have done. My dread of politics is such,
that if there is any question of politics in the matter, I
should greatly prefer to return to Pierrefonds."

"You would be quite right, if that were the case. But
with me, dear Porthos, no politics at all, that is quite
clear. You have labored hard in fortifying Belle-Isle;
the king wished to know the name of the clever engineer
under whose directions the works were carried out; you
are modest, as all men of true genius are; perhaps Aramis
wishes to put you under a bushel. But I happen to seize
hold of you; I make it known who you are; I produce
you; the king rewards you; and that is the only policy I
have to do with."

"And the only one I will have to do with either," said
Porthos, holding out his hand to D'Artagnan.

But D'Artagnan knew Porthos's grasp; he knew that
once imprisoned within the baron's five fingers, no hand
ever left it without being half-crushed. He therefore
held out, not his hand, but his fist, and Porthos did not
even perceive the difference. The servants talked a little
with each other in an undertone, and whispered a few
words, which D'Artagnan understood, but which he took
very good care not to let Porthos understand. "Our
friend," he said to himself, "was really and truly
Aramis's prisoner. Let us now see what the result will
be of the liberation of the captive."

CHAPTER XXXIV.

THE RAT AND THE CHEESE.

D'ARTAGNAN and Porthos returned on foot, as D'Artagnan set out. When D'Artagnan, as he entered the shop of the Pilon d'Or, announced to Planchet that M. de Vallon would be one of the privileged travelers, and as the plume in Porthos's hat made the wooden candles suspended over the front jingle together, a melancholy presentiment seemed to eclipse the delight Planchet had promised himself for the morrow. But the grocer had a heart of gold, ever mindful of the good old times—a trait that carries youth into old age. So Planchet, notwithstanding a sort of internal shiver, checked as soon as experienced, received Porthos with respect, mingled with the tenderest cordiality. Porthos, who was a little cold and stiff in his manners at first, on account of the social difference existing at that period between a baron and a grocer, soon began to soften when he perceived so much good-feeling and so many kind attentions in Planchet. He was particularly touched by the liberty which was permitted him to plunge his great palms into the boxes of dried fruits and preserves, into the sacks of nuts and almonds, and into the drawers full of sweetmeats. So that, notwithstanding Planchet's pressing invitations to go upstairs to the *entresol*, he chose as his favorite seat, during the evening which he had to spend at Planchet's house, the shop itself, where his fingers could always fish up whatever his nose detected. The delicious figs from Provence, filberts from the forest, Tours plums, were subjects of his uninterrupted attention for five consecutive hours. His teeth, like millstones, cracked heaps of nuts, the shells of which were scattered all over the floor, where they were trampled by every one who went in and out of the shop; Porthos pulled from the stalk with his lips, at one mouthful, bunches of the rich Muscatel raisins with their beautiful bloom, half a pound of which passed at one gulp from his mouth to his stomach. In one of the corners of the shop, Planchet's assistants, huddled together, looked at each other without venturing to open their lips. They did not know who Porthos was, for they had never seen him before. The race of those Titans who had worn the cuirasses of Hugh Capet, Philip Augustus, and Francis the First, had already begun to disappear. They could hardly help thinking he might be the ogre of the fairy tale, who was going to turn the whole contents of Planchet's shop into his insatiable stomach, and that, too, without in the slightest degree displacing the barrels and chests that were in it. Cracking, munching, chewing, nibbling, sucking, and swallowing, Porthos occasionally said to the grocer :—

"You do a very good business here, friend Planchet."

"He will very soon have none at all to do, if this sort of thing continues," grumbled the foreman, who had Planchet's word that he should be his successor. In the midst of his despair, he approached Porthos, who blocked up the whole of the passage leading from the back shop to the shop itself. He hoped that Porthos would rise and that this movement would distract his devouring ideas.

"What do you want, my man?" asked Porthos affably.

"I should like to pass you, monsieur, if it is not troubling you too much."

"Very well," said Porthos, "it does not trouble me in the least."

At the same moment he took hold of the young fellow by the waistband, lifted him off the ground, and placed him very gently on the other side, smiling all the while with the same affable expression. As soon as Porthos had placed him on the ground, the lad's legs so shook under him that he fell back upon some sacks of corks. But noticing the giant's gentleness of manner, he ventured again, and said :

"Ah, monsieur! pray be careful."

"What about?" inquired Porthos.

"You are positively putting a fiery furnace into your body."

"How is that, my good fellow?" said Porthos.

"All those things are very heating to the system."

"Which?"

"Raisins, nuts, and almonds."

"Yes; but if raisins, nuts, and almonds are heating——"

"There is no doubt at all of it, monsieur."

"Honey is very cooling," said Porthos, stretching out his hand towards a small barrel of honey which was open, and he plunged the scoop with which the wants of the customers were supplied into it, and swallowed a good half-pound at one gulp.

"I must trouble you for some water now, my man," said Porthos.

"In a pail, monsieur?" asked the lad, simply.

"No, in a water-bottle; that will be quite enough;" and raising the bottle to his mouth, as a trumpeter does his trumpet, he emptied the bottle at a single draught.

Planchet was agitated in every fiber of propriety and self-esteem. However, a worthy representative of the hospitality which prevailed in early days, he reigned to be talking very earnestly with D'Artagnan, and incessantly repeated:—"Ah! monsieur, what a happiness! what an honor!"

"What time shall we have supper, Planchet?" inquired Porthos, "I feel hungry."

The foreman clasped his hands together. The two

others got under the counters, fearing Porthos might have a taste for human flesh.

"We shall only take a sort of snack here," said D'Artagnan; "and when we get to Planchet's country-seat, we will have supper."

"Ah! ah! so we are going to your country-house, Planchet," said Porthos; "so much the better."

"You overwhelm me, Monsieur le Baron."

The "Monsieur le Baron," had a great effect upon the men, who detected a personage of the highest quality in an appetite of that kind. This title, too, reassured them. They had never heard that an ogre was ever called "Monsieur le Baron."

"I will take a few biscuits to eat on the road," said Porthos, carelessly; and he emptied a whole jar of aniseed biscuits into the huge pocket of his doublet.

"My shop is saved!" exclaimed Planchet.

"Yes, as the cheese was," whispered the foreman.

"What cheese?"

"That Dutch cheese, inside which a rat had made his way, and we only found the rind left."

Planchet looked all round his shop, and observing the different articles which had escaped Porthos's teeth, he found the comparison somewhat exaggerated. The foreman, who remarked what was passing in his master's mind, said, "Take care; he is not gone yet."

"Have you any fruit here?" said Porthos, as he went upstairs to the *entresol*, where it had just been announced that some refreshment was prepared.

"Alas!" thought the grocer, addressing a look at D'Artagnan full of entreaty, which the latter half understood.

As soon as they had finished eating they set off. It was late when the three riders, who had left Paris about six in the evening, arrived at Fontainebleau. The

journey passed very agreeably. Porthos took a fancy to
Planchet's society, because the latter was very respectful
in his manners, and seemed delighted to talk to him about
his meadows, his woods, and his rabbit-warrens. Porthos
had all the taste and pride of a landed proprietor. When
D'Artagnan saw his two companions in earnest conversation, he took the opposite side of the road, and letting
his bridle drop upon his horse's neck, separated himself
from the whole world, as he had done from Porthos and
from Planchet. The moon shone softly through the
foliage of the forest. The breezes of the open country
rose deliciously perfumed to the horses' nostrils, and they
snorted and pranced along delightedly. Porthos and
Planchet began to talk about hay-crops. Planchet admitted to Porthos that in the advanced years of his life,
he had certainly neglected agricultural pursuits for com-
merce, but that his childhood had been passed in Picardy
in the beautiful meadows where the grass grew as high
as the knees, and where he had played under the green
apple-trees covered with red-cheeked fruit ; he went on
to say, that he had solemnly promised himself that as
soon as he should have made his fortune, he would return
to nature, and end his days, as he had begun them, as
near as he possibly could to the earth itself, where all
men must sleep at last.

" Eh, eh ! " said Porthos ; " in that case, my dear Monsieur Planchet, your retirement is not far distant.'

" How so ? "

" Why, you seem to be in the way of making your
fortune very soon."

" Well, we are getting on pretty well, I must admit,"
replied Planchet.

" Come, tell me what is the extent of your ambition,
and what is the amount you intend to retire upon ? "

" There is one circumstance, monsieur," said Planchet,

without answering the question, "which occasions me a good deal of anxiety."

"What is it?" inquired Porthos, looking all round him as if in search of the circumstance that annoyed Planchet, and desirous of freeing him from it.

"Why, formerly," said the grocer, "you used to call me Planchet quite short, and you would have spoken to me then in a much more familiar manner than you do now."

"Certainly, certainly, I should have said so formerly," replied the good-natured Porthos, with an embarrassment full of delicacy; "but formerly——"

"Formerly I was M. d'Artagnan's lackey; is not that what you mean?"

"Yes."

"Well if I am not quite his lackey, I am as much as ever I was his devoted servant; and more than that, since that time——"

"Well, Planchet?"

"Since that time, I have had the honor of being in partnership with him."

"Oh, oh!" said Porthos. "What, has D'Artagnan gone into the grocery business?"

"No, no," said D'Artagnan, whom these words had drawn out of his reverie, and who entered into the conversation with that readiness and rapidity which distinguished every operation of his mind and body. "It was not D'Artagnan who entered into the grocery business, but Planchet, who entered into a political affair with me."

"Yes," said Planchet, with mingled pride and satisfaction, "we transacted a little business which brought me in a hundred thousand francs and M. d'Artagnan two hundred thousand."

"Oh, oh!" said Porthos, with admiration.

"So that, monsieur le baron," continued the grocer, "I again beg you to be kind enough to call me Planchet, as you used to do; and to speak to me as familiarly as in old times. You cannot possibly imagine the pleasure it would give me."

"If that be the case, my dear Planchet, I will do so, certainly," replied Porthos. And as he was quite close to Planchet, he raised his hand, as if to strike him on the shoulder, in token of friendly cordiality; but a fortunate movement of the horse made him miss his aim, so that his hand fell on the crupper of Planchet's horse, instead; which made the animal's legs almost give way.

D'Artagnan burst out laughing, as he said, "Take care, Planchet; for if Porthos begins to like you so much, he will caress you, and if he caresses you, he will knock you as flat as a pancake. Porthos is still as strong as ever, you know."

"Oh," said Planchet, "Mousqueton is not dead, and yet monsieur le baron is very fond of him."

"Certainly," said Porthos, with a sigh which made all the three horses rear; "and I was only saying, this very morning, to D'Artagnan, how much I regretted him. But tell me, Planchet?"

"Thank you, monsieur le baron, thank you."

"Good lad, good lad! How many acres of park have you got?"

"Of park?"

"Yes; we will reckon up the meadows presently, and the woods afterwards."

"Whereabouts, monsieur?"

"At your château."

"Oh, monsieur le baron; I have neither château, nor park, nor meadows, nor woods."

"What have you got, then?" inquired Porthos, "and why do you call it a country-seat?"

"I did not call it a country-seat, monsieur le baron," replied Planchet, somewhat humiliated, "but a country-box."

"Ah, ah! I understand. You are modest."

"No, monsieur le baron; I speak the plain truth. I have rooms for a couple of friends, that's all."

"But in that case, whereabouts do your friends walk?"

"In the first place, they can walk about the king's forest, which is very beautiful."

"Yes, I know the forest is very fine," said Porthos; "nearly as beautiful as my forest at Berry."

Planchet opened his eyes very wide. "Have you a forest of the same kind as the forest at Fontainebleau, monsieur le baron?" he stammered out.

"Yes; I have two, indeed, but the one at Berry is my favorite."

"Why so?" asked Planchet.

"Because I don't know where it ends; and, also because it is full of poachers."

"How can the poachers make the forest so agreeable to you?"

"Because they hunt my game, and I hunt them—which, in these peaceful times, is for me a sufficiently pleasing picture of war on a small scale."

They had reached this turn of the conversation, when Planchet, looking up, perceived the houses at the commencement of Fontainebleau, the lofty outlines of which stood out strongly against the misty visage of the heavens; whilst, rising above the compact and irregularly-formed mass of buildings, the pointed roofs of the château were clearly visible, the slates of which glistened beneath the light of the moon, like the scales of an immense fish. "Gentlemen," said Planchet, "I have the honor to inform you that we have arrived at Fontainebleau."

CHAPTER XXXV.

PLANCHET'S COUNTRY-HOUSE.

THE cavaliers looked up, and saw that what Planchet had announced to them was true. Ten minutes afterwards they were in the street called the Rue de Lyon, on the opposite side of the hostelry of the Beau Paon. A high hedge of bushy elders, hawthorn, and wild hops, formed an impenetrable fence, behind which rose a white house, with a high tiled roof. Two of the windows, which were quite dark, looked upon the street. Between the two, a small door, with a porch supported by a couple of pillars, formed the entrance to the house. The door was gained by a step raised a little from the ground. Planchet got off his horse, as if he intended to knock at the door; but, on second thoughts, he took hold of his horse by the bridle, and led it about thirty paces further on, his two companions following him. He then advanced about another thirty paces, until he arrived at the door of a cart-house, lighted by an iron grating; and, lifting up a wooden latch, pushed open one of the folding-doors. He entered first, leading his horse after him by the bridle, into a small courtyard, where an odor met them which revealed their close vicinity to a stable. " That smells all right," said Porthos, loudly, getting off his horse, " and I almost begin to think I am near my own cows at Pierrefonds."

" I have only one cow," Planchet hastened to say modestly.

" And I have thirty," said Porthos; " or, rather, I don't exactly know how many I have."

When the two cavaliers had entered, Planchet fastened

the door behind them. In the meantime, D'Artagnan, who had dismounted with his usual agility, inhaled the fresh perfumed air with the delight a Parisian feels at the sight of green fields and fresh foliage, plucked a piece of honeysuckle with one hand, and of sweet-briar with the other. Porthos clawed hold of some peas which were twined round poles stuck into the ground, and ate, or rather browsed upon them, shells and all : and Planchet was busily engaged trying to wake up an old and infirm peasant, who was fast asleep in a shed, lying on a bed of moss, and dressed in an old stable suit of clothes. The peasant, recognizing Planchet, called him " the master," to the grocer's great satisfaction. " Stable the horses well, old fellow, and you shall have something good for yourself," said Planchet.

" Yes, yes ; fine animals they are, too," said the peasant. " Oh! they shall have as much as they like."

" Gently, gently, my man," said D'Artagnan, " we are getting on a little too fast. A few oats, and a good bed—nothing more."

" Some bran and water for my horse," said Porthos, " for it is very warm, I think."

" Don't be afraid, gentlemen," replied Planchet; " Daddy Celestin is an old gendarme, who fought at Ivry. He knows all about horses ; so come into the house." And he led the way along a well-sheltered walk, which crossed a kitchen-garden, then a small paddock, and came out into a little garden behind the house, the principal front of which, as we have already noticed, faced the street. As they approached, they could see, through two open windows on the ground floor, which led into a sitting-room, the interior of Planchet's residence. This room, softly lighted by a lamp placed on the table, seemed, from the end of the garden, like a smiling image of repose, comfort, and happiness. In every direction where the rays of light fell, whether upon a piece of old china, or upon an article of furniture shining from excessive neatness, or upon the weapons hanging against the wall, the soft light was as softly reflected ; and its rays seemed to linger everywhere, upon something or another agreeable to the eye. The lamp which lighted the room, whilst the foliage of jasmine and climbing roses hung in masses from the window-frames, splendidly illuminated a damask tablecloth as white as snow. The table was laid for two persons. Amber-colored wine sparkled in a long cut-glass bottle; and a large jug of blue china, with a silver lid, was filled with foaming cider. Near the table, in a high backed arm-chair, reclined, fast asleep, a woman of about thirty years of age, her face the very picture of health and freshness. Upon her knees lay a large cat, with her paws folded under her, and her eyes half-closed, purring in that significant manner which, according to feline habits, indicates perfect contentment. The two friends paused before the window in complete amazement, while Planchet, perceiving their astonishment, was in no little degree, secretly delighted at it.

"Ah! Planchet, you rascal," said D'Artagnan, "I now understand your absences."

"Oh, oh! there is some white linen!" said Porthos, in his turn, in a voice of thunder. At the sound of this gigantic voice, the cat took flight, the housekeeper woke up with a start, and Planchet, assuming a gracious air, introduced his two companions into the room, where the table was already laid.

"Permit me, my dear," he said, "to present to you Monsieur le Chevalier d'Artagnan, my patron." D'Artagnan took the lady's hand in his in the most courteous manner, and with precisely the same chivalrous air as he would have taken Madame's.

"Monsieur la Baron du Vallon de Bracieux de Pierrefonds," added Planchet. Porthos bowed with a reverence which Anne of Austria would have approved of.

It was then Planchet's turn, and he, unhesitatingly, embraced the lady in question, not, however, until he had made a sign as if requesting D'Artagnan's and Porthos's permission, a permission as a matter of course frankly conceded. D'Artagnan complimented Planchet, and said, "You are indeed a man who knows how to make life agreeable."

"Life, monsieur," said Planchet, laughing, "is capital which a man ought to invest as sensibly as he possibly can."

"And you get very good interest for yours," said Porthos, with a burst of laughter like a peal of thunder.

Planchet turned to his housekeeper. "You have before you," he said to her, "the two gentlemen who influenced the greatest, gayest, grandest portion of my life. I have spoken to you about them both very frequently."

"And about two others as well," said the lady, with a very decided Flemish accent.

"Madame is Dutch?" inquired D'Artagnan. Porthos curled his mustache, a circumstance which was not lost upon D'Artagnan, who remarked everything.

"I am from Antwerp," said the lady.

"And her name is Madame Gechter," said Planchet.

"You should not call her madame," said D'Artagnan.

"Why not?" asked Planchet.

"Because it would make her seem older every time you call her so."

"Well, I call her Trüchen."

"And a very pretty name too," said Porthos.

"Trüchen," said Planchet, "came to me from Flanders with her virtue and two thousand florins. She ran away from a brute of a husband who was in the habit of beating her. Being myself a Picard born, I was always very fond of the Artesian women, and it is only a step from Artois to Flanders ; she came crying bitterly to her god-father, my predecessor in the Rue des Lombards ; she placed her two thousand florins in my establishment, which I have turned to very good account, and which have brought her in ten thousand."

"Bravo, Planchet."

"She is free and well off ; she has a cow, a maid servant, and old Celestin at her orders ; she mends my linen, knits my winter stockings ; she only sees me every fortnight, and seems to make herself in all things tolerably happy."

"And indeed, gentlemen, I *am* very happy and comfortable," said Trüchen, with perfect ingenuousness.

Porthos began to curl the other side of his mustache. "The deuce," thought D'Artagnan, "can Porthos have any intentions in that quarter ? "

In the meantime Trüchen had set her cook to work, had laid the table for two more, and covered it with every possible delicacy that could convert a light supper into a substantial meal, a meal into a regular feast. Fresh butter, salt beef, anchovies, tunny, a shopful of Planchet's commodities, fowls, vegetables, salad, fish from the pond and the river, game from the forest—all the produce in fact of the province. Moreover, Planchet returned from the cellar, laden with ten bottles of wine, the glass of which could hardly be seen for the thick coating of dust which covered them. Porthos's heart seemed to expand as he said, "I am hungry," and he sat himself beside Madame Trüchen, whom he looked at in the most killing manner. D'Artagnan seated himself on the other side of her, while Planchet, discreetly and full of delight, took his seat opposite.

"Do not trouble yourselves," he said, "if Trüchen

should leave the table now and then during supper; for she will have to look after your bedrooms."

In fact the housekeeper made her escape quite frequently, and they could hear, on the first floor above them, the creaking of the wooden bedsteads and the rolling of the castors on the floor. While this was going on, the three men, Porthos especially, ate and drank gloriously,—it was wonderful to see them. The ten full bottles were ten empty ones by the time Trüchen returned with the cheese. D'Artagnan still preserved his dignity and self-possession, but Porthos had lost a portion of his; and the mirth soon began to grow somewhat uproarious. D'Artagnan recommended a new descent into the cellar, and, as Planchet no longer walked with the steadiness of a well-trained foot-soldier, the captain of the musketeers proposed to accompany him. They set off, humming songs wild enough to frighten anybody who might be listening. Trüchen remained behind at table with Porthos. While the two wine-bibbers were looking behind the firewood for what they wanted, a sharp report was heard like the impact of a pair of lips on a lady's cheek.

"Porthos fancies himself at La Rochelle," thought D'Artagnan, as they returned freighted with bottles. Planchet was singing so loudly that he was incapable of noticing anything. D'Artagnan, whom nothing ever escaped remarked how much redder Trüchen's left cheek was than her right. Porthos was sitting on Trüchen's left, and was curling with both his hands both sides of his mustache at once, and Trüchen was looking at him with a most bewitching smile. The sparkling wine of Anjou very soon produced a remarkable effect upon the three companions. D'Artagnan had hardly strength enough left to take a candlestick to light Planchet up his own staircase. Planchet was pulling Porthos along, who was following Trüchen, who was herself jovial enough. It was D'Artagnan who found out the rooms and the beds. Porthos threw himself into the one destined for him, after his friend had undressed him. D'Artagnan got into his own bed, saying to himself, " *Mordioux!* I had made up my mind never to touch that light-colored wine, which brings my early camp days back again. Fie! fie! if my musketeers were only to see their captain in such a state." And drawing the curtains of his bed, he added, " Fortunately enough, though, they will not see me."

" The country is very amusing," said Porthos, stretching out his legs, which passed through the wooden footboard, and made a tremendous crash, of which, however, no one in the house was capable of taking the slightest notice. By two o'clock in the morning every one was fast asleep.

CHAPTER XXXVI.

SHOWING WHAT COULD BE SEEN FROM PLANCHET'S HOUSE.

THE next morning found the three heroes sleeping soundly. Trüchen had closed the outside blinds to keep the first rays of the sun from the leaden-lidded eyes of her guests, like a kind, good housekeeper. It was still perfectly dark, then, beneath Porthos's curtains and under Planchet's canopy, when D'Artagnan, awakened by an indiscreet ray of light which made its way through a peek-hole in the shutters, jumped hastily out of bed, as if he wished to be the first at a forlorn hope. He took by assault Porthos's room, which was next to his own. The worthy Porthos was sleeping with a noise like distant thunder ; in the dim obscurity of the room his gigantic frame was prominently displayed, and his swollen fist hung down outside the bed upon the carpet. D'Artagnan awoke Porthos, who rubbed his eyes in a tolerably good humor. In the meantime Planchet was dressing himself, and met at their bedroom doors his two guests, who were still somewhat unsteady from their previous evening's entertainment. Although it was yet very early, the whole household was already up. The cook was mercilessly slaughtering in the poultry-yard; Celestin was gathering white cherries in the garden. Porthos, brisk and lively as ever, held out his hand to Planchet, and D'Artagnan requested permission to embrace Madame Trüchen. The latter, to show that she bore no ill-will, approached Porthos, upon whom she conferred the same favor. Porthos embraced Madame Trüchen, heaving an enormous sigh. Planchet took both his friends by the hand.

"I am going to show you over the house," he said; "when we arrived last night it was as dark as an oven, and we were unable to see anything; but in broad daylight, everything looks different, and you will be satisfied, I hope."

"If we begin by the view you have," said D'Artagnan, "that charms me beyond everything ; I have always lived in royal mansions, you know, and royal personages have tolerably sound ideas upon the selection of points of view."

"I am a great stickler for a good view myself," said Porthos. "At my Château de Pierrefonds, I have had four avenues laid out, and at the end of each is a landscape of an altogether different character from the others."

"You shall see *my* prospect," said Planchet; and he led his two guests to a window.

"Ah!" said D'Artagnan, "this is the Rue de Lyon."

"Yes, I have two windows on this side, a paltry insignificant view, for there is always that bustling and noisy inn, which is a very disgreeable neighbor. I had four windows here, but I bricked up two."

"Let us go on," said D'Artagnan.

They entered a corridor leading to the bedrooms, and Planchet pushed open the outside blinds.

"Hollo! what is that out yonder?" said Porthos.

"The forest," said Planchet. "It is the horizon,—a thick line of green, which is yellow in the spring, green in the summer, red in the autumn, and white in the winter."

"All very well, but it is like a curtain, which prevents one seeing a greater distance."

"Yes," said Planchet; "still one can see, at all events, everything that intervenes."

"Ah, the open country," said Porthos. "But what is that I see out there,—crosses and stones?"

"Ah, that is the cemetery," exclaimed D'Artagnan.

"Precisely," said Planchet, "I assure you it is very curious. Hardly a day passes that some one is not buried there; for Fontainebleau is by no means an inconsiderable place. Sometimes we see young girls clothed in white carrying banners; at others, some of the town-council, or rich citizens, with choristers and all the parish authorities; and then, too, we see some of the officers of the king's household."

"I should not like that," said Porthos.

"There is not much amusement in it, at all events," said D'Artagnan.

"I assure you it encourages religious thoughts," replied Planchet.

"Oh, I don't deny that."

"But," continued Planchet, "we must all die one day or another, and I once met with a maxim somewhere which I have remembered, that the thought of death is a thought that will do us all good."

"I am far from saying the contrary," said Porthos.

"But," objected D'Artagnan, "the thought of green fields, flowers, rivers, blue horizons, extensive and boundless plains, is no less likely to do us good."

"If I had any, I should be far from rejecting them," said Planchet; "but possessing only this little cemetery, full of flowers, so moss-grown, shady, and quiet, I am contented with it, and I think of those who live in town, in the Rue des Lombards, for instance, and who have to listen to the rumbling of a couple of thousand vehicles every day, and to the soulless tramp, tramp, tramp of a hundred and fifty thousand foot passengers."

"But living," said Porthos; "living, remember that."

"That is exactly the reason," said Planchet, timidly, "why, I feel it does me good to contemplate a few dead."

"Upon my word," said D'Artagnan, "that fellow Planchet is born a philosopher as well as a grocer."

"Monsieur," said Planchet, "I am one of those good-humored sort of men whom heaven created for the purpose of living a certain span of days, and of considering all things good they meet with during their transitory stay on earth."

D'Artagnan sat down close to the window, and as there seemed to be something substantial in Planchet's philosophy, he mused over it.

"Ah, ah!" exclaimed Porthos, "If I am not mistaken, we are going to have a representation now, for I think I heard something like chanting."

"Yes," said D'Artagnan, "I hear singing too."

"Oh, it is only a burial of a very poor description," said Planchet, disdainfully; "the officiating priest, the beadle, and only one chorister boy, nothing more. You observe, messieurs, that the defunct lady or gentleman could not have been of very high rank."

"No; no one seems to be following the coffin."

"Yes," said Porthos; "I see a man."

"You are right; a man wrapped in a cloak," said D'Artagnan.

"It's not worth looking at," said Planchet.

"I find it interesting," said D'Artagnan, leaning on the window-sill.

"Come, come, you are beginning to take a fancy to the place already," said Planchet, delightedly; "it is exactly my own case. I was so melancholy at first that I could do nothing but make the sign of the cross all day, and the chants were like so many nails being driven into my head; but now, they lull me to sleep, and no bird I have ever seen or heard can sing better than those which are to be met with in this cemetery."

"Well," said Porthos, "this is beginning to get a little dull for me, and I prefer going downstairs."

Planchet with one bound was beside his guest whom he offered to lead into the garden.

"What!" said Porthos to D'Artagnan, as he turned round, "are you going to remain here?"

"Yes, I will join you presently."

"Well, M. D'Artagnan is right, after all," said Planchet: "are they beginning to bury yet?"

"Not yet."

"Ah! yes, the grave-digger is waiting until the cords are fastened round the bier. But, see, a woman has just entered the cemetery at the other end."

"Yes, yes, my dear Planchet," said D'Artagnan, quickly, "leave me, leave me; I feel I am beginning already to be much comforted by my meditations, so do not interrupt me."

Planchet left, and D'Artagnan remained, devouring with his eager gaze from behind the half-closed blinds what was taking place just before him. The two bearers of the corpse had unfastened the straps by which they carried the litter, and were letting their burden glide gently into the open grave. At a few paces distant, the man with the cloak wrapped round him, the only spectator of this melancholy scene, was leaning with his back against a large cypress-tree, and kept his face and person entirely concealed from the grave-diggers and the priests; the corpse was buried in five minutes. The grave having been filled up, the priests turned away, and the grave-digger having addressed a few words to them, followed them as they moved away. The man in the mantle bowed as they passed him, and put a piece of gold into the grave-digger's hand.

"*Mordioux!*" murmured D'Artagnan; "it is Aramis himself."

Aramis, in fact, remained alone, on that side at least; for hardly had he turned his head when a woman's footsteps, and the rustling of her dress, were heard in the path close to him. He immediately turned round, and took off his hat with the most ceremonious respect; he led the lady under the shelter of some walnut and lime trees, which overshadowed a magnificent tomb.

"Ah! who would have thought it," said D'Artagnan; "the bishop of Vannes at a rendezvous! He is still the same Abbé Aramis as he was at Noisy-le-Sec. Yes," he added, after a pause; "but as it is in a cemetery, the rendezvous is sacred." But he almost laughed.

The conversation lasted for fully half an hour. D'Artagnan could not see the lady's face, for she kept her back turned towards him; but he saw perfectly well, by the erect attitude of both the speakers, by their gestures, by the measured and careful manner with which they glanced at each other, either by way of attack or defense, that they must be conversing about any other subject than of love. At the end of the conversation the lady rose, and bowed profoundly to Aramis.

"Oh, oh," said D'Artagnan; "this rendezvous finishes like one of a very tender nature though. The cavalier kneels at the beginning, the young lady by and by gets tamed down, and then it is she who has to supplicate.

Who is this lady. I would give anything to ascertain."

This seemed impossible, however, for Aramis was the first to leave; the lady carefully concealed her head and face, and then immediately departed. D'Artagnan could hold out no longer; he ran to the window which looked out on the Rue de Lyon, and saw Aramis entering the inn. The lady was proceeding in quite an opposite direction, and seemed, in fact, to be about to rejoin an equipage, consisting of two led horses and a carriage, which he could see standing close to the borders of the forest. She was walking slowly, her head bent down, absorbed in the deepest meditation.

"*Mordioux! mordioux!* I must and will learn who that woman is," said the musketeer again; and then, without further deliberation, he set off in pursuit of her. As he was going along, he tried to think how he could possibly contrive to make her raise her veil. "She is not young," he said, "and is a woman of high rank in society. I ought to know that figure and peculiar style of walk." As he ran, the sound of his spurs and of his boots upon the hard ground of the street made a strange jingling noise; a fortunate circumstance in itself, which he was far from reckoning upon. The noise disturbed the lady; she seemed to fancy she was being either followed or pursued, which was indeed the case, and turned round. D'Artagnan started as if he had received a charge of small shot in his legs, and then turning suddenly round as if he were going back the same way he had come, he murmured, "Madame de Chevreuse!" D'Artagnan would not go home until he had learnt everything. He asked Celestin to inquire of the grave-digger whose body it was they had buried that morning.

"A poor Franciscan mendicant friar," replied the latter, "who had not even a dog to love him in this world, and to accompany him to his last resting-place."

"If that were really the case," thought D'Artagnan, " we should not have found Aramis present at his funeral. The bishop of Vannes is not precisely a dog as far as devotion goes : his scent, however, is quite as keen, I admit."

CHAPTER XXXVII.

HOW PORTHOS, TRÜCHEN, AND PLANCHET PARTED WITH EACH OTHER ON FRIENDLY TERMS, THANKS TO D'ARTAGNAN.

THERE was good living in Planchet's house. Porthos broke a ladder and two cherry-trees, stripped the raspberry-bushes, and was only unable to succeed in reaching the strawberry-beds on account, as he said, of his belt. Trüchen, who had become quite sociable with the giant, said that it was not the belt so much as his corporation; and Porthos, in a state of the highest delight, embraced Trüchen, who gathered him a pailful of the strawberries, and made him eat them out of her hands. D'Artagnan, who arrived in the midst of these little innocent flirtations, scolded Porthos for his indolence, and silently pitied Planchet. Porthos breakfasted with a very good appetite, and when he had finished, he said, looking at Trüchen, "I could make myself very happy here." Trüchen smiled at his remark, and so did Planchet, but not without embarrassment.

D'Artagnan then addressed Porthos :—" You must not let the delights of Capua make you forget the real object of our journey to Fontainebleau."

" My presentation to the king ? "

" Certainly. I am going to take a turn in the town to get everything ready for that. Do not think of leaving the house, I beg."

" Oh, no ! " exclaimed Porthos.

Planchet looked at D'Artagnan nervously.

"Will you be away long?" he inquired.

"No, my friend; and this very evening I will release you from two troublesome guests."

"Oh! Monsieur d'Artagnan! can you say——"

"No, no; you are a noble-hearted fellow, but your house is very small. Such a house, with half a dozen acres of land, would be fit for a king, and make him very happy, too. But you were not born a great lord."

"No more was M. Porthos," murmured Planchet.

"But he has become so, my good fellow; his income has been a hundred thousand francs a year for the last twenty years, and for the last fifty years Porthos has been the owner of a couple of fists and a backbone, which are not to be matched throughout the whole realm of France. Porthos is a man of the very greatest consequence compared to you, and . . . well, I need say no more, for I know you are an intelligent fellow."

"No, no, monsieur, explain what you mean."

"Look at your orchard, how stripped it is, how empty your larder, your bedstead broken, your cellar almost exhausted, look too . . . at Madame Trüchen——"

"Oh! my good gracious!" said Planchet.

"Madame Trüchen is an excellent person," continued D'Artagnan, "but keep her for yourself, do you understand?" and he slapped him on the shoulder.

Planchet at this moment perceived Porthos and Trüchen sitting close together in an arbor; Trüchen, with a grace of manner peculiarly Flemish, was making a pair of earrings for Porthos out of a double cherry, while Porthos was laughing as amorously as Samson in the company of Delilah. Planchet pressed D'Artagnan's hand, and ran towards the arbor. We must do Porthos the justice to say that he did not move as they approached, and, very likely, he did not think he was doing any harm.

Nor indeed did Trüchen move either, which rather put
Planchet out; but he, too, had been so accustomed to see
fashionable folk in his shop, that he found no difficulty
in putting a good countenance on what seemed disagreeable or rude. Planchet seized Porthos by the arm, and
proposed to go and look at the horses, but Porthos pretended he was tired. Planchet then suggested that the
Baron du Vallon should taste some noyeau of his own
manufacture, which was not to be equaled anywhere; an
offer the baron immediately accepted, and, in this way,
Planchet managed to engage his enemy's attention during
the whole of the day, by dint of sacrificing his cellar, in
preference to his *amour propre*. Two hours afterwards
D'Artagnan returned.

"Everything is arranged," he said; "I saw his majesty
at the very moment he was setting off for the chase; the
king expects us this evening."

"The king expects *me!*" cried Porthos, drawing himself up. It is a sad thing to have to confess, but a man's
heart is like an ocean billow; for, from that very moment
Porthos ceased to look at Madame Trüchen, in that touching manner which had so softened her heart. Planchet
encouraged these ambitious leanings as best he could.
He talked over, or rather gave exaggerated accounts of
all the splendors of the last reign, its battles, sieges, and
grand court ceremonies. He spoke of the luxurious display which the English made; the prizes the three brave
companions carried off; and how D'Artagnan, who at the
beginning had been the humblest of the four, finished by
becoming the leader. He fired Porthos with a generous
feeling of enthusiasm by reminding him of his early youth
now passed away; he boasted as much as he could of the
moral life this great lord had led, and how religiously he
respected the ties of friendship; he was eloquent, and
skillful in his choice of subjects. He tickled Porthos,

frightened Trüchen, and made D'Artagnan think. At six o'clock, the musketeer ordered the horses to be brought round, and told Porthos to get ready. He thanked Planchet for his kind hospitality, whispered a few words about a post he might succeed in obtaining for him at court, which immediately raised Planchet in Trüchen's estimation, where the poor grocer—so good, so generous, so devoted—had become much lowered ever since the appearance and comparison with him of the two great gentlemen. Such, however, is a woman's nature; they are anxious to possess what they have not got, and disdain it as soon as it is acquired. After having rendered this service to his friend Planchet, D'Artagnan said in a low tone of voice to Porthos : " That is a very beautiful ring you have on your finger."

"It is worth three hundred pistoles," said Porthos.

"Madame Trüchen will remember you better if you leave her that ring," replied D'Artagnan, a suggestion which Porthos seemed to hesitate to adopt.

" You think it is not beautiful enough, perhaps," said the musketeer. " I understand your feelings ; a great lord such as you would not think of accepting the hospitality of an old servant without paying him most handsomely for it ; but I am sure that Planchet is too good-hearted a fellow to remember that you have an income of a hundred thousand francs a year."

" I have more than half a mind," said Porthos, flattered by the remark, " to make Madame Trüchen a present of my little farm at Bracieux ; it has twelve acres."

"It is too much, my good Porthos, too much just at present . . . Keep it for a future occasion." He then took the ring off Porthos's finger, and approaching Trüchen, said to her :—" Madame, monsieur le baron hardly knows how to entreat you, out of your regard for him, to accept this little ring. M. du Vallon is one of the most

generous and discreet men of my acquaintance. He wished
to offer you a farm that he has at Bracieux, but I dissuaded
him from it."

"Oh!" said Trüchen, looking eagerly at the diamond.

"Monsieur le baron!" exclaimed Planchet, quite overcome.

"My good friend," stammered out Porthos, delighted
at having been so well represented by D'Artagnan. These
several exclamations, uttered at the same moment, made
quite a pathetic winding-up of a day which might have
finished in a very ridiculous manner. But D'Artagnan
was there, and, on every occasion, wheresoever D'Artagnan exercised any control, matters ended only just in the
very way he wished and willed. There were general em-
bracings; Trüchen, whom the baron's munificence had restored to her proper position, very timidly, and blushing
all the while, presented her forehead to the great lord with
whom she had been on such very pretty terms the evening before. Planchet himself was overcome by a feeling
of genuine humility. Still, in the same generosity of
disposition, Porthos would have emptied his pockets into
the hands of the cook and of Célestin; but D'Artagnan
stopped him.

"No," he said, "it is now my turn." And he gave one
pistole to the woman and two to the man; and the ben-
edictions which were showered down upon them would
have rejoiced the heart of Harpagon himself, and have
rendered, even him, a prodigal.

D'Artagnan made Planchet lead them to the château,
and introduced Porthos into his own apartment, where he
arrived safely without having been perceived by those he
was afraid of meeting.

CHAPTER XXXVIII.

THE PRESENTATION OF PORTHOS AT COURT.

AT seven o'clock the same evening, the king gave an audience to an ambassador from the United Provinces, in the grand reception-room. The audience lasted a quarter of an hour. His majesty afterwards received those who had been recently presented, together with a few ladies, who paid their respects first. In one corner of the salon, concealed behind a column, Porthos and D'Artagnan were conversing together, waiting until their turn arrived.

" Have you heard the news ? " inquired the musketeer of his friend.

" No ! "

" Well, look, then." Porthos raised himself on tiptoe, and saw M. Fouquet in full court dress, leading Aramis towards the king.

" Aramis ! " said Porthos.

" Presented to the king by M. Fouquet."

" Ah ! " ejaculated Porthos.

" For having fortified Belle-Isle," continued D'Artagnan.

" And I ? "

" You—oh, you ! as I have already had the honor of telling you, are the good-natured, kind-hearted Porthos ; and so they begged you to take care of Saint-Mandé a little."

" Ah ! " repeated Porthos.

" But, happily, I was there," said D'Artagnan, " and presently it will be *my* turn."

At this moment Fouquet addressed the king.

" Sire," he said, " I have a favor to solicit of your majesty. M. d'Herblay is not ambitious, but he knows when he can be of service. Your majesty needs a representative at Rome, who would be able to exercise a powerful influence there; may I request a cardinal's hat for M. d'Herblay ? " The king started. " I do not often solicit anything of your majesty," said Fouquet.

" That is a reason, certainly," replied the king, who always expressed any hesitation he might have in that manner, and to which remark there was nothing to say in reply.

Fouquet and Aramis looked at each other. The king resumed : " M. d'Herblay can serve us equally well in France; an archbishopric, for instance."

" Sire," objected Fouquet, with a grace of manner peculiarly his own, " your majesty overwhelms M. d'Herblay; the archbishopric may, in your majesty's extreme kindness, be conferred in addition to the hat; the one does not exclude the other."

The king admired the readiness which he displayed, and smiled, saying : " D'Artagnan himself could not have answered better." He had no sooner pronounced the name than D'Artagnan appeared.

" Did your majesty call me ? " he said.

Aramis and Fouquet drew back a step, as if they were about to retire.

" Will your majesty allow me," said D'Artagnan, quickly, as he led forward Porthos, " to present to your majesty M. le Baron du Vallon, one of the bravest gentlemen of France ? "

As soon as Aramis saw Porthos, he turned as pale as death, while Fouquet clenched his hands under his ruffles. D'Artagnan smiled blandly at both of them, while Porthos bowed, visibly overcome before the royal presence.

" Porthos here ? " murmured Fouquet in Aramis's ear.

"Hush! deep treachery at work," hissed the latter.

"Sire," said D'Artagnan, "it is more than six years ago I ought to have presented M. du Vallon to your majesty; but certain men resemble stars, they move not one inch unless their satellites accompany them. The Pleiads are never disunited, and that is the reason I have selected, for the purpose of presenting him to you the very moment when you would see M. d'Herblay by his side."

Aramis almost lost countenance. He looked at D'Artagnan with a proud, haughty air, as though willing to accept the defiance the latter seemed to throw down.

"Ah! these gentlemen are good friends, then?" said the king.

"Excellent friends, sire, the one can answer for the other. Ask M. de Vannes now in what manner Belle-Isle was fortified?" Fouquet moved back a step.

"Belle-Isle," said Aramis, coldly, "was fortified by that gentleman," and he indicated Porthos with his hand, who bowed a second time. Louis could not withhold his admiration, though at the same time his suspicions were aroused.

"Yes," said D'Artagnan, "but ask monsieur le baron whose assistance he had in carrying the works out?"

"Aramis's," said Porthos, frankly; and he pointed to the bishop.

"What the deuce does all this mean," thought the bishop, "and what sort of a termination are we to expect to this comedy?"

"What!" exclaimed the king, "is the cardinal's, I mean this bishop's, name *Aramis?*"

"His *nom de guerre*," said D'Artagnan.

"My nickname," said Aramis.

"A truce to modesty!" exclaimed D'Artagnan; "beneath the priest's robe, sire, is concealed the most brilliant officer, a gentleman of the most unparalleled intrepidity, and the wisest theologian in your kingdom."

Louis raised his head. "And an engineer, also, it appears," he said, admiring Aramis's calm, imperturbable self-possession.

"An engineer for a particular purpose, sire," said the latter.

"My companion in the musketeers, sire," said D'Artagnan, with great warmth of manner, "the man who has more than a hundred times aided your father's ministers by his advice—M. d'Herblay, in a word, who, with M. du Vallon, myself, and M. le Comte de la Fère, who is known to your majesty, formed that quartette which was a good deal talked about during the late king's reign, and during your majesty's minority."

"And who fortified Belle-Isle?" the king repeated, in a significant tone.

Aramis advanced and bowed: "In order to serve the son as I served the father."

D'Artagnan looked very narrowly at Aramis while he uttered these words, which displayed so much true respect, so much warm devotion, such entire frankness and sincerity, that even he, D'Artagnan, the eternal doubter, he, the almost infallible in judgment, was deceived by it. "A man who lies cannot speak in such a tone as that," he said.

Louis was overcome by it. "In that case," he said to Fouquet, who anxiously awaited the result of this proof, "the cardinal's hat is promised. Monsieur d'Herblay, I pledge you my honor that the first promotion shall be yours. Thank M. Fouquet for it." Colbert overheard these words; they stung him to the quick, and he left the salon abruptly. "And you, Monsieur du Vallon," said the king, "what have you to ask? I am truly pleased to have it in my power to acknowledge the services of those who were faithful to my father."

"Sire—" began Porthos, but he was unable to proceed with what he was going to say.

"Sire," exclaimed D'Artagnan, "this worthy gentleman is utterly overpowered by your majesty's presence, he who so valiantly sustained the looks and the fire of a thousand foes. But, knowing what his thoughts are, I—who am more accustomed to gaze upon the sun—can translate them: he needs nothing, absolutely nothing; his sole desire is to have the happiness of gazing upon your majesty for a quarter of an hour."

"You shall sup with me this evening," said the king, saluting Porthos with a gracious smile.

Porthos became crimson from delight and pride. The king dismissed him, and D'Artagnan pushed him into the adjoining apartment, after he had embraced him warmly.

"Sit next to me at table," said Porthos in his ear.

"Yes, my friend."

"Aramis is annoyed with me, I think."

"Aramis has never liked you so much as he does now. Fancy, it was I who was the means of his getting the cardinal's hat."

"Of course," said Porthos. "By the by, does the king like his guests to eat much at his table."

"It is a compliment to himself if you do," said D'Artagnan, "for he himself possesses a royal appetite."

CHAPTER XXXIX.

EXPLANATIONS.

ARAMIS cleverly managed to effect a diversion for the purpose of finding D'Artagnan and Porthos. He came up to the latter, behind one of the columns, and, as he pressed his hand, said, "So you have escaped from my prison?"

"Do not scold him," said D'Artagnan; "it was I, dear Aramis, who set him free."

"Ah! my friend," replied Aramis, looking at Porthos, "could you not have waited with a little more patience?"

D'Artagnan came to the assistance of Porthos, who already began to breathe hard, in sore perplexity.

"You see, you members of the Church are great politicians; we, mere soldiers, come at once to the point. The facts are these; I went to pay Baisemeaux a visit——"

Aramis pricked up his ears at this announcement.

"Stay!" said Porthos; "you make me remember that I have a letter from Baisemeaux for you, Aramis." And Porthos held out to the bishop the letter we have already seen. Aramis begged to be allowed to read it, and read it without D'Artagnan feeling in the slightest degree embarrassed by the circumstance that he was so well acquainted with the contents of it. Besides, Aramis's face was so impenetrable, that D'Artagnan could not but admire him more than ever; after he had read it, he put the letter into his pocket with the calmest possible air.

"You were saying, captain?" he observed.

"I was saying," continued the musketeer, "that I had

gone to pay Baisemeaux a visit on his majesty's service."

"On his majesty's service?" said Aramis.

"Yes," said D'Artagnan, "and, naturally enough, we talked about you and our friends. I must say that Baisemeaux received me coldly; so I soon took my leave of him. As I was returning, a soldier accosted me, and said (no doubt he recognized me, notwithstanding I was in private clothes), "Captain, will you be good enough to read me the name written on this envelope?" and I read, "To Monsieur du Vallon, at M. Fouquet's house, Saint-Mandé." The deuce, said I to myself, Porthos has not returned, then, as I fancied, to Belle-Isle, or to Pierrefonds, but is at M. Fouquet's house, at Saint-Mandé; and as M. Fouquet is not at Saint-Mandé, Porthos must be quite alone, or, at all events, with Aramis; I will go and see Porthos, and I accordingly went to see Porthos."

"Very good," said Aramis, thoughtfully.

"You never told me that," said Porthos.

"I had no time, my friend."

"And you brought back Porthos with you to Fontaine-bleau?"

"Yes, to Planchet's house."

"Does Planchet live at Fontainebleau?" inquired Aramis.

"Yes, near the cemetery," said Porthos, thoughtlessly.

"What do you mean by 'near the cemetery?'" said Aramis, suspiciously.

"Come," thought the musketeer, "since there is to be a squabble, let us take advantage of it."

"Yes, the cemetery," said Porthos. "Planchet is a very excellent fellow, who makes very excellent preserves; but his house has windows which look out upon the cemetery. And a confoundedly melancholy prospect it is! So this morning——"

"This morning?" said Aramis, more and more excited.

D'Artagnan turned his back to them, and walked to the window, where he began to play a march upon one of the panes of glass.

"Yes, this morning, we saw a man buried there."

"Ah!"

"Very depressing, was it not? I should never be able to live in a house where burials can always be seen from the window. D'Artagnan, on the contrary, seems to like it very much."

"So D'Artagnan saw it as well?"

"Not simply *saw* it; he literally never took his eyes off the whole time."

Aramis started, and turned to look at the musketeer, but the latter was engaged in earnest conversation with Saint-Aignan. Aramis continued to question Porthos, and when he had squeezed all the juice out of this enormous lemon, he threw the peel aside. He turned towards his friend D'Artagnan, and clapping him on the shoulder, when Saint-Aignan had left him, the king's supper having been announced, said, "D'Artagnan."

"Yes, my dear fellow," he replied.

"We do not sup with his majesty, I believe?"

"Well?—*we* do."

"Can you give me ten minutes' conversation?"

"Twenty, if you like. His majesty will take quite that time to get properly seated at table."

"Where shall we talk, then?"

"Here, upon these seats, if you like; the king has left, we can sit down, and the apartment is empty."

"Let us sit down, then."

They sat down, and Aramis took one of D'Artagnan's hands in his.

"Tell me, candidly, my dear friend, whether you have not counseled Porthos to distrust me a little?"

"I admit I have, but not as you understand it. I saw

that Porthos was bored to death, and I wished, by presenting him to the king, to do for him, and for you, what you would never do for yourselves."

" What is that ? "

" Speak in your own praise."

" And you have done it most nobly, I thank you."

" And I brought the cardinal's hat a little nearer, just as it seemed to be retreating from you."

" Ah ! I admit that," said Aramis, with a singular smile, "you are indeed, not to be matched for making your friends' fortunes for them."

" You see, then, that I only acted with the view of making Porthos's fortune for him."

" I meant to have done that myself; but your arm reaches farther than ours."

It was now D'Artagnan's turn to smile.

" Come," said Aramis, " we ought to deal truthfully with each other. Do you still love me, D'Artagnan ? "

" The same as I used to do," replied D'Artagnan, without compromising himself too much by this reply.

" In that case, thanks; and now, for the most perfect frankness," said Aramis ; " you visited Belle-Isle on behalf of the king ? "

" *Pardieu !* "

" You wished to deprive us of the pleasure of offering Belle-Isle completely fortified to the king."

" But before I could deprive you of that pleasure, I ought to have been made acquainted with your intention of doing so."

" You came to Belle-Isle without knowing anything ? "

" Of you ! yes. How the devil could I imagine that Aramis had become so clever an engineer, as to be able to fortify like Polybius, or Archimedes ? "

" True. And yet you smelt me out over yonder ? "

" Oh ! yes."

"And Porthos, too ? "

"I did not divine that Aramis was an engineer.   I was
only able to guess that Porthos might have become one.
There is a saying, one becomes an orator, one is born a
poet; but it has never been said, one is born Porthos, and
one becomes an engineer."

"Your wit is always amusing," said Aramis, coldly.
"Well, I will go on."

"Do."

"When you found out our secret, you made all the
haste you could to communicate it to the king."

"I certainly made as much haste as I could since I saw
that you were making still more.   When a man weighing
two hundred and fifty eight pounds, as Porthos does,
rides post; when a gouty prelate—I beg your pardon,
but you yourself told me you were so—when a prelate
scours the highway—I naturally suppose that my two
friends, who did not wish to be communicative with
me, had certain matters of the highest importance to conceal from me, and so I made as much haste as my lean-
ness and the absence of gout would allow."

"Did it not occur to you, my dear friend, that you
might be rendering Porthos and myself a very sad
service ? "

"Yes, I thought it not unlikely ; but you and Porthos
made me play a very ridiculous part at Belle-Isle."

"I beg your pardon," said Aramis.

"Excuse me," said D'Artagnan.

"So that," pursued Aramis, "you now know everything ? "

"No, indeed."

"You know I was obliged to inform M. Fouquet of
what had happened, in order that he would be able to
anticipate what you might have to tell the king ? "

"That is rather obscure."

"Not at all; M. Fouquet has his enemies—you will admit that, I suppose."

"Certainly."

"And one in particular."

"A dangerous one?"

"A mortal enemy. Well, in order to counteract that man's influence, it was necessary that M. Fouquet should give the king a proof of his great devotion to him, and of his readiness to make the greatest sacrifices. He surprised his majesty by offering him Belle-Isle. If you had been the first to reach Paris, the surprise would have been destroyed, it would have looked as if we had yielded to fear."

"I understand."

"That is the whole mystery," said Aramis, satisfied that he had at last quite convinced the musketeer.

"Only," said the latter, "it would have been more simple to have taken me aside, and said to me, 'My dear D'Artagnan, we are fortifying Belle-Isle, and intend to offer it to the king. Tell us frankly, for whom you are acting. Are you a friend of M. Colbert, or of M. Fouquet?' Perhaps I should not have answered you, but you would have added—'Are you my friend?' I should have said 'Yes.'" Aramis hung down his head. "In this way," continued D'Artagnan, "you would have paralyzed my movements, and I should have gone to the king, and said 'Sire, M. Fouquet is fortifying Belle-Isle, and exceedingly well, too; but here is a note, which the governor of Belle-Isle gave me for your majesty;" or, 'M. Fouquet is about to wait upon your majesty to explain his intentions with regard to it.' I should not have been placed in an absurd position; you would have enjoyed the surprise so long planned, and we should not have had any occasion to look askant at each other when we met."

"While, on the contrary," replied Aramis, "you have acted altogether as one friendly to M. Colbert. And you really are a friend of his, I suppose?"

"Certainly not, indeed!" exclaimed the captain. "M. Colbert is a mean fellow, and I hate him as I used to hate Mazarin, but without fearing him."

"Well, then," said Aramis, "I love M. Fouquet, and his interests are mine. You know my position. I have no property or means whatever. M. Fouquet gave me several livings, a bishopric as well; M. Fouquet has served and obliged me like the generous-hearted man he is, and I know the world sufficiently well to appreciate a kindness when I meet with one. M. Fouquet has won my regard, and I have devoted myself to his service."

"You could not possibly do better. You will find him a very liberal master."

Aramis bit his lips; and then said, "The best a man could possibly have." He then paused for a minute, D'Artagnan taking good care not to interrupt him.

"I suppose you know how Porthos got mixed up in all this?"

"No," said D'Artagnan; "I am curious, of course, but I never question a friend when he wishes to keep a secret from me."

"Well, then, I will tell you."

"It is hardly worth the trouble, if the confidence is to bind me in any way."

"Oh! do not be afraid; there is no man whom I love better than Porthos, because he is so simple-minded and good-natured. Porthos is so straightforward in everything. Since I have become a bishop, I have looked for these primeval natures, which make me love truth and hate intrigue."

D'Artagnan stroked his mustache; but said nothing.

"I saw Porthos and again cultivated his acquaintance;

his own time hanging idly on his hands, his presence recalled my earlier and better days without engaging me in any present evil. I sent for Porthos to come to Vannes. M. Fouquet, whose regard for me is very great, having learnt that Porthos and I were attached to each other by old ties of friendship, promised him increase of rank at the earliest promotion, and that is the whole secret."

"I shall not abuse your confidence," said D'Artagnan.

"I am sure of that, my dear friend; no one has a finer sense of honor than yourself."

"I flatter myself you are right, Aramis."

" And now "—and here the prelate looked searchingly and scrutinizingly at his friend—"now let us talk of ourselves and for ourselves ; will you become one of M. Fouquet's friends? Do not interrupt me until you know what that means."

" Well, I am listening."

" Will you become a maréchal of France, peer, duke, and the possessor of a duchy, with a million of francs ? "

" But, my friend," replied D'Artagnan, "what must one do to get all that ? "

"Belong to M. Fouquet."

" But I already belong to the king."

" Not exclusively, I suppose.'"

" Oh ! a D'Artagnan cannot be divided."

" You have, I presume, ambitions, as noble hearts like yours have."

" Yes, certainly I have."

" Well ? "

" Well ! I wish to be a maréchal; the king will make me maréchal, duke, peer ; the king will make me all that."

Aramis fixed a searching look upon D'Artagnan.

"Is not the king master ? " said D'Artagnan.

" No one disputes it; but Louis XIII. was master also."

"Oh! my dear friend, between Richelieu and Louis XIII. stood no D'Artagnan," said the muskeeter, very quietly.

"There are many stumbling-blocks round the king," said Aramis.

"Not for the king's feet!"

"Very likely not; still——"

"One moment, Aramis; I observe that every one thinks of himself, and never of his poor prince; I will maintain myself maintaining him."

"And if you meet with ingratitude?"

"The weak alone are afraid of that."

"You are quite certain of yourself?"

"I think so."

"Still the king may some day have no further need for you!"

"On the contrary, I think his need of me will soon be greater than ever; and hearken, my dear fellow, if it became necessary to arrest a new Condé, who would do it? This—this alone in France!" and D'Artagnan struck his sword, which clanked sullenly on the tesselated floor.

"You are right," said Aramis, turning very pale; and then he rose and pressed D'Artagnan's hand.

"That is the last summons for supper," said the captain of the musketeers; "will you excuse me?"

Aramis threw his arm round the musketeer's neck, and said, "A friend like you is the brightest jewel in the royal crown." And they immediately separated.

"I was right," mused D'Artagnan; "there is, indeed, something strangely serious stirring."

"We must hasten the explosion," breathes the coming cardinal, "for D'Artagnan has discovered the existence of a plot."

CHAPTER XL.

MADAME AND DE GUICHE.

It will not be forgotten how Comte de Guiche left the queen-mother's apartment on the day when Louis XIV. presented La Vallière with the beautiful bracelets he had won in the lottery. The comte walked to and fro for some time outside the palace, in the greatest distress, from a thousand suspicions and anxieties with which his mind was beset. Presently he stopped and waited on the terrace opposite the grove of trees, watching for Madame's departure. More than half an hour passed away; and as he was at that moment quite alone, the comte could hardly have had any very diverting ideas at his command. He drew his tablets from his pocket, and, after hesitating over and over again, determined to write these words :—" Madame, I implore you to grant me one moment's conversation. Do not be alarmed at this request, which contains nothing in any way opposed to the profound respect with which I subscribe myself, etc, etc." He had signed and folded this singular love-letter, when he suddenly observed several ladies leaving the château, and afterwards several courtiers too; in fact almost every one that formed the queen's circle. He saw La Vallière herself, then Montalais talking with Malicorne; he watched the departure of the very last of the numerous guests that had a short time before thronged the queen-mother's cabinet.

Madame herself had not yet passed; she would be obliged, however, to cross the courtyard in order to enter her own apartments; and, from the terrace where he was standing, De Guiche could see all that was going on in the courtyard. At last he saw Madame leave, attended by a couple of pages, who were carrying torches before her. She was walking very quickly; as soon as she reached the door, she said:

"Let some one go and look for De Guiche, he has to render an account of a mission he had to discharge for me; if he should be disengaged, request him to be good enough to come to my apartment."

De Guiche remained silent, hidden in the shade; but, as soon as Madame had withdrawn, he darted from the terrace down the steps, and assumed a most indifferent air, so that the pages who were hurrying towards his rooms might meet him.

"Ah! it is Madame then who is seeking me!" he said to himself, quite overcome; and he crushed in his hand the now worse than useless letter.

"M. le Comte," said one of the pages, approaching him, "we are indeed most fortunate in meeting you."

"Why so, messieurs?"

"A command from Madame."

"From Madame!" said De Guiche, looking surprised.

"Yes, M. le Comte, her royal highness has been asking for you; she expects to hear, she told us, the result of a commission you had to execute for her. Are you at liberty?"

"I am quite at her royal highness's orders."

"Will you have the goodness to follow us, then?"

When De Guiche entered the princess's apartments, he found her pale and agitated. Montalais was standing at the door, evidently uneasy about what was passing in her mistress's mind. De Guiche appeared.

"Ah! is that you, Monsieur de Guiche?" said Madame; "come in, I beg. Mademoiselle de Montalais, I do not require your attendance any longer."

Montalais, more puzzled than ever, courtesied and withdrew. De Guiche and the princess were left alone. The comte had every advantage in his favor; it was Madame who had summoned him to a rendezvous. But how was it possible for the comte to make use of this advantage? Madame was so whimsical, and her disposition so changeable. She soon allowed this to be perceived, for, suddenly opening the conversation, she said: "Well! have you nothing to say to me?"

He imagined she must have guessed his thoughts; he fancied (for those who are in love are thus constituted, being as credulous and blind as poets or prophets), he fancied she knew how ardent was his desire to see her, and also the subject uppermost in his mind.

"Yes, madame," he said, "and I think it very singular."

"The affair of the bracelets," she exclaimed, eagerly, "you mean that, I suppose?"

"Yes, madame."

"And you think the king is in love; do you not?"

Guiche looked at her for some time; her eyes sank under his gaze, which seemed to read her very heart.

"I think," he said, "that the king may possibly have had an idea of annoying some one; were it not for that, the king would hardly show himself so earnest in his attentions as he is; he would not run the risk of compromising, from mere thoughtlessness of disposition, a young girl against whom no one has been hitherto able to say a word."

"Indeed! the bold, shameless girl," said the princess, haughtily.

"I can positively assure your royal highness," said De Guiche, with a firmness marked by great respect, "that Mademoiselle de la Vallière is beloved by a man who merits every respect, for he is a brave and honorable gentleman."

"Bragelonne?"

"My friend; yes, madame."

"Well, and though he is your friend, what does that matter to the king?"

"The king knows that Bragelonne is affianced to Mademoiselle de la Vallière; and as Raoul has served the king most valiantly, the king will not inflict an irreparable injury upon him."

Madame began to laugh in a manner that produced a sinister impression upon De Guiche.

"I repeat, madame, I do not believe the king is in love with Mademoiselle de la Vallière; and the proof that I do not believe it is, that I was about to ask you whose *amour propre* it is likely the king is desirous of wounding? You who are well acquainted with the whole court, can perhaps assist me in ascertaining that; and assuredly, with greater certainty, since it is everywhere said that your royal highness is on very friendly terms with the king."

Madame bit her lips, and, unable to assign any good and sufficient reasons, changed the conversation. "Prove to me," she said, fixing on him one of those looks in which the whole soul seems to pass into the eyes, "prove to me, I say, that you intended to interrogate me at the very moment I sent for you."

De Guiche gravely drew from his pocket the now crumpled note that he had written, and showed it to her.

"Sympathy," she said.

"Yes," said the comte, with an indescribable tenderness of tone, "sympathy. I have explained to you how and why I sought you; you, however, have yet to tell me, madame, why you sent for me."

"True," replied the princess. She hesitated, and then suddenly exclaimed, "Those bracelets will drive me mad."

" You expected the king would offer them to you,"
replied De Guiche.

" Why not ? "

" But before you, madame, before you, his sister-in-law,
was there not the queen herself to whom the king should
have offered them ? "

" Before La Vallière," cried the princess, wounded to
the quick, " could he not have presented them to me ?
Was there not the whole court, indeed, to choose from ? "

" I assure you, madame," said the comte, respectfully.
" that if any one heard you speak in this manner, if any
one were to see how red your eyes are, and, Heaven forgive me, to see, too, that tear trembling on your eyelids,
it would be said that your royal highness was jealous."

" Jealous ! " said the princess, haughtily—" jealous of
La Vallière ! "

She expected to see De Guiche yield beneath her scorn-
ful gesture and her proud tone ; but he simply and boldly
replied, " Jealous of La Vallière ; yes, madame."

" Am I to suppose, monsieur," she stammered out, " that
your object is to insult me ? "

" It is not possible, madame," replied the comte, slightly
agitated, but resolved to master that fiery nature.

" Leave the room ! " said the princess, thoroughly exasperated ; De Guiche's coolness and silent respect having
made her completely lose her temper.

De Guiche fell back a step, bowed slowly, but with great
respect, drew himself up, looking as white as his lace cuffs,
and, in a voice slightly trembling, said, " It was hardly
worth while to have hurried here to be subjected to this
unmerited disgrace." And he turned away with hasty
steps.

He had scarcely gone half a dozen paces when Madame
darted like a tigress after him, seized him by the cuff, and
making him turn round again, said, trembling with passion

as she did so, " The respect you pretend to have is more
insulting than the insult itself. Insult me, if you please, but
at least speak."

"Madame," said the comte, gently, as he drew his
sword, "thrust this blade into my heart, rather than kill
me by degrees."

At the look he fixed upon her,—a look full of love, resolution, and despair even,—she knew how readily the
comte, so outwardly calm in appearance, would pass his
sword though his own breast if she added another word.
She tore the blade from his hands, and, pressing his arm
with a feverish impatience, which might pass for tenderness, said, " Do not be too hard upon me, comte. You see
how I am suffering, and yet you have no pity for me."

Tears, the crisis of this strange attack, stifled her voice.
As soon as De Guiche saw her weep, he took her in his
arms and carried her to an arm-chair; in another moment
she would have been suffocated.

" Oh, why," he murmured, as he knelt by her side, " why
do you conceal your troubles from me? Do you love any
one—tell me? It would kill me, I know, but not until I
should have comforted, consoled, and served you even."

" And do you love me to that extent ? " she replied, completely conquered.

" I do indeed love you to that extent, madame."

She placed both her hands in his. " My heart is indeed
another's," she murmured in so low a tone that her voice
could hardly be heard; but he heard it, and said, " Is it
the king you love ? "

She gently shook her head, and her smile was like a
clear bright streak in the clouds, through which after the
tempest has passed one almost fancies Paradise is opening.
" But," she added, " there are other passions in a high-
born heart. Love is poetry; but the real life of the heart
is pride. Comte, I was born on a throne, I am proud and

jealous of my rank.   Why does the king gather such unworthy objects round him ? "

" Once more, I repeat," said the comte, " you are acting
unjustly towards that poor girl, who will one day be my
friend's wife."

" Are you simple enough to believe that, comte ? "

" If I did not believe it," he said, turning very pale,
" Bragelonne should be informed of it to-morrow ; indeed
he should, if I thought that poor La Vallière had forgotten
the vows she had exchanged with Raoul.   But no; it would
be cowardly to betray a woman's secret ; it would be criminal to disturb a friend's peace of mind."

" You think, then," said the princess, with a wild burst
of laughter, " that ignorance is happiness ? "

" I believe it," he replied.

" Prove it to me, then," she said, hurriedly.

" It is easily done, madame.   It is reported through the
whole court that the king loves you, and that you
return his affection."

" Well ? " she said, breathing with difficulty.

" Well ; admit for a moment that Raoul, my friend, had
come and said to me, ' Yes, the king loves Madame, and has
made an impression upon her heart,' I possibly should
have slain Raoul."

" It would have been necessary," said the princess, with
the obstinacy of a woman who feels herself not easily overcome, " for M. de Bragelonne to have had proofs, before he
ventured to speak to you in that manner."

" Such, however, is the case," replied De Guiche, with
a deep sigh, " that not having been warned, I have never
examined into the matter seriously ; and I now find that
my ignorance has saved my life."

" So, then, you drive selfishness and coldness to that
extent," said Madame," that you would let this unhappy
young man continue to love La Vallière ? "

"I would, until La Vallière's guilt were revealed."

"But the bracelets?"

"Well, madame, since you yourself expected to receive them from the king, what can I possibly say?"

The argument was a telling one, and the princess was overwhelmed by it, and from that moment her defeat was assured. But as her heart and mind were instinct with noble and generous feelings, she understood De Guiche's extreme delicacy. She saw that in his heart he really suspected that the king was in love with La Vallière, and that he did not wish to resort to the common expedient of ruining a rival in the mind of a woman, by giving the latter the assurance and certainty that this rival's affections were transferred to another woman. She guessed that his suspicions of La Vallière were aroused, and that, in order to leave himself time for his convictions to undergo a change, so as not to ruin Louise utterly, he was determined to pursue a certain straightforward line of conduct. She could read so much real greatness of character, and such true generosity of disposition in her lover, that her heart really warmed with affection towards him, whose passion for her was so pure and delicate. Despite his fear of incurring her displeasure, De Guiche, by retaining his position as a man of proud independence of feeling and deep devotion, became almost a hero in her estimation, and reduced her to the state of a jealous and little-minded woman. She loved him for this so tenderly, that she could not refuse to give him a proof of her affection.

"See, how many words we have wasted," she said, taking his hand, "suspicions, anxieties, mistrust, sufferings —I think we have enumerated all those words."

"Alas! madame, yes."

"Efface them from your heart as I drive them from mine. Whether La Vallière does or does not love the

king, and whether the king does or does not love La Vallière,—from this moment you and I will draw a distinction, in the two characters I have to perform. You open
your eyes so wide that I am sure you hardly understand
me."

"You are so impetuous, madame, that I always tremble
at the fear of displeasing you."

"And see how he trembles now, poor fellow," she said,
with the most charming playfulness of manner. "Yes,
monsieur, I have two characters to perform. I am the
sister of the king, the sister-in-law of the king's wife. In
this character ought I not to take an interest in these
domestic intrigues? Come, tell me what you think?"

"As little as possible, madame."

"Agreed, monsieur; but it is a question of dignity; and
then, you know, I am the wife of the king's brother."
De Guiche sighed. "A circumstance," she added, with an
expression of great tenderness, "which will remind you
that I am always to be treated with the profoundest
respect." De Guiche fell at her feet, which he kissed, with
the religious fervor of a worshipper. "And I begin to
think that, really and truly, I have another character
to perform. I was almost forgetting it."

"Name it, oh! name it," said De Guiche.

"I am a woman," she said, in a voice lower than ever,
"and I love." He rose, she opened her arms, and their
lips met. A footstep was heard behind the tapestry, and
Mademoiselle de Montalais appeared.

"What do you want?" said Madame.

"M. de Guiche is wanted," replied Montalais, who was
just in time to see the agitation of the actors of these four
characters; for De Guiche had consistently carried out his
part with heroism.

CHAPTER XLI.

MONTALAIS AND MALICORNE.

MONTALAIS was right. M. de Guiche, thus summoned
in every direction, was very much exposed, from such a
multiplication of business, to the risk of not attending to
any. It so happened that, considering the awkwardness
of the interruption, Madame, notwithstanding her wounded
pride, and her secret anger, could not, for the moment at
least, reproach Montalais for having violated, in so bold a
manner, the semi-royal order with which she had been dismissed on De Guiche's entrance. De Guiche, also, lost his
presence of mind, or, it would be more correct to say had
already lost it, before Montalais's arrival, for, scarcely
had he heard the young girl's voice, than, without taking
leave of Madame, as the most ordinary politeness required, even between persons equal in rank and station,
he fled from her presence, his heart tumultuously throbbing, and his brain on fire, leaving the princess with one
hand raised, as though about to bid him adieu. Montalais
was at no loss, therefore, to perceive the agitation of the
two lovers—the one who fled was agitated, and the one
who remained was equally so.

"Well," murmured the young girl, as she glanced in-
quisitively round her, "this time, at least, I think I know
as much as the most curious woman could possibly wish
to know." Madame felt so embarrassed by this inquisitorial look, that, as if she had heard Montalais's muttered
side remark, she did not speak a word to her maid of
honor, but, casting down her eyes, retired at once to her
bedroom. Montalais, observing this, stood listening for

a moment, and then heard Madame lock and bolt her door. By this she knew that the rest of the evening was at her own disposal; and making, behind the door which had just been closed, a gesture which indicated but little real respect for the princess, she went down the staircase in search of Malicorne, who was very busily engaged at that moment in watching a courier, who, covered with dust, had just left the Comte de Guiche's apartments. Montalais knew that Malicorne was engaged in a matter of some importance; she therefore allowed him to look and stretch out his neck as much as he pleased; and it was only when Malicorne had resumed his natural position, that she touched him on the shoulder. "Well," said Montalais, " what is the latest intelligence you have?"

" M. de Guiche is in love with Madame."

" Fine news, truly! I know something more recent than that."

" Well, what do you know?"

"That Madame is in love with M. de Guiche."

" The one is the consequence of the other."

" Not always, my good monsieur."

" Is that remark intended for me?"

"Present company always excepted."

" Thank you," said Malicorne. " Well, and in the other direction, what is stirring?"

" The king wished, this evening, after the lottery, to see Mademoiselle de la Vallière."

" Well, and he has seen her?"

" No, indeed! "

" What do you mean by that?"

" The door was shut and locked."

" So that——"

" So that the king was obliged to go back again, looking very sheepish, like a thief who has forgotten his crowbar."

" Good."

" And in the third place ? " inquired Montalais.

" The courier who has just arrived for De Guiche came from M. de Bragelonne."

"Excellent," said Montalais, clapping her hands together.

" Why so ? "

" Because we have work to do. If we get weary now, something unlucky will be sure to happen."

"We must divide the work, then," said Malicorne, " in order to avoid confusion."

" Nothing easier," replied Montalais. " Three intrigues, carefully nursed, and carefully encouraged, will produce, one with another, and taking a low average, three love letters a day."

" Oh! " exclaimed Malicorne, shrugging his shoulders, " you cannot mean what you say, darling ; three letters a day, that may do for sentimental common people. A musketeer on duty, a young girl in a convent, may exchange letters with their lovers once a day, perhaps, from the top of a ladder, or through a hole in the wall. A letter contains all the poetry their poor little hearts have to boast of. But the cases we have in hand require to be dealt with very differently."

" Well, finish," said Montalais, out of patience with him. " Some one may come."

" Finish! Why, I am only at the beginning. I have still three points as yet untouched."

" Upon my word, he will be the death of me, with his Flemish indifference," exclaimed Montalais.

"And you will drive me mad with your Italian vivacity. I was going to say that our lovers here will be writing volumes to each other. But what are you driving at ? "

" At this. Not one of our lady correspondents will be able to keep the letters they may receive."

" Very likely not."

" M. de Guiche will not be able to keep his either."

" That is probable."

" Very well, then ; I will take care of all that."

" That is the very thing that is impossible," said Malicorne.

" Why so ? "

" Because you are not your own mistress; your room is as much La Vallière's as yours ; and there are certain persons who will think nothing of visiting and searching a maid of honor's room ; so that I am terribly afraid of the queen, who is as jealous as a Spaniard; of the queen-mother, who is as jealous as a couple of Spaniards ; and, last of all, of Madame herself, who has jealousy enough for ten Spaniards."

" You forget some one else ? "

" Who ? "

" Monsieur."

" I was only speaking of the women. Let us add them up, then : we will call Monsieur, No. 1."

" De Guiche ? "

" No. 2."

" The Vicomte de Bragelonne ? "

" No. 3."

" And the king, the king ? "

" No. 4. Of course the king, who not only will be more jealous, but more powerful than all the rest put together. Ah, my dear ! "

" Well ? "

" Into what a wasp's nest you have thrust yourself ! "

" And as yet not quite far enough, if you will follow me into it."

" Most certainly I will follow you where you like. Yet——"

" Well, yet——"

"While we have time, I think it will be prudent to turn back."

"But I, on the contrary, think the wisest course to take is to put ourselves at once at the head of all these intrigues."

"You will never be able to do it."

"With you, I could superintend ten of them. I am in my element, you must know. I was born to live at the court, as the salamander is made to live in the fire."

"Your comparison does not reassure me in the slightest degree in the world, my dear Montalais. I have heard it said, and by learned men too, that, in the first place, there are no salamanders at all, and that, if there had been any, they would have been infallibly baked or roasted on leaving the fire."

"Your learned men may be very wise as far as salamanders are concerned, but they would never tell you what I can tell you; namely, that Aure de Montalais is destined, before a month is over, to become the first diplomatist in the court of France."

"Be it so, but on condition that I shall be the second."

"Agreed ; an offensive and defensive alliance, of course."

"Only be very careful of any letters."

"I will hand them to you as I receive them."

"What shall we tell the king about Madame ? "

"That Madame is still in love with his majesty."

"What shall we tell Madame about the king? "

"That she would be exceedingly wrong not to humor him."

"What shall we tell La Vallière about Madame ? "

"Whatever we choose, for La Vallière is in our power."

"How so ? "

"Every way."

"What do you mean ?"

"In the first place, through the Vicomte de Brage-lonne."

"Explain yourself."

"You do not forget, I hope, that Monsieur de Brage-lonne has written many letters to Mademoiselle de Val-lière?"

"I forget nothing."

"Well, then, it was I who received, and I who inter-cepted those letters."

"And, consequently, it is you who have them still?"

"Yes."

"Where,—here?"

"Oh, no : I have them safe at Blois, in the little room you know well enough."

"That dear little room,—that darling little room, the antechamber of the palace I intend you to live in one of these days. But, I beg your pardon, you said that all those letters are in that little room?"

"Yes."

"Did you not put them in a box?"

"Of course ; in the same box where I put all the letters I received from you, and where I put mine also when your business or your amusements prevented you from com-ing to our rendezvous."

"Ah, very good," said Malicorne.

"Why are you so satisfied?"

"Because I see there is a possibility of not having to run to Blois after the letters, for I have them here."

"You have brought the box away?"

"It was very dear to me, because it belonged to you."

"Be sure and take care of it, for it contains original documents that will be of priceless value by and by."

"I am perfectly well aware of that indeed, and that is the very reason why I laugh as I do, and with all my heart too."

" And now, one last word."

" Why, *last ?* "

" Do we need any one to assist us ? "

" No one."

" Valets or maid-servants? "

" Bad policy. You will give the letters,—you will receive them. Oh! we must have no pride in this affair,
otherwise M. Malicorne and Mademoiselle Aure, not
transacting their own affairs themselves, will have to
make up their minds to see them done by others."

" You are quite right; but what is going on yonder in
M. de Guiche's room ? "

" Nothing ; he is only opening his window."

" Let us be gone." And they both immediately disappeared, all the terms of the compact being agreed on.

The window just opened was, in fact, that of the Comte
de Guiche. It was not alone with the hope of catching a
glimpse of Madame through her curtains that he seated
himself by the open window, for his preoccupation of
mind had at that time a different origin. He had just
received, as we have already stated, the courier who had
been dispatched to him by Bragelonne, the latter having
written to De Guiche a letter which had made the
deepest impression upon him, and which he had read over
and over again. "Strange, strange!" he murmured.
"How irresponsible are the means by which destiny hurries men onward to their fate!" Leaving the window in
order to approach nearer to the light, he once more read
the letter he had just received :—

" CALAIS.

" MY DEAR COUNT—I found M. de Wardes at Calais ;
he has been seriously wounded in an affair with the Duke
of Buckingham. De Wardes is, as you know, unques-
tionably brave, but full of malevolent and wicked feelings.
He conversed with me about yourself, for whom, he says,

he has a warm regard, also about Madame, whom he considers a beautiful and amiable woman. He has guessed your affection for a certain person. He also talked to me about the lady for whom I have so ardent a regard, and showed the greatest interest on my behalf in expressing a deep pity for me, accompanied, however, by dark hints which alarmed me at first, but which I at last looked upon as the result of his usual love of mystery. These are the facts : he had received news of the court; you will understand, however, that it was only through M. de Lorraine. The report goes, so says the news, that a change has taken place in the king's affections. You know whom that concerns. Afterwards, the news continues, people are talking about one of the maids of honor, respecting whom various slanderous reports are being circulated. These vague phrases have not allowed me to sleep. I have been deploring, ever since yesterday, that my diffidence and vacillation of purpose, notwithstanding a certain obstinacy of character I may possess, have left me unable to reply to these insinuations. In a word, M. de Wardes was setting off for Paris, and I did not delay his departure with explanations; for it seemed rather hard, I confess, to cross-examine a man whose wounds are hardly yet closed. In short, he travelled by short stages, as he was anxious to leave, he said, in order to be present at a curious spectacle the court cannot fail to offer within a short time. He added a few congratulatory words accompanied by vague sympathizing expressions. I could not understand the one any more than the other. I was bewildered by my own thoughts, and tormented by a mistrust of this man,—a mistrust which, you know better than any one else, I have never been able to overcome. As soon as he left, my perceptions seemed to become clearer. It is hardly possible that a man of De Wardes' character should not have communicated something of his own malicious nature to the statements he made to me. It is not unlikely, therefore, that in the strange hints De Wardes threw out in my presence, there may be a mysterious signification, which I might have some difficulty in applying either to myself or to some one with whom you are acquainted. Being compelled to leave as soon as possible, in obedience to the king's commands, the idea did not occur to me of running after De Wardes in order to ask him to explain his reserve; but I have dispatched a courier to you with this letter, which will explain in detail my various doubts. I regard you as myself; you have reflected and observed; it will be for you to act. M. de Wardes will arrive very shortly; endeavor to learn what he meant, if you do not already know. M. de Wardes, moreover, pretended that the Duke of Buckingham left Paris on the very best of terms with Madame. This was an affair which would have unhesitatingly made me draw my sword, had I not felt that I was under the necessity of dispatching the king's mission before undertaking any quarrel whatsoever. Burn this letter, which Olivian will hand you. Whatever Olivian says, you may confidently rely on. Will you have the goodness, my dear comte, to recall me to the remembrance of Mademoiselle de la Vallière, whose hands I kiss with the greatest respect.

"Your devoted,

DE BRAGELONNE.

"P. S.—If anything serious should happen—we should be prepared for everything—dispatch a courier to me with this one single word, 'Come,' and I will be in Paris within six-and-thirty hours after the receipt of your letter."

De Guiche sighed, folded the letter up a third time, and, instead of burning it, as Raoul had recommended him to do, placed it in his pocket. He felt it needed reading over and over again.

"How much distress of mind, yet what sublime confidence, he shows!" murmured the comte; "he has poured out his whole soul in this letter. He says nothing of the Comte de la Fère, and speaks of his respect for Louise. He cautions me on my own account, and entreats me on his. Ah!" continued De Guiche, with a threatening gesture, "you interfere in my affairs, Monsieur de Wardes, do you? Very well, then; I will shortly occupy myself with yours. As for you, poor Raoul,—you who intrust your heart to my keeping, be assured I will watch over it."

With this promise, De Guiche begged Malicorne to come immediately to his apartments, if possible. Malicorne acknowledged the invitation with an activity which was the first result of his conversation with Montalais. And while De Guiche, who thought that his motive was undiscovered, cross-examined Malicorne, the latter, who appeared to be working in the dark, soon guessed his questioner's motives. The consequence was, that, after a quarter of an hour's conversation, during which De Guiche thought he had ascertained the whole truth with regard to La Vallière and the king, he had learned absolutely nothing more than his own eyes had already acquainted him with, while Malicorne learned, or guessed, that Raoul, who was absent, was fast becoming suspicious, and that De Guiche intended to watch over the treasure of the Hesperides. Malicorne accepted the office of dragon. De Guiche fancied he had done everything for his friend, and soon began to think of nothing but his personal affairs. The next evening, De Wardes' return and first appearance at the king's reception were announced. When that visit had been paid, the convalescent waited on Monsieur; De Guiche taking care, however, to be at Monsieur's apartments before the visit took place.

CHAPTER XLII.

HOW DE WARDES WAS RECEIVED AT COURT.

MONSIEUR had received De Wardes with that marked favor light and frivolous minds bestow on every novelty that comes in their way. De Wardes, who had been absent for a month, was like fresh fruit to him. To treat him with marked kindness was an infidelity to old friends, and there is always something fascinating in that; moreover, it was a sort of reparation to De Wardes himself. Nothing, consequently, could exceed the favorable notice Monsieur took of him. The Chevalier de Lorraine, who feared this rival not a little, but who respected a character and disposition only too parallel to his own in every particular, with the addition of a bull-dog courage he did not himself possess, received De Wardes with a greater display of regard and affection than even Monsieur had done. De Guiche, as we have said, was there also, but kept in the background, waiting very patiently until all these interchanges were over. De Wardes, while talking to the others, and even to Monsieur himself, had not for a moment lost sight of De Guiche, who, he instinctively felt, was there on his account. As soon as he had finished with the others, he went up to De Guiche. They exchanged the most courteous compliments, after which De Wardes returned to Monsieur and the other gentlemen.

In the midst of these congratulations Madame was announced. She had been informed of De Wardes' arrival and knowing all the details of his voyage and duel, she was not sorry to be present at the remarks she knew would be made, without delay, by one who, she felt assured,

was her personal enemy. Two or three of her ladies
accompanied her. De Wardes saluted Madame in the
most graceful and respectful manner, and, as a commencement of hostilities, announced, in the first place, that he
could furnish the Duke of Buckingham's friends with the
latest news about him. This was a direct answer to the
coldness with which Madame had received him. The
attack was a vigorous one, and Madame felt the blow, but
without appearing to have even noticed it. He rapidly
cast a glance at Monsieur and at De Guiche,—the former
colored, and the latter turned very pale. Madame alone
preserved an unmoved countenance; but, as she knew
how many unpleasant thoughts and feelings her enemy
could awaken in the two persons who were listening to
him, she smilingly bent forward toward the traveler, as
if to listen to the news he had brought—but he was speaking of other matters. Madame was brave, even to imprudence; if she were to retreat, it would be inviting an
attack; so, after the first disagreeable impression had
passed away, she returned to the charge.

" Have you suffered much from your wounds, Monsieur
de Wardes?" she inquired, " for we have been told that
you had the misfortune to get wounded."

It was now De Wardes' turn to wince; he bit his lips,
and replied, " No, madame, hardly at all."

"Indeed! and yet in this terribly hot weather——"

"The sea-breezes were very fresh and cool, madame,
and then I had one consolation."

"Indeed! What was it?"

" The knowledge that my adversary's sufferings were
still greater than my own."

" Ah! you mean he was more seriously wounded than
you were; I was not aware of that," said the princess,
with utter indifference.

" Oh, madame, you are mistaken, or rather you pretend

to misunderstand my remark. I did not say that he was a greater sufferer in body than myself; but his heart was very seriously affected."

De Guiche comprehended instinctively from what direction the struggle was approaching; he ventured to make a sign to Madame, as if entreating her to retire from the contest. But she, without acknowledging De Guiche's gesture, without pretending to have noticed it even, and still smiling, continued,—

"Is it possible," she said, "that the Duke of Buckingham's heart was touched? I had no idea, until now, that a heart-wound could be cured."

"Alas! madame," replied De Wardes, politely, "every woman believes that; and it is this belief that gives them that superiority to man which confidence begets."

"You misunderstand altogether, dearest," said the prince, impatiently; "M. de Wardes means that the Duke of Buckingham's heart had been touched, not by the sword but by something sharper."

"Ah! very good, very good!" exclaimed Madame. "It is a jest of M. de Wardes'. Very good; but I should like to know if the Duke of Buckingham would appreciate the jest. It is, indeed, a very great pity he is not here, M. de Wardes."

The young man's eyes seemed to flash fire. "Oh!" he said, as he clenched his teeth, "there is nothing I should like better."

De Guiche did not move. Madame seemed to expect that he would come to her assistance. Monsieur hesitated. The Chevalier de Lorraine advanced and continued the conversation.

"Madame," he said, "De Wardes knows perfectly well that for a Buckingham's heart to be touched is nothing new, and what he has said has already taken place."

"Instead of an ally, I have two enemies," murmured

Madame; "two determined enemies, and in league with
each other." And she changed the conversation. To
change the conversation is, as every one knows, a right
possessed by princes which etiquette requires all to respect.
The remainder of the conversation was moderate enough
in tone; the principal actors had rehearsed their parts.
Madame withdrew early, and Monsieur, who wished to
question her on several matters, offered her his hand on
leaving. The chevalier was seriously afraid that an
understanding might be established between the husband
and wife if he were to leave them quietly together. He
therefore made his way to Monsieur's apartments, in order
to surprise him on his return, and to destroy with a few
words all the good impressions Madame might have been
able to sow in his heart. De Guiche advanced towards
De Wardes, who was surrounded by a large number of
persons, and thereby indicated his wish to converse with
him; De Wardes, at the same time, showing by his looks
and by a movement of his head that he perfectly understood
him. There was nothing in these signs to enable strangers
to suppose they were otherwise than upon the most friendly footing. De Guiche could therefore turn away from
him, and wait until he was at liberty. He had not long
to wait; for De Wardes, freed from his questioners,
approached De Guiche, and after a fresh salutation, they
walked side by side together.

" You have made a good impression since your return,
my dear De Wardes," said the comte.

" Excellent, as you see."

" And your spirits are just as lively as ever ? "

" Better."

" And a very great happiness, too."

" Why not? Everything is so ridiculous in this world,
everything so absurd around us."

" You are right."

" You are of my opinion, then ? "

" I should think so!   And what news do you bring us from yonder ? "

" I?   None at all.   I have come to look for news here."

" But, tell me, you surely must have seen some people at Boulogne, one of our friends, for instance; it is no great time ago ? "

" Some people—one of our friends——"

" Your memory is short."

" Ah! true; Bragelonne, you mean."

" Exactly so."

" Who was on his way to fulfil a mission, with which he was entrusted to King Charles II."

" Precisely.   Well, then, did he not tell you, or did not you tell him——"

" I do not precisely know what I told him, I must confess: but I do know what I did *not* tell him."   De Wardes was *finesse* itself.   He perfectly well knew from De Guiche's tone and manner, which was cold and dignified, that the conversation was about to assume a disagreeable turn. He resolved to let it take what course it pleased, and to keep strictly on his guard.

" May I ask what it was you did not tell him ? " inquired De Guiche.

" All about La Vallière."

" La Vallière. . . What is it? and what was that strange circumstance you seem to have known over yonder, which Bragelonne, who was here on the spot, was not acquainted with ? "

" Do you really ask me that in a serious manner ? "

" Nothing more so."

" What ! you, a member of the court, living in Madame's household, a friend of Monsieur's, a guest at their table, the favorite of our lovely princess ? "

Guiche colored violently from anger. " What princess are you alluding to?" he said.

" I am only acquainted with one, my dear fellow. I am
speaking of Madame herself. Are you devoted to another princess, then? Come, tell me."

De Guiche was on the point of launching out, but he saw
the drift of the remark. A quarrel was imminent between the two young men. De Wardes wished the quarrel to be only in Madame's name, while De Guiche would
not accept it except on La Vallière's account. From this
moment, it became a series of feigned attacks, which would
have continued until one of the two had been touched
home. De Guiche therefore resumed all the self-possession
he could command.

" There is not the slightest question in the world
of Madame in this matter, my dear De Wardes," said
Guiche, " but simply of what you were talking about just
now."

" What was I saying?"

" That you had concealed certain things from Bragelonne."

" Certain things which you know as well as I do,"
replied De Wardes.

" No, upon my honor."

" Nonsense."

" If you tell me what they are, I shall know, but not
otherwise, I swear."

" What! I, who have just arrived from a distance of
sixty leagues, and you who have not stirred from this
place, who have witnessed with your own eyes that which
rumor informed me of at Calais! Do you now tell me
seriously that you do not know what it is about? Oh!
comte, this is hardly charitable of you."

" As you like, De Wardes; but I again repeat, I know
nothing."

" You are truly discreet—well!—perhaps it is very prudent of you."

" And so you will not tell me anything, will not tell me any more than you told Bragelonne? "

" You are pretending to be deaf, I see. I am convinced that Madame could not possibly have more command over herself than *you* have."

" Double hypocrite," murmured De Guiche to himself, " you are again returning to the old subject."

" Very well, then," continued De Wardes, " since we find it so difficult to understand each other about La Vallière and Bragelonne, let us speak about your own affairs."

" Nay," said De Guiche, " I have no affairs of my own to talk about. You have not said anything about me, I suppose, to Bragelonne, which you cannot repeat to my face ? "

" No ; but understand me, Guiche, that however much I may be ignorant of certain matters, I am quite as conversant with others. If, for instance, we were conversing about the intimacies of the Duke of Buckingham at Paris, as I did during my journey with the duke, I could tell you a great many interesting circumstances. Would you like me to mention them ? "

De Guiche passed his hand across his forehead, which was covered with perspiration. "No, no," he said, " a hundred times no ! I have no curiosity for matters which do not concern me. The Duke of Buckingham is for me nothing more than a simple acquaintance, whilst Raoul is an intimate friend. I have not the slightest curiosity to learn what happened to the duke, while I have, on the contrary, the greatest interest in all that happened to Raoul."

" In Paris ? "

" Yes, in Paris, or Boulogne. You understand, I am on

the spot; if anything should happen, I am here to meet it; whilst Raoul is absent, and has only myself to represent him; so, Raoul's affairs before my own."

" But he will return?"

" Not, however, until his mission is completed. In the meantime, you understand, evil reports cannot be permitted to circulate about him without my looking into them."

" And for a better reason still, that he will remain some time in London," said De Wardes, chuckling.

" You think so," said De Guiche, simply.

" Think so, indeed! do you suppose that he was sent to London for no other purpose than to go there and return again immediately. No, no; he was sent to London to remain there."

"Ah! De Wardes," said De Guiche, grasping De Wardes' hand, " that is a very serious suspicion concerning Bragelonne, which completely confirms what he wrote to me from Boulogne."

De Wardes resumed his former coldness of manner: his love of raillery had led him too far, and by his own imprudence, he had laid himself open to attack.

" Well, tell me, what did he write to you about?" he inquired.

" He told me that you had artfully insinuated some injurious remarks against La Vallière, and that you had seemed to laugh at his great confidence in that young girl."

" Well, it is perfectly true I did so," said De Wardes, " and I was quite ready, at the time, to hear from the Vicomte de Bragelonne that which every man expects from another whenever anything may have been said to displease him. In the same way, for instance, if I were seeking a quarrel with you, I should tell you that Madame after having shown the greatest preference for the Duke of Buckingham, is at this moment supposed to have sent the handsome duke away for your benefit."

" Oh ! that would not wound me in the slightest degree, my dear De Wardes," said De Guiche, smiling, notwithstanding the shiver that ran through his whole frame. "Why, such a favor would be too great a happiness."

" I admit that, but if I absolutely wished to quarrel with you, I should try and invent a falsehood, perhaps, and speak to you about a certain arbor, where you and that illustrious princess were together—I should speak also of certain genuflections, of certain kissings of the hand; and you who are so secret on all occasions, so hasty, so punctilious——"

" Well," said De Guiche, interrupting him, with a smile upon his lips, although he almost felt as if he were going to die; "I swear I should not care for that, nor should I in any way contradict you ; for you must know, my dear marquis, that for all matters which concern myself I am a block of ice; but it is a very different thing when an absent friend is concerned, a friend who, on leaving, confided his interests to my safe-keeping; for such a friend, De Wardes, believe me I am like fire itself."

" I understand you, Monsieur De Guiche. In spite of what you say, there cannot be any question between us just now, either of Bragelonne or of this insignificant girl, whose name is La Vallière."

At this moment some of the younger courtiers were crossing the apartment, and having already heard the few words which had just been pronounced, were able also to hear those which were about to follow. De Wardes observed this, and continued aloud;—" Oh! if La Vallière were a coquette like Madame, whose innocent flirtations, I am sure, were, first of all, the cause of the Duke of Buckingham being sent back to England, and afterwards were the reason of your being sent into exile ; for you will not deny, I suppose, that Madame's pretty ways really had a certain influence over you ? "

The courtiers drew nearer to the speakers, Saint-Aignan at their head, and then Manicamp.

"But, my dear fellow, whose fault was that?" said De Guiche, laughing. "I am a vain, conceited fellow, I know, and everybody else knows it too. I took seriously that which was only intended as a jest, and got myself exiled for my pains. But I saw my error. I overcame my vanity, and I obtained my recall, by making the *amende honorable*, and by promising myself to overcome this defect; and the consequence is, that I am so thoroughly cured, that I now laugh at the very thing which, three or four days ago, would have almost broken my heart. But Raoul is in love, and is loved in return; he cannot laugh at the reports which disturb his happiness —reports which you seem to have undertaken to interpret, when you know, marquis, as I do, as these gentlemen do, as every one does in fact, that all such reports are pure calumny."

"Calumny!" exclaimed De Wardes, furious at seeing himself caught in the snare by De Guiche's coolness of temper.

"Certainly—calumny. Look at this letter from him, in which he tells me you have spoken ill of Mademoiselle de la Vallière; and where he asks me, if what you reported about this young girl is true or not. Do you wish me to appeal to these gentlemen, De Wardes, to decide?" And with admirable coolness, De Guiche read aloud the paragraph of the letter which referred to La Vallière. "And now," continued De Guiche, "there is no doubt in the world, as far as I am concerned, that you wished to disturb Bragelonne's peace of mind, and that your remarks were maliciously intended."

De Wardes looked round him, to see if he could find support from any one; but, at the idea, that De Wardes had insulted, either directly or indirectly, the idol of the day, every one shook his head; and De Wardes saw that there was no one present who would have refused to say he was in the wrong.

"Messieurs," said De Guiche, intuitively divining the general feeling, " my discussion with Monsieur de Wardes refers to a subject so delicate in its nature, that it is most important no one should hear more than you have already heard. Close the doors, then, I beg you, and let us finish our conversation in the manner which becomes two gentlemen, one of whom has given the other the lie."

"Messieurs, messieurs!" exclaimed those who were present.

"Is it your opinion, then, that I was wrong in defending Mademoiselle de la Vallière?" said De Guiche. "In that case, I pass judgment upon myself, and am ready to withdraw the offensive words I may have used to Monsieur de Wardes."

"The deuce! certainly not!" said Saint-Aignan. "Mademoiselle de la Vallière is an angel."

"Virtue and purity itself," said Manicamp.

"You see, Monsieur de Wardes," said De Guiche, "I am not the only one who undertakes the defense of that poor girl. I entreat you, therefore, messieurs, a second time, to leave us. You see, it is impossible we could be more calm and composed than we are."

It was the very thing the courtiers wished; some went out at one door, and the rest at the other, and the two young men were left alone.

"Well played," said De Wardes, to the comte.

"Was it not?" replied the latter.

"How can it be wondered at, my dear fellow; I have got quite rusty in the country, while the command you have acquired over yourself, comte, confounds me; a man always gains something in women's society; so, pray accept my congratulations."

" I do accept them."

" And I will make Madame a present of them."

" And now, my dear Monsieur de Wardes, let us speak as loud as you please."

" Do not defy me."

" I do defy you, for you are known to be an evil-minded man; if you do that, you will be looked upon as a coward, too; and Monsieur would have you hanged, this evening, at his window-casement. Speak, my dear De Wardes, speak."

" I have fought already."

" But not quite enough, yet."

" I see, you would not be sorry to fight with me while my wounds are still open."

" No; better still."

" The deuce! you are unfortunate in the moment you have chosen; a duel, after the one I have just fought, would hardly suit me; I have lost too much blood at Boulogne; at the slightest effort my wounds would open again, and you would really have too good a bargain."

" True," said De Guiche; " and yet, on your arrival here, your looks and your arms showed there was nothing the matter with you."

" Yes, my arms are all right, but my legs are weak; and then, I have not had a foil in my hand since that devil of a duel; and you, I am sure, have been fencing every day, in order to carry your little conspiracy against me to a successful issue."

" Upon my honor, monsieur," replied De Guiche, " it is six months since I last practiced."

" No, comte, after due reflection, I will not fight, at least, with you. I will await Bragelonne's return, since you say it is Bragelonne who finds fault with me."

" Oh no, indeed! You shall not wait until Bragelonne's return," exclaimed the comte, losing all command over himself, " for you have said that Bragelonne might, pos-

sibly, be some time before he returns; and, in the mean-
while, your wicked insinuations would have had their
effect."

"Yet, I shall have my excuse. So take care."

"I will give you a week to finish your recovery."

".That is better. We will wait a week."

"Yes, yes, I understand; a week will give time to. my
adversary to make his escape. No, no; I will not give
you one day, even."

"You are mad, monsieur," said De Wardes, retreating
a step.

"And you are a coward, if you do not fight willingly.
Nay, what is more, I will denounce you to the king, as
having refused to fight, after having insulted La Vallière."

"Ah!" said De Wardes, "you are dangerously treacherous, though you pass for a man of honor."

"There is nothing more dangerous than the treachery,
as you term it, of the man whose conduct is always loyal
and upright."

"Restore me the use of my legs, then, or get yourself
bled, till you are as white as I am, so as to equalize our
chances."

"No, no; I have something better than that to propose."

"What is it?"

"We will fight on horseback, and will exchange three
pistol-shots each. You are a first rate marksman. I have
seen you bring down swallows with single balls, and at
full gallop. Do not deny it, for I have seen you myself."

"I believe you are right," said De Wardes; "and as that
is the case, it is not unlikely I might kill you."

"You would be rendering me a very great service, if
you did."

"I will do my best."

"Is it agreed? Give me your hand upon it."

"There it is: but on one condition, however."

" Name it."

" That not a word shall be said about it to the king."

" Not a word, I swear."

" I will go and get my horse, then."

" And I, mine."

" Where shall we meet ? "

" In the plain ; I know an admirable place."

" Shall we go together ? "

" Why not ? "

And both of them, on their way to the stables, passed beneath Madame's windows, which were faintly lighted ; a shadow could be seen behind the lace curtains. " There is a woman," said De Wardes, smiling, " who does not suspect that we are going to fight—to die, perhaps, on her account."

CHAPTER XLIII.

THE COMBAT.

DE WARDES and De Guiche selected their horses, and saddled them with their own hands, with holster saddles. De Guiche, having two pairs of pistols, went to his apartments to get them ; and after having loaded them, gave the choice to De Wardes, who selected the pair he had made use of twenty times before—the same, indeed, with which De Guiche had seen him kill swallows flying. " You will not be surprised," he said, " if I take every precaution. You know the weapons well, and, consequently, I am only making the chances equal."

" Your remark was quite useless," replied De Guiche, " and you have done no more than you are entitled to do."

" Now," said De Wardes, " I beg you to have the good-

ness to help me to mount; for I still experience a little
difficulty in doing so."

" In that case, we had better settle the matter on foot."

" No; once in the saddle, I shall be all right."

" Very good, then; we will not speak of it again," said
De Guiche, as he assisted De Wardes to mount his
horse.

" And now," continued the young man, " in our eagerness to murder one another, we have neglected one
circumstance."

" What is that ? "

" That it is quite dark, and we shall almost be obliged
to grope about, in order to kill."

" Oh! " said De Guiche, " you are as anxious as I am
that everything should be done in proper order."

" Yes; but I do not wish people to say that you have
assassinated me, any more than, supposing I were to kill
you, I should myself like to be accused of such a crime."

" Did any one make a similar remark about your duel
with the Duke of Buckingham ? " said De Guiche, " it took
place precisely under the same conditions as ours."

" Very true; but there was still light enough to see by;
and we were up to our middles almost, in the water; besides, there were a good number of spectators on shore,
looking at us."

De Guiche reflected for a moment; and the thought
which had already presented itself to him became more
confirmed—that De Wardes wished to have witnesses
present, in order to bring back the conversation about
Madame, and to give a new turn to the combat.   He
avoided saying a word in reply, therefore; and, as De
Wardes once more looked at him interrogatively, he replied, by a movement of the head, that it would be best to
let things remain as they were.   The two adversaries
consequently set off, and left the château by the same gate,

close to which we may remember to have seen Montalais and Malicorne together. The night, as if to counteract the extreme heat of the day, had gathered the clouds together in masses which were moving slowly along from the west to the east. The vault above, without a clear spot anywhere visible, seemed to hang heavily over the earth, and soon began, by the force of the wind, to split into streamers, like a huge sheet torn to shreds. Large and warm drops of rain began to fall heavily, and gathered the dust into globules, which rolled along the ground. At the same time, the hedges, which seemed conscious of the approaching storm, the thirsty plants, the drooping branches of the trees, exhaled a thousand aromatic odors, which revived in the mind tender recollections, thoughts of youth, endless life, happiness, and love. "How fresh the earth smells," said De Wardes; "it is a piece of coquetry to draw us to her."

"By the by," replied De Guiche, "several ideas have just occurred to me; and I wish to have your opinion upon them."

"Relative to——?"

"Relative to our engagement."

"It is quite time, in fact, that we should begin to arrange matters."

"Is it to be an ordinary combat, and conducted according to established custom?"

"Let me first know what your established custom is."

"That we dismount in any particular open space that may suit us, fasten our horses to the nearest object, meet, each without our pistols in our hands, and afterwards retire for a hundred and fifty paces, in order to advance on each other."

"Very good; that is precisely the way in which I killed poor Follivent, three weeks ago, at Saint-Denis."

"I beg your pardon, but you forget one circumstance."

"What is that?"

"That in your duel with Follivent you advanced towards each other on foot, your swords between your teeth, and your pistols in your hands."

"True."

"While now, on the contrary, as I cannot walk, you yourself admit that we shall have to mount our horses again, and charge; and the first who wishes to fire will do so."

"That is the best course, no doubt; but it is quite dark; we must make allowance for more missed shots than would be the case in the daytime."

"Very well; each will fire three times; the pair of pistols already loaded, and one reload."

"Excellent! Where shall our engagement take place?"

"Have you any preference?"

"No."

"You see that small wood which lies before us."

"The wood which is called Rochin?"

"Exactly."

"You know it?"

"Perfectly."

"You know that there is an open glade in the center?"

"Yes."

"Well this glade is admirably adapted for such a purpose, with a variety of roads, by-places, paths, ditches, windings, and avenues. We could not find a better spot."

"I am perfectly satisfied, if you are so. We are at our destination, if I am not mistaken."

"Yes. Look at the beautiful open space in the center. The faint light which the stars afford seems concentrated in this spot; the woods which surround it seem, with their barriers, to form its natural limits."

"Very good. Do as you say."

" Let us first settle the conditions."

" These are mine; if you have any objection to make you will state it."

" I am listening."

" If the horse be killed, its rider will be obliged to fight on foot."

" That is a matter of course, since we have no change of horses here."

" But that does not oblige his adversary to dismount."

" His adversary will, in fact, be free to act as he likes."

" The adversaries, having once met in close contact, cannot quit each other under any circumstances, and may consequently, fire muzzle to muzzle."

" Agreed."

" Three shots and no more will do, I suppose? "

" Quite sufficient, I think. Here are powder and balls for your pistols; measure out three charges, take three balls; I will do the same; then we will throw the rest of the powder and the balls away."

" And we will solemnly swear," said De Wardes, " that we have neither balls nor powder about us ? "

" Agreed; and I swear it," said De Guiche, holding his hand towards heaven, a gesture which De Wardes imitated.

" And now, my dear comte," said De Wardes, " allow me to tell you that I am in no way your dupe. You already are, or soon will be, the accepted lover of Madame. I have detected your secret, and you are afraid I shall tell others of it. You wish to kill me, to insure my silence; that is very clear; and in your place, I should do the same." De Guiche hung down his head. " Only," continued De Wardes, triumphantly, " was it really worth while, tell me, to throw this affair of Bragelonne's on my shoulders? But, take care, my dear fellow; in bringing the wild boar to bay, you enrage him to madness; in running down the fox, you endow him with the ferocity of the jaguar. The consequence is, that brought to bay by you, I shall defend myself to the very last."

" You will be quite right to do so."

" Yes; but take care; I shall work more harm than you think. In the first place, as a beginning, you will readily suppose that I have not been absurd enough to lock up my secret, or your secret rather, in my own breast. There is a friend of mine, who resembles me in every way, a man whom you know very well, who shares my secret with me; so, pray understand, that if you kill me, my death will not have been of much service to you; whilst, on the contrary, if I kill you—and everything is possible, you know—you understand?" De Guiche shuddered. " If I kill you," continued De Wardes, "you will have secured two mortal enemies to Madame, who will do their very utmost to ruin her."

" Oh! monsieur," exclaimed De Guiche, furiously, " do not reckon upon my death so easily. Of the two enemies you speak of, I trust most heartily to dispose of one immediately, and the other at the earliest opportunity."

The only reply De Wardes made was a burst of laughter, so diabolical in its sound, that a superstitious man would have been terrified. But De Guiche was not so impressionable as that. " I think," he said, " that everything is now settled, Monsieur de Wardes; so have the goodness to take your place first, unless you would prefer me to do so."

" By no means," said De Wardes. I shall be delighted to save you the slightest trouble." And spurring his horse to a gallop, he crossed the wide open space, and took his stand at that point of the circumference of the cross road immediately opposite to where De Guiche was stationed. De Guiche remained motionless. At this distance of a hundred paces, the two adversaries were absolutely invisible to each other, being completely concealed by the thick

shade of elms and chestnuts. A minute elapsed amidst
the profoundest silence. At the end of the minute, each
of them, in the deep shade in which he was concealed,
heard the double click of the trigger, as they put the pistols
on full cock. De Guiche, adopting the usual tactics, put
his horse to a gallop, persuaded that he should render his
safety doubly sure by the movement, as well as by the
speed of the animal. He directed his course in a straight
line towards the point where, in his opinion, De Wardes
would be stationed ; and he expected to meet De Wardes
about half-way ; but in this he was mistaken. He continued his course, presuming that his adversary was impatiently awaiting his approach. When, however, he had
gone about two-thirds of the distance, he beheld the trees
suddenly illuminated and a ball flew by, cutting the plume
of his hat in two. Nearly at the same moment, and as if
the flash of the first shot had served to indicate the direction of the other, a second report was heard, and a second
ball passed through the head of De Guiche's horse, a little
below the ear. The animal fell. These two reports proceeding from the very opposite direction to that in which
he expected to find De Wardes, surprised him a great
deal ; but as he was a man of amazing self-possession, he
prepared himself for his horse falling, but not so completely, however, that the toe of his boot escaped being
caught under the animal as it fell. Very fortunately the
horse in its dying agonies moved so as to enable him to
release the leg which was less entangled than the other.
De Guiche rose, felt himself all over, and found that he
was not wounded. At the very moment he had felt the
horse tottering under him, he placed his pistols in the
holsters, afraid that the force of the fall might explode
one at least, if not both of them, by which he would have
been disarmed, and left utterly without defense. Once
on his feet, he took the pistols out of the holsters, and ad-

vanced towards the spot, where, by the light of the flash, he had seen De Wardes appear. De Guiche had, at the first shot, accounted for the maneuver, than which nothing could have been simpler. Instead of advancing to meet De Guiche, or remaining in his place to await his approach, De Wardes had, for about fifteen paces, followed the circle of the shadow which hid him from his adversary's observation, and at the very moment when the latter presented his flank in his career, he had fired from the place where he stood, carefully taking aim, and assisted instead of being inconvenienced by the horse's gallop. It has been seen that, notwithstanding the darkness, the first ball passed hardly more than an inch above De Guiche's head. De Wardes had so confidently relied upon his aim, that he thought he had seen De Guiche fall; his astonishment was extreme when he saw he still remained erect in his saddle. He hastened to fire his second shot, but his hand trembled, and he killed the horse instead. It would be a most fortunate chance for him if De Guiche were to remain held fast under the animal. Before he could have freed himself, De Wardes would have loaded his pistol and had De Guiche at his mercy. But De Guiche, on the contrary, was up, and had three shots to fire. De Guiche immediately understood the position of affairs. It would be necessary to exceed De Wardes in rapidity of execution. He advanced, therefore, so as to reach him before he should have had time to reload his pistol. De Wardes saw him approaching like a tempest. The ball was rather tight, and offered some resistance to the ramrod. To load carelessly would be simply to lose his last chance; to take the proper care in loading meant fatal loss of time, or rather, throwing away his life. He made his horse bound on one side. De Guiche turned round also, and, at the moment the horse was quiet again, fired, and the ball carried off De Wardes' hat from his head.

De Wardes now knew that he had a moment's time at his own disposal; he availed himself of it in order to finish loading his pistol. De Guiche, noticing that his adversary did not fall, threw the pistol he had just discharged aside, and walked straight towards De Wardes, elevating the second pistol as he did so. He had hardly proceeded more than two or three paces, when De Wardes took aim at him as he was walking, and fired. An exclamation of anger was De Guiche's answer; the comte's arm contracted and dropped motionless by his side, and the pistol fell from his grasp. But De Wardes observed the comte stoop down, pick up the pistol with his left hand, and again advance towards him. His anxiety was excessive. " I am lost," murmured De Wardes, "he is not mortally wounded." At the very moment, however, De Guiche was about to raise his pistol against De Wardes, the head, shoulders, and limbs of the comte seemed to collapse. He heaved a deep-drawn sigh, tottered, and fell at the feet of De Wardes' horse.

" That is all right," said De Wardes, and gathering up the reins, he struck his spurs into his horse's sides. The horse cleared the comte's motionless body, and bore De Wardes rapidly back to the château. When he arrived there, he remained a quarter of an hour deliberating within himself as to the proper course to be adopted. In his impatience to leave the field of battle, he had omitted to ascertain whether De Guiche were dead or not. A double hypothesis presented itself to De Wardes' agitated mind; either De Guiche was killed, or De Guiche was wounded only. If he were killed, why should he leave his body in that manner to the tender mercies of the wolves; it was a perfectly useless piece of cruelty, for if De Guiche were dead, he certainly could not breathe a syllable of what had passed; if he were not killed, why should he, De Wardes, in leaving him there uncared for, allow himself to be regarded as a savage, incapable of one generous feeling? This last consideration determined his line of conduct.

De Wardes immediately instituted inquiries after Manicamp. He was told that Manicamp had been looking after De Guiche, and, not knowing where to find him, had retired to bed. De Wardes went and awoke the sleeper, without any delay, and related the whole affair to him, which Manicamp listened to in perfect silence, but with an expression of momentarily increasing energy, of which his face could hardly have been supposed capable. It was only when De Wardes had finished, that Manicamp uttered the words, "Let us go."

As they proceeded, Manicamp became more and more excited, and in proportion as De Wardes related the details of the affair to him, his countenance assumed every moment a darker expression. "And so," he said, when De Wardes had finished, "you think he is dead?"

"Alas, I do."

"And you fought in that manner, without witnesses?"

"He insisted upon it."

"It is very singular."

"What do you mean by saying it is singular?"

"That it is so very unlike Monsieur de Guiche's disposition."

"You do not doubt my word, I suppose?"

"Hum! hum!"

"You do doubt it, then?"

"A little. But I shall doubt it more than ever, I warn you, if I find the poor fellow is really dead."

"Monsieur Manicamp!"

"Monsieur de Wardes!"

"It seems you intend to insult me."

"Just as you please. The fact is, I never did like people who come and say, 'I have killed such and such a gentleman in a corner; it is a great pity, but I killed him in a perfectly honorable manner.' It has an ugly appearance, M. de Wardes."

" Silence! we have arrived."

In fact, the glade could now be seen, and in the open space lay the motionless body of the dead horse. To the right of the horse, upon the dark grass, with his face against the ground, the poor comte lay, bathed in his blood. He had remained in the same spot, and did not even seem to have made the slightest movement. Manicamp threw himself on his knees, lifted the comte in his arms, and found him quite cold, and steeped in blood. He let him gently fall again. Then, stretching out his hand and feeling all over the ground close to where the comte lay, he sought until he found De Guiche's pistol.

" By Heaven! " he said, rising to his feet, pale as death and with the pistol in his hand, "you are not mistaken, he is quite dead."

" Dead! " repeated De Wardes.

" Yes; and his pistol is still loaded," added Manicamp, looking into the pan.

" But I told you that I took aim as he was walking towards me, and fired at him at the very moment he was going to fire at me."

" Are you quite sure that you fought with him, Monsieur de Wardes ? I confess that I am very much afraid it has been a foul assassination. Nay, nay, no exclamations! You have had your three shots, and his pistol is still loaded. You have killed his horse, and he, De Guiche, one of the best marksmen in France, has not touched even either your horse or yourself. Well, Monsieur de Wardes, you have been very unlucky in bringing me here; all the blood in my body seems to have mounted to my head; and I verily believe that since so good an opportunity presents itself, I shall blow out your brains on the spot.   So Monsieur de Wardes, recommend yourself to Heaven."

" Monsieur Manicamp, you cannot think of such a thing ! "

" On the contrary, I am thinking of it very strongly."

" Would you assassinate me ? "

" Without the slightest remorse, at least for the present."

" Are you a gentleman ? "

" I have given a great many proofs of it."

" Let me defend my life, then, at least."

" Very likely ; in order, I suppose, that you may do to me what you have done to poor De Guiche."

And Manicamp slowly raised his pistol to the height of De Wardes' breast, and with arm stretched out, and a fixed, determined look on his face, took a careful aim.

De Wardes did not attempt a flight ; he was completely terrified.   In the midst, however, of this horrible silence, which lasted about a second, but which seemed an age to De Wardes, a faint sigh was heard.

" Oh," exclaimed De Wardes, " he still lives !   Help, De Guiche, I am about to be assassinated ! "

Manicamp fell back a step or two, and the two young men saw the comte raise himself slowly and painfully upon one hand.   Manicamp threw the pistol away a dozen paces, and ran to his friend, uttering a cry of delight. De Wardes wiped his forehead, which was covered with a cold perspiration.

" It was just in time," he murmured.

" Where are you hurt ? " inquired Manicamp of De Guiche, " and whereabouts are you wounded ? "

De Guiche showed him his mutilated hand and his chest covered with blood.

" Comte," exclaimed De Wardes, " I am accused of

having assassinated you; speak, I implore you, and say that I fought loyally."

"Perfectly so," said the wounded man; "Monsieur De Wardes fought quite loyally, and whoever says the contrary will make an enemy of me."

"Then, sir," said Manicamp, "assist me, in the first place, to carry this gentleman home, and I will afterwards give you every satisfaction you please; or, if you are in a hurry, we can do better still; let us stanch the blood from the comte's wounds here, with your pocket-handkerchief and mine, and then, as there are two shots left, we can have them between us."

"Thank you," said De Wardes. "Twice already, in one hour, I have seen death too close at hand to be agreeable; I don't like his look at all, and I prefer your apologies."

Manicamp burst out laughing, and Guiche too, in spite of his sufferings. The two young men wished to carry him, but he declared he felt quite strong enough to walk alone. The ball had broken his ring-finger and his little finger, and then had glanced along his side, but without penetrating deeply into his chest. It was the pain rather than the seriousness of the wound, therefore, which had overcome De Guiche. Manicamp passed his arm under one of the count's shoulders, and De Wardes did the same with the other, and in this way they brought him back to Fontainebleau, to the house of the same doctor who had been present at the death of the Franciscan, Aramis's predecessor.

CHAPTER XLIV.

THE KING'S SUPPER.

THE king while these matters were being arranged was sitting at the supper-table, and the not very large number of guests invited for that day had taken their seats too, after the usual gesture intimating the royal permission. At this period of Louis XIV.'s reign, although etiquette was not governed by the strict regulations subsequently adopted, the French court had entirely thrown aside the traditions of good fellowship and patriarchal affability existing in the time of Henry IV., which the suspicious mind of Louis XIII. had gradually replaced with pompous state and ceremony.

The king, therefore, was seated alone at a small separate table, which, like the desk of a president, overlooked the adjoining tables. Although we say a small table, we must not omit to add that this small table was the largest one there. Moreover, it was the one on which were placed the greatest number and quantity of dishes, consisting of fish, game, meat, fruit, vegetables, and preserves. The king was young and full of vigor and energy, very fond of hunting, addicted to all violent exercises of the body, possessing, besides, like all the members of the Bourbon family, a rapid digestion and an appetite speedily renewed. Louis XIV. was a formidable table-companion; he delighted in criticising his cooks; but when he honored them by praise and commendation, the honor was overwhelming. The king began by eating several kinds of soup, either mixed together or taken separately. He intermixed, or rather separated, each of the soups by a glass of old wine. He ate quickly and somewhat greedily. Porthos, who from the beginning had, out of respect, been waiting for a jog of D'Artagnan's arm, seeing the king make such rapid progress, turned to the musketeer and said in a low tone—

"It seems as if one might go on now; his majesty is very encouraging, from the example he sets. Look."

"The king eats," said D'Artagnan, "but he talks at the same time; try and manage matters in such manner, that, if he should happen to address a remark to you, he will not find you with your mouth full—which would be very disrespectful."

"The best way in that case," said Porthos, "is to eat no supper at all; and yet I am very hungry, I admit, and everything looks and smells most invitingly, as if appealing to all my senses at once."

"Don't think of not eating, for a moment," said D'Artagnan; "that would put his majesty out terribly. The king has a saying, 'that he who works well, eats well,' and he does not like people to eat indifferently at his table."

"How can I avoid having my mouth full if I eat?" said Porthos.

"All you have to do," replied the captain of the musketeers, "is simply to swallow what you have in it, whenever the king does you the honor to address a remark to you."

"Very good," said Porthos; and from that moment he began to eat with a certain well-bred enthusiasm.

The king occasionally looked at the different persons who were at table with him, and, *en connoisseur*, could appreciate the different dispositions of his guests.

"Monsieur du Vallon!" he said.

Porthos was enjoying a *salmi de lièvre*, and swallowed half of the back. His name, pronounced in such a manner,

made him start, and by a vigorous effort of his gullet he
absorbed the whole mouthful.

"Sire," replied Porthos, in a stifled voice, but sufficiently intelligible, nevertheless.

"Let those *filets d'agneau* be handed to Monsieur du
Vallon," said the king; "do you like brown meats, M. du
Vallon?"

"Sire, I like everything," replied Porthos.

D'Artagnan whispered: "Everything your majesty
sends me."

Porthos repeated: "Everything your majesty sends
me," an observation which the king apparently received
with great satisfaction.

"People eat well who work well," replied the king,
delighted to have *en tête-à-tête* a guest who could eat as
Porthos did. Porthos received the dish of lamb, and put
a portion of it on his plate.

"Well?" said the king.

"Exquisite," said Porthos, calmly.

"Have you as good mutton in your part of the country,
Monsieur du Vallon!" continued the king.

"Sire, I believe, that from my own province, as everywhere else, the best of everything is sent to Paris for
your majesty's use; but, on the other hand, I do not eat
lamb in the same way your majesty does."

"Ah! ah! and how do you eat it?"

"Generally, I have a lamb dressed whole."

"*Whole?*"

"Yes, sire."

"In what manner, Monsieur du Vallon?"

"In this, sire: my cook, who is a German, first stuffs
the lamb in question with small sausages he procures
from Strasburg, force-meat balls from Troyes, and larks
from Pithiviers; by some means or other, which I am not
acquainted with, he bones the lamb as he would do a fowl,

leaving the skin on however, which forms a brown crust all over the animal; when it is cut in beautiful slices, in the same way as an enormous sausage, a rose-colored gravy pours forth, which is as agreeable to the eye as it is exquisite to the palate." And Porthos finished by smacking his lips.

The king opened his eyes with delight, and, while cutting some of the *faisan en daube*, which was being handed to him, he said:

"That is a dish I should very much like to taste, Monsieur du Vallon. Is it possible! a whole lamb!"

"Absolutely an entire lamb, sire."

"Pass those pheasants to M. du Vallon; I perceive he is an amateur."

The order was immediately obeyed. Then, continuing the conversation, he said: "And you do not find the lamb too fat?"

"No, sire, the fat falls down at the same time as the gravy does, and swims on the surface; then the servant who carves removes the fat with a spoon, which I have had expressly made for that purpose."

"Where do you reside?" inquired the king.

"At Pierrefonds, sire."

"At Pierrefonds; where is that, M. du Vallon—near Belle-Isle?"

"Oh no sire! Pierrefonds is in the Soissonnais."

"I thought you alluded to the lamb on account of the salt marshes."

"No, sire, I have marshes which are not salt, it is true, but which are not the less valuable on that account."

The king had now arrived at the *entremets*, but without losing sight of Porthos, who continued to play his part in the best manner.

"You have an excellent appetite, M. du Vallon, said the king, "and you make an admirable guest at table."

"Ah! sire, if your majesty were ever to pay a visit to Pierrefonds, we would both of us eat our lamb together; for your appetite is not an indifferent one by any means."

D'Artagnan gave Porthos a severe kick under the table, which made Porthos color up.

"At your majesty's present happy age," said Porthos, in order to repair the mistake he had made, "I was in the musketeers, and nothing could ever satisfy me then. Your majesty has an excellent appetite, as I have already had the honor of mentioning, but you select what you eat with quite too much refinement to be called for one moment a great eater."

The king seemed charmed at his guest's politeness.

"Will you try some of these creams?" he said to Porthos.

"Sire, your majesty treats me with far too much kindness to prevent me speaking the whole truth."

"Pray do so, M. du Vallon."

"Well, sire, with regard to sweet dishes I only recognize pastry, and even that should be rather solid; all these frothy substances swell the stomach, and occupy a space which seems to me to be too precious to be so badly tenanted."

"Ah! gentlemen," said the king, indicating Porthos by a gesture, "here is indeed a model of gastronomy. It was in such a manner that our fathers, who so well knew what good living was, used to *eat*, while we," added his majesty, "do nothing but tantalize with our stomachs." And as he spoke, he took the breast of a chicken with ham, while Porthos attacked a dish of partridges and quails. The cupbearer filled his majesty's glass. "Give M. du Vallon some of my wine," said the king. This was one of the greatest honors of the royal table. D'Artagnan pressed his friend's knee. "If you could only manage to swallow the half of that boar's head I see yonder," said he to Porthos,

I shall believe you will be a duke and peer within the next twelvemonth."

"Presently," said Porthos, phlegmatically; "I shall come to that by and by."

In fact it was not long before it came to the boar's turn, for the king seemed to take a pleasure in urging on his guest; he did not pass any of the dishes to Porthos until he had tasted them himself, and he accordingly took some of the boar's head. Porthos showed that he could keep pace with his sovereign ; and, instead of eating the half, as D'Artagnan had told him, he ate three-fourths of it. "It is impossible," said the king in an undertone, "that a gentleman who eats so good a supper every day, and who has such beautiful teeth, can be otherwise than the most straightforward, upright man in my kingdom."

"Do you hear?" said D'Artagnan in his friend's ear.

"Yes ; I think I am rather in favor," said Porthos, balancing himself on his chair.

"Oh ! you are in luck's way."

The king and Porthos continued to eat in the same manner, to the great satisfaction of the other guests, some of whom, from emulation, had attempted to follow them, but were obliged to give up half-way. The king soon began to get flushed, and the reaction of the blood to his face announced that the moment of repletion had arrived. It was then that Louis XIV., instead of becoming gay and cheerful, as most good livers generally do, became dull, melancholy, and taciturn. Porthos, on the contrary, was lively and communicative. D'Artagnan's foot had more than once to remind him of this peculiarity of the king. The dessert now made its appearance. The king had ceased to think anything further of Porthos ; he turned his eyes anxiously towards the entrance-door, and he was heard occasionally to inquire how it happened that Monsieur de Saint-Aignan was so long in arriving. At last, at the moment when his majesty was finishing a pot of preserved plums with a deep sigh, Saint-Aignan appeared. The king's eyes, which had become somewhat dull, immediately began to sparkle. The comte advanced towards the king's table, and Louis rose at his approach. Everybody got up at the same time, including Porthos, who was just finishing an almond-cake capable of making the jaws of a crocodile stick together. The supper was over.

CHAPTER XLV.

AFTER SUPPER.

THE king took Saint-Aignan by the arm, and passed into the adjoining apartment. "What has detained you, comte?" said the king.

"I was bringing the answer, sire," replied the comte.

"She has taken a long time to reply to what I wrote her."

"Sire, your majesty deigned to write in verse, and Mademoiselle de la Vallière wished to repay your majesty in the same coin; that is to say in gold."

"Verses! Saint-Aignan," exclaimed the king in ecstasy. "Give them to me at once." And Louis broke the seal of a little letter, inclosing the verses which history has preserved entire for us, and which are more meritorious in intention than in execution. Such as they were, however, the king was enchanted with them, and exhibited his satisfaction by unequivocal transports of delight; but the universal silence which reigned in the rooms warned Louis, so sensitively particular with regard to good breeding, that his delight might give rise to various interpretations. He turned aside and put the note in his pocket, and then advancing a few steps, which brought him again to the

threshold of the door close to his guests, he said, " M. du
Vallon I have seen you to-day with the greatest pleasure, and my pleasure will be equally great to see you
again." Porthos bowed as the Colossus of Rhodes would
have done, and retired from the room with his face towards
the king. M. d'Artagnan continued the king, you will
await my orders in the gallery; I am obliged to you for having made me acquainted with M. du Vallon. Gentlemen,"
addressing himself to the other guests, " I return to Paris
to-morrow on account of the departure of the Spanish
and Dutch ambassadors. Until to-morrow then."

The apartment was immediately cleared of the guests.
The king took Saint-Aignan by the arm, made him read
La Vallière's verses over again, and said, " What do you
think of them ?"

" Charming, sire."

" They charm me, in fact, and if they were known——"

" Oh! the professional poets would be jealous of them;
but it is not at all likely they will know anything about
them."

" Did you give her mine ?"

" Oh! sire, she positively devoured them."

" They were very weak, I am afraid."

" That is not what Mademoiselle de la Vallière said of
them."

" Do you think she was pleased with them?"

" I am sure of it, sire."

" I must answer, then."

" Oh! sire, immediately after supper? Your majesty
will fatigue yourself."

" You are quite right; study after eating is notoriously
injurious."

" The labor of a poet especially so; and, besides, there
is great excitement prevailing at Mademoiselle de la
Vallière's."

" What do you mean ? "

" With her as with all the ladies of the court."

" Why ? "

" On account of poor De Guiche's accident."

" Has anything serious happened to De Guiche, then ? "

" Yes, sir, he has one hand nearly destroyed, a hole in his breast ; in fact, he is dying."

" Good heavens ! who told you that?"

" Manicamp brought him back just now to the house of a doctor here in Fontainebleau, and the rumor soon reached us all."

" Brought back ! Poor De Guiche ; and how did it happen ? "

" Ah ! that is the very question,—how did it happen ? "

" You say that in a very singular manner, Saint-Aignan. Give me the details. What does he say himself ? "

" He says nothing, sire ; but others do."

" What others ? "

" Those who brought him back, sire."

" Who are they ? "

" I do not know, sire ; but M. de Manicamp knows. M. de Manicamp is one of his friends."

" As everybody is indeed," said the king.

" Oh ! no ! " returned Saint-Aignan, " you are mistaken, sire ; every one is not precisely a friend of M. de Guiche."

" How do you know that ? "

" Does your majesty require me to explain myself ? "

" Certainly I do."

" Well, sire, I believe I have heard something said about a quarrel between two gentlemen."

" When ? "

" This very evening, before your majesty's supper was served."

" That can hardly be. I have issued such stringent

and severe ordinances with respect to duelling, that no one, I presume, would dare to disobey them."

" In that case, Heaven preserve me from excusing any one!" exclaimed Saint-Aignan. " Your majesty commanded me to speak, and I spoke accordingly."

" Tell me, then, in what way the Comte de Guiche has been wounded ? "

" Sire, it is said to have been at a boar-hunt."

" This evening ? "

" Yes, sire."

" One of his hands shattered, and a hole in his breast. Who was at the hunt with M. de Guiche ? "

" I do not know, sire ; but M. de Manicamp knows, or ought to know."

" You are concealing something from me, Saint-Aignan."

" Nothing, sire, I assure you."

" Then, explain to me how the accident happened ; was it a musket that burst ? "

" Very likely, sire. But yet, on reflection, it could hardly have been that, for De Guiche's pistol was found close by him still loaded."

" His pistol ? But a man does not go to a boar-hunt with a pistol, I should think."

" Sire, it is also said that De Guiche's horse was killed and that the horse is still to be found in the wide open glade in the forest."

" His horse ? —Guiche go on horseback to a boar-hunt ? —Saint-Aignan, I do not understand a syllable of what you have been telling me. Where did the affair happen ? "

" At the Rond-point, in that part of the forest called the Bois-Rochin."

" That will do. Call M. d'Artagnan." Saint-Aignan obeyed, and the musketeer entered.

" Monsieur d'Artagnan," said the king, " you will leave

this place by the little door of the private staircase."

" Yes, sire."

" You will mount your horse."

" Yes, sire."

"And you will proceed to the Rond-point du Bois-Rochin. Do you know the spot?"

"Yes, sire. I have fought there twice."

" What!" exclaimed the king, amazed at the reply.

" Under the edicts, sire, of Cardinal Richelieu," returned D'Artagnan, with his usual impassibility.

" That is very different, monsieur. You will, therefore, go there, and will examine the locality very carefully. A man has been wounded there, and you will find a horse lying dead. You will tell me what your opinion is upon the whole affair."

" Very good, sire."

" As a matter of course it is your own opinion I require, and not that of any one else."

" You shall have it in an hour's time, sir."

"I prohibit your speaking with any one, whoever it may be."

" Except with the person who must give me a lantern," said D'Artagnan.

" Oh ! that is a matter of course," said the king, laughing at the liberty, which he tolerated in no one but his captain of musketeers. D'Artagnan left by the little staircase.

" Now, let my physician be sent for," said Louis. Ten minutes afterwards the king's physician arrived, quite out of breath.

" You will go, monsieur," said the king to him, " and accompany M. de Saint-Aignan wherever he may take you ; you will render me an account of the state of the person you may see in the house you will be taken to." The physician obeyed without a remark, as at that time people began to obey Louis XIV., and left the room preceding Saint-Aignan.

"Do you, Saint-Aignan, send Manicamp to me, before the physician can possibly have spoken to him." And Saint-Aignan left in his turn.

CHAPTER XLVI.

SHOWING IN WHAT WAY D'ARTAGNAN DISCHARGED THE
MISSION WITH WHICH THE KING HAD INTRUSTED HIM.

WHILE the king was engaged in making these last-mentioned arrangements in order to ascertain the truth, D'Artagnan, without losing a second, ran to the stable, took down the lantern, saddled his horse himself, and proceeded towards the place his majesty had indicated. According to the promise he had made, he had not accosted any one; and, as we have observed, he had carried his scruples so far as to do without the assistance of the stable-helpers altogether. D'Artagnan was one of those who in moments of difficulty pride themselves on increasing their own value. By dint of hard galloping, he in less than five minutes reached the wood, fastened his horse to the first tree he came to, and penetrated to the broad open space on foot. He then began to inspect most carefully, on foot and with his lantern in his hand, the whole surface of the Rond-point, went forward, turned back again, measured, examined, and after half an hour's minute inspection, he returned silently to where he had left his horse, and pursued his way in deep reflection and at a foot-pace to Fontainebleau. Louis was waiting in his cabinet; he was alone, and with a pencil was scribbling on paper certain lines which D'Artagnan at the first glance recognized as unequal and very much touched up.

The conclusion he arrived at was, that they must be verses. The king raised his head and perceived D'Artagnan. "Well, monsieur," he said, "do you bring me any news?"

"Yes, sire."

"What have you seen?"

"As far as probability goes, sire," D'Artagnan began to reply.

"It was certainty I requested of you."

"I will approach it as near as I possibly can. The weather was very well adapted for investigations of the character I have just made; it has been raining this evening, and the roads were wet and muddy——"

"Well, the result, M d'Artagnan?"

"Sire, your majesty told me that there was a horse lying dead in the cross-road of the Bois-Rochin, and I began, therefore, by studying the roads. I say the roads, because the center of the cross-road is reached by four separate roads. The one that I myself took was the only one that presented any fresh traces. Two horses had followed it side by side; their eight feet were marked very distinctly in the clay. One of the riders was more impatient than the other, for the footprints of the one were invariably in advance of the other about half a horse's length."

"Are you quite sure they were travelling together?" said the king.

"Yes, sire. The horses are two rather large animals of equal pace,—horses well used to maneuvers of all kinds, for they wheeled round the barrier of the Rond-point together."

"Well—and after?"

"The two cavaliers paused there for a minute, no doubt to arrange the conditions of the engagement; the horses grew restless and impatient. One of the riders spoke, while the other listened and seemed to have contented himself by simply answering. His horse pawed the ground, which proves that his attention was so taken up by listening that he let the bridle fall from his hand."

" A hostile meeting did take place then?"

" Undoubtedly."

"Continue; you are a very accurate observer."

" One of the two cavaliers remained where he was standing, the one, in fact, who had been listening; the other crossed the open space, and at first placed himself directly opposite to his adversary. The one who had remained stationary traversed the Rond-point at a gallop, about two-thirds of its length, thinking that by this means he would gain upon his opponent; but the latter had followed the circumference of the wood."

" You are ignorant of their names, I suppose?"

"Completely so, sire. Only he who followed the circumference of the wood was mounted on a black horse."

" How do you know that?"

" I found a few hairs of his tail among the brambles which bordered the sides of the ditch."

"Go on."

" As for the other horse, there can be no trouble in describing him, since he was left dead on the field of battle."

" What was the cause of his death?"

" A ball which had passed through his brain."

" Was the ball that of a pistol or a gun."

" It was a pistol-bullet, sire. Besides, the manner in which the horse was wounded explained to me the tactics of the man who had killed it. He had followed the circumference of the wood in order to take his adversary in flank. Moreover, I followed his foot-tracks on the grass."

" The tracks of the black horse, do you mean?"

" Yes, sire."

" Go on, Monsieur d'Artagnan."

" As your majesty now perceives the position of the two adversaries, I will, for a moment, leave the cavalier who had remained stationary for the one who started off at a gallop."

" Do so."

" The horse of the cavalier who rode at full speed was killed on the spot."

" How do you know that?"

" The cavalier had not time even to throw himself off his horse, and so fell with it. I observed the impression of his leg, which, with a great effort, he was enabled to extricate from under the horse. The spur, pressed down by the weight of the animal, had plowed up the ground."

" Very good; and what did he do as soon as he rose up again?"

" He walked straight up to his adversary."

" Who still remained upon the verge of the forest?"

" Yes, sire. Then, having reached a favorable distance, he stopped firmly, for the impression of both his heels are left in the ground quite close to each other, fired, and missed his adversary."

" How do you know he did not hit him."

" I found a hat with a ball through it."

" Ah, a proof, then!" exclaimed the king.

" Insufficient, sire," replied D'Artagnan, coldly; " it is a hat without any letters indicating its ownership, without arms; a red feather, as all hats have; the lace even, had nothing particular in it."

" Did the man with the hat through which the bullet had passed fire a second time?"

" Oh, sire, he had already fired twice."

" How did you ascertain that?"

" I found the waddings of the pistol."

" And what became of the bullet which did not kill the horse?"

" It cut in two the feather of the hat belonging to him against whom it was directed, and broke a small birch at the other end of the open glade."

" In that case, then, the man on the black horse was disarmed, whilst his adversary had still one more shot to fire ? "

" Sire, while the dismounted rider was extricating himself from his horse, the other was reloading his pistol. Only, he was much agitated while he was loading it, and his hand trembled greatly."

" How do you know that ? "

" Half the charge fell to the ground, and he threw the ramrod aside, not having time to replace it in the pistol."

" Monsieur D'Artagnan, this is marvelous you tell me."

" It is only close observation, sire, and the commonest highwayman could tell as much."

" The whole scene is before me from the manner in which you relate it."

" I have, in fact, reconstructed it in my own mind, with merely a few alterations."

" And now," said the king, " let us return to the dismounted cavalier. You were saying that he walked towards his adversary while the latter was loading his pistol."

" Yes ; but at the very moment he himself was taking - aim, the other fired."

" Oh ! " said the king ; " and the shot ? "

" The shot told terribly, sire ; the dismounted cavalier fell upon his face, after having staggered forward three or four paces."

" Where was he hit ? "

" In two places ; in the first place, in his right hand, and then, by the same bullet, in his chest."

" But how could you ascertain that ? " inquired the king, full of admiration."

"By a very simple means; the butt end of the pistol was covered with blood, and the trace of the bullet could be observed with fragments of a broken ring. The wounded man, in all probability, had the ring finger and the little finger carried off."

"As far as the hand goes, I have nothing to say; but the chest?"

"Sire, there were two small pools of blood, at a distance of about two feet and a half from each other. At one of these pools of blood the grass was torn up by the clenched hand; at the other, the grass was simply pressed down by the weight of the body."

"Poor De Guiche!" exclaimed the king.

"Ah! it was M. de Guiche, then?" said the musketeer quietly. "I suspected it, but did not venture to mention it to your majesty."

"And what made you suspect it?"

"I recognized the De Grammont arms upon the holsters of the dead horse."

"And you think he is seriously wounded?"

"Very seriously; since he fell immediately, and remained a long time in the same place; however, he was able to walk, as he left the spot, supported by two friends."

"You met him returning, then?"

"No; but I observed the footprints of three men; the one on the right and the one on the left walked freely and easily, but the one in the middle dragged his feet as he walked; besides, he left traces of blood at every step he took."

"Now, monsieur, since you saw the combat so distinctly that not a single detail seems to have escaped you, tell me something about De Guiche's adversary."

"Oh, sire, I do not know him."

"And yet you see everything very clearly."

"Yes, sire, I see everything; but I do not tell all I see;

and, since the poor devil has escaped, your majesty will permit me to say that I do not intend to denounce him."

" And yet he is guilty, since he has fought a duel, monsieur."

" Not guilty in my eyes, sire," said D'Artagnan, coldly.

"Monsieur ! " exclaimed the king, " are you aware of what you are saying ? "

" Perfectly, sire ; but, according to my notions, a man who fights a duel is a brave man ; such, at least, is my own opinion; but your majesty may have another, it is but natural, for you are master here."

" Monsieur d'Artagnan, I ordered you, however——"

D'Artagnan interrupted the king by a respectful gesture. " You ordered me, sire, to gather what particulars I could, respecting a hostile meeting that had taken place ; those particulars you have. If you order me to arrest M. de Guiche's adversary, I will do so; but do not order me to denounce him to you, for in that case I will not obey."

"Very well !   Arrest him, then."

" Give me his name, sire."

The king stamped his foot angrily ; but after a moment's reflection, he said, " You are right—ten times, twenty times, a hundred times right."

" That is my opinion, sire : I am happy that, this time, it accords with your majesty's."

" One word more.   Who assisted Guiche ? "

" I do not know, sire."

" But you speak of two men. There was a person present, then, as second."

" There was no second, sire.   Nay, more than that, when M. de Guiche fell, his adversary fled without giving him any assistance."

" The miserable coward ! " exclaimed the king.

" The consequence of your ordinances, sire. If a man

has fought well, and fairly, and has already escaped one chance of death, he naturally wishes to escape a second. M. de Botteville cannot be forgotten very easily."

"And so, men turn cowards."

"No, they become prudent."

"And he has fled, then, you say?"

"Yes; and as fast as his horse could possibly carry him."

"In what direction?"

"In the direction of the château."

"Well, and after all that?"

"Afterwards, as I have had the honor of telling your majesty, two men on foot arrived, who carried M. de Guiche back with them."

"What proof have you that these men arrived after the combat?"

"A very evident proof, sire; at the moment the encounter took place, the rain had just ceased, the ground had not had time to imbibe the moisture, and was, consequently, soaked; the footsteps sank in the ground; but while M. de Guiche was lying there in a fainting condition, the ground became firm again, and the footsteps made a less sensible impression."

Louis clapped his hands together in sign of admiration. "Monsieur d'Artagnan," he said, "you are positively the cleverest man in my kingdom."

"The identical thing M. de Richelieu thought, and M. de Mazarin said, sire."

"And now, it remains for us to see if your sagacity is at fault."

"Oh! sire, a man may be mistaken; *humanum est errare*," said the musketeer, philosophically.

"In that case, you are not human, Monsieur d'Artagnan, for I believe you never are mistaken."

"Your majesty said, that we were going to see whether such was the case, or not."

"Yes."

"In what way, may I venture to ask?"

"I have sent for M. de Manicamp, and M. de Manicamp is coming."

"And M. de Manicamp knows the secret?"

"De Guiche has no secrets from M. de Manicamp."

D'Artagnan shook his head. "No one was present at the combat, I repeat; and unless M. de Manicamp was one of the two men who brought him back——"

"Hush!" said the king, "he is coming; remain, and listen attentively."

"Very good, sire."

And, at the very same moment, Manicamp and Saint-Aignan appeared at the threshold of the door.

CHAPTER XLVII.

THE ENCOUNTER.

THE king signified with an imperious gesture, first to the musketeer, then to Saint-Aignan, "On your lives, not a word." D'Artagnan withdrew, like a sentinel, to a corner of the room; Saint-Aignan, in his character of favorite, leaned over the back of the king's chair. Manicamp, with his right foot properly advanced, a smile upon his lips, and his white and well-formed hands gracefully disposed, advanced to make his reverence to the king, who returned the salutation by a bow. "Good-evening, M. de Manicamp," he said.

"Your majesty did me the honor to send for me," said Manicamp.

"Yes, in order to learn from you all the details of the unfortunate accident which has befallen the Comte de Guiche."

"Oh! sire, it is grievous indeed."

"You were there?"

"Not precisely, sire."

"But you arrived on the scene of the accident, a few minutes after it took place?"

" Sire, about half an hour afterwards."

"And where did the accident happen?"

"I believe, sire, the place is called the Rond-point du Bois-Rochin."

"Oh! the rendezvous of the hunt."

"The very spot, sire."

"Good; give me all the details you are acquainted with, respecting this unhappy affair, Monsieur de Manicamp."

"Perhaps your majesty has already been informed of them, and I fear to fatigue you with useless repetitions."

"No, do not be afraid of that."

Manicamp looked round him; he only saw D'Artagnan leaning with his back against the wainscot—D'Artagnan, calm, kind, and good-natured as usual—and Saint-Aignan whom he had accompanied, and who still leaned over the king's arm-chair with an expression of countenance equally full of good feeling. He determined, therefore, to speak out. " Your majesty is perfectly aware," he said, " that accidents are very frequent in hunting."

"In hunting, do you say?"

"I mean, sire, when an animal is brought to bay."

"Ah! ah!" said the king, "it was when the animal was brought to bay, then, that the accident happened?"

"Alas! sire, unhappily, it was."

The king paused for a moment before he said: " What animal was being hunted?"

"A wild boar, sire."

" And what could possibly have possessed De Guiche to go to a wild boar-hunt by himself; that is but a clownish idea of sport, only fit for that class of people who, unlike the Maréchal de Grammont, have no dogs and huntsmen, to hunt as gentlemen should do."

Manicamp shrugged his shoulders. "Youth is very rash," he said, sententiously.

"Well, go on," said the king.

"At all events," continued Manicamp, not venturing to be too precipitate and hasty, and letting his words fall very slowly one by one, "at all events, sire, poor De Guiche went hunting—all alone."

"Quite alone? indeed?—What a sportsman! And is not M. de Guiche aware that the wild boar always stands at bay?"

"That is the very thing that really happened, sire."

"He had some idea, then, of the beast being there?"

"Yes, sire, some peasants had seen it among their potatoes."

"And what kind of animal was it?"

"A short, thick beast."

"You may as well tell me, monsieur, that De Guiche had some idea of committing suicide; for I have seen him hunt, and he is an active and vigorous hunter. Whenever he fires at an animal brought to bay and held in check by the dogs, he takes every possible precaution, and yet he fires with a carbine, and on this occasion he seems to have faced the boar with pistols only."

Manicamp started.

"A costly pair of pistols, excellent weapons to fight a duel with a man and not with a wild boar. What an absurdity!"

"There are some things, sire, which are difficult of explanation."

"You are quite right, and the event which we are now discussing is certainly one of them. Go on."

During the recital, Saint-Aignan, who probably would have

made a sign to Manicamp to be careful what he was
about, found that the king's glance was constantly fixed
upon himself, so that it was utterly impossible to communicate with Manicamp in any way.   As for D'Artagnan, the statue of Silence at Athens was far more noisy
and far more expressive than he.   Manicamp, therefore,
was obliged to continue in the same way he had begun,
and so contrived to get more and more entangled in his
explanation.   " Sire," he said, " This is probably how the
affair happened.   Guiche was waiting to receive the boar
as it rushed towards him."

" On foot or on horseback ? " inquired the king.

" On horseback. He fired upon the brute and missed
his aim, and then it dashed upon him."

" And the horse was killed."

" Ah! your majesty knows that, then."

" I have been told that a horse has been found lying
dead in the cross-roads of the Bois-Rochin, and I presume
it was De Guiche's horse."

" Perfectly true, sire, it was his."

" Well, so much for the horse, and now for De Guiche ? "

" De Guiche, once down, was attacked and worried by the
wild boar, and wounded in the hand and in the chest."

" It is a horrible accident, but it must be admitted it
was De Guiche's own fault.   How could he possibly have
gone to hunt such an animal merely armed with pistols ;
he must have forgotten the fable of Adonis ? "

Manicamp rubbed his ear in seeming perplexity. " Very
true," he said, " it was very imprudent."

" Can you explain it, Monsieur Manicamp ? "

" Sire, what is written is written ! "

" Ah! you are a fatalist."

Manicamp looked very uncomfortable and ill at ease.

" I am angry with you, Monsieur Manicamp," continued
the king.

" With me, sire ? "

" Yes. How was it that you, who are De Guiche's intimate friend, and who know that he is subject to such acts of folly, did not stop him in time ? "

Manicamp no longer knew what to do; the tone in which the king spoke was anything but that of a credulous man. On the other hand, it did not indicate any particular severity, nor did he seem to care very much about the cross-examination. There was more of raillery in it than menace. " And you say, then," continued the king, " that it was positively De Guiche's horse that was found dead ? "

" Quite positive, sire."

" Did that astonish you ? "

" No, sire; for your majesty will remember that, at the last hunt, M. de Saint-Maure had a horse killed under him, and in the same way."

" Yes, but that one was ripped open."

" Of course, sire."

" Had Guiche's horse been ripped open like M. de Saint-Maure's horse, I should not have been astonished."

Manicamp opened his eyes very wide.

" Am I mistaken," resumed the king, " was it not in the frontal bone that De Guiche's horse was struck? You must admit, Monsieur de Manicamp, that that is a very singular place for a wild-boar to attack ? "

" You are aware, sire, that the horse is a very intelligent animal, and he doubtless endeavored to defend himself."

" But a horse defends himself with his heels and not with his head."

" In that case, the terrified horse may have slipped or fallen down," said Manicamp, " and the boar, you understand, sire, the boar——"

" Oh! I understand that perfectly, as far as the horse is concerned ; but how about his rider ? "

"Well! that, too, is simple enough; the boar left the horse and attacked the rider; and, as I have already had the honor of informing your majesty, shattered De Guiche's hand at the very moment he was about to discharge his second pistol at him, and then, with a gouge of his tusk, made that terrible hole in his chest."

"Nothing is more likely; really, Monsieur de Manicamp, you are wrong in placing so little confidence in your own eloquence, and you can tell a story most admirably."

"Your majesty is exceedingly kind," said Manicamp, saluting him in the most embarrassed manner.

"From this day henceforth, I will prohibit any gentleman attached to my court going to a similar encounter. Really, one might just as well permit dueling."

Manicamp started, and moved as if he were about to withdraw. "Is your majesty satisfied?"

"Delighted; but do not withdraw yet, Monsieur de Manicamp," said Louis, "I have something to say to you."

"Well, well!" thought D'Artagnan, "there is another who is not up to the mark;" and he uttered a sigh which might signify, "Oh! the men of *our* stamp, where are they *now?*"

At this moment an usher lifted up the curtain before the door, and announced the king's physician.

"Ah!" exclaimed Louis, "here comes Monsieur Valot, who has just been to see M. de Guiche. We shall now hear news of the man maltreated by the boar."

Manicamp felt more uncomfortable than ever.

"In this way, at least," added the king, "our conscience will be quite clear." And he looked at D'Artagnan, who did not seem in the slightest degree discomposed.

CHAPTER XLVIII.

THE PHYSICIAN.

M. VALOT entered. The position of the different persons present was precisely the same; the king was seated, Saint-Aignan leaning over the back of his arm-chair, D'Artagnan with his back against the wall, and Manicamp still standing.

"Well, M. Valot," said the king, "did you obey my directions?"

"With the greatest alacrity, sire."

"You went to the doctor's house in Fontainebleau?"

"Yes, sire."

"And you found M. de Guiche there?"

"I did, sire."

"What state was he in?—speak unreservedly."

"In a very sad state, indeed, sire."

"The wild boar did not quite devour him, however?"

"Devour whom?"

"De Guiche."

"What wild boar?"

"The boar that wounded him."

"M. de Guiche wounded by a boar!"

"So it is said at least."

"By a poacher, rather, or by a jealous husband, or an ill-used lover, who, in order to be revenged, fired upon him."

"What is that you say, Monsieur Valot? Were not M. de Guiche's wounds produced by defending himself against a wild boar?"

"M. de Guiche's wounds are the result of a pistol-bullet

that broke his ring-finger and the little finger of the right hand, and afterwards buried itself in the intercostal muscles of the chest."

"A bullet! Are you sure Monsieur de Guiche was wounded by a *bullet?*" exclaimed the king, pretending to look much surprised.

"Indeed I am, sire; so sure, in fact, that here it is." And he presented to the king a half-flattened bullet, which the king looked at, but did not touch.

"Did he have that in his chest, poor fellow?" he asked.

"Not precisely. The ball did not penetrate, but was flattened, as you see, either upon the trigger of the pistol or upon the right side of the breast-bone."

"Good Heavens!" said the king, seriously, "you said nothing to me about this, Monsieur de Manicamp."

"Sire——"

"What does all this mean, then, this invention about hunting a wild-boar at nightfall? Come, speak, monsieur."

"Sire——"

"It seems, then, that you are right," said the king, turning round towards his captain of musketeers, "and that a duel actually took place."

The king possessed, to a greater extent than any one else, the faculty enjoyed by the great in power or position, of compromising and dividing those beneath him. Manicamp darted a look full of reproaches at the musketeer. D'Artagnan understood the look at once, and not wishing to remain beneath the weight of such an accusation, advanced a step forward, and said: "Sire, your majesty commanded me to go and explore the place where the cross-roads meet in the Bois-Rochin, and to report to you, according to my own ideas, what had taken place there. I submitted my observations to you, but without denouncing any one. It was your majesty yourself who was the first to name the Comte de Guiche."

" Well, monsieur, well," said the king, haughtily; " you have done your duty, and I am satisfied with you. But you, Monsieur de Manicamp, have failed in yours, for you have told me a falsehood."

" A falsehood, sire. The expression is a hard one."

" Find a more accurate, then."

" Sire, I will not attempt to do so. I have already been unfortunate enough to displease your majesty, and it will, in every respect, be far better for me to accept most humbly any reproaches you may think proper to address to me."

" You are right, monsieur, whoever conceals the truth from me, risks my displeasure."

"Sometimes, sire, one is ignorant of the truth."

"No further falsehood, monsieur, or I double the punishment."

Manicamp bowed and turned pale. D'Artagnan again made another step forward, determined to interfere, if the still increasing anger of the king attained certain limits.

" You see, monsieur," continued the king, " that it is useless to deny the thing any longer. M. de Guiche has fought a duel."

" I do not deny it, sire, and it would have been truly generous on your majesty's part not to have forced me to tell a falsehood."

" Forced? Who forced you?"

" Sire, M. de Guiche is my friend. Your majesty has forbidden duels under pain of death. A falsehood might save my friend's life, and I told it."

"Good!" murmured D'Artagnan, " an excellent fellow, upon my word."

" Instead of telling a falsehood, monsieur, you should have prevented him from fighting," said the king.

"Oh! sire, your majesty, who is the most accomplished

gentleman in France, knows quite as well as any of us other gentlemen that we have never considered M. de Botteville dishonored for having suffered death on the Place de Grève. That which does in truth dishonor a man is to avoid meeting his enemy—not to avoid meeting his executioner!"

"Well, monsieur, that may be so," said Louis XIV.; "I am desirous of suggesting a means of your repairing all."

"If it be a means of which a gentleman may avail himself, I shall most eagerly seize the opportunity."

"The name of M. de Guiche's adversary?"

"Oh! oh!" murmured D'Artagnan, "are we going to take Louis XIII. as a model?"

"Sire!" said Manicamp, with an accent of reproach.

"You will not name him, then?" said the king.

"Sire, I do not know him."

"Bravo!" murmured D'Artagnan.

"Monsieur de Manicamp, hand your sword to the captain."

Manicamp bowed very gracefully, unbuckled his sword, smiling as he did so, and handed it for the musketeer to take. But Saint-Aignan advanced hurriedly between him and D'Artagnan. "Sire," he said, "will your majesty permit me to say a word?"

"Do so," said the king, delighted perhaps at the bottom of his heart, for some one to step between him and the wrath he felt had carried him too far.

"Manicamp, you are a brave man, and the king will appreciate your conduct; but to wish to serve your friends too well, is to destroy them. Manicamp, you know the name the king asks you for?"

"It is perfectly true—I do know it."

"You will give it up then?"

"If I felt I ought to have mentioned it, I should have already done so."

"Then I will tell it, for I am not so extremely sensitive on such points of honor as you are."

"You are at liberty to do so, but it seems to me, however——"

"Oh! a truce to magnanimity; I will not permit you to go to the Bastile in that way. Do you speak; or I will."

Manicamp was keen-witted enough, and perfectly understood that he had done quite sufficient to produce a good opinicn of his conduct; it was now only a question of persevering in such a manner as to regain the good graces of the king. "Speak, monsieur," he said to Saint-Aignan; "I have on my own behalf done all that my conscience told me to do; and it must have been very importunate," he added, turning towards the king, "since its mandates led me to disobey your majesty's commands; but your majesty will forgive me, I hope, when you learn that I was anxious to preserve the honor of a lady."

"Of a lady?" said the king, with some uneasiness.

"Yes, sire."

"A lady was the cause of this duel?"

Manicamp bowed.

"If the position of the lady in question warrants it," he said, "I shall not complain of your having acted with so much circumspection; on the contrary, indeed."

"Sire, everything which concerns your majesty's household, or the household of your majesty's brother, is of importance in my eyes."

"In my brother's household," repeated Louis XIV., with a slight hesitation. "The cause of the duel was a lady belonging to my brother's household, do you say?"

"Or to Madame's."

"Ah! to Madame's?"

"Yes, sire."

"Well—and this lady?"

"Is one of the maids of honor of her royal highness Madame la Duchess D'Orleans."

"For whom M. De Guiche fought—do you say?"

"Yes, sir, and, this time, I tell no falsehood."

Louis seemed restless and anxious. "Gentlemen," he said, turning towards the spectators of this scene, "will you have the goodness to retire for a moment. I wish to be alone with M. de Manicamp; I know he has some important communication to make for his own justification, and which he will not venture before witnesses. . . . Put up your sword, M. de Manicamp."

Manicamp returned his sword to his belt.

"The fellow decidedly has his wits about him," murmured the musketeer, taking Saint-Aignan by the arm, and withdrawing with him.

"He will get out of it," said the latter in D'Artagnan's ear.

"And with honor, too, comte."

Manicamp cast a glance of recognition at Saint-Aignan and the captain, which luckily passed unnoticed by the king.

"Come, come," said D'Artagnan, as he left the room, "I had an indifferent opinion of the new generation. Well, I was mistaken after all. There is some good in them, I perceive."

Valot preceded the favorite and the captain, leaving the king and Manicamp alone in the cabinet.

CHAPTER XLIX.

WHEREIN D'ARTAGNAN PERCEIVES THAT IT WAS HE WHO WAS
MISTAKEN, AND MANICAMP WHO WAS RIGHT.

THE king, determined to be satisfied that no one was
listening, went himself to the door, and then returned
precipitately and placed himself opposite to Manicamp.

"And now we are alone, Monsieur de Manicamp, explain yourself?"

"With the greatest frankness, sire," replied the young
man.

"And, in the first place, pray understand," added the
king, "that there is nothing to which I personally attach
a greater importance than the honor of *any* lady."

"That is the very reason, sire, why I endeavored to
study your delicacy of sentiment and feeling."

"Yes, I understand it all now. You say that it was
one of the maids of honor of my sister-in-law who was the
subject of dispute, and that the person in question, De
Guiche's adversary, the man, in point of fact, whom you
will not name——"

"But whom M. de Saint-Aignan will name, Monsieur."

"Yes, you say, however, that this man insulted some
one belonging to the household of Madame."

"Yes, sire. Mademoiselle de la Vallière."

"Ah!" said the king, as if he had expected the name,
and yet as if its announcement had caused him a sudden
pang; "ah! it was Mademoiselle de la Vallière who was
insulted."

"I do not say precisely that she was insulted, sire."

"But at all events——"

"I merely say that she was spoken of in terms far enough from respectful."

"A man dares to speak in disrespectful terms of Mademoiselle de la Vallière, and yet you refuse to tell me the name of the insulter?"

"Sire, I thought it was quite understood that your majesty had abandoned the idea of making me denounce him."

"Perfectly true, monsieur," returned the king, controlling his anger; "besides, I shall know in good time the name of this man whom I shall feel it my duty to punish."

Manicamp perceived that they had returned to the question again. As for the king, he saw he had allowed himself to be hurried away a little too far, and therefore continued:—"And I will punish him—not because there is any question of Mademoiselle de la Vallière, although I esteem her very highly—but because a lady was the object of the quarrel. And I intend that ladies shall be respected at my court, and that quarrels shall be put a stop to altogether."

Manicamp bowed.

"And now, Monsieur de Manicamp," continued the king, "what was said about Mademoiselle de la Vallière?"

"Cannot your majesty guess?"

"I?"

"Your majesty can imagine the character of the jest in which young men permit themselves to indulge."

"They very probably said that she was in love with some one?" the king ventured to remark.

"Probably so."

"But Mademoiselle de la Vallière has a perfect right to love any one she pleases," said the king.

"That is the very point De Guiche maintained."

" And on account of which he fought, do you mean."

" Yes, sire, the sole and only cause."

The king colored. " And you do not know anything more, then ? "

" In what respect, sire ? "

" In the very interesting respect which you are now referring to."

" What does your majesty wish to know ? "

" Why, the name of the man with whom La Vallière is in love, and whom De Guiche's adversary disputed her right to love."

" Sire, I know nothing—I have heard nothing—and have learnt nothing, even accidentally ; but De Guiche is a noble-hearted fellow, and if, momentarily, he substituted himself in the place or stead of La Vallière's protector, it was because that protector was himself of too exalted a position to undertake her defense."

These words were more than transparent ; they made the king blush, but this time with pleasure. He struck Manicamp gently on the shoulder. " Well, well, Monsieur de Manicamp, you are not only a ready, witty fellow, but a brave gentleman besides, and your friend De Guiche is a paladin quite after my own heart ; you will express that to him from me."

" Your majesty forgives me, then ? "

" Completely."

" And I am free ? "

The king smiled and held out his hand to Manicamp, which he took and kissed respectfully. " And then," added the king, " you relate stories so charmingly."

" I, sire ! "

" You told me in the most admirable manner the particulars of the accident which happened to Guiche. I can see the wild boar rushing out of the wood—I can see the horse fall down fighting with his head, and the boar rush from the horse to the rider. You do not simply relate a story well: you positively paint its incidents."

" Sire, I think your majesty condescends to laugh at my expense," said Manicamp.

"On the contrary," said Louis, seriously, " I have so little intention of laughing, Monsieur de Manicamp, that I wish you to relate this adventure to every one."

" The adventure of the hunt?"

" Yes; in the same manner you told it to me, without changing a single word—*you understand?*"

" Perfectly, sire."

" And you will relate it, then?"

" Without losing a minute."

" Very well! and now summon M. D'Artagnan; I hope you are no longer afraid of him."

" Oh, sire, from the very moment I am sure of your majesty's kind disposition, I no longer fear anything!"

" Call him, then," said the king.

Manicamp opened the door, and said, " Gentlemen, the king wishes you to return."

D'Artagnan, Saint-Aignan, and Valot entered.

" Gentlemen," said the king, " I summoned you for the purpose of saying that Monsieur de Manicamp's explanation has entirely satisfied me."

D'Artagnan glanced at Valot and Saint-Aignan, as much as to say, " Well! did I not tell you so?"

The king led Manicamp to the door, and then in a low tone of voice said—" See that M. de Guiche takes good care of himself, and particularly that he recovers as soon as possible; I am very desirous of thanking him in the name of every lady, but let him take special care that he does not begin again."

" Were he to die a hundred times, sire, he would begin again if your majesty's honor were in any way called in question."

This remark was direct enough. But we have already said that the incense of flattery was very pleasing to the king, and, provided he received it, he was not very particular as to its quality.

"Very well, very well," he said, as he dismissed Manicamp, "I will see De Guiche myself, and make him listen to reason." And as Manicamp left the apartment, the king turned round towards the three spectators of this scene, and said, "Tell me, Monsieur d'Artagnan, how does it happen that your sight is so imperfect?—you, whose eyes are generally so very good."

"My sight bad, sire?"

"Certainly."

"It must be the case since your majesty says so; but in what respect, may I ask?"

"Why, with regard to what occurred in the Bois-Rochin."

"Ah! ah!"

"Certainly. You pretend to have seen the tracks of two horses, to have detected the foot-prints of two men; and have described the particulars of an engagement, which you assert took place. Nothing of the sort occurred; pure illusion on your part."

"Ah! ah!" said D'Artagnan.

"Exactly the same thing with the galloping to and fro of the horses, and the other indications of a struggle. It was the struggle of De Guiche against the wild boar, and absolutely nothing else; only the struggle was a long and a terrible one, it seems."

"Ah! ah!" continued D'Artagnan.

"And when I think that I almost believed it for a moment; but, then, you told it with such confidence."

"I admit, sire, that I must have been very short-sighted," said D'Artagnan, with a readiness of humor which delighted the king.

"You do admit, then?"

"Admit it, sire, most assuredly I do."

"So that now you see the thing——"

"In quite a different light from that in which I saw it half an hour ago."

"And to what, then, do you attribute this difference in your opinion?"

"Oh! a very simple thing, sire; half an hour ago I returned from the Bois-Rochin, where I had nothing to light me but a stupid stable lantern——"

"While now?"

"While now, I have all the wax-lights of your cabinet, and more than that, your majesty's own eyes, which illuminate everything, like the blazing sun at noonday."

The king began to laugh; and Saint-Aignan broke out into convulsions of merriment.

"It is precisely like M. Valot," said D'Artagnan, resuming the conversation where the king had left off; "he has been imagining all along, that, not only was M. de Guiche wounded by a bullet, but still more, that he extracted it, even, from his chest."

"Upon my word," said Valot, "I assure you——"

"Now, did you not believe that?" continued D'Artagnan.

"Yes," said Valot; "not only did I believe it, but, at this very moment, I would swear it."

"Well, my dear doctor, you have dreamt it."

"I have dreamt it!"

"M. de Guiche's wound—a mere dream; the bullet, a dream. So, take my advice, and prate no more about it."

"Well said," returned the king, "M. d'Artagnan's advice is sound. Do not speak of your dream to any one, Monsieur Valot, and, upon the word of a gentleman, you will have no occasion to repent it. Good-evening, gentlemen; a very sad affair, indeed, is a wild boar hunt!"

"A very serious thing, indeed," repeated D'Artagnan, in a loud voice, "is a wild-boar hunt!" and he repeated it in every room through which he passed; and left the château, taking Valot with him.

"And now we are alone," said the king to Saint-Aignan, "what is the name of De Guiche's adversary?"

Saint-Aignan looked at the king.

"Oh! do not hesitate," said the king; "you know that I am bound beforehand to forgive."

"De Wardes," said Saint-Aignan.

"Very good," said Louis XVI.; and then, retiring to his own room, added to himself, "To forgive is not to forget."

CHAPTER L.

SHOWING THE ADVANTAGE OF HAVING TWO STRINGS TO ONE'S BOW.

MANICAMP quitted the king's apartment, delighted at having succeeded so well, when, just as he reached the bottom of the staircase and was passing a doorway, he felt that some one suddenly pulled him by the sleeve. He turned round and recognized Montalais, who was waiting for him in the passage, and who, in a very mysterious manner, with her body bent forward, and in a low tone of voice, said to him, "Follow me, monsieur, and without any delay, if you please."

"Where to, mademoiselle?" inquired Manicamp.

"In the first place, a true knight would not have asked such a question, but would have followed me without requiring any explanation."

"Well, mademoiselle, I am quite ready to conduct myself as a true knight."

"No; it is too late, and you cannot take the credit of it. We are going to Madame's apartment, so come at once."

"Ah! ah!" said Manicamp. "Lead on, then."

And he followed Montalais, who ran before him as light as Galatea.

"This time," said Manicamp, as he followed his guide, "I do not think that stories about hunting expeditions would be acceptable. We will try, however, and if need be—well, if there should be any occasion for it, we must try something else."

Montalais still ran on.

"How fatiguing it is," thought Manicamp, "to have need of one's head and legs at the same time."

At last, however, they arrived. Madame had just finished undressing, and was in a most elegant *dishabille*, but it must be understood that she had changed her dress before she had any idea of being subjected to the emotions now agitating her. She was waiting with the most restless impatience; and Montalais and Manicamp found her standing near the door. At the sound of their approaching footsteps, Madame came forward to meet them.

"Ah!" she said, "at last!"

"Here is M. Manicamp," replied Montalais.

Manicamp bowed with the greatest respect; Madame signed to Montalais to withdraw, and she immediately obeyed. Madame followed her with her eyes, in silence, until the door closed behind her, and then, turning towards Manicamp, said, "What is the matter?—and is it true, as I am told, Monsieur de Manicamp, that some one is lying wounded in the château?"

"Yes, madame, unfortunately so—Monsieur de Guiche."

"Yes, Monsieur de Guiche," repeated the princess. "I had, in fact, heard it rumored, but not confirmed. And so, in truth, it is Monsieur de Guiche who has been thus unfortunate?"

"M. de Guiche himself, madame."

"Are you aware, M. de Manicamp," said the princess, hastily, "that the king has the strongest antipathy to duels?"

"Perfectly so, madame; but a duel with a wild beast is not answerable."

"Oh, you will not insult me by supposing that I credit the absurd fable reported, with what object I cannot tell, respecting M. de Guiche having been wounded by a wild boar. No, no, monsieur; the real truth is known, and, in addition to the inconvenience of his wound, M. de Guiche runs the risk of losing his liberty if not his life."

"Alas! madame, I am well aware of that, but what is to be done!"

"You have seen the king?"

"Yes, madame."

"What did you say to him?"

"I told him how M. de Guiche went to the chase, and how a wild boar rushed forth out of the Bois-Rochin; how M. De Guiche fired at it, and how, in fact, the furious brute dashed at De Guiche, killed his horse, and grievously wounded himself."

"And the king believed that?"

"Implicitly."

"Oh, you surprise me, Monsieur de Manicamp; you surprise me very much."

And Madame walked up and down the room, casting a searching look from time to time at Manicamp, who remained motionless and impassible in the same place. At last she stopped.

"And yet," she said, "every one here seems unanimous in giving another cause for this wound."

"What cause, madame?" said Manicamp; "may I be

permitted, without indiscretion, to ask your highness?"

"You ask such a question! You, M. de Guiche's intimate friend, his confidant, indeed!"

"Oh, madame! his intimate friend—yes; confidant —no. De Guiche is a man who can keep his own secrets, who has some of his own certainly, but who never breathes a syllable about them. De Guiche is discretion itself, madame."

"Very well, then; those secrets which M. de Guiche keeps so scrupulously, I shall have the pleasure of informing you of," said the princess, almost spitefully; "for the king may possibly question you a second time, and if, on the second occasion, you were to repeat the same story to him, he possibly might not be very well satisfied with it."

"But, madame, I think your highness is mistaken with regard to the king. His majesty was perfectly satisfied with me, I assure you."

"In that case, permit me to assure you, Monsieur de Manicamp, it only proves one thing, which is, that his majesty is very easily satisfied."

"I think your highness is mistaken in arriving at such an opinion; his majesty is well known not to be contented except with very good reason."

"And do you suppose that he will thank you for your officious falsehood, when he will learn to-morrow that M. de Guiche had on behalf of his friend, M. de Bragelonne, a quarrel which ended in a hostile meeting?"

"A quarrel on M. de Bragelonne's account," said Manicamp, with the most innocent expression in the world; "what does your royal highness do me the honor to tell me?"

"What is there astonishing in that? M. de Guiche is susceptible, irritable, and easily loses his temper."

"Oh the contrary, madame, I know M. de Guiche to be

very patient, and never susceptible or irritable except upon very good grounds."

"But is not friendship a just ground?" said the princess.

"Oh, certainly, madame; and particularly for a heart like his."

"Very good; you will not deny, I suppose, that M. de Bragelonne is M. de Guiche's friend?"

"A great friend."

"Well, then, M. de Guiche had taken M. de Bragelonne's part; and as M. de Bragelonne was absent and could not fight, he fought for him."

Manicamp began to smile, and moved his head and shoulders very slightly, as much as to say, "Oh, if you will positively have it so——"

"But speak at all events," said the princess, out of patience; "speak!"

"I?"

"Of course; it is quite clear you are not of my opinion, and that you have something to say."

"I have only one thing to say, madame."

"Name it!"

"That I do not understand a single word of what you have just been telling me."

"What!—you do not understand a single word about M. de Guiche's quarrel with M. de Wardes," exclaimed the princess, almost out of temper.

Manicamp remained silent.

"A quarrel," she continued, "which arose out of a conversation scandalous in its tone and purport, and more or less well founded, respecting the virtue of a certain lady."

"Ah! of a certain lady,—this is quite another thing," said Manicamp.

"You begin to understand, do you not?"

"Your highness will excuse me, but I dare not——"

"You dare not," said Madame, exasperated; "very well, then, wait one moment, I will dare."

"Madame, madame!" exclaimed Manicamp, as if in great dismay, "be careful of what you are going to say."

"It would seem, monsieur, that, if I happened to be a man, you would challenge me, notwithstanding his majesty's edicts, as Monsieur de Guiche challenged M. de Wardes; and that, too, on account of the virtue of Mademoiselle de la Vallière."

"Of Mademoiselle de la Vallière!" exclaimed Manicamp, starting backwards, as if that was the very last name he expected to hear pronounced.

"What makes you start in that manner, Monsieur de Manicamp?" said Madame, ironically; "do you mean to say you would be impertinent enough to suspect that young lady's honor?"

"Madame, in the whole course of this affair there has not been the slightest question of Mademoiselle de la Vallière's honor."

"What! when two men have almost blown each other's brains out on a woman's behalf, do you mean to say she has had nothing to do with the affair, and that her name has not been called in question at all? I did not think you so good a courtier, Monsieur de Manicamp."

"Pray forgive me, madame," said the young man, "but we are very far from understanding one another You do me the honor to speak one language while I am speaking altogether another."

"I beg your pardon, but I do not understand your meaning?"

"Forgive me then; but I fancied I understood your highness to remark that De Guiche and De Wardes had fought on Mademoiselle de la Vallière's account?"

" Certainly."

" On account of Mademoiselle de la Vallière, I think you said?" repeated Manicamp.

" I do not say that M. de Guiche personally took an interest in Mademoiselle de la Vallière, but I say that he did so as representing or acting on behalf of another."

" On behalf of another?"

" Come, do not always assume such a bewildered look. Does not every one here know that M. de Bragelonne is affianced to Mademoiselle de la Vallière, and that before he went on the mission with which the king intrusted him, he charged his friend M. de Guiche to watch over that interesting young lady."

" There is nothing more for me to say, then. Your highness is well-informed."

" Of everything. I beg you to understand that clearly."

Manicamp began to laugh, which almost exasperated the princess, who was not, as we know, of a very patient disposition.

" Madame," resumed the discreet Manicamp, saluting the princess, " let us bury this affair altogether in forgetfulness, for it will probably never be quite cleared up."

" Oh, as far as that goes there is nothing more to do, and the information is complete. The king will learn that M. de Guiche has taken up the cause of this little adventuress, who gives herself all the airs of a grand lady ; he will learn that Monsieur de Bragelonne, having nominated his friend M. de Guiche his guardian-in-ordinary, the latter immediately fastened, as he was required to do, upon the Marquis de Wardes, who ventured to trench upon his privileges. Moreover, you cannot pretend to deny, Monsieur Manicamp—you who know everything so well—that the king on his side casts a longing eye upon this famous treasure, and that he will bear no slight grudge against M. de Guiche for constituting him-

self its defender.   Are you sufficiently well informed now,
or do you require anything further? If so, speak, monsieur."

"No, madame, there is nothing more I wish to know."

"Learn, however—for you ought to know it, Monsieur
de Manicamp—learn that his majesty's indignation will
be followed by terrible consequences. In princes of a
similar temperament to that of his majesty, the passion
which jealousy causes sweeps down like a whirlwind."

"Which you will temper, madame."

"I!" exclaimed the princess, with a gesture of indescribable irony; "I! and by what title, may I ask?"

"Because you detest injustice, madame."

"And according to your account, then, it would be an
injustice to prevent the king arranging his love affairs as
he pleases."

"You will intercede, however, in M. de Guiche's favor?"

"You are mad, monsieur," said the princess, in a
haughty tone of voice.

"On the contrary, I am in the most perfect possession
of my senses; and, I repeat, you will defend M. de Guiche
before the king."

"Why should I?"

"Because the cause of M. de Guiche is your own,
madame," said Manicamp, with ardor kindling in his
eyes.

"What do you mean by that?"

"I mean, madame, that, with respect to the defense
which Monsieur de Guiche undertook in M. de Bragelonne's absence, I am surprised that your highness has
not detected a pretext in La Vallière's name having been
brought forward."

"A pretext? But a pretext for what?" repeated the
princess, hesitatingly, for Manicamp's steady look had
just revealed something of the truth to her.

"I trust, madame," said the young man, "I have said sufficient to induce your highness not to overwhelm before his majesty my poor friend, De Guiche, against whom all the malevolence of a party bitterly opposed to your own will now be directed."

"You mean, on the contrary, I suppose, that all those who have no great affection for Mademoiselle de la Vallière, and even, perhaps, a few of those who have some regard for her, will be angry with the comte?"

"Oh, madame! why will you push your obstinacy to such an extent, and refuse to open your ears and listen to the counsel of one whose devotion to you is unbounded? Must I expose myself to the risk of your displeasure,— am I really to be called upon to name, contrary to my own wish, the person who was the real cause of this quarrel?"

"The person?" said Madame, blushing.

"Must I," continued Manicamp, "tell you how poor De Guiche became irritated, furious, exasperated beyond all control, at the different rumors now being circulated about this person? Must I, if you persist in this willful blindness, and if respect should continue to prevent me naming her,—must I, I repeat, recall to your recollection the various scenes which Monsieur had with the Duke of Buckingham, and the insinuations which were reported respecting the duke's exile? Must I remind you of the anxious care the comte always took in his efforts to please, to watch, to protect that person for whom alone he lives,—for whom alone he breathes? Well! I will do so; and when I shall have made you recall all the particulars I refer to, you will perhaps understand how it happened that the comte, having lost all control over himself, and having been for some time past almost harassed to death by De Wardes, became, at the first disrespectful expression which the latter pronounced respecting the person in question, inflamed with passion, and panted only for an opportunity of avenging the affront."

The princess concealed her face with her hands. "Monsieur, monsieur!" she exclaimed; "do you know what you are saying, and to whom you are speaking?"

"And so, madame," pursued Manicamp, as if he had not heard the exclamations of the princess, "nothing will astonish you any longer,—neither the comte's ardor in seeking the quarrel, nor his wonderful address in transferring it to a quarter foreign to your own personal interests. That latter circumstance was, indeed, a marvelous instance of tact and perfect coolness, and if the person in whose behalf the comte so fought and shed his blood does, in reality, owe some gratitude to the poor wounded sufferer, it is not on account of the blood he has shed, or the agony he has suffered, but for the steps he has taken to preserve from comment or reflection an honor which is more precious to him than his own."

"Oh!" cried Madame, as if she had been alone, "is it possible the quarrel was on my account!"

Manicamp felt he could now breathe for a moment— and gallantly had he won the right to do so. Madame, on her side, remained for some time plunged in a painful reverie. Her agitation could be seen by her quick respiration, by her drooping eyelids, by the frequency with which she pressed her hand upon her heart. But, in her, coquetry was not so much a passive quality, as, on the contrary, a fire which sought for fuel to maintain itself, finding anywhere and everywhere what it required.

"If it be as you assert," she said, "the comte will have obliged two persons at the same time; for Monsieur de Bragelonne also owes a deep debt of gratitude to M. de Guiche—and with far greater reason indeed, because everywhere, and on every occasion, Mademoiselle de la

Vallière will be regarded as having been defended by this generous champion."

Manicamp perceived that there still remained some lingering doubt in the princess's heart. "A truly admirable service indeed," he said, "is the one he has rendered to Mademoiselle de la Vallière! A truly admirable service to M. de Bragelonne! The duel has created a sensation which, in some respects, casts a dishonorable suspicion upon that young girl; a sensation, indeed, which will embroil her with the vicomte. The consequence is that De Wardes' pistol-bullet has had three results instead of one; it destroys at the same time the honor of a woman, the happiness of a man, and, perhaps, it has wounded to death one of the best gentlemen in France. Oh, madame! your logic is cold—even calculating; it always condemns—it never absolves."

Manicamp's concluding words scattered to the winds the last doubt which lingered, not in Madame's heart, but in her mind. She was no longer a princess full of scruples, nor a woman with her ever-returning suspicions, but one whose heart had just felt the mortal chill of a wound. "Wounded to death!" she murmured, in a faltering voice, "oh, Monsieur de Manicamp! did you not say, wounded to death?"

Manicamp returned no other answer than a deep sigh.

"And so you said that the comte is dangerously wounded?" continued the princess.

"Yes, madame; one of his hands is shattered, and he has a bullet lodged in his breast."

"Gracious heavens!" resumed the princess, with a feverish excitement, "this is horrible! Monsieur de Manicamp! a hand shattered, do you say, and a bullet in his breast? And that coward! that wretch! that assassin, De Wardes, did it!"

Manicamp seemed overcome by a violent emotion. He

had, in fact, displayed no little energy in the latter part
of his speech. As for Madame, she entirely threw aside
all regard for the formal observances of propriety society
imposes; for when, with her, passion spoke in accents
either of anger or sympathy, nothing could restrain her
impulses. Madame approached Manicamp, who had subsided in a chair, as if his grief were a sufficiently powerful excuse for his infraction of the laws of etiquette.
" Monsieur," she said, seizing him by the hand, " be frank
with me."

Manicamp looked up.

" Is M. de Guiche in danger of death ? "

" Doubly so, madame," he replied; " in the first place
on account of the hemorrhage which has taken place, an
artery having been injured in the hand; and next, in consequence of the wound in his breast which may, the
doctor is afraid, at least, have injured some vital part."

" He may die, then ? "

" Die, yes, madame; and without even having had the
consolation of knowing that you have been told of his
devotion."

" You will tell him."

" I ? "

" Yes; are you not his friend ? "

" I ? oh, no, madame; I will only tell M. de Guiche—if,
indeed, he is still in a condition to hear me—I will only
tell him what I have seen; that is, your cruelty to
him."

"Oh, monsieur, you will not be guilty of such bar-
barity ! "

" Indeed, madame, I shall speak the truth, for nature
is very energetic in a man of his age. The physicians are
clever men, and if, by chance, the poor comte should survive his wound, I should not wish him to die of a wound
of the heart, after surviving one of the body."   Manicamp

rose, and, with an expression of profound respect, seemed to be desirous of taking leave.

" At least, monsieur," said Madame, stopping him with almost a suppliant air, " you will be kind enough to tell me in what state your wounded friend is, and who is the physician who attends him ? "

" As regards the state he is in, madame, he is seriously ill; his physician is M. Valot, his majesty's private medical attendant. M. Valot is moreover assisted by a professional friend, to whose house M. de Guiche has been carried."

" What! he is not in the château? " said Madame.

" Alas, madame! the poor fellow was so ill, that he could not even be conveyed thither."

" Give me the address, monsieur," said the princess, hurriedly ; " I will send to inquire after him."

" Rue du Feurre; a brick-built house, with white outside-blinds. The doctor's name is on the door."

" You are returning to your wounded friend, Monsieur de Manicamp? "

" Yes, madame."

" You will be able, then, to do me a service."

" I am at your highness's orders."

" Do what you intended to do ; return to M. de Guiche, send away all those whom you may find there, and have the kindness yourself to go away too."

" Madame——"

" Let us waste no time in useless explanations. Accept the fact as I present it to you ; see nothing in it beyond what is really there, and ask nothing further than what I tell you. I am going to send one of my ladies, perhaps two, because it is now getting late ; I do not wish them to see you, or rather I do not wish you to see them. These are scruples you can understand—you particularly,

Monsieur de Manicamp, who seem capable of divining so much."

"Oh, madame, perfectly; I can even do better still,—I will precede, or rather walk, in advance of your attendants; it will, at the same time, be the means of showing them the way more accurately, and of protecting them, if occasion arises, though there is no probability of their needing protection."

"And, by this means, then, they would be sure of entering without difficulty, would they not?"

"Certainly, madame; for as I should be the first to pass, I thus remove any difficulties that might chance to be in the way."

"Very well. Go, go, Monsieur de Manicamp, and wait at the bottom of the staircase."

"I go at once, madame."

"Stay."

Manicamp paused.

"When you hear the footsteps of two women descending the stairs, go out, and, without once turning round, take the road which leads to where the poor count is lying."

"But if, by any mischance, two other persons were to descend, and I were to be mistaken?"

"You will hear one of the two clap her hands together softly. Go."

Manicamp turned round, bowed once more, and left the room, his heart overflowing with joy. In fact, he knew very well that the presence of Madame herself would be the best balm to apply to his friend's wounds. A quarter of an hour had hardly elapsed when he heard the sound of a door opened softly, and closed with like precaution. He listened to the light footfalls gliding down the staircase, and then heard the signal agreed upon. He immediately went out, and, faithful to his promise, bent his way, without once turning his head, through the streets of Fontainebleau, towards the doctor's dwelling.

CHAPTER LI.

M. MALICORNE THE KEEPER OF THE RECORDS OF FRANCE.

Two women, their figures completely concealed by their mantles, and whose masks effectually hid the upper portion of their faces, timidly followed Manicamp's steps. On the first floor, behind curtains of red damask, the soft light of a lamp placed upon a low table faintly illumined the room, at the other extremity of which, on a large bedstead supported by spiral columns, around which curtains of the same color as those which deadened the rays of the lamp had been closely drawn, lay De Guiche, his head supported by pillows, his eyes looking as if the mists of death were gathering; his long black hair, scattered over the pillow, setting off the young man's hollow temples. It was easy to see that fever was the chief tenant of the chamber. De Guiche was dreaming. His wandering mind was pursuing, through gloom and mystery, one of those wild creations delirium engenders. Two or three drops of blood, still liquid, stained the floor. Manicamp hurriedly ran up the stairs, but paused at the threshold of the door, looked into the room, and seeing that everything was perfectly quiet, he advanced towards the foot of the large leathern arm-chair, a specimen of furniture of the reign of Henry IV., and seeing that the nurse, as a matter of course, had dropped off to sleep, he awoke her, and begged her to pass into the adjoining room.

Then, standing by the side of the bed, he remained for a moment deliberating whether it would be better to awaken Guiche, in order to acquaint him with the good

news. But, as he began to hear behind the door the
rustling of silk dresses and the hurried breathing of his two
companions, and as he already saw that the curtain
screening the doorway seemed on the point of being impatiently drawn aside, he passed round the bed and followed
the nurse into the next room. As soon as he had disappeared the curtain was raised, and his two female companions entered the room he had just left. The one who
entered first made a gesture to her companion, which
riveted her to the spot where she stood, close to the door,
and then resolutely advanced towards the bed, drew back
the curtains along the iron rod, and threw them in thick
folds behind the head of the bed. She gazed upon the count's
pallid face; remarked his right hand enveloped in linen
whose dazzling whiteness was emphasized by the counter-
pane patterned with dark leaves thrown across the couch.
She shuddered as she saw a stain of blood growing larger
and larger upon the bandages. The young man's breast
was uncovered, as though for the cool night air to assist
his respiration. A narrow bandage fastened the dress-
ings of the wound, around which a purplish circle of ex-
travasated blood was gradually increasing in size. A
deep sigh broke from her lips. She leaned against one
of the columns of the bed, and gazed, through the aper-
tures in her mask, upon the harrowing spectacle before
her. A hoarse harsh groan passed like a death-rattle
through the count's clenched teeth. The masked lady
seized his left hand, which scorched like burning coals.
But at the very moment she placed her icy hand upon it,
the action of the cold was such that De Guiche opened
his eyes, and by a look in which revived intelligence was
dawning, seemed as though struggling back again into
existence. The first thing upon which he fixed his gaze
was this phantom standing erect by his bedside. At that
sight, his eyes became dilated, but without any appear-

ance of consciousness in them. The lady thereupon made a sign to her companion, who had remained at the door; and in all probability the latter had already received her lesson, for in a clear tone of voice, and without any hesitation whatever, she pronounced these words:—"Monsieur la comte, her royal highness Madame is desirous of knowing how you are able to bear your wound, and to express to you, by my lips, her great regret at seeing you suffer."

As she pronounced the word Madame, Guiche started; he had not as yet remarked the person to whom the voice belonged, and he naturally turned towards the direction whence it proceeded. But, as he felt the cold hand still resting on his own, he again turned towards the motionless figure beside him. "Was it you who spoke, Madame?" he asked, in a weak voice, "or is there another person beside you in the room?"

"Yes," replied the figure, in an almost unintelligible voice, as she bent down her head.

"Well!" said the wounded man, with a great effort, "I thank you. Tell Madame that I no longer regret to die, since she has remembered me."

At the words "to die," pronounced by one whose life seemed to hang on a thread, the masked lady could not restrain her tears, which flowed under her mask, and appeared upon her cheeks just where the mask left her face bare. If De Guiche had been in fuller possession of his senses, he would have seen her tears roll like glistening pearls, and fall upon his bed. The lady, forgetting that she wore her mask, raised her hand as though to wipe her eyes, and meeting the rough velvet, she tore away her mask in anger, and threw it on the floor. At the unexpected apparition before him, which seemed to issue from a cloud, De Guiche uttered a cry and stretched his arms towards her; but every word perished on his lips, and his

strength seemed utterly abandoning him.   His right hand,
which had followed his first impulse, without calculating
the amount of strength he had left, fell back again upon
the bed, and immediately afterwards the white linen was
stained with a larger spot than before.   In the meantime,
the young man's eyes became dim, and closed, as if he
were already struggling with the messenger of death;
and then, after a few involuntary movements, his head
fell back motionless on his pillow;—his face grew livid.
The lady was frightened; but on this occasion, contrary
to what is usually the case, fear attracted.   She leaned
over the young man, gazed earnestly, fixedly at his pale
cold face, which she almost touched, then imprinted a
rapid kiss upon De Guiche's left hand, who, trembling as
if an electric shock had passed through him, awoke a
second time, opened his large eyes, incapable of recognition, and again fell into a state of complete insensibility.
"Come," she said to her companion, "we must not remain
here any longer; I shall be committing some folly or
other."

"Madame, Madame, your highness is forgetting your
mask!" said her vigilant companion.

"Pick it up," replied her mistress, as she tottered
almost senseless towards the staircase, and as the outer
door had been left only half-closed, the two women, light
as birds, passed through it, and with hurried steps returned to the palace.   One of them ascended towards
Madame's apartments, where she disappeared: the other
entered the rooms belonging to the maids of honor, namely,
on the *entresol*, and having reached her own room, she sat
down before a table, and without giving herself time even
to breathe, wrote the following letter:—

"This evening Madame has been to see M. de Guiche.
Everything is going on well on this side.   See that your

news is equally exemplary, and do not forget to burn this paper."

She folded the letter, and leaving her room with every possible precaution, crossed a corridor which led to the apartments appropriated to the gentlemen attached to Monsieur's service. She stopped before a door, under which, having previously knocked twice in a short quick manner, she thrust the paper, and fled. Then, returning to her own room, she removed every trace of her having gone out, and also of having written the letter. Amid the investigations she was so diligently pursuing she perceived on the table the mask which belonged to Madame, and which, according to her mistress's directions, she had brought back but had forgotten to restore to her. "Oh! oh!" she said, "I must not forget to do to-morrow what I have forgotten to-day."

And she took hold of the velvet mask by that part which covered the cheeks, and feeling that her thumb was wet, looked at it. It was not only wet, but reddened. The mask had fallen upon one of the spots of blood which, we have already said, stained the floor, and from the black velvet outside which had accidentally come into contact with it, the blood had passed through to the inside, and stained the white cambric lining. "Oh! oh!" said Montalais, for doubtless our readers have already recognized her by these various maneuvers, "I shall not give back this mask; it is far too precious now."

And rising from her seat, she ran towards a box made of maple wood, which inclosed different articles of toilette and perfumery. "No, not here," she said, "such a treasure must not be abandoned to the slightest chance of detection."

Then, after a moment's silence, and with a smile that was peculiarly her own, she added:—"Beautiful mask, stained with the blood of that brave knight, you shall go and join that collection of wonders, La Vallière's and Raoul's letters, that loving collection, indeed, which will some day or other form part of the history of France, of European royalty. You shall be placed under M. Malicorne's care," said the laughing girl, as she began to undress herself, "under the protection of that worthy M. Malicorne," she said, blowing out the taper, " who thinks he was born only to become the chief usher of Monsieur's apartments, and whom I will make keeper of the records and historiographer of the house of Bourbon, and of the first houses in the kingdom. Let him grumble now, that discontented Malicorne," she added, as she drew the curtains and fell asleep.

CHAPTER LII.

THE JOURNEY.

THE next day being agreed upon for the departure, the king, at eleven o'clock precisely, descended the grand staircase with the two queens and Madame, in order to enter his carriage drawn by six horses, that were pawing the ground in impatience at the foot of the staircase. The whole court awaited the royal appearance in the *Fer-à-cheval* crescent, in their traveling costumes; the large number of saddled horses and carriages of ladies and gentlemen of the court, surrounded by their attendants, servants, and pages, formed a spectacle whose brilliancy could scarcely be equaled. The king entered his carriage with the two queens; Madame was in the same one with Monsieur. The maids of honor followed their example, and took their seats, two by two, in the carriages destined for them. The weather was exceedingly warm; a light breeze, which, early in the morning, all had thought would have proved sufficient to cool the air, soon became fiercely heated by the rays of the sun, although it was hidden behind the clouds, and filtered through the heated vapor which rose from the ground like a scorching wind, bearing particles of fine dust against the faces of the travelers. Madame was the first to complain of the heat. Monsieur's only reply was to throw himself back in the carriage, as though about to faint, and to inundate himself with scents and perfumes, uttering the deepest sighs all the while; whereupon Madame said to him, with her most amiable expression:—" Really, Monsieur, I fancied that you would have been polite enough, on account of the terrible heat, to have left me my carriage to myself, and to have performed the journey yourself on horseback."

"Ride on horseback!" cried the prince, with an accent of dismay which showed how little idea he had of adopting this unnatural advice; " you cannot suppose such a thing, madame! My skin would peel off if I were to expose myself to such a burning breeze as this."

Madame began to laugh.

" You can take my parasol," she said.

"But the trouble of holding it!" replied Monsieur, with the greatest coolness ; " besides, I have no horse."

" What, no horse?" replied the princess, who, if she did not secure the solitude she required, at least obtained the amusement of teasing. No horse! You are mistaken, Monsieur; for I see your favorite bay out yonder."

" My bay horse!" exclaimed the prince, attempting to lean forward to look out of the door ; but the movement he was obliged to make cost him so much trouble that he soon hastened to resume his immobility.

" Yes," said Madame ; " your horse, led by M. de Malicorne."

" Poor beast," replied the prince ; " how warm it must be ! "

And with these words he closed his eyes, like a man on the point of death. Madame, on her side, reclined indolently in the other corner of the carriage, and closed her eyes also, not however to sleep, but to think more at her ease. In the meantime the king, seated in the front seat of his carriage, the back of which he had yielded up to the two queens, was a prey to that feverish contrariety experienced by anxious lovers, who, without being able to quench their ardent thirst, are ceaselessly desirous of seeing the loved object, and then go away partially satisfied, without perceiving they have acquired a more insatiable thirst than ever. The king, whose carriage headed the procession, could not from the place he occupied perceive the carriages of the ladies and maids of honor, which followed in a line behind it. Besides, he was obliged to answer the eternal questions of the young queen, who, happy to have with her " *her dear husband,*" as she called him in utter forgetfulness of royal etiquette, invested him with all her affection, stifled him with her attentions, afraid that some one might come to take him from her, or that he himself might suddenly take a fancy to quit her society. Anne of Austria, whom nothing at that moment occupied except the occasional cruel throbbings in her bosom, looked pleased and delighted, and although she perfectly realized the king's impatience, tantalizingly prolonged his sufferings by unexpectedly resuming the conversation at the very moment the king, absorbed in his own reflections, began to muse over his secret attachment. Everything seemed to combine—not alone the little teasing attentions of the queen, but also the queen-mother's interruptions—to make the king's position almost insupportable; for he knew not how to control the restless longings of his heart. At first, he complained of the heat—a complaint merely preliminary to others, but with sufficient tact to prevent Maria Theresa guessing his real object. Understanding the king's remark literally, she began to fan him with her ostrich plumes. But the heat passed away, and the king then complained of cramps and stiffness in his legs, and as the carriages at that moment stopped to change horses, the queen said :—" Shall I get out with you? I too feel tired of sitting. We can walk on a little distance ; the carriage will overtake us, and we can resume our places presently."

The king frowned ; it is a hard trial a jealous woman makes her husband submit to whose fidelity she suspects, when, although herself a prey to jealousy, she watches herself so narrowly that she avoids giving any pretext for an angry feeling. The king, therefore, in the present case, could not refuse ; he accepted the offer, alighted from the carriage, gave his arm to the queen, and walked up and down with her while the horses were being changed. As he walked along, he cast an envious glance upon the courtiers, who were fortunate enough to be on horseback. The queen soon found out that the promenade she had suggested afforded the king as little pleasure as he had experienced from driving. She accordingly expressed a wish to return to her carriage, and the king conducted her to the door, but did not get in with her. He stepped back a few paces, and looked along the file of carriages for the purpose of recognizing the one in which he took so strong an interest. At the door of the sixth carriage he saw La Vallière's fair countenance. As the king thus stood motionless, wrapt in thought, without perceiving that everything was ready, and that he alone was causing the delay, he heard a voice close beside him, addressing him in the most respectful manner. It was M. Malicorne, in a complete costume of an equerry, holding over his left arm the bridles of a couple of horses.

"Your majesty asked for a horse, I believe," he said.

"A horse? Have you one of my horses here?" inquired the king, trying to remember the person who addressed him, and whose face was not as yet familiar to him.

"Sire," replied Malicorne, "at all events I have a horse here which is at your majesty's service."

And Malicorne pointed at Monsieur's bay horse, which Madame had observed. It was a beautiful creature royally caparisoned.

"This is not one of my horses, monsieur," said the king.

"Sire, it is a horse out of his royal highness's stables; but he does not ride when the weather is as hot as it is now."

Louis did not reply, but approached the horse, which stood pawing the ground with his foot. Malicorne hastened to hold the stirrup for him, but the king was already in the saddle. Restored to good-humor by this lucky accident, the king hastened towards the queen's carriage, where he was anxiously expected; and notwithstanding Maria-Theresa's thoughtful and preoccupied air, he said: "I have been fortunate enough to find this horse, and I intend to avail myself of it. I felt stifled in the carriage. Adieu, ladies."

Then bending gracefully over the arched neck of his beautiful steed, he disappeared in a second. Anne of Austria leaned forward, in order to look after him as he rode away; he did not get very far, for when he reached the sixth carriage, he reined in his horse suddenly and took off his hat. He saluted La Vallière, who uttered a cry of surprise as she saw him, blushing at the same time with pleasure. Montalais, who occupied the other seat in the carriage, made the king a most respectful bow. And, then, with all the tact of a woman, she pretended to be exceedingly interested in the landscape, and withdrew herself into the left-hand corner. The conversation between the king and La Vallière began, as all lovers' conversations generally do, namely, by eloquent looks and by a few words utterly devoid of common-sense. The king explained how warm he had felt in his carriage, so much so indeed that he could almost regard the horse he then rode as a blessing thrown in his way. "And," he added, "my benefactor is an exceedingly intelligent man, for he seemed to guess my thoughts intuitively. I have now only one wish, that of learning the name of the gentleman who so cleverly assisted his king out of his dilemma, and extricated him from his cruel position."

Montalais, during this colloquy, the first words of which had awakened her attention, had slightly altered her position, and contrived so as to meet the king's look as he finished his remark. It followed very naturally that the king looked inquiringly as much at her as at La Vallière; she had every reason to suppose that it was herself who was appealed to, and consequently might be permitted to answer. She therefore said: "Sire, the horse which your majesty is riding belongs to Monsieur, and was being led by one of his royal highness's gentlemen."

"And what is that gentleman's name, may I ask, mademoiselle?"

"M. de Malicorne, sire."

The name produced its usual effect, for the king repeated it smilingly.

"Yes, sire," replied Aure. "Stay, it is the gentleman who is galloping on my left hand;" and she pointed out Malicorne, who, with a very sanctified expression, was galloping by the side of the carriage, knowing perfectly well that they were talking of him at that very moment, but sitting in his saddle as if he were deaf and dumb.

"Yes," said the king, "that is the gentleman; I remember his face, and will not forget his name;" and the
king looked tenderly at La Vallière.

Aure had now nothing further to do; she had let Malicorne's name fall; the soil was good; all that was now
left to be done was to let the name take root, and the
event would bear fruit in due season. She consequently,
threw herself back in her corner, feeling perfectly justified
in making as many agreeable signs of recognition as she
liked to Malicorne, since the latter had had the happiness
of pleasing the king. As will readily be believed, Montalais was not mistaken; and Malicorne, with his quick
ear and his sly look, seemed to interpret her remark as
"All goes on well," the whole being accompanied by a
pantomimic action, which he fancied conveyed something
resembling a kiss.

"Alas! mademoiselle," said the king, after a moment's
pause, "the liberty and freedom of the country is soon
about to cease; your attendance on Madame will be more
strictly enforced, and we shall see each other no more."

"Your majesty is too much attached to Madame," replied Louise, "not to come and see her very frequently;
and whenever your majesty may chance to pass across the
apartments——"

"Ah!" said the king, in a tender voice, which was
gradually lowered in its tone, "to perceive is not to see,
and yet it seems that it would be quite sufficient for you."

Louise did not answer a syllable; a sigh filled her heart
almost to bursting, but she stifled it.

"You exercise a great control over yourself," said the
king to Louise, who smiled upon him with a melancholy
expression. "Exert the strength you have in loving
fondly," he continued, "and I will bless Heaven for having
bestowed it on you."

La Vallière still remained silent, but raised her eyes.

brimful of affection toward the king. Louis, as if overcome by this burning glance, passed his hand across his
forehead, and pressing the sides of his horse with his knees
made him bound several paces forward. La Vallière leaning back in her carriage, with her eyes half closed, gazed
fixedly upon the king, whose plumes were floating in the
air; she could not but admire his graceful carriage, his
delicate and nervous limbs which pressed his horse's sides
and the regular outline of his features, which his beautiful
curling hair set off to great advantage, revealing occasionally his small and well-formed ear. In fact the poor girl
was in love and she reveled in her innocent affection. In
a few moments the king was again by her side.

"Do you not perceive," he said, "how terribly your
silence affects me? Oh! mademoiselle, how pitilessly
inexorable you would become if you were ever to resolve
to break off all acquaintance with any one; and then, too,
I think you changeable; in fact—in fact, I dread this deep
affection which fills my whole being."

"Oh! sire, you are mistaken," said Vallière; "if ever
I love, it will be for all my life."

"If you love, you say," exclaimed the king; "you do
not love now, then?"

She hid her face in her hands.

"You see," said the king, "that I am right in accusing
you; you must admit that you are changeable, capricious,
a coquette, perhaps."

"Oh, no! sire, be perfectly satisfied as to that. No, I
say again; no, no!"

"Promise me, then, that to me you will always be the
same."

"Oh! always, sire."

"That you will never show any of that severity which
would break my heart, none of that fickleness of manner
which would be worse than death to me."

"Oh! no, no."

"Very well, then! but listen. I like promises, I like to place under the guarantee of an oath, under the protection of Heaven in fact, everything which interests my heart and my affections. Promise me, or rather swear to me, that if in the life we are about to commence, a life which will be full of sacrifice, mystery, anxiety, disappointment, and misunderstanding; swear to me that if we should in any way deceive, or misunderstand each other, or should judge each other unjustly, for that indeed would be criminal in love such as ours; swear to me, Louise——"

She trembled with agitation to the very depths of her heart; it was the first time she had heard her name pronounced in that manner by her royal lover. As for the king, taking off his glove, and placing his hand within the carriage, he continued:—"Swear, that never in all our quarrels will we allow one night even to pass by, if any misunderstanding should arise between us, without a visit, or at least a message, from either, in order to convey consolation and repose to the other."

La Vallière took her lover's burning hand between her own cool palms, and pressed it softly, until a movement of the horse, frightened by the proximity of the wheels, obliged her to abandon her happiness. She had vowed as he desired.

"Return, sire," she said, "return to the queen. I foresee a storm yonder, which threatens my peace of mind and yours."

Louis obeyed, saluted Mademoiselle de Montalais, and set off at a gallop to rejoin the queen. As he passed Monsieur's carriage, he observed that he was fast asleep, although Madame, on her part, was wide awake. As the king passed her she said, "What a beautiful horse, sire! Is it not Monsieur's bay horse?"

The young queen kindly asked, "Are you better now sire?"

www.ingramcontent.com/pod-product-compliance
Lightning Source LLC
Chambersburg PA
CBHW032257020726
47495CB00001B/150